Mary Ann Sate, Imbecile

ALICE JOLLY

Unbound

This edition first published in 2018

Unbound
6th Floor Mutual House, 70 Conduit Street, London W1S 2GF

www.unbound.com

Text Design by PDQ Digital Media Solutions, Bungay UK

A CIP record for this book is available from the British Library

ISBN 978-1-78352-549-2 (trade hbk)
ISBN 978-1-78352-550-8 (ebook)
ISBN 978-1-78352-551-5 (limited edition)

Printed in Great Britain by Clays Ltd, St Ives Plc

1 3 5 7 9 8 6 4 2

MIX
Paper from
responsible sources
FSC
www.fsc.org   FSC® C018179

For my brilliant mother Jan Jolly
whose love and courage never fail

Dear Reader,

The book you are holding came about in a rather different way to most others. It was funded directly by readers through a new website: Unbound. Unbound is the creation of three writers. We started the company because we believed there had to be a better deal for both writers and readers. On the Unbound website, authors share the ideas for the books they want to write directly with readers. If enough of you support the book by pledging for it in advance, we produce a beautifully bound special subscribers' edition and distribute a regular edition and ebook wherever books are sold, in shops and online.

This new way of publishing is actually a very old idea (Samuel Johnson funded his dictionary this way). We're just using the internet to build each writer a network of patrons. At the back of this book, you'll find the names of all the people who made it happen.

Publishing in this way means readers are no longer just passive consumers of the books they buy, and authors are free to write the books they really want. They get a much fairer return too – half the profits their books generate, rather than a tiny percentage of the cover price.

If you're not yet a subscriber, we hope that you'll want to join our publishing revolution and have your name listed in one of our books in the future. To get you started, here is a £5 discount on your first pledge. Just visit unbound.com, make your pledge and type **sate5** in the promo code box when you check out.

Thank you for your support,

Dan, Justin and John
Founders, Unbound

NOTE

This manuscript was found at a house called Mount Vernon that is at the top of Butterrow Hill, just outside the town of Stroud, in the county of Gloucestershire. My husband and I purchased this house earlier this year. It was previously owned by a Mrs Isabella Harbingham, née Greylord, whose recent death brought about the sale of the house. She had apparently inherited Mount Vernon in her youth from her great-uncle.

Upon arriving at the house, my husband and I ascertained that some maintenance works would be necessary. So it happened that a few weeks ago, I found myself in the lower tower room assessing some damage to a wooden panel beneath a window. My husband being away from home, and I myself being a person who enjoys practical tasks, I set out to sand the edges of that broken panel, so that the carpenter might more easily repair it.

It was in this way that I realized that certain papers were enclosed behind the panel. Seeing that these papers were a recollection written in this house, I sat down and started to read. My intention was to read but a few pages, as I had many other tasks to complete. However, when I finally laid down the dusty and tattered manuscript, I remarked that the first light of dawn was already rising.

Initially I thought to edit the manuscript I had discovered before typing it out. To this end, I marked in the geographical location of certain sections of the story so as to reduce some confusion that might otherwise arise. Having done that, I then considered how I might improve and correct the text itself but, after some reflection, I decided to type it out just as I found it, without revision.

Sarah Jane Moffatt
July 1938

MOUNT VERNON

If you tell a story oft enough
So it become true ·

Words like the twisting grain of wood
Or the course of a slow running river
Have ways they must evr go

Who might I be to wield the axe cross the grain
Or try to untwist the flow of water

Yet I take up this my pen
To set down here my story
Bone blood brain

What does a soul look like
If you write him on paper
Yes soil also how may he be held
Within this fragile mesh of words

Yet so tis certain
Soil hisself must find his tongue
My story being but one speck of grit
In the swelling ballad of these Valleys

Oh how I do love to see them once again
The light brush cross their emerald edges
As the sun bloom and wither day on day

Soil soul and sin too
Soon all one
The hours hurry at my shoulder
The words will not wait

Yea these Valleys were my beginning
I come here first on the black ridge of the night
A coach tumbling falling many clattering mile
I know nothing afore

I sit on the back next a basket of chickens
The coach roll and pitch stars unspool behind me
Through a banner of black

The coach cut through all
Chickens screaming feathers poking out
Through the thick twist basket weave
My hand numb as I grip tight head nodding

Not a house a tree a man a beast or a Devil
Only the road
Slap of the horses hooves creak of a wheel
Tear and drag of a wind
Tips and tussles distant trees
Til sudden the coach falls forward into stillness

A man come round lamp light furrows of his face
He reach up lift me down
My skirt catching in the chicken basket
So wood stiff I can barely stand
From above a man cries out
You not leave a child here

Tis well knowd the history of this place

These are my instructions
No No the voice above says
Then many on the roof nodding their heads
Saying Nay
One splutters and coughs
A thick hand waves down

These are my instructions
She must be left

The door of the coach open
A fat whisker man pale britches call out
What is the delay We must drive on
Other on the roof
They say No Yes You cannot Cough cough Hurry up now

Another say You must go on to the Bear
In the name of Christian charity
You may not leave her

The furrow face man say to me close
Only you wait Wait He will come

Left with my one cloth bag
On the high shelf of the night
Though old man the coach call
Shame on you

Still the coach grow narrow
Small the light flicker

Flicker smaller and smaller
Flicker again is gone

Around me nothing flat land only nothing
Not a hedge or a tree but as my sight clear I see
Here the place many roads meet

The wind does sweep in now
From somewhere close
Creak creak creak like door grate on rustd hinge

Above the stars sway and pray God His mercy
This place many ghosts and ghouls
Gather thick the air
Their hiss and spit their foul smell
Tether my throat

I would turn out my pockets to protect myself
Yet my hands are too froze
So I cruck my thumbs in my fists instead

Fall upon my knees in the grass fix my eyes
On that shadowd line far in the distance
Black on black
Feel my fears calm

Were it not for that moment I look up see
Some dark shadow hang ovrhead
Black and spreading but also fragile
Maybe some girt dark bird
Moves with clanks and whistles

I know not what
But the Devil is certainly in it

My bones shudder cold fingers tight at my throat
Mercy mercy on my soul

I know well the Bible does say

That you call and He come
Even though you be no one and nothing

I never know if this be right
But now can only call and call
Hope and faith

Is the Lord there Does He hear
For many a long moment it seems not
Still I believe

Then gradually it begins
A sound comes from far away
High up in the heavens
A swishing and rustling
The drawing back of fine cloth

The flickers of whiteness small
Like light touching
The wings of flock of geese
A coming always closer

Then gathering round You cannot see them clear
Only their wings white curvd on the darkly grass

Gentle and still gathering softly
The sound a soft beating as of many hearts

Angels many Angels
Drive out legion of Devils dwell here

Such is His majesty and mercy
With them come girt certainty
Ease and courage I feel sure my hour has come

I go with them gladly to meet my Maker

Only instead the sound of horses hooves
Echo the same road the coach departd

The Angels wings fold away
Yet still I am in their care
So watch the horseman swell
Out through the shadows
The bridle of the horse clunking
As he snuffles and chomps

There the horse stops The man looks down
His face in the shadow of a tall hat so he barks
You are Mary Ann Sate

I say Yes Sir that is I

Then he reaches down
Grips tight the bone of my arm
I see his black knottd hair and wide cut lips
A red and white spottd kerchief tied his neck

He swings me up heels knees kicking struggling
My legs come to rest
Either side the horse waxen withers

Then all swings round the shape of the hill turn
The horse is striding out brisk the way he come
My hand twistd tight in his greasy mane

The mans arm round me not warm but rootd firm
In this way we travel on
Soon passing a coaching inn

This the Bear of Rodborough
Though I know it not at the time
Lights sway in the winders

Scrape of boots in the yard
A sudden shout of laughter
Smell of log fire hay and goose fat

But we stop not there
Dive down deep into trees
Then behind me feel the swell of lungs
The man begins to sing
Not loud but his voice is fine
It rolls and swoops carries all round

Heres a health to the barley mow my brave boys
We drink it out the jolly brown bowl

Sets the heart spinning I would sing too

When he stops for a moment laughs to hisself
Wraps his arm tighter round me
Only then I find heart tongue say
Sir where are we head

The man say only

The Heavens

MOUNT VERNON

I write this down for my Master tell me I must
His name is Mr Blyth Cottrell

Mark well my words

I cannot deny him or argue make any answer
My Master is not a man whose will is evr movd

I say this assurdly
Having knowd him many a distant year
Even since we were both green and but half growd

I workd for his father then Mr Harland Cottrell
A slippery saviour God Bless his soul
Twas another house another time

These few short weeks since
I bring my creaking body back
To these Valleys of Stroudwater
Return to work for my Master here
In the Grace of God I come back to my beginnings

Yet my soul is tossd and troubld sore
I did so want these Valleys again

Longd for them as dry earth yearns water

Yet I did not want to see my Master again
Yet so in Gods judgement it has fall out

Only do I find my peace
When I wake early the day yet thin
In the small tower room I take for mine

Walk out into the embrace of the garden
Stand gainst the white railing
See the dawn grey pink come up
Drawn like a veil off the town
Which has growd now so far along the Valley
Railway come cutting all
I would hardly know

These the most sacred hours
For once there is settling quiet
A drop down into deep stillness

Sometime if I am sure he is sleeping
I lie down in the weeping grass
As I did when a child

Put my ear to the ground
Can hear the creaking
Turn of the day starting the suck of the sap
The sly settling of the earth
In this the blessd early spring of all creation

Then look up at the blue above scatter of clouds
Flies buzz in spirals birds chatter

Course I should work but how might I
This is a fine noble house

Solid in the hill but fluttering also
Light as a childs toy
So many winders the light glance

They call it Mount Vernon
Was built here when I was but a child
By a Mr Partridge a dyer from Bowbridge
Workd down below in the pit of the Valley

A delicate house all latest style from London
Turret tower battlements shutters
Water tank gather rain from the many roofs
But needs butler gardener indoor maid and out

There was the man servant Mr Gains
But he is gone
Now only me

Thanks be to our Almighty God
My Master beyond the care of such matters

Now I hear him calling so go once again to the
Downstairs front drawing room
Where he sit in a chair by the winder
Swollen with age

Even a few weeks since had still top hat
Satin waistcoat gold rings and buckle shoe
Kept his stub arm neatly hid away

Now he is bare head shirt hang open
Putrid leg prop on a spindle chair

He made his fortune as a chirurgeon
In the East of India among the pagan Hindoo
So they say

Though in his family this a vex question
Who is chirurgeon or carpenter and who is no
I suppose they Hindoo would not know

Comes back here to the land of his birth
Buy hisself this lofty house
Though I think he has not so much money
As you would think

The whole place already furnishd
Everything left behind by the people afore
All now soaking slipping sliding
Into damp decay and dusty mould

Though this room still glitter vast winders
Draw in wavering pools of sun light
All cross the panes twistd leads like lace
You never saw a thing so fine

The air all about bright silver today
Though the rain come oft splatter the glass
In sharp early zummer squalls

One winder look out the front of the house
One to the side and about the garden
Where the land drops away
Steep almost as a cliff right down to the town
Then rise up sharp a wall of green the other side

He say Ah Mary Ann there you are
What would I do without you

This sometimes is his mood
But he has evr been fickle as the weather
A storm may come in at any time Take care of he

I have an idea he says
Snuffles and coughs tries to shift
His poison heavy leg

I want a story writ down

I look cross at him and think Oh so now it start
He never would leave alone

I know now what he will say
I do not want to hear the words

The dead are best left
Under the moist comfort of soil
Left to whatevr peace they may find

We have all the time he says So much time

But I know we have v little
He know it too for all he talks it out

He will go afore me
Yet I shall not be many days to follow

This story he does say must now be told
All the events that our times have led to
For there have been some as have
Engagd in deceits and misrepresentations
Such as must be correctd

I had thought perhaps to ask Mr Gains
His assistance in this matter
Yet he being gone now

I should like to write myself course he say
Then waves at me the sleeve of his shirt

Flapping white and empty

Yes Sir I say
Polite and quiet not look at him direct
Yet inside me anger flush like fever

How dare he How dare he
Age have growd him mad

He takes my peace again he takes my peace

Aye he say I want my brothers story to be told

The word brother drop into the room
Like a smouldering coal
Fallen from the grate and lie there betwixt us
We neither move to stamp it out We cannot
Twill not be snuffd so

Yr brother Sir I say
The words flare in my throat
Make my voice burst sudden loud

Yes Yes he say but as his hand reach out
Long and white still it trembles sharp
As he takes a kerchief
Wipes at the sweat now blooms his brow

I look at him then
Have not lookd him arrow shaft in the eye
For more than forty years

Then I were powerless gainst he
So tis again now

His eyes fugitive from mine

Wipes again at his bead brow

Go he says
Open up that tallboy drawer in the corner
So I do as he say and take out paper pen ink
But as I come back past him I stumble a little
Fall gainst his leg
God help me it were done a purpose

He draw tight in pain whimper
Like a whippd animal
I did enjoy to see it

Yet soon he takes a hold upon hisself

So I sit beside he at the desk
Take up the pen
The balance of it feel precious
In my hand

The steel nib made finer far
Than those I did use at the gaol in Gloucester

Take down moderate and careful what he say
Even now write a fair hand as his father taught

The title of this book he say
The Strange and Courageous History
Of Mr Ned Cottrell
As did live in the county of Gloucester
Being born there on the date of 1812
As did advance the rights of the common man

This I can abear no more so do now say
Perhaps the title should it be
The History of the Cottrell Brothers

Again I look him straight
Only once like this afore
He knows it He understands
He never was a fool

He divines that I know all
Aye every last bone marrow all
He may deceive others but never me

Tries he then to roll on with his words
But we have not gone one step more
Cross the white acres of the page
Afore his breath come sudden
His face bloom purple and groan

Maybe I change the dressing for you Sir I say

He nods his head tries to inch his leg
Cries out again
Sweat run the deep rivulets of his face

So steps I down to the kitchen
Which in this house a low room half under earth
Much linen and bandage tear in strip
Dry there now a cause the squalling flisks
On the range boil pots of herbs
Prescriptions and receipts

So I do find Muriatic quicksilver three grains
Rosewater six ounces sugar of lead one ounce
I would know these cures in my dreams
I done the same for his father

Then back I goes to the drawing room
Finds there my Master
Has stood up holding hisself

With the barrel of a musket

This musket he did ask me to bring down
Line of fine matchlocks
Standing to attention in a cabinet upstairs
Their wood silk to the touch
Metal engravd like fine embroidery

Now he use such as a walking stick
Lowers hisself down the armchair
As is near the fire

So I do set to and dress his leg
Hoping that now he may perhaps
Settle into some rest

Yet no no he will go on
Write write we must
So back I then to the desk
Wait to hear what I must write next

Yet though I wait many stilld minutes
No word does come

Perhaps Sir I say might I suggest
I could continue for you
If that would assist you

He considers me then eyes cat narrow

So I do say Course Sir you would then
Correct what I write
As would be need I am sure

He now is sliding into sleep
The pain having draind he deep

So yes yes he say
Perhaps you may continue
His eyes dropping down now
Even as he speak

So there I am left
Alone with the page

Such a v fine page tis
I have hardly words to tell

Paper the like I never did see
Clear and smooth pourd like buttermilk
So many pages Hundreds maybe
All unstaind

I am rippld by it
The silken cream the space and light
Paper cool to the touch and waiting

Yet I can find not one word to write

Sitting there in the stillness
The rain fling gainst the winder

Yet all its sound gather together
In one loud beat fills not just this room
But echoes all cross the Valleys

That one word Brother Brother Brother

I stand up then from the desk
Gasp as though invisible hands
Do constrict tight my throat

My eyes then do light

On that musket usd as a stick to walk
Still prop long and lean beside he

I move toward it
Run my finger up and down the black shine barrel
Feel the stipple of the metal reach up
Run my finger once twice
Round the open toothless mouth

Take it up
Measure the weight and length in my hands

Tis a long time since
I took a musket to my shoulder
Ambrose taught me and I was once a fine shot

Tis nearly as long as I and heavily to balance
The barrel almost too much weight to raise

The powder in the cabinet upstairs
Dry and ready

He could not run and though he cry for help
There is no one would hear

I seed what a musket can do
When it blasts in a mans face
The blackend flesh the splinterd bone
See straight through into the globe of the head
Dark deep red the teeth there
Tiny chips of white still bright like stars
Blown inward

I crook my finger into the trigger
It fits neatly there

THE HEAVENS

That first morning I wake
The rock and rattle of the carriage
Still sway through my bones
Bump in my teeth

I look round the dawn gathering chamber
See myself in bed next another maybe more

I know I am not at home
Yet could not say where home is

I want to twist ovr see where I find myself
Yet I turn the bed make an animal squeaking
So I must ease myself slow

Look up the gloom plaster shadow of the ceiling
Crackd and sagging and toward the winder
Hangs only a white cloth
The light blur like milken mist

Turn creak groan
Another shifts stop turn again
The sheet and blankets warm gainst my leg
Still I ease myself out into a clap of cold

I walk the grey shadows furrd boards
To the winder The cold fit to crack the air
There been a hard frost the winder thick ice
Inside and out the pattern delicate as
Lace on the cuff of a fine gentleman

I put my finger up to touch
Look up above the ice
A girt fiery sun rises up

Below all is white
The house floating light on a bed of cloud
I thank God for bringing me safe to His side

Then I remember again the night afore
How I did arrive here
I must have slept

My thoughts immediately interruptd by a boy
Who rises upright out of the bed
Throwing back the covers
He but a rough shape in the bluntd light

Who are you What are you doing here
He stands in his night shirt eyes gaping

What are you

I have no answer to give him

I am come to heaven I say

Since we float high on the clouds
This must be so

The boy tosses his head back

Laughs a bursting laugh
Comes toward me
Hits me cross the side of the head
V friendly

Heaven Heaven Who are you Where are you from

This is a place called The Heavens he say
Yet nothing to do with the heavens
Made God Almighty so they say
Tis only a name as all villages and hamlets
Even fields and coppice must have
Tis The Heavens but v far from heaven

I fix my eyes on the floor boards feeling fool
Yet wonder also if what he tells me is true

He laughs again puts out his hand
Says I am Ambrose

Then a voice comes from below
No words just an angry voice

At this sound a girl jumps also from the bed
She has long brown hair in a plait moves sprite
Taking clothes from a pile on a chair

She considers me briefly
Her lip snarl pushes clothes at me
You must dress the baby she says

Only then I notice a cradle wedgd in the corner
A tiny child lying turnd on its front head up
Bonnet hanging crookd

Who is she the boy still say

You were told Ambrose the girl says
You are not to ask

Come on come on she says to me
I start to pull on clothes
Vest calico chemise drop my knees drawers flannel petticoat
Clothes I never did see afore
Know not how to put on

You are no good for anything the girl say
Pushes me Now I must get Baby Fern dressd
You are too slow

I pull on the many clothes follow the childers
The stairs narrow tipping straight down a door

The air is biting sharp on the skin the light red
We go down through vegetables and past pigs
Around are sheds as I splash ice water hear
Shuffle of animals the white of breath rising
All gasp and laugh at the clip of cold

This is two cottages now I see
As I follow the others indoors

The room is low with a long table a range
Pot hanging and long handle for the bread
Far in the corner bags of wool
A trestle table and hazel twigs

Three men sitting at table
Eating barley bread and dripping
Their hands crackd their boots scuffle
Drops of tea glisten in their uncut beards
Their shallow eyes watch

The girl tells me we are to clear the table
She pass me plates but I am not ready
The greasy rim slips and juggles in my fingers
Crashes to the stones of the floor
The metal of it clattering
Loud as a musket fird

After come a silence while I pick up the plate
I raise my head to see a woman looking at me
Her eyes are big as the moon
White of them bright as best china
The ball blue dazzling
Eye lashes thick as flowr petal
Sweeping down on china cheek frame perfect
Her yeller hair pulld tight from her face
So the skin stretch back with it

A fine woman blessd with Beauty and Grace
Yet tis her mouth I notice
Which tell another tale
Sewd up pulld wrinkld
With a thread will not fray
Teeth tiny and bleach white
Going inward sharp like a fox

The woman stares at me a long while
Then she turn to a man
Tis the same man from last night
Head of ebony curls and swollen lips laughing

We were not told about her mouth she say

Tis the mark of the Devil another say

I hang my head

Yet the man from last night
I shall know he soon as Mr Abel Woebegone

He does say Enough of that
All is all the same
In the spread of Gods creation

Then say to the girl Sybilla
Shew her where is the scullery
Get these dishes clear I want no more said

So I follow Sybilla to the scullery make haste
The water is cold to clean the dishes
They must be rubbd with grit many atimes
I am a fast worker and all is soon done

Then the woman calls breakfast and we go back
The men are leaving now

The woman points at me and say
That one eat in the scullery
Yet the man from last night say
I want no more of it We must remember our Christian charity

So I sit down at the table
Bread and dripping much I eat quick and well
Thank God for my good fortune in this meal

The woman holds the baby now screaming for food
She pull out her nipple rub it with coal dust
Then puts the baby on it
Keening more and worse

Then puts milk in a cup and pours that down
The baby coughing and choking

Ambrose foot kick gainst mine
He is laughing flick a crumb toward me

Straight up the woman is on her feet
Baby still grippd and yelling
Slams her hand down flat on the table
Even the walls shake

Out You go out
This she shouts at Ambrose and he move quick

No no she say to him You leave that bread
He puts down the chunk
Shrug his shoulders smirk
Then out the door

The woman turn then to get more milk
Sybilla go to help her

Moving quick I slide the bread off the table
Hide it tight under my apron

Soon I say Let me please help with the table
So I get out to the scullery

There is Ambrose as I thought
Pull on his boots
Silent I pass him the bread

He smiles A sudden blooming easy smile
Pulls my ear and nods
Laughs

MOUNT VERNON

My Master call me and so I go to him

Tis a morning blessd with strengthening sun
My Master sit as he do so oft
In that front drawing room

The room is crowd now for only yesterday
He had me move a bed downstairs
It took me many a long hour to get it down
Take to piece oak frame struggle bed head down
Rattle and bash gainst the fine wood the stair
Push and fold the horse hair mattress

After that all my strength
Washd right out of me
Yet still he starts again this morning
That I am to write this book

Though first the dressing once again to change
I have the ointment now for bathing
Tis ready made

Drop on stiff knee down
Strip the bandages off

This does make he grunt in pain
For the bandages were tied as tight
As he could be borne so it must be

Put they aside for boiling

The leg underneath is soft and swollen
Like marrow ovr ripe and split all open
Fat and purple and also green in some place
Smell sharp sweet dead flesh

So I swab with cloth and bathe it well
Draw the poison off
Take now the bandage higher up the thigh

My head jerk back
A cry rise to my lips
I cut it short
But he has seed my face

There are maggots in his leg

The time is short so v soon now
I do not look at he

Maybe he send for a chirurgeon or a barber
Have the leg saw off
This being now not so difficult
As twas when his father
So oft did chop and cut

This done his arm a few years back
But they cannot saw and chop saw and chop

Soon nothing left to chop

Is need a different regimen of life
But my Master has already tried that
Give me instructions in all the medicaments
As should bring healing inside
Yet they have not

His face is freezd tight now
His mouth turn down his eyes roll

Even he cannot ignore this omen

I kneel again clean all maggot egg
Use vinegar salt to burn all out

My hands I do hold steady
Though he is not the only one afeard

For when he is gone
What chance is there then for me

Always the choices are but few
All ends in the Workhouse
You keep yrself out as long as you may
But all paths end there
No matter how respectable you come
I cannot think on this

Work steady and tender touch
Still he wince in pain

After I done I pour him some whisky
He has always been too fond of hard liquor
Though his father never permit it
Never was in that house
But now with the pain what choice he has

Then as I finish he ask me again
About the writing of his cursd book
He will not leave it
Though has hardly strength to speak

This matter he want settld
Afore his soul is takd

Again I do suggest to he
I may well write a few words
For he to correct

He rambling now again some such
The county of Gloucestershire on this date
Such heroic deed in advancement progress

Yet afore many words is gone in sleep

Once again I am left with the page
Yet can find not a word to say

The problem being this
Where might one begin such a story

Tis like you pull up the root of a tree
Which runs deeper and further
Than evr you can know
The beginning found far distance
From where the tree now stand

Yet so it happen as I sit there puzzling
I do look up and see a boy
Who steps away from the house

His stride is long and easy
Clean and sharp as a March breeze

I know course who the boy is
For it does happen that the son of Ambrose
Does live in the toll house down below

Sends sometimes this boy
Being the grandson of Ambrose
Sometime with bread milk egg

Now just this glimpse of him
Does grip at my heart for even in his stride
He is like his grandfather

I would know him anywhere

This thought leading me back then
Into the many tributaries of mine own past

My question being this
Where now is the girl who felt no fear
The lass Mr Abel Woebegone did make
Who did believe in the power of the truth

For despite me poor and without family
I was in the care of the Angels
Flourishd in mine own strength

Oh for that time again
Would the pen could return me there

Then of a sudden start to write
My hand run on tumbling fast
The words gallop so I can hardly keep pace

Not write as he writ
As an educatd person writ

Yet it do not matter
His father said we have a language
Which belong equal to all

The voice of the flowring meadow
The product of our own soil
The voice of our own dear country of England
The words we speak in mill or field or lane
Of which we should not be shamd

I write not the story of his brother
But the story of my beginning
Which must start with these Valleys
With my life at The Heavens With Ambrose Aye

What does a soul look like
If you write him on paper
And soil also

Soil soul and sin too
Soon all one

Ah Mr Abel Woebegone
May God keep safe his generous soul
His were a life that seem blight and thwartd
Yet so much he gave to me

That I must write down so all would know
He must not be completely forgot

So my pen goes on galloping ahead of me
In pursuit of she who livd without fear
Who believd the truth could save

THE HEAVENS

My life at The Heavens is blessd with much
Grace and Good

Lives I there in the care
Of her with the draw string mouth
Stretchd hair Mrs Freda Woebegone

The childers Ambrose Sybilla and Baby Fern
She I love head thick with knottd curls
Eyes wide and blue as zummer skye
Tiny hands damp and grasping
When she wake at night I hold her close

Mr Abel Woebegone a gardener for Clutterbucks
At Lower Lypiatt

Though tis said he write a fair hand
I never see it not til the end

Next door to us the Forresters
Also Claypits Farm and Mr Wood
Down the end of the garden
Beyond the vegetables sheds and pigs

Tis for Mr Wood
I am sent up the hill to tend the sheep
The Heavens already perchd up high
Yet still I go higher

This pleases me much
From the ceiling on which I am placd
I can see the whole world

There on the top
You feel the power and majesty of the Lord
Though the winter thickening day on day

The land is pale and lonesome
The night come early and the frost
Digs into the v bone
Nose red and running
Hands swelld with it

Oft the sheep is lost in hedge or wood
I must not go til they is all pulld out
Sometimes in places thick with thorns
Catch in my clothes blood scratchd my face

Yet I am never without courage

One of the early days
Ambrose come to find me
That day I remember well

Memory is not this day leads to that
Tis where the heart is touchd

Ambrose is sent with a message to Mack House
Stops by me on his way home
Even though he must take another road

Mrs Freda would not like if she knew

Course I see Ambrose morning and evenings
Never talk to he much
Mrs Freda does not care for idle chatter
In particular not from he
Must be careful or she will beat raw

Twas raining that day the drops so thick
All the Valleys lost behind a curtain
Just the grey slant arrows tumbling down
Gather thick every rut mud ankley deep
Even at this girt height

I sit on a log at the end of a small copse
Soon time to get the sheep back in

Yet I wait hoping that the rain may stop
The sheep pushd in gainst a hedge theysselfs
Sodden sagging grey bleating pitiful

I see him walk toward me
With an easy swing to his stride
Take no care of the rain
His hand raisd to wave

His cheeks are red his eyes fire his face round
He come in under the trees stand near to me

The rain it comes thick as a stream he say
Tis true even through the branches of the trees
Water is still splatting down

He takes from his pocket a piece of cheese
This he does for me
Food steal from pantry

After I do so for he

I do not know then what I should say
But break the cheese and try to give he half
He say no I must eat all and we stand
Look out ovr the muffld shadows cross
To where the other side of the Valleys should be

So you are Mr Woebegones son I say

This is bold of me but I want to know
For it has not been clear to me
Though he does use the name Woebegone
I know he is not the son of Mrs Woebegone
She makes that clear
But I think him perhaps the child
Of a woman Mr Woebegone was marrid to afore

No No he say I am not
He take me from the Workhouse
I am an orphan

When I hear the word Workhouse I breathe sharp
No matter how small child
All know what that mean

Where is orphan I say

He laugh at me then but kindly and say
No No An orphan is someone who has no family

Oh I say Oh Then I am an orphan as well

This knowledge gives me pleasure
I enjoy to be something
Particular as Ambrose is as well

So he and I now closy be

Though it also seem strange
As he is so v like Mr Woebegone
Close as my two thumbs
But I say none of that

Then he say
Do you not cry to sit here alone and cold

No I say I am not alone I like the rain

You like the rain he say
I had not thought anyone should say that

I feel foolish then but he seeing that
Clouts my capper gently give me such a smile

You never see a smile so wide and clean
Full of such clear delight
That evr were his gift

I like the rain too he say
Also storms and burning sun
Cool days pale brown neither hot nor cold
I like all those days
You see them cross these hills
The way they change the colours
Sometimes you see all things the same time
You understand

Yes I say I understand
When I speak these words
I never had such a feeling afore

I do not think most people are like this

Ambrose say

Most people like the spring the zummer
The good days

Yes I say You are right

But you must have it all Ambrose says
All the seasons even blackest winter when the
Land is dark and grasping and boots numb
Without feeling for the cold

Yes I say You are right
I wish then I had words such as he
To say the things I felt

Then I shiver through every bone
A happy shiver

But he see it and say You must not sit still
Twill not answer

See see You must stamp yr feet a bit
Swing yr arms

I do not want to do that
My face burn hide my eyes

Look look he say He catches hold of my arms
Swings them around Stamps his feet to shew

Come come Here Like this Stamp stamp

Slap his thighs raise the toes of boots
The music sudden quicken through him

Like this and this
He makes me stand beside he
First my feet bang only heavy up and down

Here here he say Like this like this
Then slowly it starts
No no Here Like this

My feet go heel and toe heel and toe
Turn turn and turn again then No Listen
Clap clap clap

The raining wood rattle our twisting turning
Our rising laughter Clap clap Heel toe turn
The blood floods warm through our hearts
Hardly notice the swelling dark

Til Ambrose says Come Look tis clearing now
I help you get the sheep in

No no I say There is no need

Yes he say No need but I shall do it anyway
Since we are family now Mary Ann Sate

If evr I think the world
Is a dark and terrible place
Tis Ambrose I think of and remember
Heel toe turn turn

*

Mr and Mrs Woebegone are good Christians
Of the Methodist Chapel of Mr John Wesley

I am told oft how Mrs Woebegone has

Out of the mercy of her Christian heart
Takd on the weighty burden of her husbands sin

Mr Wood at the farm Methodist also
Tis the true and proper path
The only hope we may have of redemption

The way of the upright is to depart from evil
He that keep his way so preserves his soul

Are you savd they say Are you savd

Mrs Woebegone read the Bible always
Break yr arm to lift it down from the shelf
A gold cross dug into the front
To remind of our Lords suffering
So many girter than any we can know

Hell is always but two step away
Where the unrighteous boil in pots of fire
Or are pushd off cliffs by forks
Into burning chasms licking orange and red
Even those as young as Baby Fern So she say

The Devil dwell in every corner
We must be fearful of he

I know this from my experience
For I have seed he
Just beyond the pig pens walkd

As they say shining like a bright morning star
Coverd also in many magnificent jewel
Such as ruby topaz diamond and jasper

Such is my shock I am took dead

Fall down on the path

Mrs Woebegone slapping my legs
Shouting the true Gospel at me

Yet so tis good she do not find cider bottles
Stone and corkd hidden up in the rafters
Of the hay loft
Ambrose and me know

I do not like to consider on it
Mr Woebegone is not savd
Yet he is a heart full man merry and kind
Though bend like a sapling always

Afore we go to the chapel
Sybilla evr a peart and pinnikin girl
Twist her hair braid
Scream if she get dirt on her apron

She is a proper girl and I watch her
To see how I must behave

No one braid my hair
Thick and knotty as a thicket they say
Must be choppd at the shoulder

I do not care better that way

Mrs Woebegone also wear bonnet button boot
She is a woman likes things kept spick neat
Tis a shame for her
To live as she does at The Heavens
Where she wather all the day
About the dirt the farm men brings in
The ceilings held up in several corner

By thick pillars of wood
Water pour in the back door
Many a winder banging
When the gale worries and the rain floods

Tis not what she were born to

The Methodist Chapel at Acre Hedge in Stroud
Visitd many atime Mr John Wesley hisself
Two mile along the Valley side

Tis glorious to walk that way
Ovr the stream at the Coombs down Dry Hill
Past Way House Farm and then ovr Lyme Stream
Where the brokd down mill is

Many a field you see from here is spread
With scarlet cloth drying out in the air
Does come from the mills and dyehouses below

The fall of the fulling stocks sound always
The heart beat that does keep
The life to flow through all these Valleys

Then through Creese Gate
Til you come to the hem of Stroud
Where are many gabld houses
Some also poke holes
No bigger than a kennel

You must take care for the pigs
Rooting through the many gardens

Water running the churs and many middens
You must step round

All being on a perilous slide
So the front door of one house
Almost on a level with the roof
Of the lower

This being the nature of Stroud

The smell of seg ripe from the currier
Hops brewing the corner of Acre Street
John Prices workshops where is made
The spinning mule for the mills

Come you then to the many side chapel
Multitudes are there maybe a hundred or more
All come to give thanks to the Almighty

I am to walk with Mr and Mrs Woebegone
Ambrose Sybilla
All the way there but when we arrive
I am not to go in the pew
Am to stay at the back
With cripples and old people smell bad
Blatchy and not Properly Dress

One man has only a bloody hole
Where his eyes should properly be
They say is done in the war in France
Defending the freedom and bounty
Of our heroic country of England
From foreign tyranny

I am not to speak any
Only meet them again as we walk back
After we been in the Sunday school
Where you may get a cup of milk
Play there with some carvd figures

The ark Noah built and many animals
Paintd neat you may arrange in rows

Ye must all grow up good Christians
Mr Woebegone say
Ye must not go wrong as I did
But as he suck on his pipe he is smiling

The people at the chapel do not care for he
I see it in their bitter eyes
The tip of a hat contempt like spit

When the sermon come
I do not understand the word
Though this is the true path
The Devil come in my mind
Coverd with those many shining jewels
Cannot be movd from there
Stuck in tight

Then oft we must go up to the front
Me and some others kneel down afore the altar

Are you savd Are you savd

My knees are pressd into the rock floor
I cannot keep myself up straight
Are you savd Are you savd

The stick come down cross the back of a head
I wait for it on mine
Are you savd Are you savd

When we leave Mr Woebegone shake his shoulders
Swing his arms Toss his hat
I think he pleasd to be gone

I pray she do not see

On the way home back above Stroud Fields
Through Creese Gate and all the jade rich ways
Mrs Woebegone and Sybilla shout to scurry up
As I am left far behind from thinking
Too much of the Devil and his questions

I ask Ambrose what he think
He say little laughs trips me up
Flicks at my hair with a long switch
Catch hold of me and spin me round
Like a spinning top full of laughing
As all pass in a swirl of verdant green

Then just as he catch hold me again
The path turn past Way House Farm
A coming up to Dry Hill
We happen then upon Mr Woebegone
Who is stood in the way
Looking down the moss green folds of the Valley
Smoking his pipe scratching his head
Tis only now I notice
How he smell of cider
God save him

He was evr a man with a crookd elbow

Ambrose say to him So what then you think Sir
He oft speak to Mr Woebegone in this way
Bold but only when she is not round

The Devil he say What I think on him
Then he laughs a little licks his lips

I look round for we close the weavers cottages

45

I should not want any hears
We cannot know how far is Mrs Woebegone
She may be only in the fringe of trees

Mr Woebegone stares down the Valley smiles
Shakes his head lay a hand on Ambrose shoulder

I never seed him do that afore
At the same time rustle a breeze
Shiver all the leaves
Turn their silver back
Flickering and glistening to us

Mr Woebegone says I think not much on he
Nor on God neither

I am filld with terrible fear
And excitement both
I remember to this day that feeling how it come

Say Mr Woebegone
For why would any think on sin and punishment
When one sees here all of Gods creation
Spread round us in these Valleys
All that we might need to know
Do you not think so

Is this not miracle and revelation enough

As he speaks he stretches out his hand
In a long arc to take in all the Valley
Such majesty in the gesture
As though he create it all
Just then and there
With the twitch of his fingers

Then he shouts out heart rent loud
Tears bubbling in his eyes
Laying his hand cross his chest saying
The world is my country
All mankind are my brethren
To do good is my religion

He turns to Ambrose and then to me
I welling tears his talk does tempt torment so
Surely he must be heard
Ambrose and me shall be beat

Then comes calm and I hear it whisper
That tender sound which tells me
The Angels are closy by and we are safe

So I laughs then and Mr Woebegone
Does lay his hand gentle on my head

Tis not til we are at the Coombs
We hear above us Sybilla running in the path

Hurry up Hurry up Do not banter about there
Mother says come You come now
So we all go on
But I remember

*

That same night I lie awake long
From down below I hear Ambrose and Mr Woebegone
I get up watch them see them pointing up
Hear fragments of words mysterial and veild

They are naming them the stars in the heavens
I never thought they might have names

When Ambrose come in I am still awake
He is flushd ruddy laughing

Come come he says I will shew you something
I not want to get up but he makes me
Come come You must see

I follow him down to the front parlour
Our feet whispering through the shadowd house

The front parlour we are not allowd to go
The moon at the winder a shining coin
Fill the room with silver surfaces
Touch on the tapestry seat of a chair

Ambrose move the wood basket quiet
So none above may hear
Then he pull back floor boards
I shiver listen breath tight

Here he says See here

At first I see nothing but then knees down
My eyes strengthen I see the yellerd paper
In a hole down under the boards
A pile of raggd papers curld at the edges
The one on top a pamphlet
Some letter printd big and some small
A black line cross the bottom

Something in it afears me

I stand back
Ambrose look up at me from where he kneel

You know he was in prison he say

Mr Woebegone In Horsley
Wearing the county livery he
And walking the burster
You know what that means

I do know for tis talkd oft enough
What happens to those who go there

Now I say tis not true

So I turn and go
Heading back to bed

My mind knocking and banging gainst itself
For Mr Abel Woebegone is surely a good man
Yet good men do not go to prison

I do not want to know any more
But those hidden books smoulder in my head

When I go back to bed lie awake til Ambrose come
Lie down next to me his legs tangld with mine
His breath close on my face

Are you savd Are you savd he say
His voice deep and mocking his face pulld grim

I push at him laughing but afeard

Do you not care he say
I know you do not care if you are savd

I stop then and sit right up
Feel the room round me
As though the weight gone from it
Walls ceiling winders beds scatterd clothes

No more substantial than tree branches
The heavens close to us

My mind goes back to Mr Woebegone
Stood on the Valley side
His hand stretchd out as though he
Hisself the creator of all

I am thinking of Ambrose question
Remembering what Mr Woebegone say
Then I know the answer

I whisper the words into the floating bedroom

No I do not think on it
A cause me I know right well that I am savd
I have always been savd
I will be savd forevr
Tis certain I will

For I know what is true
What is not
Being all I need to know

Ambrose and I lie together laughing then
But I am frightd of myself
Yearning now always always

To go back to that moment
When Mr Woebegone spoke
To hear those words again
On the skirt of the Valley

*

Time come when I must go to school

I did not know if I evr would
Being not proper of the family

I do not think it would a come to pass
But for Mr Abel Woebegone for I hear oft words
Twixt him and Mrs Freda harsh and angry
Yet quiet and snake hiss venom

She will go She will not
She will go I tell you
What point there be for such as she
All she can learn is work hard
Be of good Christian virtue

The most such as she expect
Is the dignity earn her living
Best she start now

Finally I go in the morning
As do Ambrose and Sybilla
Many at the school go the mornings
Work the mill in the afternoons

Tis but a short walk to school
Down Dry Hill pass Way House Farm
To Creese Gate and then on to Acre Street
All in one room tall winders stretching high
Warm oft on account a massy furnace at the back
Filld up with logs

Like in the chapel
I am not to sit with Ambrose and Sybilla
Yet still I am given slate and chalk
Here for the first time I see books
Which is not the Bible

They teach us how to write
Must be from left to right
Fill up all the space
One line lead on to next
No gap in betwixt or down the side

I like blank spaces
Areas of black and nothing there
I like to give the words their breath

But no no no I am told that is not the way
Girl for the love of God
Will you but listen to what you are told
Left to right fill up all the slate

I love to form the letters
See them grow the easy twist and curl
The world caught and orderd
Put down straight

No no Mary Ann
How many times must I tell you
Fill up all the space

I like the words to roam free
I relish the books also
Though I not get to see them much
That for older children whose hands are clean

Is best when we can all go out in the yard
For there play many rickety boys rabble games
The best is kill Mr Bonny Part
The French tyrant who is a stocking
Stuffd all full of straw
Who chase and hit as hard as you may
With a long banging stick

A hard woman is the Mistress there
Did beat Ambrose once thwack thwack thwack
The sound of stick gainst moleskin bash

Saying to him afterwards
I hope now Ambrose Woebegone you understand
Where do you stand

That I most certainly do he then reply
For one thing I can know for sure
I shall not be sitting for some long time

I did think then she might beat he again
Except at that moment three large geese
Did walk in the room passing up the aisle
Through all the childers
Trying hard not to laugh

By the time the geese shoo out
Ambrose was forgot

*

So my time at school go on quite merry
Though at this time one circumstance
Cause me much worry and trembling
Some days Ambrose does not go to school
He come with us
All the way
Take his pail for his lunch
All as should

Then afore he get to the school
He go laiking off down hill
I do not know where he go
Perhaps to the mills or dye works

Down Stroud Fields just below
You hear the crashing of the fulling stocks
Makes the earth leap and shudder
Even so far up as the school

I been down there myself
Takes me on a Sunday afternoon
Down through the tumpy fields all dressd
In the cloth they call Stroudwater scarlet
Which ripples red in the worrying wind

Tis made this singing colour of red
So when the bullet hit the soldier
You may not see the stain

To mill building three time higher any you see
The chimbley reach nearly to the rushing clouds
So many winders and gables

The new toll road cut through all

The noise smashing to make yr ears jump
Many is made deaf by it

The rush of the water
White splashing gasping a jumping
Press through narrow walls and into
The spanning wheel

Sometimes the water running blue or red
Or even yeller as dandelion
From the dyes they do make

Maybe that is where he goes
I do not know but when we reach school
We must say he is sick with fever

54

Sybilla do not want to say it but he tell
If you not do what I say then in the night
With the shears cut off all yr hair
Right to the white of the scalp
Twill never never grow back

After but a while of this
Ambrose really is took sick fever and coughing
Which is maybe a punishment
For feneaguing out of school

Many days he is at home
Too sick to get from his bed
Mr Abel Woebegone down to the dispensary
Many atime he does go

Sometimes Ambrose is better for a day or two
A week maybe then sick again

Makes me downcast when Ambrose is not there
The other childers will have no hands with me
On account of my face

When winter come
I long for the school for the furnace
At night at The Heavens we cannot sleep
Wake again and evr with the cold

At school I am near the white wash wall
Place my head gainst it
Look far up at the bleachd winter light
Slant in the high winders
The air thick as a wool glove
Soon there must be snow

Others sleep as well

Those that work at the mill always tird

Left to right Left to right
Fill up all the slate

*

It must a been a day when I slept
As I do not remember him a coming

By he I mean Mr Harland Cottrell Yes was he

He come in the school with one other a chirurgeon
Walk down the rows of childers
That the first time I see he

As he come near he turn
Look me pierce in the candle of my eye
I see him full I never forget

For he were a singular looking man
Tall thin as a coffin about as sombre too

His face long and gaunt
His hair surprising thick and straight
Swept back sideways from his brow
Held up then in a club the old fashion way

His lips well formd and full His teeth even

But what you notice most about he was his eyes
Fixd on one thing another with a terrible hunger
As though he might draw strength or knowledge
From anything he saw

Though so many in the room

You could not look at any but he

Held his white hands together
Long dandling fingers
Something in his hands would make you step away

I ask myself did I see all this then
Or only later

Yet I think it true that all who met him felt
Some attraction Some dread Some foreboding Always so

Then I wake as from a trance
See that the benches must now be push aside
All must line up though I know not for why

Try to follow what is now happening
At the front tables are pull up
Mr Harland Cottrell about some business
With bottle rag and such like

Then all is told you must pull up yr clothes
So yr arm is bare
I watch the others and do the same

Up the front is a murmur and a wheeze of fear
In the air there might be whimpers
A shuffling of feet a snuffle of tears
But I hear naught

You best not argue with the Mistress
Nor would you ask question or complain
So though the room curdld with fear
Not a whisper is

They come down the line of us

Mr Harland Cottrell and the other man
They have bottles and cloths
Take each child You cannot see proper
You must not look

As they come close to us they grow
Evr bigger and bigger
Their heads almost touching the high beams
The whole room full of stifld air
What happens I do not know
I think to run but I cannot
A girl ahead step out of line
The Mistress go for her with the rod

The faces of the two men stern careful solemn
Come come they say Calm yrselfs
Tis nothing at all

Only then I do look up and see at the winders
Gathering white the wings of the Angels
So then I am strong in the strength of the Lord
Who does send mercy and succour to even
Such lowly as me

So they come My teeth clench tight
I try to keep my arm away
Mr Harland Cottrell catches it
Holds it out

I look up into his scouring eyes
Again I am calm You a good girl he say
You know this can save yr life

He hold a knife with a thin blade
With two pieces of casing held to each side
The needle blade he then dip in the bottle

Then quite sudden goes deep in my arm
Digs through flesh blood spike pain sharp

The tip of it pierce right through to my heart
Is all I can do to keep on my feet
Then rubbing rubbing arm with a cloth
The room turn round sudden floor go to ceiling
My stomach clutches itself all together

There there he say
All done now and my arm is release

Not til many years later
I understand what is done
Was said at the time Sarah Mayne who is older
Die soon after from it
Tis true she is never seed more

I do not comprehend also at that time either
Who is Mr Harland Cottrell

But now I tell
He is the father of the Master
In whose employ now old crustd I find myself

More I do not know
That our ways are soon to bind together again
Soon soon

That all the shape of my life
Come from he The good and the bad
The two wound so tight
Separate one from the other
You never could
You must not try

*

I remember those days the glory of all
Ambrose and I on Sunday afternoons
Always off cross the fields

Swinging oft down the Cut
Where is the canal far dip of our Valley
Where gypsies tinkers and Irish
Do call out from the barges
Their faces oft blatchy
Drinking and singing rolling songs

One there does lift us up
To the peck of a towering horse
As does pull the boats
So we sit our legs spread wide
The two of us behind
The girt leather collar
Feel the strain of the horse
As he pulls on and on
We so high can see far
Ovr hedge scatterd buttercup yeller
Clouds yawn above

Then we helps also to pull the locks
Runs on then all the tow path
Right down to Brimscombe Port
Thick with so many boats
The ground under yr feet
Black where the coal from Gloucester
Is unload

Ambrose tell me about water wheels
Gig mills and fulling stocks all

At the Coombs he makes his own water wheel
Cut from planks of wood and twine
I to help him work it

Tells me also of these many innovations
These girt and marvellous machines
To maintain the wonder of the cloth mills
All the pride of our Valleys

Yet I am oft tird and sleep instead
Drowsy under the sailing clouds
The butter touch of the sun

So we stay out til the cricket whispers
The hour of waking spirits

As we walk home see up ahead
The lofty battlements floating above

So says I to Ambrose See you well
Look look Tis the walls of the City of God

He only laugh at me and soon my head does ache
So I took dead down by the path

He sit beside me til I strong again

*

Was it then that zummer following
I cannot lay the months out straight
As the years do turn and turn again

But it were Midzummer
When the fires of St John are lit
All must pray full the night long

Though more oft fall into gluttony

At that time also when the ancient folk
Come out the trees
Fayries Unicorns and Giants also
To dance with us under the stars
While the fires flash and flicker
Til those folk melt away into the dawn
Of Midzummer day

Ambrose say tis not true
But I take no note of he

So at that time it come Mrs Freda Woebegone
Must go out to Frampton at the Severn River
Help her sister took bad in the bellers

So Sybilla is left in charge of the house
Though really it be me only
As Sybilla keep her hands clean
She her mothers daughter

Anyways when Mrs Freda goes
Then I see what I always know
How Mr and Mrs Woebegone
How they evr come to get marrid
Such an oil and water match you never see

She like a tree tall straight unbending
He like a song bird tied to the tree
By a collar round his neck
Always try to break away
But never can

Fragile and bright and foolish
But beautiful for all that

This I had always knowd

Soon she go out of the house it start
The cider bottles stone and corkd
I am sent out to fetch them down off
The rafters in the barn
The men drinking much at night

I am sent to the Forresters down the way
Many atimes to get those bottles filld up

Mr Woebegone with the fiddle out
Push his lustrous dark hair back out his eyes
His lips as red as the kerchief he wears
His white teeth sparkle laughing

The fiddle she normally does not allow
But now he play and sing when he like
All the winders of the house hang open

I find Baby Fern climbing the fence to the pigs
Bring her back and intend to speak to her firm
But instead hold her warm and wriggle gainst me
Remember I must watch her now
For surely no one else will

The house like a tinder box take fire and blaze
Crackle with music and drink

That first time I heard many ballads sing
Oh how they did ignite my mind
Such were the stories and the music
Lilting rattling swaying sweeting
Stories of lost love and betrayal
Did race in my veins

I could have listend to those songs forevr
Such was their pleasure to me

Come the evening I am sent out again
To the Forresters
For to bring back ale
Though I do not want to go
I cannot say no

That night we childers go up to bed
Sybilla weeping for her mother
Things must be kept neat
For her mothers sake

I say Come come now
I will help you
We will get all set to rights

Then I brush her hair
Tuck her up in bed

Ambrose only mock
Go back down to join the men
Little Fern mercifully firm asleep

The noise go on long into the night
The tap tap tapping of feet the swaying songs
The violent laughter and clink of tankards
Sit by Sybilla a while stroke her hair

I do love Sybilla much though she pinch me
Kick me when no one sees

Finally she sleeps but I do not
The swing of the music runs fast through me
The tipping jolting fiddle set me alight

I get up and go to the winder
The night sprinkld all cross with many stars
The Valleys swallowing all in silent sleep

There stand Mr Woebegone on a wall
His head throwd back and arm flung wide
Toss his hand high to declaim

What is that of England
Tis a market where every man has his price
Where corruption is the common traffic
At the expense of a delude people

The words stir in my stomach
I go down the stairs and see
The men and Ambrose their faces plush
Their legs unsteady
Slap their thighs and raise their tankards
The light still hold outside
A blood red sun set glint
Make all the room stain red edges caught bright
Their long shadows dance and drink as well
Swing turn crash as a chair go ovr

I am afeard and excitd disgustd and blessd
Ambrose sees me and pulls me outside

The night air touch cold and shiver me through
Ambrose holds a tankard and pass it

No no no I say but he say Go on She is not here
You may do as you please

Tis wrong I say but he only laugh
I tip the tankard
Cold hard the lip of it gainst my own

Choke hard then drink again
Feel flames lick inside
The cider swelling in my head

Ambrose says Let us dance and shews me again
Just like when I first come here watch the sheep
My feet bare ovr the hard earth now
The stars all rattling round above

Turn turn clap clap
Ambrose catch me and swirl me round
I drink from the tankard again

In my mind swirl many thoughts for I know
That this is wrong That Mr Woebegone ought not

Think of the books under the parlour boards
What Ambrose says which is not true
None must find them hid there

For all my fear I feel my life beginning
The world generous eager stretchd out afore me
Like many yards of fine cloth

Ambrose and me dance long
Then walk on down the field and he tell me now
Look up and I tip back So many stars never seed
Stretch into blackness without end

Do you know them he say Let me shew
So we lie down on our backs in the grass
He does hold my wavering finger
Tell me of horses and riders in the skye

I laughing at first think it but a game
Then I see all he say

The pole star the plough the girt bear
A whole world up above
You join one star with yr finger to another
How was all this always in the skye I never see

If those in the stars look down
They do not even see us
Neither do the fields
Still they care for us
More than God Hisself maybe
I think this though I know it blasphemy

My certainty is the world

Then come Fayries Unicorns and Giants
Shadows we see in the fields down below
Tall as trees swaying
A Unicorn carrying his proud horn
The dash of his hooves thunder the Valley
As he gallops away into Midzummers Day

Then my stomach heave and I am mortal tird
Fall asleep where I lie out in the field
Do not wake til the sun far up

Feel sick and frightd and alone

*

A day come when Ambrose and me
Did take a brute beating

It came about like this that he Sybilla me
Sent with a cratch to clear droxy and fullock
Left there by the scrag end of winter
Go with a flint to make a fire and burn all up

This we do for Mr Wood as he is took sick
Back bent near double and cannot straight it
So all must help where they may

We were glad enough away down the field
Through Home Piece to Burglis Ground
For Mrs Freda Woebegone in a witching temper
Mr Woebegone gone fresh with drink again
As was his way

I do not know how twas
He did not lose his job
Except it were said he were a gardener
Could grow and splice and graft
Many exotic plants

I want to go to the Manor to see
But Ambrose thought it matter nothing
Water wheels sluices and shuttles
That was his passion
Think nothing on flowrs

So twas waking early spring
The first tips of sage green shewing
The sun clean and new but its light not strong
The cold of the sombre days still hold the earth

We stand down on Burglis Ground and from there
You see all the Valley cross

Even to where they build a grand new house
A tower rise from a cloud of black tangle trees

Course I do not know it then but that the house
This Mount Vernon where I now live out my days
How things come around is God alone to know

Eyes drop down then to the floor of the Valley
Where the River Frome twists and rushes
The wagons pull all along
Staffords Griffin even Ham Mills
Chimbleys thrust high above the tips of trees
Ambrose says Look you there to Ham
Do you see

When I am growd I shall work there
Ambrose tells me
That shall be soon now
Maybe next year even

But I shall not be a weaver he say

This I know for all does say
There is no purpose to be weaver more
Though so many in these Valleys are
For the weaver his day is all pourd away
His vessel echo empty now

Ambrose talking of this strikes me cold
How will the seasons turn without he

What then will I do when he is not here
To take me out Sunday afternoon
For skiddy hunting

Or lying on our backs in the long grass
Seeing shapes in the clouds
Hearing the sweeing flight of the woodpecker
Cuckoo nightingale pigeon thrush
Swallow rise high and plunge down steep

See together the greens of the wood
White poplar grey sally mellow lime

Stand wavering on his shoulders
As he lift me high to raise warm eggs
From knottd nest and suck them out slow

Yet I have not more time to think on this
For we strike the flint and light the fire
Fetch carry pull toss all the scrub
All soon flizzie up

After that Sybilla went back up home
Ambrose and I stayd on
The flames leap warm green and copper crackles
The light of the evening brokd and silver
The edge of the clouds hemmd steel
But still the sun bright at the rim
Bring a gleam to all the fields

Together we put in sticks to get them burning
Then waving them through the wind
Twisting and turning tumbling on the bank
Following always the flicker of red
Twizzle it through the watery air

Then Ambrose need to relieve hisself
Which he done close to the fire so to keep warm

I laughing so at the neat little pile it made
So twas we decide to make it into a patty

So I did also relieve myself
That we should have a smart pair of them
Agreed we should cook the two up on the fire
Though laughing so much bent near double
Pushing gainst each other guffawing so

We could not stop ourselves

So bewitchd and befoxd were we
We never notice Mrs Freda Woebegone
Come fly down the field sleeve flapping
Black crow tongue flaying eyes scouring

Straightway she shout us stern
For unseemly behaviour

Still not worried I thought
She cannot tell the difference
One sort of mud same as other

Yet I was much deceive
For she seemd to know right well
Her temper already flaring high
Afore she reach to us

Now spark sharp fire up a fraddling rage
Arms flailing hands ready to slap
I thought she would burst open
Be spread all up the Valley side
Such were she taking on

Caught hold of Ambrose and me
Face red as a radish
Pinching sharp one each ear
Drag us shrilling back up the hill
Slipping and sliding in the dirt
She never let go our stinging ears
All the way shouting
Under the grey wash and struggling sun
Even the lace trees bend away as she shriek
About the fearful and unbelieving
The murderers sorcerers and idolators
How all have their part in the burning lake
That is the second death

When she got us back
She strippd my apron and blouse from me
Beat me raw cross the shoulders
All the while holding me down
The heavy flat of her hand

Yet this the question Ambrose and me
We were thicker stronger than we had been
No childers more but growing fast
She but a sapling woman
Though flint hard never to be broke

So when she start on Ambrose
I snatch hold of the cane
Held on tight she snarling wild dog
Fight me for it fingers scratching
Try to gouge out my eyes
Bring all the curse of God and Bible
Down on me

Til Mr Woebegone come in from the yard
Pull Ambrose out the way

She say The child is filthy Satan in her
You can see it in her face
She is not right she say
We should not have her
Christian charity or no

Hear no any more for Ambrose and me
Heels flickaway to the hay loft
First me crying for the pain
The weight of sin that was in me
For the Devil got in me made me do such wrong

Still Ambrose was fooling

It were not long afore I rollicking again

I should not have done so

When we come out the loft I see Mrs Woebegone
She sitting by the range and rub eye weeping
Her hands wrung tight together
Her shoulder slump right down

The world is not as she would want it to be
I can find pity for that

She will not always
Keep the fiddle in the cupboard so
The cider hidden out on barn beam

Perhaps it were that thought kept me awake

I do not know for why
Yet those pamphlets always alive in my mind

So I went down to the parlour
Careful not to creak even one board
Move the chair and look down in that hole

Those pamphlets were vanishd
In some way I knew it even afore I saw

What now will happen I ask myself
Who took them and where

For some tiny moment I did consider
Tell Mrs Woebegone
Like her I want things put straight
She keeps the house tetherd down tight
She is cruel but safe

Of course I would not tell her

As I go back upstairs
A wind blew gainst the chimbleys
Rattle around inside them
Whistle and hoot

Could blow all the house away
Like a dandelion clock as we make
One puff
Gone

MOUNT VERNON

Last night as I write those last word
The silence of the house split open
A horrible growling yell burst up all the stairs

I hurry to my Master though a lump in my chest
Does strangle all my breath

When I get there my Master is sat up in bed
His hands stretchd out veins clinging red
His hair that grows thick even at this late age
All ruckld on his head His eyes standing out

He says He was here My brother
I saw him here He stand at the foot of my bed

Now come come I say You know tis not true
Only the fever takes you

This is how I speak to him now
As child to mother
Yet so it evr was
With both those two
Though I always the younger

Takes hold of his shoulders now
Shakes the nightmare out of he
Til he falls back on the bed
Groaning shifting like a girt tormentd beast
The linen all knot around

Yet still he is seizd by terror

Nay nay I say
Let me fetch water for you
Put a poultice on yr leg

Go to the kitchen then fetch
Calomel and tar ointment
Bandages wrap weeping ulcers
And venomd nabcess tight

Still the Master turns in the bed
Speaks again saying
I saw him He was here

Aye aye I think So tis true
I may not have seed he myself
Yet tis sure he is back among us now
Moving through the shadows of this house
As once he move through Stocton Hill
That was his fathers house

How can we lay him back in his grave again
Get the lid of the coffin bang down once more
Fold the welcoming earth ovr he

Standing at the foot of the Masters bed
What is it that his brother want
Vengeance Justice What he never had in life
He has a right to ask

Yet I shall not be the one
To give that to he

I made my decision many years ago
Cannot go back

Nothing can give it to him now

Except perhaps God Hisself
When all shall come to stand afore
His Judgement Seat

But in truth Vengeance Justice
He were not that mould of man

Perhaps all he wants
That he should have his voice heard
Should be listend to after all these years

That his span upon this mortal earth
Should end in something more than dust

This we must all desire
That some person bear witness to our lives
Know us in all our deepest parts

As Ambrose know me all those years ago
Under the dripping field where we dancd

THE HEAVENS

Always I am caught in the balance
Mr Woebegone Mrs Woebegone
Tip one way then tother

One day he will lose his battle
Then will trouble come

Yet afore that happen come a day
Turn the balance my way
Or not my way I do not know
For better or worse
I cannot say

It fell out like this
Sybilla and I walk back from school
Up Dry Hill and through the wood
As we do most every day
Ambrose is not with us now

Tis meant he stay at school all day
Which cost some pence extra
But he is sick at home

None at The Heavens know

Those pence all waste
Even when he is healthful
He not go there evr
One day will be discoverd

So Sybilla and I walk alone
The shoulder of the Valley side
Pass the weavers cottages
Come to the Coombs where the stream flow
Where we stop to build a dam sometime
Boys swing on a piece of rope high above
But we dare not daddle long
On account of Mrs Woebegone
Must get home start the fire in the wash house
Mash up food to give to Baby Fern

So we turn up the way to The Heavens
A track all inclosd on both sides by steep banks
Surround thick on all sides by trees

We walk on up as we do each day
Hitting at the banks and bushes with sticks
Hear the flick and hollow echo
All happy as the day is caressing warm
School is done
For supper may be peas and gooseberries
As is the season now

So we rounds the corner not far from home
When a terrible sight appears afore us

Standing in the way is a white bull
Such is the width and height
He fill out all cross the lane
His rock shoulders near up to the branch above

He come from Claypits Farm
Seed him when we go down the garden
Cross the farm yard next door
Climbing on the fence to tease he
With long sticks of grass

But now he is not pennd or fencd

Sybilla steps back
Opens her mouth as if to scream
But I steps smart up behind her
Slaps hand ovr her mouth
Holding her firm
Feeling her heart beating
Like the wings of trappd bird
Gainst my chest

The bull stands watching us
Head down horns point at us

I look up to one side and then tother
The banks are up right steep
I am strong and a lithe climber
So might perhaps get up
Use the roots of trees
As ladder in the mud

Yet I could not pull Sybilla as well
Her arms being thin as ribbons
Though she can be a spiteful pinching miss
Yet she is a sister to me
I cannot leave her

All this I think in the space of a second
The bull lowers his head
Paws the earth opens his mouth

In a growling bellow

Sybilla makes again to shout
But still I holds her tight
Says do not move Do not move one muscle

For some how I know
In this moment of dire extremity
That the Lord God will decide
If the bull sees not our fear
He may not charge

So that is my decision
I stand still and straight chin up
In the strength of the Almighty
Fix my eyes firm on his
Scowling darkly eyed visage

He bellows again tips his weight forward
Lowers head

Now he comes I think
I pray Lord save our souls
Save now our mortal souls

Many I know is haunchd by bulls
Gone dead in an instant

I feel the air thicken
Hear the beating of wings

The Angels are come
Massd above the banks in the trees
They hold the bull where he is
Though his head is low hoof scraping
Forward and back forward and back

The Angels hold me where I am
Quite strong and firm and God strengthend
My eyes fixd straight on his

I know not how long we stand like that

Then behind the bull
I see men come from the farm
Mr Woebegone hisself
Know now the bull is loose

At first they come waving pitchfork rake
But then praise God they see how we are placd

If they run on
They will trap the bull make him run scard
So drive him on into us rather than away

So quick and stealthy they mount the banks
Side of the road is not as steep where they are

I do not watch
Hear only the silent snap of a twig
I must not look up at them
Only keep my eyes on the bull
Fix the deep candles of his eyes
See right in the dark inside of he

Another shuffle and a snap
I know the men are above
Then a coming from either side they appear high
Start a terrible shouting hollering
Banging of sticks waving cratch and duns pick

They jump down now into the lane
The bull is afeard

Begins to turn away

Mr Abel Woebegone comes beside me
Lifts Sybilla out my arms
She turns fantomy and now gone dead

The bull bellows turns gallops away
Mr Woebegone lift Sybilla away up the bank

Iron arms lift me aloft also
While others run after the bull afeard of what
Further damage he may do

Mr Woebegone hold Sybilla tight in his arms
Like the Good Lord Our Shepherd found His flock

I laugh and brush my hands together Pleasd
For I have got upsides of that bull

*

That not the finish of the story of the bull
For that eve in the kitchen talk much

Among those present was that same
Mr Harland Cottrell

I recognizd him straightway from the school
Think Oh yes Tis he
For now I hear his name
I realize I have heard much talk

He livd the other side of Stroud
At a place they call Stocton Hill

He a man live close up tight to God they say

Take no flesh or fish or strong liquor

Yet more than that he is a cunning man
Having travelld to many far countries
Skilled in physic and herb

So having a certain gift for the healing of
Rare and stubborn ailments

Mr Woebegone know him but I know not for why

Mrs Woebegone do not hold with he
Not want he come to The Heavens
She considers him heathen
As he not of our faith
But Ambrose been ill now so long a time

Others have come with potions salves
Plasters on his chest blood letting
Leeches stuck on behind his ears
The wounds being sufferd to bleed
For some long hours

Yet none has made him well so tis
Mr Woebegone send for Mr Harland Cottrell

Mrs Woebegone say he waste his money
Tis well known Mr Harland Cottrell
Not a real doctor or even an apothecary

Now he has already tend Ambrose
Says he has got the Vipers Dance
But this receipt will heal soon enough

Since the boy seem straightway rather better
We must all be respectful to such as

Mr Harland Cottrell
Pagan or no he is a gentleman
So Mr Woebegone say Sit you down
Eat afore you go

He does not eat only drink water but still
He hear the story of the bull

He listen to it carefully
His head turn sprightly
So he may catch each word

His long face is solemn
He wipe at his lips with a napkin
Held precise betwixt those root like fingers
Clear his throat

His eyes move and move round the room
Always restless always searching

A cause of the story of the bull
So I am calld to the table
To be given a piece of cold beef
Still rimmd with much fat
I ate it quick
I never had such a thing afore

One of the farm men say
Two of them both be dead
If it had not been for our Mary Ann
Scard off the bull

All is laughing a little and say
What a thing twas a bull staring scard
Into the eyes of such a small lass

Even Mrs Woebegone say
Indeed I done well
I glowing at such praise

If only then it had been left like that
But then things went on
I could not stop myself
Saying what I never should have said

But one of the farm hands speaks up
So Mary Ann what you do
How you stop such a girt
And fiercesome bull

I did not want to make myself too large
For in truth it were nothing that I done
So I say quite clear

Twas not me as did it
It were the Angels

So a silence fell

Then after a while What Angels I am askd
I say then it were the Angels of the Lord

Then what fool am I cannot stop myself
Say I seed them afore felt their wings

Soon as I spoke Mrs Woebegone grow
Blood red in the face
Eyes bulging and say in a voice hissing steam

What say you child
What say you

I step back as I know well her temper
The walls of the room draw in tight around us

Then it were Mr Harland Cottrell
Spoke up his voice calm and polite
As had been silent to that time

No no says he Let the child speak

Yet I have nothing more to say
Stood back gainst the wall

Still he waits for me to speak
There is something in his face
Draws words from all who look at he
As the fingers of the fiddle player draw music
From his instrument

Yet finally all I can say again is
Were the Angels of the Lord stoppd the bull
Not me

So you saw these Angels Mr Harland Cottrell say
I know not what to say for I feel
The room crowd all about now with
Anger and Fear

Yet surely I must speak the truth
That above all else
So I say Yes I saw the Angels

Around me a hubble of voices start

Mr Harland Cottrell say
You seed them afore these Angels

I say Yes Sir I have

Well I suppose it could be so
Say Mr Woebegone

What do they look like say another

I find it hard to say
I have not the words
Maybe I say like animals
Small Maybe like a goose

I only say this last
For the damage is done already
Yet still the Devil set me to make it worse

Loud guffaw of laughter grow large the room

That is enough Mrs Woebegone say
I will not have such blasphemy
In this a Christian house

She reaches to take hold of me and I look to run
But there is no gap to fit through

Others catch hold of Mrs Woebegone
Say Nay Nay
She is but a stripling
A silly prattling moppet

Then Mr Woebegone come forward and say
That is enough Mary Ann
You get you to bed now
Come not down again

I were not sorry to depart

Hurry nippling to the stair to avoid the beating
Definitely stinging in her chappd fingers

Yet as I make the first step of the stair
I look back
I know not why but I did

I find the eyes of that Mr Harland Cottrell
Fixd on me clear and still
Looking through into every corner of my soul
As only the Lord God surely should

＊

The night of the bull and the Angels
So changd many things at The Heavens

You could not see it clearly not at first
Only you feel it

As you are touchd sometime
By the chill of winter
Gathering yet on a September eve

Perhaps things were changing anyways
The harvest poor bellies swollen sore

Many wandering land pull berries from hedges
Pilching carrots from gardens
Getting in the pigs pen to take back
Even the scraps givd for them
Sleeping in the woods and hedges
Their faces all hollow out
As though the flesh scrap off

Mrs Woebegone take in more wool picking

Which we must all work together
Out in the shed with no windows there
Though all the while she say
That this is beneath her
Oh how she does take on

Though at least the wool now she says
Being German not from Spain a mercy that is
That of Spain being cakd in filth

Though does seem to me what we have
Is nastry enough as we do beat with hazel twig
Wash out afterwards

Mrs Woebegone read to us from the Bible
How the Lord will come in fire
His chariots flashing like a whirlwind
Render His anger with red hot fury
Execute His eternal judgement

Yet Mr Woebegone say
Tis a cause the weavers
Who are compelld to take their looms now
Into the weaving shops all together
Where they must pay a shameful rent
Just for the standing of their looms
Many an industrious man
Brought to the parish in this way

I not go to school any more now
Neither Sybilla only Ambrose
The money does not run far enough
Ambrose will not go much longer neither
Soon to work for a weaver
Or go in one mill or another

Mr and Mrs Woebegone argue
Back and forth

Ambrose want to go in the mills
Despite all his father say
That tis gainst all reason
That any should work shut away from the sun

Yet Ambrose talk all the time
Shuttles wheels and an engine drivd by steam
Made by Mr Boulton and Watt
Which he walk ovr The Vatch to see
A man let him help shovel the coal

Then also at this time Mr Wood
He must give up the farm
As his wife falls down the well
His back still crookd as a bent nail
He with two small childers
Tis a pity

We weep to see him go
All that they own pild on a creaking cart
On top a cock horse with a felt nose
I remember how Mr Wood found the stick
His wife make the nose
Dark wool fluff for a mane

All goes off bumping down the lane
The childers following
The one pull the other by the hand

This same does happen to many now
Honest yeomen who must give up their land
All cross Oxfordshire and Nottingham also
So tells us Mr Abel Woebegone

So is notd down the ownership
Of every acre rood and perch
So the position of every road footway
Public drain fence gate

Mr Woebegone say Here here
Many now does make bitter protest
For they even stop a stream in his running
Lay him straight in a ditch
Label him who owns

Tis a lawless law this inclosing
So tis said

I am set to work now for a farmer
In field down the dip of the Valley
New Leaze above The Thrupp
Pull turnips for which six pence I earn

The tops of the turnips are already gone off
So tis the root that we must get
Stuck deep and sucking in the sodden earth

The winter come upon us early and strike hard
The ground solid with frost October even

The work is bitter my hands sore
The land deathly for the sun may not
Pierce down into these deep parts
The Valley sides all around steep as walls
The wind whistle through like a tunnel
Scrape all life out of me

Others who pull are mainly fully growd
They say tis not right but I say naught
I am a hard worker

One day as I step down there dawn rising
The skye v low and red above the frost
Seeping colours pink and orange

I come off Dry Hill start cross the fields
A man step out the hedge I never saw such a man

His clothes tord and blatchy his hair mattd
He come at me and I nowhere to run
Fear that I shall be cornobbld

Seizing he turn me wrong ways up
Push hands into my clothes
The smell of him his black teeth
His cracked hands grabbing
Me press gainst
His sticking ribs
Breath rasping

I am too afeard even to scream
Then I realize this desperd man has let me go
Droppd me back on the ground like a rag doll
He only stolen from me the cleat of bread
Which is in my pocket for my lunch

He eat it down sparking eyes still watching me
I run on do not look back
I hate him for it

When I reach to the turnip field
I sink down craiky and sobbing
But old Mrs Madden come to help me
Others with her

Come come child You are safe Do not you cry
They pick me up and wipe me down

Say Take heart Now now

Young Jack a gallus lad get me some milk
From a bottle clap me firm on the shoulder
Be you not scard Mary Ann You a brave girl

So I am but that time of my life is unforgiven

My hands is the main trial They bleed much
From grapping in the mud after the turnips

The cuts cannot heal from one day to the next
Bleed and pull open again as I work

Tis not right Tis not right say old Mrs Madden
Who were evr blob mouth though kind in heart

That witch she cast her spell on Woebegone
Him a gentle soul though fird by wrong passion
Never should have matchd with her
What a cooten was he
You must at least be givd gloves

One day that young Jack
Walk up The Heavens with me
Many do call him a Jerry Me Diddler

But I do like him heartily
For he is bold and quick of tongue
Walk straight in the kitchen
Mrs Woebegone be there gutting a rabbit
With Baby Fern crawling under the table

Say Jack What do you Why she not have gloves
Mrs Woebegone have none of it
Scream him right out the kitchen

Call him a hobbledehoy and a Neddy then

Still my hands paind and skinless
So I ask later again
Mrs Woebegone can I not be givd gloves
This time she not bullock at me but still say
Yr hands must harden to the work

What use will you be to anyone in the world
If you cannot earn yr keep
So I suppose she has a purpose

Yet the day come when the pain is too much
I take fever Can stand up no longer

Jack and another lad then lift me up the fields
Mrs Madden come after as well spitting curse bad
Place me down on the kitchen floor
Where my legs do not hold me

Mrs Woebegone is stakd firm there
Mrs Madden hiss at her
So this what you want is it

I know Mrs Woebegone would like to beat me
But Mr Woebegone just come back and see all

Why she no gloves he say

I am put to bed and rest there several days
Til my hands is heald

After that I go back to the fields
Am given gloves
Still I have sores and cuts but not so raw now
My hands is hardend and me as well

So the work goes much better
In gratitude to the Lord

Still Mrs Woebegone has not finishd with me
She talk to her husband I hear not all but some

They mean to be rid of me I know it
What can I do

One day I come back from the field
The Minister is a come
I know him closy from the chapel
Yet never spoke him

Others come as well
The men from the end cottage
Mr Woebegone though he shakes his head
Say There is no cause for it

The Minister take hold of me
Stand me tall on the table
He look me in the eye say Be not afraid Mary Ann
I think you know right well the Devil is in you
That he must be bought out

Is it not true Mary Ann Sate
Do you feel the Devil is in you

Oh yes Sir I say I know that he is

At this Mrs Woebegone look v pleasd
Her point is well made

Ah then say the Minister
We must pull him out

Yr adversary the Devil
Prowls around like a roaring lion
Seeking someone to devour
Take care

I do not know what a lion is
But wonder how this Devil be got out
I suppose I will be beat
Perhaps tis best
I have tussld with him long
Seed him oft times
Hides by the path as we do walk
I know him by his red eyes
Following us home
Do want him banishd

We must take care say one of the men
She may writhe strongly
Also vomit needles
Tis oft so

The Minister take no cane but holy water and oil
A cloth of gold embroidery hung ovr his arm
A crucifix of wood curld with much fine silver
All is laid out and then he speak

Ask the Devil inside me what is his name
The Devil say naught

Then he calls on him in a thunder voice
Come out of the child thou unclean spirit

Then he say to me
Take on you the whole Armour of the Lord
That you may be able to withstand the evil day
And having done all still to stand

Says many more words
Some in a language I do not understand
I feel him tug at the Devil inside me
I hope him soon gone
Pull him out I think
Pull him out

I am near fantomy such is the struggle

This I say unto you
Beelezebub Beelezebub
You come out now you cunning Fiend

All are watching
I wait to feel some girt groaning wrench
Like when a tooth is drawd
A horrible scream and a tearing sound
As the root come away from bone

This is how twill be when he is pulld out
But nothing nothing nothing

I do not know the Minister say
I do not think it right
I find no Devil here

I am sorely disappointd in he
Both in the Minister and in that cunning Fiend
Knows so well how to hide hisself

There is There is say Mrs Woebegone
Much put out

Ay ay say one of the men from the end cottage
He is there but he hide well and stubborn
You must wrestle with he long

You do not tell me what I do the Minister say
Flapping his embroiderd arms
Like a trappd bird

I still wearing my gloves from the fields
Take these off the Minister say

I take them off and he looks long at my hands
Then he stares deep at Mrs Woebegone
She not like this one penny worth

You go child he say to me
Lift me off the table
I hurry out glad to be there no more
I did not understand
I should have let the Devil go from me
But how is that to be done

You might think that given that no Devil found
Then all would be easier in these afterclaps
But no no Mrs Woebegone not like to be gainsay

I must take much care

Yet twas that v evening
Just as I walk out
I saw the first of the spring blow in
A breath of daffodilly lickorish on the wind

A change in the air and I knew then
That better times were a coming

I told Ambrose about the Minister and he laughd
Most disrespectful yet as always
I like him for it

Soon soon the days longer
No more turnips to pull
May get a job pot scouring
Turning hay or pick up kindle
For this I thank the Lord

Then just as the blossom sweep
All the scatterd way cross the Valleys
Like a late fall of snow
So is the time come for Ambrose to go
It has been talkd about long and bitterly argud

He is to go to Bowbridge Mill
As a dyer to learn that trade
This there is always need

He does not want that work
He prefer to be a millwright or carpenter
Or work where is a steam engine
Yet is glad enough to get away any place

I am downcast he will go
Who will I turn to now

Tis only a mile or more down the dropping hill
Below Stroud Fields and Creese Gate
Yet still I will not see he
Except Sunday maybe

When the day comes I say naught
I stay out in the scullery I will not cry

He comes then to look for me Opens the door

Do not fear he says Do not fear
I shall be back to see you oft

I slam the door in his face
Shout I do not care You go You go
I do not care

After he is gone I am sick with shame

*

Yet the spring rise soon after
Life flow back into heart and limb
I am happy have no sense of the darkness gather

I am given a job scaring birds
By Mr Bartlett the new man at Claypits Farm
This I like well

Though I know full heavily
The state of our Valleys is no better

Many join The Stroud Valleys Weavers Union
So they may do now for
The Act of Parlement is repeald

That Union being made gainst the shop looms
Also to fight the falling wage

I hear all from Ambrose I see him Sundays
How is organizing committees and delegations
For to strike work

He shew me a paper he tell me is calld
The True British Weaver
Has no printers name on it

Meetings held on Break Heart Hill
Some also going to the loom shops

Pulling the flying shuttles
Out the looms with many malign threats
Gainst those who might break the strike
For the level of wages must be maintaind

Tearing unfinishd cloths out also
Stamping him on the ground
Right in the face the manufacturer

Ambrose tell he is all for fair conditions
All must be paid the same
Yet those who blame the shuttle
They have no more brain than a dromedary

For tis new machinery which is need
To save our proud tradition of cloth

I do not know Some I do not understand
But I interestd to hear and mombld oft
As to what he may do

Mrs Woebegone call them all ruffians
Jacobins work shy traitors

So tis that when one day come
The top end of the month of May
When I am out in the fields
I see several men in the lanes below
All moving the same way

Have you heard Have you heard
Now is the trouble starting Mark well

They say they go to Ham Mill
Some story I do not understand
What does happen there

Ay Ay It would always come
Three pence per yard on a chain of broadcloth
They will not take less

Then I am much troubld
No one should leave their work
Tis not right

Yet I am sore heartd for Ambrose
What might happen to him there

So I stand sometime in thought
But more and more come down the lane
So I am swept along with they

Along the top of Bowrey Grove
Through Four Acres toward Park Wood

We tumble down the long hill together
Through the tunnels of trees
Passing then the many quarries
Light stipple the lane shift sway
Blind yr eyes and then gone

The men ahead of me heading on fast
Their faces scarlet step boots stomping
Arms swing breathing high

All singing and shouting
Now let us all while in our bloom
Drink success to the weavers loom

All the time the thrill grow in our chests
Though I know not what tis we will see

Stopping then low down the Green Hill

See down below the way as leads to Stroud
The Gate House to Ham Mill
So we start to hear much bullocking
The sound of many people gatherd

One is high in drink and sing loud and tuneless

But the weavers they are valiant men
As you will understand
Then for our wages we stand out
No more be at command

Down below a crowd such as I never seed
All gatherd about the mill buildings the stream

Men stand with long sticks in their hands
Along the stream bank
Gatherd close round the mill pond
Some shaking fists and shouting

All round I hear the name of Edward Perrin
Yet I know not who or what is he

A wagon is being usd as a platform
From which some weavers
Do address the gathering

They best take care one behind me say
For a troop of hussars is on their way
Even now a coming as fast as hoof may fly
From Stroud sent out by the Clothiers
And others of the King and Country men

Then I see one tied up high
On the beam take from a loom
He is one of Marlings men they say

All jeering and hesselling
Drop he in the pond
Duck he down

Outside the gates of the mill
Some there are on horses fine gentlemen
High collar top hat and cane shining gold button
Bridles of the horses glitter also
Foam at the mouth clatter and shine

One comes forward and begins to read
In voice bracd firm The Riot Act

This is perhaps the special constables
As tis knowd many has been sweard in
Also with them the vicar
Gripping the Bible in his hands

All singing then and punch fist the air

Til a soldier jump his horse
Right on to the wagon where the weavers is
Scattering all about

A swelling shout goes up Duck him down
The man toppling on the loom beam
Raisd high above the crowd
Struggling and crying
Yet tied on tight

But then I see no more
For others climb beside me on the stile
Push and pull
I get down afore I fall
Cannot see much no more except the russet
Backs of fustian jackets knottd hair

Shoulder edging through the crowd

I not understand but my heart is bubbling
Swelling with the excitement of such a number
All holding together breathing together
The feeling of anger knots them all tight

Behind it all a sense as of a fire starting
The harsh snap and crackle the kindling flizzie

So so they duck him now one say
In the mill pond another speaks
Others is jeering staggering high above me
All clamberd on the stile

But I do not laugh I am not sure tis right
Tis Gods design they must work
As all must work
Not for them to say what money they should have

Then I see Ambrose push up the hill toward me
The light fall full on his face
His black hair curl loose and thick
His limbs as always have that long easy swing

So so he say You come to see
I hope not Mrs Woebegone hear word of it

Til that moment I had not thought much of her
Now I know that trouble will come
Word will go back

What think you Ambrose I say Is it right

Oh yes yes Ambrose say
All have the right to live

All must have money to eat

From below harsh cries and the crowds press
Shove jostle some shouting out
As they is nearly pushd down

I should go I should stay
Tis the work of the Devil
We shall fall in temptation this way
But still I am held fixd

I want to join my voice to the hollering Though tis wrong
They shall get their way now
Ambrose tell me

Then many come running up the hill
Get down they shout Go back

Then among the pushing throng
We see one of the men from the Forresters
Quick Quick Ambrose pull away
Go back up the hill
Keep in close under the hedge
Ambrose say Be careful Keep yrself hid
I will come later

We shall be beat til the flesh hung off
If we is found
Now others is striding the hill

Mary Ann one shouts
I know him from the chapel
A string thin whisker and bristle man
With a glout face and a nooching stride
Cause by a bumble foot
How dare you What you do

You keep away from all that

Run Ambrose tells me Run and say naught
I break away from him and slide myself into
A narrow slip of woodland as edges the lane

When I a come back to The Heavens
Ambrose is there at the gate afore me
He say he call to see Mr Woebegone

I am glad of that If there is to be trouble
Then he and I together

Soon as we come to the house all is silent
Is the silence of gathering anger
Of tight woven fear

Mrs Woebegone dance with wrath

Do you not know for the love of God
They are Jacobins and revolutionaries all
Will chop off our heads with guillotines

You Mary Ann gone down with them
Tis gainst the Lord
I will not have you in my house one day more

Mr Woebegone is there but he cannot stop her now

Child child say Mr Woebegone
Why go you there

Ambrose speak then for me
She want to see what will happen
Such are the injustices they do suffer

What say you Father
But Mr Woebegone will not be drawd
Sit smoke his pipe in the corner by the hearth
As he so oft does

Father Father say Ambrose
Still Mr Woebegone say naught

Mrs Woebegone will not be set aside
She leave work
She go down there You think I see nothing

Then she say from the Bible
Obey them that have the rule ovr you
Submit yrselfs
For they watch for yr souls

I say naught keep my eyes hid

Ambrose say
She goes for she is like me
She cares for Justice
Mrs Woebegone go for him then
Take hold of he
Has he in a corner

Come now come now say Mr Woebegone
Enough enough

Yet Mrs Woebegone take hold of Ambrose
She not a head taller than he and thin bond
But as I know well
She has a fearful strength
Ambrose strong but she hold him tight
Gainst the wall pressd in a corner

Tis only then I see she has a carving knife

The sight of its silver slice of length
Trembles through me
Never has she done such afore

You do not think that
So she scream at he

Ambrose only smirk and shrug
For he not see the knife
Then she raise it up
Lay it close gainst the white of his neck

I see his eye change
What can I do
What can he do
If I go into her she may slice him
I hold my ground
Watch Feel breath flare my nostrils
Press down the scream in my throat

What say you now
She say and hold the knife gainst he

What say you

He cannot move
He must feel the knife
Closy gainst him
We both know
She is possessd
She can use it if she decide

Pray God he dispute with her no more

No Ambrose say finally I do not think it
I do not I know he hates to say it
What else may he do

For he is feard of the knife
As well he might

Yet no sooner she drop the knife from him
Than she turn on me   I should have got away
But foot catch on the table and fall
She then is set on me

Sit astride my back pull up my head
Tear back the collar
Hold the knife gainst my throat
I feel it tremble close the shivering white
Of my sunless stretchd skin

Mr Woebegone and Ambrose both above me
Nay Nay Come come Enough now enough

But they now in the place I was in
Just minutes afore
If they try to take the knife from her
They may provoke her worse
One flick of her wrist and I am done

What say you now she say What say you now

Mary Ann Mary Ann say Ambrose from above
You save yr soul You say what evr you say
Take care Take care

A picture comes to me then of Mr Woebegone
As he was on the hillside his arm stretchd wide
All mankind are my brethren

To do good is my religion
He was a different man from now

The moment hold long
I can see naught but floor
Table legs boots
Little Fern scream in the corner
Her tiny hands lockd to her face
Mrs Woebegone pull back my hair
My neck crick
Still the blade gainst me

What say you now What say you now

I am fire I am sure

A certain knowledge come to me in that moment
Sudden and certain A knowledge all must have

Mary Ann I say to myself
You think tis the knife kills
But you do not die that way
Not you Not any other

Fear not them which kill the body
For they cannot kill the soul

The knife may kill yr mortal body that it may
But death the deep death come another way
It come when you say what you know is not true

This I am sure This I know
The courage of the Lord in me
I have a power could tread on serpent or scorpion

What say you now What say you now

Speak child or I shall do my worse

Though she spit this
I feel her body gainst mine
Feel her weaken Give
I am stronger than she

So I say
I think all men have the right to bread

I hear Ambrose gasp He thinks the knife to move
Yet I know twill not

She say
No No You do not bring that talk in this house
I slit yr throat I slit it

What Devil in it I do not know
Still I say it Again and again
She will not have the best of me

I think all men have the right to bread

Knowledge still in me like a burning light
You can never put it out
She will not kill me with that knife
No one will evr kill me with knife
Or chain or gun or rope or poison No

She still has the knife at my throat
But her hand unclasp and I turn my head
See her spitting inward bending white fox teeth
Her skin red and blotchd
Where the hair held tight back enough
To stretch the chin at ear and forehead

No one will evr kill me this way

Tis as though she sees it and knows it too
The breath goes from her She shakes her head
Tears are fountain all down her face
Her twig bones shaking
Sobs her shoulders hard wrack

Lay down the knife
Instead drag me out in the yard
Where two of the men the other cottage stand
Shaking their heads Nay nay

The evening now is all about red and gold
Down through the vegetables we go
Will she push me in the pig pen
Or throw me in the well

For a moment I look up at the high clouds
Oh that I might reach up and lift myself
Away up high where I might look down
See all below hills farms sheep cottage stream
All come one green and peaceful

Push me in the stable there shut up both doors
Is fixd with heavy bolts
Silence fall liquid dark and quiet
I wait I am not afeard

Later much later Ambrose come
He speak to me through the stable door say
I must go back Mary Ann I must go back
Mr Woebegone will come He will let you out
Even as he said the words I wonder

*

I tell it to you now
I am in that stable three days three nights
No food no light
Only a sip of water
From a bucket left in the corner
Crustd green

First I think she do not mean to kill me
She will let me out
As the time go by I wonder

I listen all the time for Mr Woebegones voice
But I never hear it All is hush

I listen men in the yard splashing of the pump
The cows in the sheds shift and sigh
The pigs root and snuffle

Once I hear the voices of the cottage men
Tis enough Tis enough

Nay she deserve all she get
Why they keep her here

Then the voices scatter and hush
I know no more
They will not stand gainst her
Never have

All the time I plan how I am to get out

Many many times I try
Tis easy to get half way
Can stand on a ridge there
But there is no way further
The roof is well built tiles and wood

Tight upon each other
Many stars of light
No way to move even one

I think of digging out and make a fine deep hole
Push aside all the straw
Dig til my fingers skinless
She made sure my hands were good

But this building is old
The wall sunk deep
The earth is dry and hard
I cannot get underneath he

So I lie in the straw witherd and weak
She means me now to die

Drink again from the brakish drip of water
Greening in the pail

I pray again and again to the Lord God
Do not forsake me now in this my hour of need
Have mercy on Thy humble servant
That I pray

All the time waiting for the Angels to come
But they do not

Lying there I think even if I get out
What then am I to do

I cannot stay no longer at The Heavens

Might I go to Bowbridge Mill or Griffin
Or even further on to Chalford
St Marys or Iles which I have seed with Ambrose

Find out what is there
Ambrose would help me this I know
Now that I am ten year old I can decide myself

So people say the work break you the pay poor
Oh for the days when you work in yr own home
With yr own family
But family matter not to me

When I think of winter a coming
I prefer mill to turnip

Yet I might never see the winter
So I think

Next day find a long flint amidst the straw
This my best hope
I begin to work on the bolts
I am fantomy now my stomach gnawing
Still my fingers edge and scrape

I am pushing gainst the metal
That I might move the bolts
I must throw all my weight gainst it
Sometimes it move a whiskers breadth
Mostly not at all

Scrap scrap scrap back and forwards
I shift it but a little once twice
But I am fammeld and gasping adry
Must lie down in the straw a while
Then back again scrap scrap
Move a whisper Nothing more

All that time as I remember
I did know the heat in that stable

Burnt more than any general zummer day

I did think the silence strange
Still I had no sense of what comes

Oh what blessing finally a time
When the flint work stronger slides back faster
It opens sudden The bolt come back

Who knows not that
The hand of the Lord hath wrought this

I am free Step out into the sun light
My eyes blind My hands stretch out
As I tumble to the pump grab at the handle
Push my whole head under it

I notice then how the day hang strangely
Hot and still The sun come straight down
On the Valleys No shade
Not under tree or roof

Not a breath of breeze
Even the water from the pump
Warm to the touch Dust blow thick

Herbs hung in bunches at the door
Their sharp smell swollen the air

Then I hear it
A sound from the kitchen
Choking twisting

Something is brokd all pulling out of joint

*

So there is always danger
Yet the danger you fear
That is never the one that strike

Watch therefore for you know neither
The day nor the hour

That noise I hear is Mrs Woebegone
She lie on the kitchen floor
Her night dress pull up around her knees
Hands grip stomach head strain

All round is the foulest stench and vomit
Spread cross the kitchen

When Mrs Woebegone see me she struggle upright
Eyes staring wide and say
Tis you Mary Ann as brought the Devil
In this house

I say from the beginning the Devil in you
I try to drive it out
You know right well as I did try
But he is too strong for me
Now you bring plague and poison

For all she say these words I go to help her

Just then Mr Woebegone steps in
Smell that tugging stinging smell
Watch her hunchd green stomach grip

I run to get a bucket a cloth wash out the floor
He take Mrs Woebegone lift her up the stairs

Soon he come stumbling back down eyes roll

119

God save us all God save us
It come here now So it would

Mary Ann he say I need you quick
Yes Sir I say

I need you to take a letter
Also to go to the dispensary
You know where he is

You go now to the George Inn
Find a person as may take that letter
Get to the dispensary Do not delay
If you see Sybilla tell her come home now
Though what safety now we have
I do not know

First I take a dabbit of bread in the pantry
For I am still craiky weak
Then goes straightway
Following all the greenly ways down

As I near Stroud I come level with Jack
Who I did know in the turnip field

Oh he says You like I
Do flee this place while you may
But I did not understand his meaning
Til he said So Woebegones took sick also

Then tells he this sickness all ovr the Valley
Yet what care I he say
The wages no good here
I not wait til I took sick as well
I to Gloucester see what work there may be there

I wish him luck hurry on though boffld
Sick at heart what might come to pass

When I get to the town of Stroud
All is worse than I feard
For many are weeping in the streets
A man is carrid down dead
Wrappd in a closet sheet
A child lies side of the road
Bubbling mouth flat eyes seeing nothing

I go to the dispensary but many is already
Lind up gainst the wall there
What salvation is there here
Who will walk out to The Heavens offer succour
When so many sick in the town

Still I go to the George with the letter
A man there takes the letter I do give
Though who know whether any will go

Find many shops with the shutters down
Packing bundles and carts to get away

O Lord have mercy on our souls thinks I
As I go on through asking each person I see
Where is a doctor though I know is no purpose
None is to be found

Then an old man black teeth waving hat say
No no girl Tis no good
You are young and strong yet
Get you out of the town to the clearer air
While you may

Tis true I were sorely worrit

How might I help those at The Heavens
If I took sick myself
So I set off back

When I come the situation is yet worse
Who could think such could happen
With the sun so merry and laughing
In the skye and fields high with corn
The bounty of God all round us

At The Heavens little Fern is took sick
I cry out when I see it
I cannot abide to see her so
Sweat bead her brow jewel eyes dull

Sybilla stand in the kitchen crying
Mr Woebegone say to her Sybilla
Pack food and water now
Take some linen be quick
I have writ yr aunt at Frampton
Now we cannot wait
You must walk there
If you not go now twill be too late

I am hoping that Mr Woebegone will say
You also Mary Ann You must go with Sybilla

But no no He does not say it
I must be one to stay
So it always is

I help Sybilla to pack
I cannot leave Fern she say
I cannot leave

I promise I will take care of Fern

Though Sybilla never care me any
It were a sad and sticking bitter
Leave taking we made

She knew her life break to bits
God save Fern she say
I say Yes yes so it shall be
Yet having seed what happen in the town
I do not know

After Mr Woebegone send me upstairs
To tend Mrs Woebegone knottd now in the bed
I never been in that room afore

See Mrs Woebegone shivering and rattling
Again when she see me she accuse me of all

So so I think You may say all that
But then I not come to help you

So I turn from the room back down the stairs
See little Fern motionless on the hearth
I go to her and she turn
She is meeking and dry all ovr
Her tongue pushing out her mouth
The sheet she lie on soild

I find water and pour some down her throat
Take the sullid linen outside
Bring some fresh spread it flat
As I lay it under her she hold out her hand
Grip mine tight then lie back
Drift gently into sleep as I hold

After that I do not know
Hardly I remark that day follow night

None comes to the house
All is hushd and tight lippd
The air v sultry and sticking
Enough to maggle you to the grave
No wind at all

All again come without form and void

Mr Woebegone is soon takd
When he know it comes
He sits by the hearth calm and even
Say to me So so Mary Ann we are all undone

I can say naught
He is a man I have lovd
Brokd long afore I come
Yet beautiful in his ruin

I think of him stand on the side of the Valley
Speaking words that make the heart leap
I wipe at my eyes

Nay nay he say Come now Mary Ann
Take courage You are a strong girl
A good worker You may yet have life

As for the rest
The Lord take our mortal souls as He must
We go forth happy to meet Him

I am creasd with crying
Yet he lays a hand soft on my shoulder

Say I hope when they write down my testimony
They will remember my soul always live free
Though my body chafd always and sorely cagd

We all meet soon in a better place
So he say and pull from his neck
That kerchief he does oft wear
To wipe up my tears

All I can do is carry water wash clean change
Soon there are no more linen
The house reek so I try not to breathe deep
I sleep on the kitchen floor
Hold Fern in my arms

None now to feed the animals except me
So I must carry hay and water
Push them ovr the bellowing doors

In the house I make beef broth
In the hope it might revive them

But they want only water

All the time I am listening to my own heart beat
Ready for the moment this plague strike me
Which it surely must

Yea though I walk through the Valley of the Shadow of Death
I will fear no evil

One evening I go out into the kitchen garden
Stand look out ovr the Valley

So much corn a coming tall and proud
But like to wither in the fields afore it ripen
There is no one now well enough to bring it in
What will the winter be

In the distance I see

As I seed so oft afore
A cart small as an insect
Move along the brow of the hill opposite
He has still life I think
He goes on his way
Maybe there is a breeze in that place
Maybe life

I think of Mr Woebegone
All here is done
We meet soon in a better place

But I cannot bather long there go back inside
Taking with me beans from the garden
To eat for supper

Fern lie silent wastd
All the rich vigour of life gone
I stay up with her all that night
Sit in the big chair by the hearth
Hold her in my arms

Beside me is a pail of water
I bathe her burning body
Put water on her dry lips
Try to tempt her to drink
But she is too far away now

All that night
Though since tis near Midzummer
Is only a few dipping dark hours
But in that time she is gone
Still I hold her tight waiting
For what I do not know

Yet soon the dawn come

With it the Angels
I hear them from a far off

So then I go upstairs
Fern now stiff heavy in my arms
I watch them come from that high winder
The white light the featherd wings
Such blessing they bring
I know they come to take the soul of
Blameless Fern

I feel them when they come in the room
Her breath long ceasd her tiny hand cold in mine
Then with motherly gentleness
They lift her mortal soul
From her body

She is gone into the arms of the Almighty
Nothing now to do except
Lay tender her mortal remains down where
She always slept

Go downstairs still hear that gentle beating
Lie down on the hearth where she did lay
Fall asleep

When I wake the sun is growd high
I hear the voice of Mr Woebegone take him water
Mrs Woebegone stiff in the bed aside he
But he do not know it
I have not strength to move her
What can I do

Downstairs I eat uncookd potaters beans
Then I crack fat from the top of the broth
Drink some of that I cannot make a fire

The food brings me strength I am yet alive
But what life can there be for me now

Just as I am sit on the back door step
Thinking these thoughts
A stirring of wind does come
I stand up to feel it on my face

With it my courage returns
I am young and strong
I will find work
Should I go down the mills
Stroud or even Nailsworth

So I pack up my belongings that is only one bag
Am ashamd to say I dress myself in the pinafore
Which belong to Sybilla and also button boots
Such as I have never word afore

On the bedroom shelf
Are ribbons she did put in her hair
I take those as well
Even tie one beside my own face
I should not have done

I must look clean for a job

Then I stand on the landing outside the room
But hear then again Mr Woebegone cry out
Go downstairs again to get water for him
Pour some ovr his lips wipe his hands
The room is full of flies
The v wall sweat with plague

So God help me
I turns and goes down the stairs

Leaves him there though he is yet living
For I am already in my new life mint pinafore
Hair ribbon button boots
The life is high in me

Thank the Lord for the abiding mercy of my life
Pray God for the souls
Of all who are lost

I know that He has savd me
Because I gave no ground to Mrs Woebegone
I spoke the truth and always will
So I did think then

Walk out through the kitchen
Only as I am going I see on the chair
That kerchief Mr Woebegone did so oft wear
Put that in my pocket

Also chemise as belong to little Fern

Twas put there days afore
When the world was upright
The intention was I must sew the button

A job never to be done now
No reason to do it

Still I pick up that button
Hold tight in my hand
As I set off down the tree shade lane
Walk firm into whatevr world
Now await me

Feel no fear but certain and sure in
The care of the Lord

Always ready to defend His truth

*

I have not walkd but many steps
When I must decide

What purpose is there to go to Claypits Farm
Or even the cottages at Drybrook
Some person would have come from there
If there was any alive to come

So am I to go cross the skirt of the Valley
To Stroud or down the lane
Down down to where the mills is

As I stand there thinking I know not which
I sudden see below a figure I know

A coming the lane through deep turning shadows
Walking fast face sweat
The light touch him sometime
Then he move on is lost again the shadows close

Is Ambrose
I gather my new skirts run down toward him

Ambrose Ambrose Ambrose

As I stand afore him
All the tears that never fell
Come flowing now
Drip down onto the dry dust of the lane

So tis true then he says

I cannot look at him

Are they all takd he ask

Sybilla gone to her aunt in Frampton I say

Aye and the others

I do not speak partly for grief
Also for shame
Because I left
A cause I stole the pinafore and boots

Fern and Mrs Woebegone I start to say
The words choke

Ambrose knows anyway
Mr Woebegone he ask

The words wedge in my throat
I know not if Mr Woebegone his father
I always think yes though I am told no
Is certain he the only father Ambrose know

His kerchief is stinging in my pocket

He does live yet I say
I will come with you now

No Mary Ann he say No You go on

No no I cannot I must help you Ambrose

For why Mary Ann he say
He is sure and stern
For why you must help them

What good they evr done you

I shake my head I cannot answer
We look at each other long
His face now is stretchd and slappd
But still it has that shine from deep inside
He look me up and down

You look v fine Mary Ann he say
I like to see you look so well

Now I look him clear in the eye
See the depth of his strength

I must find a job I say
Shall I go to Bowbridge

No Ambrose say No I do not think so
The mill is stoppd for the moment anyway
So many is plagud

Go into Stroud town
Yr chances are better

I nod my head and say And you go on

Yes I go on

So it comes we must say good bye
Ambrose is the closest to family I know
He cleave so to my heart
How can I leave he

He see the look in my eye
Lay a heavy hand on my shoulder

Come come Mary Ann he say All is not lost
We have our lives yet
I know tis hard to say farewell
Twill be but for a brief time

How can you know I say

I just do know he say I am sure of it Sure
You and I will meet again not so long from now
The circumstances be better then

All you must do is wait on that time
If you need me you know where to find me

Thank you I say Thank you

Now set yr shoulders square he say
Be of good cheer
All will be well

With that he and I part
He for The Heavens
I to walk to Stroud

A new heaven and earth creatd
The light divide anew from the darkness
The whole world made new like the first day

*

So as I walk me then that day
Toward the town

The air still breathe hot
Yet now a hush of wind
Stir the trees the shrivelld

Sticks of grass

Lower Street mute and closd in on itself
Rubbage rotten vegetables
Lie in the street People wander purposeless
Houses eyeless dusty hanging limp

No washerwomen taking their laundry
Up to Gaineys Well No not this day

So I go on in the town heart where I only been
Two or three times afore
Past the coach maker and the White Hart
Which lies at the Cross

See the bone house and the stocks
Where the meat market usually is
The many weavers workshops all about

I gaitle then among the fine buildings
Sun glint on yeller and high winders
Still sharp enough to split yr eye

Pass fine gentlemen in glimmering soft coats
The fabric pull the fingers the desire to touch

A fine docksy lady I do stare at long
For she parade the streets
With a red silk petticoat
Held up above her head on a stick

In grocers shop many vegetables never seed afore
Though some split open and rotting
None to buy

All the scene eye stretchd wide to me

New pinafore and ribbon I feel I belong

Stand staring up to the White Hill
A place well namd for the light shine there
Do turn the hill glimmer pale

So for some time I did not properly consider
How I might find work
Need a recommendation
Wait for Hiring Day

Then hunger nag in my belly sharp
The sun start to slide the hills grow pale
The day lay itself down adry and fritchety
Fear take I must spend the night on the ground
How will I find food

Thinking this walk back to the Acre Hedge
Tis the only place I know well
But there being no one there
Continue on up the hill

A coming of a sudden to the Workhouse
You would always know it
Long and grim with many high winders
Tis a building hung with sorrow

Outside stand some raggd their head shavd
Their hands and eyes strangely large
I do not want to look

If I am to end there
The plague might have rather takd me

Just as I think this
A group of lads comes round a corner

Trousers tord at the knee scabs thick
No shoes sores running

What is yr name they say

Mary Ann Sate I say
Though I do not want to converse such as they

I step then smartly away
Making pretence I am not afeard
Though this is not purely the case

Stepping down the hill
Turning into this muddy chur and that
Finding my way through gardens
Past middens and pig pens

Find when I look back they yet follow me
Step then through wide stone gates
Find myself in a grave yard

Everywhere around signs of much activity
With many heaps of earth
Spades cratches and boards of wood
For many new graves are being dug
But now all is quiet for the day is end

I should not go in but my feet carry me on
Mounds of earth like the work of many moles
The shadows now growing ovr them

My mind sudden crowd with The Heavens
All I now lost there
My little sister Fern has not a Christian burial

The boys now are close again

Get out of here they shout
We do not want you Devil mouth here

I do not move
If I did not bend for Mrs Woebegone
Then I do not submit for these

They point to a gaping hole ovr to one side
Run right along the metal railing

You know what that is they say
But I say naught

Get out of here Get out
A Devil hare did cross yr mothers path

I will not move for them

Put paupers in the Workhouse there they say
Put them all in together pild v deep
One on top the other Many many

All come close foul breath on my cheek
Their voice grate like metal scrape
Nastry feet up close gainst my new button boot

Now I think
This is my punishment for leaving The Heavens
So it seem for these boys grab hold of me
Though I scream and plead for mercy
Pull me toward one of the newly dug graves
Narrow and deep the sides cut square

Here they stand me on the edge
Then they push me in
My head hit gainst the side my hands scrabble

Earth fall in my mouth my teeth crack grit

The skye narrow to a slice
The cold closes in like a lid pushd down
Smell of roots and decay all round
The earth cut clean on each side
Not a foot hold or a crack to use
A narrow fringe of green above
Jaggd jutting steeple the church needles skye

There I fix my eyes
I cannot look down
Unsteady I stand feel planks
But they are not firm

I stretch up my arms
The sleeves of my pinafore all streakd mud
Underneath me the board shift
The hands of the dead reach for me

I scream and scream my lungs raw
But tis eve now and who to hear

The dead below pild many
The boards shift and twist
My feet sinking
Still I scream and scream

Try to get some purchase on the clean cut sides
Scrambling and pulling with nails hands feet

Alas the earth is soft and starts to give way
A massy pile of earth falling upon me
So I think myself like to be burid alive

Only with girt difficulty

I pull myself out from under it
Hands touch the planks what mess lie beneath

Start I then once more to try to climb out
Which might now be possible where earth fell in

Then a shadow fall and a face appear
I cannot see right for the light behind him
But such is the power of this moment
That I think to myself without any doubt
So this now is God hisself
Who does come to save me

A hand come down
Fingers long and white root dangle
The touch soft but v strong
I take hold and feel the press of a gold ring
Sharp gainst my fingers
Then I am liftd out of the grave
Into the embracing grey light

Such is the shock and shame
I cannot look up
None can see the face of God

Why tis Mary Ann Sate a voice says
I see above me Mr Harland Cottrell
He looks at me knife pierce sharp

What do you here Mary Ann

I do not know what I can tell him but say
All at The Heavens took sick I cannot stay

So Woebegone is called home is he

Yes Sir I say God save me
Tis not the whole truth

Ah Ah say Mr Harland Cottrell
He was a man of goodness much mistreatd
Such are the times in which we live
The price of the truth can be high
Ah yes

Mr Harland Cottrell consider me then a while
Peer away far beyond the town
Up into the pleatd distant hills

Ah Ah he say
So many gone I have never seed such contagion
The wrath of God so many say but I do not agree
A God of love does not this

Then he considers me again and I could weep
For the mud on my dress and much else beside

He say What do you now Mary Ann Sate

I say surprisd at my own boldness
I look for a position Sir
Perhaps as a kitchen maid
I am a good worker

A silence gathers the shadows of the church yard
Grow long round us air chill the breeze growing

What of the Angels Mary Ann Sate
Do they not help you now

Yes I reply They can help me
Yet I need also human hands

So God has provide

I do not know why I said this
· Perhaps I read something in his face
For after a while longer he say
V well Mary Ann
Do you know where is Stocton Hill

I had heard the name but knew naught of it

Still say I can find my way easy Sir

Yes Yes he say
You go out past the grist mill at Stratford
Along the stream or the new road to Salmon Mill
Then up the fields at Cally Well Ground
Up Cleeve and Dry Leaze
You will find it well

Oh yes Sir I say Do not doubt it

V well he says
For I must call upon Mr Hawkins Fisher
Afore I go home

But you walk on and find me there
I will see what can be done for you Mary Ann

Thank you Sir I say and set out to walk

Though my legs drag tird
Hunger tear and wretch my stomach
I made good progress through warm blue shadows

A coming to Stratford House I do stare long
For I never seed a house so large and fine

A wide lake stretch cross the way

Walking then the path along the jostling brook
Skirt round the mill buildings
Catch sight of the girt wheels turning
The crash of water

But where tis I must turn up hill
I do not know

So I ask a drover that is herding sheep
He is a radish man red all ovr
With whiskers sticking out his ears
Spitting as he speaks

Why go you there he say

For work I say
He laugh at me then Oh aye Oh so you do
You work then for the Kettle Boil Cutter
Could be useful if you need yr leg off

He laugh loud then
Rub his hand cross his forehead

I say no more
You take care my lass

I am not afeard for what this man say
If I have chance of work then that is all
I keep good care my soul

Walk up the Painswick Road pass the mills there
Which I heard spoke of afore but never seed

Now I tird and weak with hunger

The ways about me are all confusion
I do not know which path to go

Yet seeing ahead of me such mercy
The figure of a woman dressd in blue
She holds a babe in her arm

So this then the blessd Virgin
I do follow the way then gladly
For she does come to shew me

Though soon she is gone into the bosky light
I must lie down then a while under a sally tree
For such weariness ovr take me

Yet soon pull myself up turnd up the hill
The last of the sun away behind my shoulder
Through the gwalleys of cut hay
All merge together in many yellers

Ahead saw the place must be his
Girt gabld farm roof heavy with many chimbleys
Sat on its own shelf on the Valley side
A wall round the garden
Close it from the falling fields
Around about other barns and stone cottages
Though some fallen in disrepair

This then was Stocton Hill Farm
And though I never been there afore
I feel all my life
I have been sickening for the want of this place

MOUNT VERNON

My Master now does find again some life
Wish to go out in the garden

Tis true the weather stretch out kind arms now
The chestnut trees the garden heavy with green
White candles drip many held high

The clouds float still and distant
The skye evr brightening blue
Its light a sparkling stain
Everywhere

The grass grow ankley long on the lawns
Creepers climb cross roses
Field daisies push up gainst the house
For there is no one to cut

This is the day that the Lord has made
We will rejoice and be glad in it

I see why my Master should wish
To take also his share of it

Yet how can I take him out

He has little strength and neither have I
I cannot bear his weight

He can lean upon that musket
Also we use a chair
Push a little in front of he

I step out to arrange this
Though I have little enough breath
My stomach oft gone griggly
So I may eat but little

First I position a chair in the garden
The white iron rails near
Tis a good spot to sit if we can get him out

As we go out the front door he slows
Take the door frame to steady hisself
Maybe he will never get round the corner
Into the garden

Wait I tell him Wait
I bring the chair back
So tis not so far out from the front door

So we move on   Scraping and gasping slow

Every step does wince pain through he
Finally I get him sat in the chair
Then go to get the whisky
Despite the warmth of the day a blanket

Today he is the kinder part of hisself
He does not shout or blame

So he says

You say that from here one may see the house
Where you were born

Not where I was born Sir No
The cottage where I livd as a child
Yes Sir You can Tis at The Heavens

Ah yes he say for he know the name
So where then

I raise my finger and point cross the Valley
Though the trees block our sight

I think then of that cottage at The Heavens
As I saw when I first came back here
Afore the leaves come
So still and unchangd I felt I could
Walk cross that way Push open the door
Find they all still there

Ah Dry Hill he says and Claypits
Up on the lofty top there

Yes Sir that is it

You livd there afore you came to my father

Yes Sir I did

It surprises me he takes an interest

We neither of us move our eyes round the Valley
Neither of us want to see that other house

So so the Master says
Perhaps you may bring a table out here

For I have need that you write

My heart does wilt at these words
Surely not the book again

Yet still I go and fetch a table
Mercifully tis a dainty piece
Of hardly any weight

Also chair paper ink pen
So all is set ready

Then say he I have decide that my affairs
Must now be set straight

You know I have relatives in Gloucester
A lady by the name of Mrs Constance Greylord
Has a daughter also Miss Isabella Greylord

Mrs Constance Greylord my niece by marriage
Miss Isabella granddaughter
Of my mothers brother
One Solomon Greylord
So he say it all

Then send me inside to fetch a miniature
Does represent the two of they

Both finely dressd lace at cuff and neck
A fine jewel lie at the centre
The old womans dress

The young woman
It quakes me when I see her face
For she is the pictures I seed at Stocton Hill
Has walkd straight out of the canvas

Her dress less severe but otherwise all the same

I suppose Mount Vernon will come to her
Think then of her fondly

She will be like the Masters mother
Who was left alone in charge of Stocton Hill
Fell into the hands of that Mr Harland Cottrell
God rest her soul

She could not have knowd

Life has many paths and by ways
You cannot help but think back

What if those boys had had a proper mother
It would not then had fallen out the same

Yet little time have I to think on this
For my Master sets out to dictate the letter
Though I do write neatly all he says
Yet my mind is wheeling fast

What now will come
A man like my Master is eldering
Rich or appear to be so
Now took sick

Tis clear enough where that must lead
Soon our peace here will be takd
All will be set about in other ways

Surely they will take the Master to Gloucester

I will have to leave this place
I nowhere else to go

I am ready for the Lord to claim me
Been ready this many an endless year
But still He keeps me here on this earth
I know not His purpose

Maybe the Master read my mind
For hasty he say
You need not worry Mary Ann
I know you have servd me well
Whatevr arrangements are made
I will be sure and certain
Some provision is made for you

Yes yes he is right I serve he to the end
A loyal servant that I am

For so you see tis oft easy to forget
You tell a story long enough it become true

He play his role I play mine
We all feel happy with our lot
Sickening master loyal servant
Happy memories all

Yet this matter of the house
To whom twill be left
Seems not to be my Masters primary interest

Instead he is writing to these relatives
They may perhaps help to find a book binder
To assist in the making public
Of a book of much interest

So he does go on
I keep my eyes down on the page
Yet I do understand what passes here

He does not place his trust in me
He never was a fool

Finally he is done with all
So I then offer my assurance
I will take the letter down
To the cottages below
Find some person there to post it

Yet dictating the letter has tird he much
So he sags in the chair shakes his head

Soon enough our eyes move again
Cross all the sides of the Valley
Come to rest drawn by invisible thread
On that Stocton Hill Farm

Out beyond the town
Above Cally Well and Rock Mill
Just aside of the doorway to Painswick

Green on greener hill fold in on hill
Roll and toss Path and hedge hidden deep
The farm stands there on its own proud shelf
A place of dreams you cannot quite believe
It casts its spell still

Our minds can easily fill the detail our eyes
Cannot behold

You know he says
I bought this house now Mount Vernon
A lofty place
When I returnd partly
A cause I knew you could spy Stocton Hill
From this precise spot

I know that surely
Know also that this house
Does call him to mind of Stocton Hill
As it must me as well

Oh yes he says I remember
Just then is seizd by such a gasp of coughing
As nearly take him off the chair

His head bows down and he fights for breath

Why does he take me back there with him
Better to forget

Yet I know for I dream of it still
So do he I am certain

For all he did destroy it

STOCTON HILL

At Stocton Hill Farm is Nettie
Has the care of all that passes in that house
Her eyes not good but good enough to see
She wants none of me

Nettie is a vussock woman
Her shape square and plubby not many teeth
With one snag stuck out straight
So she spits and splutters when she speaks
Wheezes bad her breath drawn shallow

No no no Mr Cottrell she say Tis not right
The Devil crossd her mothers path
If yr good wife were still above the grass
She would not jape and jest with me like thee

But Nettie not Mrs Freda Woebegone
She not Mistress here
Still she say No no
You know right well Sir

So Nettie say nose running red and sore
Face inflamd and red with many spots
And marks of boils and scabs

Though finding me yet a piece of bread
Spread thick with dripping
The taste do bring me strength

Nettie Nettie Mr Harland Cottrell say
Standing near the kitchen door
His head nearly up to the top frame
His long hand resting gainst the side
His shirt tails hanging
Long feet bare on the stone floor
Certainly it may be the end a maggle hot day
But surely is unproper
In such as he

Come come have you no charity he say
Do you not see that God gives us here
The privilege to take care
Of some unfinishd part of His creation

Finishd or not I want none of it say she
Or finishd I shall be without no doubt

Now now come come say he You need help
If she stays not here she is for the Workhouse
She has no friends no connections
Have you no heart

She can go to the Workhouse now
That is all I care
So does Nettie spit and wheeze

I wonder she dare speak such a way to her Master
I stand crooch the side of the winder stare down
But she not Mrs Freda and he not Mr Abel

Nettie Nettie You have said enough

153

This is all ignorant superstition
That deformity of her face
But an accident of birth
There is no meaning to it
I can cause the flesh to close up
In but a day or so
Will do so when I find the time

Now come now come She is a hearty girl
Oft those who are simple are closest to God
I think you may yet find her a good worker

Nettie give me then a look would curdle milk
Walks away her struggling walk
For she is bumble footd
With one leg shorter tother

Yet for all that she do find me a good worker
I am well gatd that night again dawn next day

Work all day and never stop
Never speak anything much

Sweeping washing wind the mangle fetch wood
Poke the sheets in the copper with a long stick
Stand on a chair press down hard the flat iron
Make all fresh Count it all joy

Nettie hockle after me shout
You do this You do that
Call me a noaf and a ninny hammer

Yet she has little satisfaction in it
For oft I have done what she say
Afore she gets the words out

Those first days soon in this way
I see all ovr the rooms of the house
Two on each side the staircase
All with deep set mulliond winders

For this is an ancient creaking house
The date 1685 set in the giant stone
As stands above the fire place
Downstairs Mr Harland Cottrells study
Also the dining room that makes use also
For a school room being crammd with many books
Up above another drawing room

Velvet curtains silver plates in cabinets
Many japannd tables and turkey rugs
Chairs with spreading wing arms
You would not sit down in them
Lest you be swallowed in their depth

Much wood near black and dusty
All in need of polish
Dark oil paintings strung on the wall
Many with curld ringlets long sniffing noses
I do not like the way they stare

Except for one which I know to be his wife
The one who is dead
Her face is clean and kind full of questions
She might step out the frame
To laugh with me

Books books books everywhere
Line all the walls not only the dining room
I dust down their spines carefully
Dare not lift them out
Though the shelves behind need cleaning sore

Come on girl come on hurry up get on
Stop yr gaitling and friggling around
So say Nettie when she can stir herself
From the kitchen table

All this I see and the bedrooms above
Four poster with many dusty hangings
Wooden presses and chests heavy to open

I know not then that this not his house
But the house of his wife who died young
She in the portrait with kindness and questions
Of her I shall later tell

Two of the rooms belong to the young Masters
But I do not see them those first days
Only hear their boots bang the stairs
Barking whooping laughter sometimes
As they rantipole through the house

Even hear them once up the roof
They can get up there
For many long pieces of scaffold birch wood
Are set up gainst the house
I suppose so the roof can be mend
That certainly does need fixing
There being many signs of damp
And water dribbling

Can it be safe I think
For them to climb up there
But of course tis not for me to say

In one of their rooms
Move then a box to clean
Discover it full of weeds with a bowl of water

Hiding therein grass snakes and a toad
I put it back and keep away
Who would do such as that

All ovr the house I go bucket mop brush
Clean scrub scrape all up and down
At least Nettie does not get up the stairs well
So can say not much to me
While I am in these many chambers above

No one has done this in many endless day
Mould grow low down the walls
Creepers climb in at the winders
Cobwebs thick the ceilings
I make it all shining polish surface bright

Though the need for this surprise me
Mr Harland Cottrell is surely a rich man
So why is his house kept no better
Than at The Heavens

There was not Mrs Freda Woebegones fault
Was no money
So how could she keep things right
With the winders broke and floors failing

That I do not understand
For Mr Harland Cottrell is a fine gentleman
Speaking many languages writing letters
To educatd folk in Oxford even London

Nor the food either
For you think that rich people
Have always side of beef or bacon
But not here no only vegetables boild in water

The fields will provide all
So say Mr Harland Cottrell
Tis only the nourishment of the soul we need

Is not the life more than meat
The body more than raiment

I do not think much to this
For sure pigs and cows enough in the yard
But it is only my part to clean all

Even the back kitchen
Where herbs are set in pots to boil
Filling all the house with scents
Both lickorish sweet and cloying dank

This room I do not like
For lying sometimes in a basin
Is blood clottd bits of some such
I know not what

Buckets full of sawdust staind scarlet
It makes my stomach griggly to look
Sometimes also I do find
This same blood soakd sawdust
Spread round the soil and roots
Where the vegetables do grow

I do not understand or want to know

Neither the spacious place out the back
He calls his Cabinet of Curiosities
Even though twas formerly a barn

There I do not go

You never open the door Nettie say You never

This Cabinet is just across the lane
That lead to the place call Whites Hill
This entrance usd by those
Who come to see him for his healing skills

I go not go even near the door if I can avoid
But that is not always possible as tis near
The pigs and the pump

Even that first day I hear weeping pain
I keep well away The smell is bad
Does carry on the wind back to the kitchen
The byre the creamery the vegetables

Maybe that first day maybe the second
I come back in the kitchen and Nettie is there
With a man I not know then is Mr Birch Nazareth
Who is the Steward of the farm and organize all
For Mr Harland Cottrell

He is a timberous man thick like a tree trunk
With arms which are surpassing long
Stick out a little at his sides
For such is the size of he
They may not hang flat
His face half cover by a black beard
Falls all down his chest
His eyes merry and sharp
But lost in so many weatherd folds his face
With ready laugh comes bursting
Up in a sudden howl
As claps his girt hands together

So he drinks some tea as Nettie made him

Sat stiff at the kitchen table
His hand like a chunk joint of meat
Resting there upon the boards
The other grip a cup
Making it no more than a toy

Hurry up Mary Ann Do not you dawdle
So she spit and wheeze at me

Then she and he laugh together
Talk about Mr Harland Cottrell
Not respectful

Today I think it were only two so Nettie say

Oh only killd two today say Mr Birch Nazareth
So a good day for Mr Harland Cottrell then
So they splutter to hold back laughter
Slap their hands down on the table

I think of the weeping behind the door
Wonder how they laugh
Think of the older girl at school Sarah Mayne
Who never was seed again after

But nay nay I tell myself
You can make no judgement so
For poor Mr Abel Woebegone did always say
To any who would hear
How Mr Harland Cottrell did cure Ambrose

Who could know then Who can know now

Hurry past head down
Dinging on with my work

Mary Ann come hurry now
Get on with you
I never seed a girl so tardy

                              *

The first time I see the two brothers
Twas after I been at Stocton Hill
I do not know maybe a week

I am sent down to find them
They come late for lunch
Will be down the hill where is the mill
Called Jenners but also Pitchcombe
They swim there I am told

So I go down to the Wick Stream
Which they do call the never failing stream
Diving deep the secret shades of that Valley
Down through the orchards heavy laden
Into the racing toss of the stream

Follow it away from Stroud
Under the drooping sally trees
Walk on til I hear splashes and shouts
Comes to a spinney thickly knit
Where the stream run slow
Stretches hisself wide

Hear louder the heart beat of the fulling stocks
As come from Pitchcombe Mill ahead

As I come close I move cautiously
Those notmatots as threw me in the grave
In the Stroud church yard did fright me
So I move through the thicket

Try not to foot break a twig rustle leaves

So I come where I am able to see the water
The rushes tall at the spring edge
Though I am well hid within the trees
Hear still hollering and mirth bright splashing

I do not know whether I should call out
Or what I should do

Sudden a noise close at hand
Footsteps gust of crackling laughter
They are there

Two well grown boys all dangling legs and arms
I am ashamd to say quite nakd
So turn my eyes away
How am I to deliver my message to them

I have seldom seed nakedness afore
Their limbs so long and strong and round
Strange parts such as only men have
I blush red my blood rising in shame to see

In the reeds close to the waters edge
They push and wrestle flesh gainst flesh

Their whiteness touchd green by the trees around
Limbs flickerd the shadows brindld
Hair flat gainst their head

Both have the face of their father
Long and narrow with full lips
Drops of bright water spraying
Catching jewels in the sun
In all their youth and joy and certainty of life

For a moment I think then of Ambrose
How we lit sticks flashd them through the air
My limbs then do want to run to the water
To throw myself in leave every care aside

Course I cannot Think instead
How strange it be that in the town
But three mile endways from here
The bodies still pile up in the cemetery
The bell still toll
Such is the piebald nature
Of our God glorious world

I watch then til the one boy wins the fight
So he takes the other by the shoulders
Push him down into the shallow reed thick water
The two still laughing

Then with a howl falls on top of him
Two roll together splashing heaving
In the shallow mud water

Til the one struggles up the other rolls away
They chase each other again legs pulling
Through the heavy water and then away

Still they are fighting
Laughing but fighting
So the one catch hold of his brother
Cup his hands on the top of his head
Push he down

The whole glade drops then into quiet
The surface of the water settle calm
Sun up above pierce through the trees
Come down in glittering rays

Each like the blade of sword

I see the head of one boy but not the other
Above a rook is cawing circling
Black gainst the sun

He will come up soon I think
He does not hold him down
But he is He is
He is pushing him down

Tis too long Minutes pass
The air spin out v thin
All breath stop
The crow still cawing
The sun still watch all with uncaring eye
Still the boy under the water does not come up

I run from the glade and start to shout
You will drown him
Stop stop You must

The boy watch me his eyes squint the sun
Then he smiles a huge smile
Cracks open that long serious face

Sudden the other comes up breaking the surface
Spluttering and gulping
Grasping at his brother
But the other boy only laugh

Together they move to where
The water is shallower
To a spot their feet might meet the ground
Closer to where I stand

What a fool I have made of myself
There never was any danger
Except that in my own understanding

You are sent to get us for lunch
The taller boy enquire

Then they both start guffawing again

I have not laugh for some long time
The machinery in me does not work well
I smile and nod

Then slowly I feel the merriment a coming
Spilling out of me

We are all three there in the watery glade
What a neddy I was to be so scard

The breeze touch the leaves above dapple us all
Light and shade catch us as it moves

Bobbing above the water they are together fine

They speak to me of what life can be
It seem for a moment I take some part
Of what they have

That I believe the whole world made for me
Just for the long sun still moment

*

Nettie is old her joint swolld
Her fingers crookd as her short leg back
Soon sees what advantage I am for her

165

Sit down by the hearth she does
Go in the stretching warm afternoons
When the shadows stunt
The Valley below yawn long
Lie down for a sleep while I do all

This she may well do
For Mr Harland Cottrell is oft out from home
Walking the farm or ministering to the sick
Master Blyth also closy by him

Mr Harland Cottrell also writing letters
Making speeches signing this and that
For to put an end to the
Horrors of the West Indian Slavery

I oft put to cut the quills and mix the ink
Which Mr Harland Cottrell say I do
With care For that he is most grateful

It does not trouble me that Nettie sleep
I have bed and board
In this fine house
I am a maid of all work
I have a place

Nettie and I take a room to share
Up above the creamery
The stove below does heat rise up
Many warm blankets on the bed

That part of the house
The roof does not leak
Though shame to say it do
Most everywhere else

Even after only a week Nettie say
Though you are ugly you are not a bad girl

How dare she say that when she herself
Is hunch back and one leg crookd
Yet I say naught

Then one afternoon
I have been there maybe two weeks
I am sweeping the hall I comes upon a mouse
They are everywhere in the house
They have need of a cat

I am good at killing mice
Even Mrs Woebegone do not deny this
I bang many with a shovel at The Heavens
This one will be easy
He goes cross the hall
I am carrying the shovel

I look around and see he trappd
There is no hole he can go in
I advance on him with the shovel
Intent to bang he down
Think how pleasd Nettie will be
We have one less of he

Yet just as I come to raise the shovel
I hear a noise behind me
The door to the study open
Mr Harland Cottrell stand there
Surely he will be pleasd also

But instead he say No No No Mary Ann
Do not strike
So I drop my arm

The mouse flits away as he must

I turn to look at Mr Harland Cottrell
The shovel hang useless in my hand
No No No he say

I bow my head though I do not understand

You must not kill he says
You know the Bible

Thinks I
I do know the Bible
But I not think it writ for varmint

All Gods creatures must be precious to us he say

I am sorry Sir I reply
Though I think he stupid

All is well Mary Ann he say
But you remember Do not kill in this house

I want to ask if this apply even to beetle
Of which there are more than a fair few

Yet just as my mind rebel
I look up and see him stare down at me
There is in his eyes such kindness
That I feel my whole self warmd by it

Then it comes to me that he is right
That the mouse too have his life
Want to keep it
Just as I do

I look up see Nettie standing at the door
Which lead back to the kitchen

Mary Ann she say You come here
So I go shovel and all

I expect her to speak to me harsh
But instead she finds slickut for me
Sit down a moment she say

Then she comes to sit opposite me watch me close
Arms folded cross her chest

So you stay here she say
So you may since he decide
She nods her head then speaks v quiet
Hissing and wheezing
With that one snag tooth stick out at me

Yet let me tell you something
You see it now for yrself
You watch carefully how things stand

This house is not as it should be
Tis not right
Mr Harland Cottrell
He does not know the proper place
Believe that God live in the tail of a mouse

Say to me I may sit in the dining room
Why you not do so he say
You a servant only because you decide

Not Master Ned nor Master Blyth neither
All touchd with the same madness

And so so she say leaning in close on me
As we sit there at the table
I keep my eyes down say naught

There is something else you shall see
Much witchcraft in this house
Ghosts and evil spirits do lurk here
So disturb the proper workings

Her face is close to mine
The skin flowsy red like it scrubbd sore
So I do nod my head as though I understand

But inside I do remind myself
What both Ambrose and Mr Woebegone say
That all stories of ghouls and ghosts
Of hobgoblins elves witches and their powers

All of this is but superstitious talk
As is believd only by the stupid and credulous
Those who have not the wit to use their own mind
Or they would see their error

So that is what they always say to me
Yet the truth is that I am not always so sure
For how can this be knowd
Much cannot be explaind
Except you look outside the power
Of God and man

You know also Nettie say tis well knowd
That Mr Harland Cottrell is a mesmerist
Also Master Blyth have that gift

You know what is that

I nod my head like it bounce on a spring
Though know not what this means

So you listen to me girl Nettie say
Then she sit back and snoffling say again
Listen careful to what I say

I do hear what she say and take it well

For ovr time I will see her meaning
There is danger this is true
Yet it does not lie where she say

*

Tis true there is much that cannot be explaind

Such as the people as come to Stocton Hill
Late the eve gather close night

Even from the top of the house I hear them
Talking scuffling stifld laughter in the lane
Their boots turn and clatter on the track
Hear the creaking swing of the gate

Is this what Nettie mean by witchcraft
Even she cannot be so fool

But I not been there many a week
Afore I come to understand

This happen for I adry for water
So must cross the few steps
From the creamery to the kitchen

Twas the top of the zummer

The night fittd close and muffle
The smell of new hay blown on its breath

I carry a candle though I hardly need one
For the dark has not entirely settld

Soon as I slide into the kitchen
I know many are gatherd close
The house fair strain at the seams with them
Though they make hardly a slither of sound
Still I hear the scrape of a chair
A cough a rustling of breath

I think of Nettie and what she tell me
But curiosity soon ovrcome
As it too oft does

I blow my candle so I cannot be seed
Move close to the door
Where is the dining room

This room I am told is where
Master Ned and Master Blyth do their studying
Though precious little studying there I seed
Since tis ripe zummer yet
I suppose they do not start til autumn

This it did surprise me to be told
For why they not go to school
Surely there is more than enough money
Their father an educatd man

But Nettie has told me wagging her finger
Laughing a little as she speak
Oh no tis not money course not no

Tis that Mr Harland Cottrell
Does not believe in the schools as are here
They being not about the education
As he takes the word to mean

I found that strange
For what must a school do but teach you
But it were naught to me
I polish the door handles in that room
The winder fittings dust the surfaces
Lay the grate straight
That is all

But now I come close the door that room
Many are gatherd round the table
Candles white waver and dance vivid

The men are all young not gentlemen
Men in their working clothes and boots
The circles of candle lit touch their foreheads
The folds of brow and hair
Hands lie on the table crustd and strong

Books have been takd down from the shelves
Laid out on the table slates chalk
Quills and powderd ink and paper also

I feel my breath quicken as I understand
My back stay fixd gainst the door
Yet I do not want to go back to bed

Soon Mr Harland Cottrell begin to speak
For he tis who stands at the table top

Education is the only path out of death and sin
Into the light of the Lord that each may have

The glory of his own God given life

That he may be a channel of Gods Grace
We may see how that Grace live in he

All live now in dirt and poverty and ignorance
But tis our duty to the Lord our God
To rise out of this state

So now we go to work to copy and learn
Study here not the works of the Classical World
But the tradition and language of this
Our own dear country of England
The words we speak in mill or field or lane
Of which we should not be shamd
For this a pure language
The voice of the flowring meadow
The product of our own soil
Which can express the myriad prayers
Thoughts and ideas we vessels hold
Without the need of foreign adornment

So we think always of Mr William Tyndale
As does say I defy the Pope and all his laws
If God spare my life afore many years
I shall cause the plough boy to know
More of the Bible than he

So all falls to work with chalk or pen
I stand watching unseed
See the light from the candles jig

Winders open onto the garden fields below
Girt gratitude that such as this can be
The Lord God must truly smile at what He see
For this is good and acceptable in his sight

*

That following morning
After the range is lit
The coppies fed the milk in the cowl
The dough for the bread put to prove

I go to the dining room
To set all straight
Some glasses and tankards
Left on the table

Otherwise I might not be sure
Of what I saw the night afore

The winders still open
The dew gather thick

I push the chairs straight
Then look up and see
A book is left open on the table

I know I must not look at the book
But still I must put it away
So why not just peep the pages
Afore I put it back

I climb on a leather seatd chair
The book on the dark wood shine the table
Its pages wide open like welcoming arms

I take a deep breath and look at what is there

But am disappointd I expect to see words
Laid out as they should be in long rows
Yet there are not many words in this book

Only in small clumps
The rest of the page is takd up with many lines
Betwixt a multitude of dots
I know not what tis

There I am about to climb down in disappointment
When I sees something I recognize
A figure A girt bear
Then all of a sudden
A leap inside me a gasp from my lips
I know what tis I see here

Tis a drawing of the heavens
As Ambrose did shew me
Here are several of the figures I know
Just as his finger did point to me
So in this book the lines drawn in

Bewitchd I cannot stop myself
The next page make my breath hang still
Tis all ink in blue a picture of the heavens

Blue gold lines finer than the finest net
So carefully drawn
Angels blowing trumpets
Banner waving cross the heavens
I know it I am sure
The words in clumps tell what you see

I try to read them Try to remember the letters
But tis all gone from me
All I can do is enjoy
The shapes the patterns and swirls

I want to put my finger out
Follow them round and round again

As I did in those short days of school

Yet I know well I must not touch the book
So only hold my finger high ovr
The letter and the golden lines
Travel through the skye
Lose myself in the blue and gold
Come close to the round cheekd Angels
The gleam of light on their trumpets

What do you there

I jump back
Master Ned is stood at the door
His eyes are narrow and he steps toward me

So you look at my fathers books

No I say No Sir I never
I was just getting up on the chair to put it away

You touchd it
With yr nastry soot coverd fingers
He say

No No I never did Only trace the shape

I am trembling in every limb and muscle
I know what I done is v wrong
I should have listend to Nettie

Master Ned stand ovr me
His full lips are turnd to a thin line
He uses his hand to sweep aside his thick hair

You know what happen to you Mary Ann he say

You know what comes
You will be put out of the house
Put with the dog in the kennel
Not be fed these several days

I begin to get down from the chair
Though he will catch me wherevr I go

Then just as my foot touch the floor
His face change entirely he start to laugh

Mary Ann Mary Ann You silly goose
Do you not know I am only jesting

But I think it not any prank
Back away still thinking
I must run

No no he say
For goodness sake
Come come
You must know that I am only playing
You can look at the books any time
Anyone can look at them
They are for whoevr wants them

But I do not trust him
All I want to do is get away

Do you not believe me he say
Right then wait here and I will ask
So he steps out toward his fathers study

Just as he does so Mr Harland Cottrell appear

Father Father the boy say

Mary Ann can look at the books
She can look Is that not right

Then I hear them both return
Mr Harland Cottrell look ovr his eye glasses
Why Mary Ann you like to read

They make a fool of me I know it

Or perhaps to look at the books
Mr Harland Cottrell say
His voice kind and quiet his head nod
Course you may look at the books

Now he comes to see the page of the open book
Ah he say Ah Now here you make a good choice
Who would not want to look at so fine a book

Then he turn to me
I suppose you do not know what tis you see

The sound of his voice the softness of his look
Have calmd me

He asks the question not to mock
But in all sincerity

I do Sir Tis the heavens
Not the heavens in the Bible Sir
But those we see through the winder at night

Why yes yes yes
How wonderful you should know
How come you by such knowledge

A friend shewd me I say

For the heavens we see in the skye
They are free for all to share

Ah yes Mary Ann say he
Gods heaven equally
Tis there for us all
Even the poor and deformd
Do you not think it so

I do not know what to say to this

The friend who shewd you was Mr Abel Woebegone
I nod my head cannot explain
In truth was Ambrose

Ah yes yes say Mr Cottrell Poor Woebegone

For a moment his mind seem to falter
He shakes his head sighs but then

Course you may look at the book say he
You examine any book you like
But first you wash yr hands
Touch only the side of the pages
Take care that nothing tears

I should be glad of this and say thank you
Yet all I want to do is come away

I shall shew you Master Ned say

Yes yes say Mr Harland Cottrell
That is quite right
Ned shall shew you
He can read the words to you
Now now I must be back to my work

With that he is gone
Master Ned and I left together

Come then he say
I will shew you

Thank you Sir tis v kind
But I must get back to work

No no I insist I want to shew you
Come now Get up on this chair

So I have no choice must climb back on the chair
Listen to what he say

At first I cannot listen proper
I am too scard
I wish I had stayd out the back

Yet gradually my eye begin to follow his finger
He read out words I do not understand
They are not words I know
Sound solemn grand but have no meaning at all
This is Latin he tell me

Then he says the words in English
Some I still not understand
Yet again I leave the dining room there
All the swelling morning
Am carrid away to other worlds

I watch his finger
Sit close to the smooth sweep of his hair
Sometimes he turns to look at me
His eyes are like the deepest tunnels
His voice wind me in

He is like his father
The same power is in him

I am caught like a fish on a hook wriggling
To get away gasping and dying
But then fight no more
Hand ovr my mortal soul to him willingly
That he may skin gut prepare for the fire

Such is the silkness of his hair the way
He repeats the words for me again and again

Asks do you understand it now Do you see

*

Stocton Hill Farm is not as should be
Tis not right
So say Nettie

There is witchcraft here
She tell me this many a time

So I find it
Though tis hard to name
Where lies the difficulty
Not witchcraft no but how do I say

You see it in small things
A thimble you leave on the kitchen winder sill
Then you find on a chest on the landing

Pies that goes missing from the larder
Winders that you fix shut and are open again
Nettie say to me Mary Ann Mary Ann
Girl you are a fool

You know not what you do
You must take more trouble in yr work

But I know tis not me
So then who could it be

Hobgoblins maybe or an imp or some such
I do not think so for I never see
Any of that kind

Sometimes also screaming in the night
An unholy sound fird by terror and pain
Door open then footsteps running
Til the screaming stop

Is this Master Blyth or Master Ned I do not know

Then comes a day I am making a rice pudding
It must have been the zummer after I come there

That was the time when Mrs Miles and her son
Clothiers who were at Rock Mill down below
Has gone bankrupt
Many lost their living there

Not long after Vatch Mill blaze up in fire

Mr Harland Cottrell much concernd in this
Many a system for help those without work
That is much need for White Hill Ruscombe
Bread Street as lies beyond tis widely knowd
Live there many rough folk of a low state
Spending their days in ale houses
Lost to the Lord
So there I was with the rice pudding
Sugar and milk all finishd off

Sprinkld light with nutmeg

I hear Mr Birch Nazareth out in the yard
He is calling for someone to hold a horse

So I go out but when I come back
Nettie staring at the floor spitting ire
There the pudding bowl on the floor
Smashd and the pudding all spoild

You must not leave the dish close the table edge
So Nettie tell me though is a touch of mirth
As she speaks

Know right well I never leave
The dish near the edge

Am meant to go upstairs to fetch the linen down
But instead I go in the garden
For I cannot stop my tears
I am afeard they will make me leave

I go down the end past the byre
Where the vegetables are
Also odorous cuttings peelings

Normally the garden give me much pleasure
The tall fox gloves and nodding poppies
Tis not a place well tend
But abundant in colours and scent
The butterflies thick about

But on that day I felt no pleasure
Thinking myself alone there let go my tears
But then straightway the head of Master Ned
Pop up ovr the garden wall

He must have been in the field below
Hear me sobbing sore

I am ashamd that he should see me cry
I must get back to my work
Afore Nettie find me

I turn away but Master Ned pull me back
Twist me round to face him then
Though he is but two years older than me
His head is far above mine

He uses his hand to push back
That thick lock of brown hair cross his forehead
Then his eyes fix on me soft and sure

Come come Mary Ann he say
We all know you are v careful
But Nettie Nettie you must be patient with her

I wonder then what does he know
Was he down the field or near the kitchen
Did he hear Nettie and me talk

He do not say more
Do not say she push the bowl
But such is the meaning behind his words

I am grateful to he for he tries to be kind
So I stay standing there a moment
Just to feel his hand upon my arm
Feel his eyes touch me

I should like to push my crying head gainst he
Course I may not do such as that
Instead I say thank you to he

Turnabout to go back inside

But all the time my thoughts are turning
For it does not seem right
That Nettie touchd the bowl

She do not care for me
Yet she and I are the same
Though she plenty of lard on her now
Keeps herself well
With many a scrap of meat or fat or pudding
Brought in by Mr Birch Nazareth

Who says oft How many kill today
Nettie say only but the one

Oh oh they laugh
A good day then for Mr Harland Cottrell

Mr Birch Nazareth does bring in these scraps for Nettie
Sometimes says God Bless he
That some crinch must be given to me

For he does not believe the many physic virtues
Of water vegetables as does Mr Harland Cottrell

Yet for all that Nettie know the gnaw of hunger
She would not waste good food
Even out of spite she would not

Or so I think

Then some hobgoblin or sprite maybe
Who else be there
Well of course only Master Blyth
Who I know little and rarely see

For he is to be traind to work for his father
So in that Cabinet room cross the lane
Where I have never be

Or out with Mr Harland Cottrell
Making his many rounds
Which oft bring them back to Stocton Hill
Late at night and off the next morning early

Even sometimes as far as Oxford
Where they go to hear the work
Of learnd societies

So this it would suggest that Master Blyth
Is the favourd son to work so with his father

But no no I do not think so
Mr Harland Cottrell peck upon Master Blyth
As Nettie does with me
You hear all the time
Criticize berate scold

Master Blyth does seem to do all the rough work
Which increasingly I discover is rough indeed
For now I understand the Kettle Boil Cutter

Which is a comment made privily
On Mr Harland Cottrells skill
In amputating limbs
That he may have yr leg off
Afore the kettle boils

Which Master Blyth does help him with
Is sent after to pour the blood on the garden
For this will make the vegetables grow better

I seed Master Blyth tip the bucket
Smelt the blood afterwards seed the tar stain
Spreading on the soil

Dreamt that night of limbs do push up
Through the earth growing tall
The white fingers reaching up to the skye

I wake then shaking and crying
The shadow of Master Blyths face in my head

Yet this is all my imagining
For in truth I know little of him
But I tell you this

You think they two brothers are similar
Being only three years apart in age
Both the same thick hair high on their forehead
Both clear seeing hazel eyes long straight nose
Flourishing lips being much the same

Even near the same height as Master Ned
Being v well growd and his brother not so

Yet even at that time I had understood
In character they not similar at all
For though Master Blyth is near
The same stature as his brother
Yet strange he seems always low and dark
Always something of a Will Jill he

Some fragility to he unfixd and wavering
Hands knottd ockerd together in front
Wind seems to blow through his bones
Shake them like leaves tremble on a tree

Some baff of his speech he also suffer
He say oft G G G
You know he mean Good Morning
Though his tongue throb hard in his mouth
Leap and jerk Yet oft no word do produce

You cannot see or know him proper

Nay they are not the same character at all
This I tell you well
For within that knot of circumstance
Does lie much of the story
Which I shall go on to tell

*

One other memory I have of that early time
I cannot fix it exact
Still I do not like to write it down
For even now I do wonder
At the sin we did commit
The risk we did take

Only I can say I were young
Could only do as I were told
Even if I knew it were wrong

Oft think it were a dream but know twas not

The details now I cannot fully recall
Except that Master Ned and Master Blyth
Did take me out one night
Waking me up and dragging me down
From the creamery

I did not want to go

Long after all was asleep
Walking the high lane to White Hill
Picking our ways under the high light
Of a sprinkling blanket of stars

The night was sharp enough to make the lips sore
They held me tight by the hand pulling me on
My heart risd up to stop my throat
Holding onto those boys tight
For what other safety was there

I do not remember how we got to the place
Only there were many people crowd in
It must have been a barn or some such
I could see nothing til Master Ned
Pull me up to sit beside he
On a low beam

See then many heads bobbing all looking
The smell of drink and snuff and smoke
Pressing in tight

Tis a galantee showman who has come
So tell me Master Ned
But I know not what the word means

Soon all is dark breathing tight close
Lights then up ahead and a man in a black cloak
Swings his hand out wide
A woman starts to sob hysterical

Tis then I see it
Dark figures moving on the wall
First the figure of our Lord
The Blessd Virgin
Adam and Eve walks in the garden

Such Glory and Peace there was to see it
I was warmd by their blessd light

That they should come down to earth

But then the Devil come and his eyes move
I were weeping in fear
Many pushing to get out
Master Blyth though only laughing
Rocking back and forwards on that beam

Master Ned keep hold me tight
So I not fall or trample on

I do not remember how we got back
Only that no one else evr knew or saw
That Devil with the rolling eyes

It stayd in my head
There with the bloodied limbs
Which do grow evr in the garden

Some how in my mind
It cannot be right I know it cannot
Yet that night as I did unknot the boots
Of Master Blyth and he take out his foot

It were all scald like a snake
Clawd like an eagle

I were taken then in fear
Also always sure that Master Blyth
He has creatd it all

He was the showman in the black cape
Swinging his hand wide

He twas who summond the staring eye Devil

Always afterwards behind his smiling face
I saw the magician the worker of black magic

The Devil who laughd and cackld
His eyes rolling round the room
Holding us all in his dark power

Master Blyth also his feet and legs
Always scald and clawd
Could never clean it from my mind

MOUNT VERNON

The house Mount Vernon I do say
Tis all crowd with zummer now
The plunging Valleys too

The sap push out in the bud
The earth itself bloom
All chargd full with the Grace of God

I see it there as I work
Do not raise my head from the page

Fill this paper with the breathings of my heart

Though the garden call and Valleys
Though I be dragging terrible tird
The earth sucking down my bones

The pain in my chest now sharp

Reading also sometime some books
I did take from his boxes and trunks
As is placd in an upstairs room
A fine chamber with winders at each end

One packd with wooden boxes contain
Metal instruments as doctors use
The same his father had

In those boxes find also
The poetry I have always lovd
Of Mr Wordsworth and Southey

Also Mr Milton the Tale How Paradise Was Lost
Romance of Robinson Crusoe Pilgrims Progress
The poems of Mr William Barnes John Clare

Deep in the night wrap myself in blanket
Sit in the arm chair there
Read to myself as once I read
To Mr Harland Cottrell

Such as Mr Blake his chimbley sweeps
Stuck long in their black flues

By came an Angel had a bright key
He opend a coffin set them all free
Down a green plain leaping they ran
Wash in a river and shine in the sun

Hearing again those same rolling words
Fires in yr head like a gasp of cider
Time then flies away
The days fall in upon each other

Yet still oft my Master cry

His eyes bulge and sweat bead his forehead
His leg when I change the dressing not worse
But certainly not heald any road at all

After he is gone there is no future for me
Who employ a broken down old crone
In particular one call Mary Ann Sate
The name still knowd by some of these Valleys

They build a new Workhouse now
I see it high up the Valley side
A grand building so they say
Yet I do not think he so

It pains me now that I should come to that
Yet so I fear it shall
The poison high in his leg
Soon enter the chambers of his heart

Though still he does tell me
Infuse two ounces the root of black hellebore
Bruise it well soak in a pint of proof spirit
Then filter the tincture through paper

I hear him call me so I do go
Imagine then my surprise to find he
Up and walking balancd the musket barrel

See then that he is standing near the desk
Worse worse he does hold in his hand
Some papers I have writ
Also left there is a book of poetry

Oh how careless I have been

I did not think he to move so far

Reading now those papers he does say
Yes yes Mary Ann Of course I see

Perhaps I not consider yr concerns as I must
You may hardly write about my family
Without writing also of yr own life

That cottage you did shew cross the hill
Where you were born

There have been books publishd in London
Give the life of a coach man
A boot black a maid servant
Quite a sensation they do create

Oh aye I say V interesting I am sure

Ah yes say he Also these poems
Do bring remembrance do they not
You having quite a taste for poetry then
Did you not Mary Ann

Yes Sir and also no
I like some parts of it and some not

I see his face clear
The illness has strippd
Many of the layers of deceit
Laid down by the years

What in poetry you did not admire he ask

Sometimes the language Sir
It sound fine oft I think
Yet it does not lead us to truth

For that we have need of different language
One perhaps does not suit so well the ear

And you Mary Ann he say
Is that what you write for
The truth

Yes Sir I say
When you ask me to write
I know you expect
No less

The truth I say
Was evr all were important to me

Oh yes he say I do remember well

But whose truth
That he asks now

The truth of all I say
Who did live in that distant time

What I expect is a look of anger
A look which say You do not challenge me
You write only my story
Put it down as I say

Yet instead his look is sorrowful
I seldom seed that look afore
It bring back the boy never quite gone

Slowly he get hisself to the bed
I pull back the covers settle he down
Pour whisky for he
Wipe cold water on his creasd forehead

Still he not comfortable
Pull hisself straight up on the bolster

Gestures to me I should sit down
This heat he say
It fit to burn the soil from the earth

His face hollow now the lips pinchd
Rest gainst the bolster as he sail into sleep

His hand stretchd out close to me
Witherd and pale as candle wax

My own lie close to it

Now he sleeps and I sit down
In the chair next the bed
Drift into sleep also
For my strength is all burnd out

Am lost firm many an hour

Then comes dusk and a cooler breeze wakes me
Go down to the kitchen to boil up tea

There is cool and shade earth damp

Is there I see that while I wrote
Someone has come into the house

For on the table there lies a basket full of eggs
I stare at them lay my hand on the white
Moon glimmer of their shells feel their shape
As they lie in their basket of straw

I know who must have left them
Tis the boy the grandson of Ambrose

Sometimes these gifts do come

Eggs milk bread
I am sure the boy is sent up the Pitch
Through the woods

Tis good he do
For how else do we eat

I lay my hand on whatevr he send
Now the eggs and feel a hand
Stretch out through the past

Take hold of mine strong and gripping
This the past that I want
Ambrose back with me

I sit then a long time my hand grippd
Round that egg

STOCTON HILL

The life at Stocton Hill Farm
I cannot measure it well gainst other lives
For I am not widely travelld in the world
I do not know how many conduct theysselfs

Still I feel it were different
I ask myself now how that were

Mainly it were the words
Perhaps that is what I remember

The way people spoke
Oft and loud

Yes many times words in a tone of contention
Yet never was there any malice or contempt

In particular this were so for Mr Birch Nazareth
Who live in a cottage out the back
Tries his best to manage the farm

This were not a down hill job
Mr Harland Cottrell want an income
Yet has no interest or understanding

Of what Mr Birch Nazareth do intend

Mr Harland Cottrell make no contribution
Except for some wild farming wonderments
Which always go awry

Such as the spreading of human waste
Oh I do remember well the stench of that
Also the ground bones and hair
As must be spread

Master Ned tell me also that human bones
Is also usd by his father on the land
Yet it were never true
Or I do not think twas

Mr Birch Nazareth does come in to him
Berate him furious as surely someone
Who is but employd for a Steward
Ought not to do

Still they goes at it
Like a scolding husband and wife
The study door open so all can hear
Mr Harland Cottrell has no shame in this

For he enjoys a good set to
A fine pair they make
One thin thoughtful mild
With no head fit for this world
The other firm as a tree trunk

So back and forth we hear them go
Though there is something merry in the sound

Always by the end of it

When hands have been bangd on the table
Mr Birch Nazareth has said many a time
I am finishd I am done I away from here

Yet always it comes out well
Mr Harland Cottrell slapping Mr Birch Nazareth
Fondly on the shoulder
Saying to him God Bless you for yr patience
A true soul of the soil you are
An excellent toad of a man
Where should I be without yr good guidance

Or some other like that
For such was Mr Harland Cottrell
A man of uneven temper
Yet soon jovial and hearty again
No never blame nor bitterness nor hurt

So oft like father like son
For Master Ned much the same

Also like his father clever
This no one doubts about Mr Harland Cottrell
A man with a love of a new idea
Creator inventor of schemes tests wonderments
Though not all of them leading
Where perhaps he thought they would

I am at Stocton Hill a while afore I understand
Sometimes Mr Harland Cottrell away from home
Is engagd in what is calld vaccinations
Such as he did nocklate when I was at school
Though I did not understand it then

Nettie tells me some who is nocklatd
Does grow the head of a cow

But this is only neddy talk

That and other healing practices
Does Mr Harland Cottrell travel out to make
For all Nettie and Mr Birch Nazareth laugh
How many is killd today
I know that sometimes he did much good
Or certainly intend much

For sure I recall times when some accident
It does befall in the mill
Such as a mans smock takd in the machines
His arm chest ploughd open
The screaming I do not forget

Mr Harland Cottrell was well gatd
With Master Blyth also
To fix that man back together
So to talk firm to Mr Biddulph
How compensation must be paid

Had also many opinions on doctors in general
In particular those does work in Stroud
Who he tells many a time are nothing
But butchers carpenters poisoners barbers all

Even I am not exempt from his care
Though I should well like to be
For he make Master Blyth adry out eggshells
In the range and then in that back kitchen
Grind them up then mix in boild milk
Which must then be usd to soak my bread
Make me grow taller and more hearty
As I still not much higher
Than first I came to this place

I think he blow his time to the wind
The bread taste gritty stick in my teeth

God has made me of short stature
No man will change it so I think

Worse he insists that a plaster
Made of sheep leather soakd in oil of elder
Must be put on my lip for to heal up

So for many days the plaster sit there
Feel like a slug stuck on my mouth
But it change nothing

How many killd today Mr Birch Nazareth say
Though bring me a crinch of meat
When no one sees
More likely to make me grow
So I should say

Yet for all that I know Mr Harland Cottrell
Speak several languages is exceptional educatd
Master Ned for sure has inheritd his abilities
For I oft am sweep up in the school room
Sat there long is Master Blyth
Struggle oft ovr his work
Scratching late into the night

Yet Master Ned despite he is the younger
Finish all at high speed
Make no effort in it

You could not fail to be impressd by he

Tall and straight and lither with pinning eyes
A ready laugh a quick mind

Long white hands waving as he speaks
Kind oft and thoughtful
I did like to be in a room
When he was there

I also like to hear him talk
For he has the same way of fighting with words
As does his father

Tis from him I first do hear
Some of that poetry that I do love
Such as Mr Wordsworth and Shelley

This he do read aloud striding cross the room

Though less I do enjoy his talk
As takes from other books such as William Godwin
Gainst those does doubt the guilt
Of the recently martyrd French King

How the clergy must be strippd of their wealth
So it be applid to the alleviation
Of the National Misery

This I hear particular
As we all walk back from chapel on Sundays

Oft we go to the Ruscombe Chapel
There Mr Harland Cottrell work with one
Mr John Burder the completion of a new chapel
Being much need for the low types there

Also sometime walk to Stroud
For to worhip with the Methodists in Acre Hedge
Those same ones did go Mrs Freda Woebegone

These followers of Mr Wesley
Have fallen in many grievous spiritual errors
So say Mr Harland Cottrell

Yet he keeps peace with they
For these folk are ardent in their work
Gainst the West Indian slavery
So much else must be forgiven they

I did not know you could pick and choose
In this way and argue with what is said

Surely God cannot be only what we make He

Yet Mr Harland Cottrell care not for all that
Going oft through the sermon
He and Master Ned commenting on it both
Mr Harland Cottrell encouraging Master Ned

Master Blyth is not part of this conversation
Should he evr try to add anything
He is quickly talkd down by his father
Or by Master Ned

So those two debate and argue on and on
As we walk back from Stroud or Ruscombe

How reason have more value than revelation
Nor can be miracles or the Trinity

How man can surely achieve the perfection of God
By studying the natural world
Which does reflect divine perfection

How this is truth and that is not
As though they argue with God hisself

This I do not think it right
But oh I love to hear it
For at moments like that I am remind
Both of Mr Abel Woebegone and of Ambrose

He I have lost and never think to find again
Did consider of asking at the Acre Hedge Chapel
But dare not for he like not that place

Also went down one Sunday afternoon
To ask for him at the Bowbridge Dye Works
One there told me he gone to Playnes
At Dunkirk in the Nailsworth Valley

I know no more yet never cease to think on he
Mr Abel Woebegone too how he talkd

Why would anyone think on sin and punishment
When one sees here all Gods creation
Spread round us in these Valleys

The world is my country
All mankind are my brethren
To do good is my religion

That I do remember
Yet also worrid for I still did not know
Is it true he were sent to prison

This does trouble me much
For if it be true then will he be savd

Sometimes would like to ask Mr Harland Cottrell
What he think to that

But I do not

*

Then comes one night
I understand a little more

It happens like this I wake
To hear a screaming in the house

I have heard it sometime afore

Usually such a noise as this does stop soon
Yet this time it does not
So I am afeard and get up
The noise is so wracked with pain
I must see what assistance I can give

In the house are hushd voices also
Doors opening and feet moving ovr the boards
Go I then to the foot of the stairs

Just at that moment the screaming stop
Mr Harland Cottrell does then appear
His long white legs under his night shirt
Descending the narrow shadowd stair

I would like to hide but he comes on me too quick

Ah Mary Ann he say Do not trouble yrself
Fetch me only a pitcher of water

So I go then bring back without delay

Aye thank you now he say
Do not worry yrself Master Blyth is calm now
Tis always thus

What would he do without his brother
A young man who as you must have noticd
Has such prodigious kindness sympathy
This is his blessd gift givd of God
Tis the purpose for which he was born
For which we must all give thanks

I nod in agreement say amen to that
Slide back through the house
Settle myself next to Nettie
Scratches snores wheezes
Yet has heard nothing

Sleep though has flown and will not return
So I do lie awake crampd under the eaves
Thinking of what was said
Which seems to me true and right

*

Nettie say to me the next day eve
So you are hookd in by Master Ned

No I say Her question vex me
Tis not my place to have an idea of him
Or she neither

Course many believe he blessd she say

This she speak when the work is done
Sitting at the kitchen table
On a chair which have no seat in it
Which Master Blyth did make for her
Oft she cannot sit down
Having weeping tetters on her private parts

Me finishing a piece of coppies leg
Brought in by Mr Birch Nazareth
This we must keep hid
But do not worry as Mr Harland Cottrell
Not back til tomorrow

Despite myself I cannot deny an interest
In what Nettie say

Why I say Why they think he blessd

No one tell you she say
About Master Ned
How he should not rightfully be on this earth
About the circumstances of his birth

No I do not know
What do you mean

Ah ah So no one tell you then
About the Mistresses death
Tis all the same story
I was there
I saw it all

I do not take the meaning from it as some do
But I saw certainly
It were a shocking thing
Shall never forget

So we sat in the eve bronzd kitchen
All cleard away but the darkness not yet come
It being still zummer
The shadows slide in at the back door
Yet not time to light the candle

So she tell me then the story
Through her hissing teeth
Keeping me fixd firm
With her flat pig eyes
Nodding oft her head

What she say printd itself
Inside my head forevr
The outline of it always there
Never can be rubbd out

Oft think I was there and saw it all myself
Such is the way she tell it

It come she say at a time
When Mr Harland Cottrell not marrid long
Master Blyth but three years old
The Mistress heavily burdend
Soon expect Master Ned

Nettie know all this she work for the family
Since the time Mr Harland Cottrell come here
She like the Mistress well

A peart piece light on her feet laughing
Yet all alone in this farm sudden orphand
Meet Mr Harland Cottrell quite puckfoistd by he
As many are and he also like this house

I not say he see hisself well set up say Nettie
I not say that

He lovd her well I am sure
Yet he is not blind
He see all that is here
It suit him fine well

For he has his schemes and his healing
His ideas about the simple life
All of that cafuddle

Want none of the management of the farm
So she organize most
He work at his healing

Master Blyth a good and healthful boy
His mother love so much

It come that time
An aunt of the Mistress died
She of the Greylord family
Livd at Gloucester

So some furniture was inheritd
Twas a chest of some sort so was thought

The Mistress did not care so much for this
Twas many miles endways to bring it back
She not sure what value it had
Heavy with child she thought perhaps to ask
Some person in Gloucester to sell it for her
Send the money on

Mr Harland Cottrell did not like that idea
Already money was not as plentiful as he hopd

He evr was a man see only the good
Thought perhaps the furniture had much value
Should be brought here to be examind
Afore a decision was made

Anyway they had other business in Gloucester
So twas agree they go cart harnessd

Could bring the chest back

All this despite the fact it were early December
The air cloud with rising frost
The jaws of the cold clamping hard

Nettie here take pause

She know the chest turnd out not a chest
But a large oak dresser the drawers lockd
Twas a difficult business to load it
On the cart and bring it back all the long way
Ovr the top at Painswick
Down the Valley

They drive off from Gloucester that morning
Took them all day to come
The dresser slipping sometime on the cart
Startd to freeze deep from Painswick

So that road as had been thick with mud
Running with water
Turn sudden cracking hard and slipping

Course they should never have gone
On such a wild venture
Nettie say to me

Yet you not a child Mary Ann
You know what is the situation here
A gentleman does not become involvd
In the shifting of furniture

But you see how this family is placd
A fine house this but hardly a shilling

If only he had not gone to Gloucester
If only he had done as she say
Sell the dresser there

It were evr like him though to be curious
To believe it might contain
Something to his advantage

Anyways they descend the Painswick Valley
Rough way for the new turnpike not finishd
The cold clench still the skye growd tar black
So they come down just below this farm

You know well how we are situate here
On the ledge above the way below

Tis pitifully steep to come
So Mr Harland Cottrell know as well

He should have takd the cart
The long way round up through Cally Well
Or even pass through Pakenhill
The way is better made there
Yet no he think to come up the hill
Tis no problem in fine weather

The Mistress say no
Tis best not the day is ending
The child Master Blyth tird and hungry

Yet Mr Harland Cottrell say No no
Scant trouble twill be
They can go up the twisting track
The horse is strong the cart well made
Tis a simple matter

So the cart turn up the track
Which goes cross the hill one way
Back tother again and again
Too steep to go up direct

The skye now is low and gatherd thick
The dark collied as a black wool cloak

At first they make good progress
The horse is sinuous strong
He dig in hoof and pull pull up
The dresser well tied on
The way it lie then
Fall of the hill favour

Then they turn the corner
Tis hard to get round
Wheels and hooves slatting on ice
Weight shift
Still Mr Harland Cottrell go on
Apply whip Come on Come on
Tis not so much trouble
We go up

In the cart the Mistress draind pale
Master Blyth sit gainst her
The two shuddering with the cold
Yet they say naught

The cart on the flat again
Cut sideway cross the hill
The horse pull on
No moon no stars ice thicken

The horse go on capital well
Pull strain groan creak

The cart go round
For a moment drop back
Mr Harland Cottrell apply the whip
Not like him that
He is always soft with all things living

The horse strain on
Yet a coming out of the bend the cart stick
Mr Harland Cottrell whip and whip
The horse strain and creak
Massy dresser rock and sway
High wind sweep down the hill

The horse panic sliding on the ice
Hooves scrape and flail squealing rear back
The coach begin to tip
Sliding slipping cracking
Goes sudden ovr the side
Crashing back down the hill

Mr Harland Cottrell thrown well clear
Also little Master Blyth jump far
They both land up hill
Master Blyth screaming
Mr Harland Cottrell slabberd in mud and ice
Shoulder bent pulld the socket

But he jump up
See the cart below
All break up
The horse down
Fighting in the harness
Trying still to gain a footing

Yet where is the Mistress
Mr Harland Cottrell hurry down feet slurry slip

As he come round look up from below
See then Oh a terrible sight
Her body he can see
Yet her head is under the fallen dresser
The brokd side of the cart

He climb up quick try free her
But in the chilling darkly light
He see the streams of blood running
He knows her head is broke
Clasp her china white hand
Still wear the ring he gave her
That hand already growing cold
The life retreating from her

There she is on the hillside
Her head smashd under the carriage
Yet her belly still lie proud and high
Where the unborn babe lie

I come down from the house by then
He shout to me Nettie Nettie
Get a knife from my Cabinet
The largest and sharpest

Run now Go quick I look at tiny Master Blyth
Stood on the high bank shaking screaming
Yet I must not stop for he
Just get the knife as I am told
I think he mean to cut harness
In that way perhaps lift the wood
That lie on her head

So I come back with the knife
By this time little Master Blyth
Has climbd down closy by his father

But that Mr Harland Cottrell shout at him
Stay back Come not near
Still the child see all

I watch wait for Mr Harland Cottrell
To start on the harness
Though I know there is no purpose
Yet still the horse must sometime be free
Though he kneel now in the crackd ice
Still and blowing heavy

So listen well now Nettie say
Believe what I say
I saw it all Tis as twas told
I never thought to see such a thing as this

Mr Harland Cottrell take the knife
But he not touch the harness
Instead he kneeling down
Beside the body of her his wife
Slit open first her bodice and chemise

Then draw no breath afore slit open her flesh
A long clean cut
A swathe of blood run thick
All cross the ground round

Cut her open all down the belly
Not hesitate or tremble
But clean strong and straight deep

Then pulls her open as you gut a fish
Fold back the flesh
Pulld her far right open

In goes his hands diving deep her ruind body

The arms in near to the elbow
Dig dig within
All his white shirt turnd wine red
His face calm certain

Sudden he holds up
Red and writhing screaming
The body of a living boy child
Full growd and strong
Twisting in his hand

Then he sit back in the mud
Lay the babe cross his knee
Cut the cord
Another clean fine sweep
Like slicing a piece of meat

He stoppd to take two deep breath
Shut his eyes a moment
Then held up the babe and shout to me
Take him in to the fire warm him through Nettie

I step down and seize the babe
Hold him gainst me despite all the blood
So much there was

Blood all down the hillside
Thick with the ice mud
I could not even look at her
Her fine young body
All split open and broke
He sitting beside her
Blood cover he face hands chest legs
What not coverd with blood soakd by ice
Wet with mud

Yet still does he clean off the knife
On his britch leg

Still Master Blyth sit on the hill
His hands pressd to his head
Screaming screaming
The sound so sharp and shrill and hurt
You would think he the one cut
It fill the entire Valley

Pray that the Almighty abide with us always

I then go to take he in with me
But Mr Harland Cottrell call out
No no You look to the babe

After that others come
News travel fast to White Hill
The men from Ruscombe Farm they come
Cross the Valley from Hammonds also

Still I hold the babe
Now swaddld well
While others bring Master Blyth in
Though they must hold tight
Pin his arms to his body
Keep clear his kicking legs

Screaming screaming for his mother
She never come more
May God hold tender her precious soul

Yet others cut the harness and get the horse up
He exhaustd and frightd
But otherwise unharmd
Were a good horse they say later

It were not he made the decision
To come up that hill
When the mud were ankley deeper
Fetlock the ice crackd ovr it
It were evr a treacherous spot
No not he

Men then try to pick up what piece they could
Though the dresser the cart all crackd to bits
Only so many pieces of wood and snappd shafts
One of the wheels roll off down the hill

All the time the Master sat there
Still beside her body
Even as they lift off wooden side
As crackd into her head
They could not make he come in
He would not do it

Master Blyth scream long into the night

Yet the babe Master Ned for course it were he
Not cry at all but settle down happy
Course know nothing of all that passd

Many come to the house to peer at he
They do not believe he live
They do not think it possible
See him there pure white and strong
Eyes watching sharp even then

Course they ask how such could happen
What is the meaning of it
What we could expect from a boy savd
From such a Devil wrought disaster

The Master when he come to his senses
Not stop the talk but only add to it

For what has he been savd
That is the question askd
Tis askd still

More than that folk know there was no wet nurse
No no Mr Harland Cottrell say We have no need of such
Make up chicken broth he say
The boy will do well enough on that

So he say though he take no meat hisself

Well well I did not like it
I will not Sir I will not
You will poison he that way

Give to me say Mr Harland Cottrell
So he start to feed he on chicken broth
No ill did come of it

People do not believe it now
But I was there and tis so

Mr Harland Cottrell after that night
He go on the same
Tell all the blessing of his son
Who is chosen and belovd of God

As the years go on
It were hard not to see the touch of God
On the burnish of his pallid skin
That thick straight hair

His smiling smirking sullen face

So say Nettie then purse up her mouth

I do not say Mr Harland Cottrell did not grieve
Yet you know how he is made
All is the will of God
Whatevr happen is His Grace

Though others say behind their hands
That God cannot be held responsible
For those as cannot drive a cart

Nettie stop her story wheeze and laugh then
Shake her head look ovr her shoulder

How the shadows creep in at the door
For we are come to edge of the night
Who has drawd his curtain now
All cross the Valleys

The air itself does draw in breath
As she finishes this her story

So that how they said it after she say
But I myself think nothing of that talk
I do not divine it that way

I see other things that night

I tell you all

You see it now for yrself

*

I do not know if twas Netties story
Made me think so much on Master Ned

Perhaps no
It were more he were everywhere in the house
Lift down books for me to look at
Knock my brush from my hand
Then pick it up again
Present it to me with a deep bow
Evr fool like that he

Yet anyway it soon come about
Many were expectd at the house
I knew not why

All were shrammd with cold then
Not long after Candlmass
A glitter snipple of frost
Sparkle ovr all and the Valley lost in white

Mr Harland Cottrell and Master Blyth
Engagd in preparation
Nettie and I set to clean well
Get all the dust of every fousty corner
Of which there were many

Mr Birch Nazareth told farm yard
Must be put straight
Though he did rumple and humple
Take little notice of this

Tis a farm yard he say
Course tis a full of muck

Master Ned was not hisself
A part of these preparations
That were evr so

Master Ned you see

He was intend for to be a lawyer
For only through the proper reform of the law
Can the world be brought to divine perfection
So tell us Mr Harland Cottrell

So Master Ned must keep up his studies
Though as I say he seldom in the school room
Til such time as he must go
For two years education afore he can begin

Master Ned not happy with that plan
For he wants to go to school now as others do
Oft dispute this with Mr Harland Cottrell

Yet Mr Harland Cottrell say Nay nay
You will get no knowledge in such place

Master Ned does not agree I know
Yet still think he glad he is not expectd
To take any interest in the study of healing
For that he talk of most contemptuous

Sometimes when he hear Mr Birch Nazareth say
How many has he killd today
He say Only one killd but a leg sawd off
Another gone stone blind
Not a bad day then

I thought it disrespectful
Though still I could not help but laugh

So anyway that was how all stood
That preparations were being made

When Mr Harland Cottrell say to me

You are a careful girl are you not
You have gentle hands You move quiet

I know you I can trust

I do not take his meaning but only say
I hope that I to be trust in all matters Sir

Good good say he
Usual I do not like my Cabinet be disturbd
But now tomorrow I have visitors
I do not want people take the wrong idea

You cannot know say he
The poisons and diseases
That may be wedgd tween the cracks in a tile
Or press down the gaps in the floor boards
This now we understand more fully every day

So you will clean Mary Ann Is that so
But touch nothing Make sure nothing fall
Only work with girt care

Yes Sir course I take good care

So I say though I think it a little contrary
That he should speak of keeping things clean
When I think how blatchy was this house
When first I come

Sometimes not so much better now
For I can clean well
But not mend what is broke

What else can I say He is my Master
There is no choice I must do as he say

Though I prefer not to enter that room
I cannot quite say why

You must work in the evening he say
I am busy there all day
I have many preparations to make
But you can light candles

Yes I say and so that eve
I know that I must be dinging long
Nettie already gone to bed
Goes as soon as she may
Leave all to me I do not care

Take candles broom mop soap
Bucket blacking feather duster
No one is in the room by now or so I think
Mr Harland Cottrell already gone his chamber

So then I am surprise when I push back the door
See a candle burn at a desk
In the far corner of the room

The light touch the brow lip cheek
Tis Master Blyth
Who work at a desk
His head come up as I enter

He nod at me
Eyes shut with concentration
To make a word Finally say

You you you can can come in
Then the words flow more free
I shall continue to work
His head drop back down

Ovr the book

Yes Sir I say Begin to spread my tools
Light another candle the room begin to form
Push back the shadows

Walls lind with many books
At the centre heavy wooden furniture
As I begin to sweep see what look like a bed
Yet high up and round it many wooden seats

Also a wooden tray nearby
I move the candle so I may see more clear
The light leaps and jumps
Playing up the walls of books
Glittering on brass handles
Lighting the edge of a vast bone
Must surely be the jaw of a cow

Saws pliers knives
So many metal instruments
Wooden cases and leather bags
Much like a carpenter have
But something tells me this not the same
Move the light jagging away

At one wall a winder fullsome curtains close
My candle move cross the furrow of the fabric

Keep yr eyes now on the surfaces I say
Make all clean wipd shine

There is much to do
Still my eyes oft wander
See the visage of Master Blyth

It were strange how a face
Could be so like another
Yet not like at all
All the features being a true copy
But the light within quite different
The character shadowd and knit tight

Come come Mary Ann I say to myself
You have much work to do here
Stop bathering about

Yet even then as I speak to myself thus
I move the candle It touches blood letting bowls
Then glass bottles with black lids
Many many lind on the shelves and all labelld
In a neat slanting hand
Some hardly the length of my finger
Others will be heavy to lift
I should be afeard to drop them

All dusty and rightly each must be liftd out
Cleand all about yet there are so many
That may be another time

I move the candle on so I can measure
The scale of all must be done

Then feel a shiver pass up my spine
My hands tremble
My stomach rise up in my throat
For there are other bottles
Which gleam white in the candle
Things move

White clumps like sheeps wool
Marked with fine lines all running together

Like the grains of wood
Bottle pulling shapes round stretchd horribly

Made bright by the light
I cannot say what they are
I hold on tight to the candle
Must not drop it
Must not cry out

Then I see out of a glass jar
A human face peering at me

Terror breaks in a scream from my lips

Master Blyth I never hear him move
Sudden he is at my side
Take my candle

M M M Mary Ann Y Y Y you not be afeard

I cannot speak but only point

Y Y yes he say Sometime they use a pigment
To give a colour so it looks quite real
Does it not

I want him to lower the candle
I want to get away
Tis only my job to clean dust
Use my eyes only for that

Still I cannot help but look
What I see is moon touchd and shining
But also hazy like seed through water

S S S see here an adder and here a piglet

His voice is chargd with wonder
More than that a hunger
How can he speak so

These things swimly nakd in glass bottles
Alive and not alive Trappd Floating
My teeth are screeching my bones squeeze

Y Y Y you have nothing to fear say Master Blyth
Hold the candle higher

There is no harm in it
These things are dead anyway
Only put h h h here so that we may study
To know better the world in which we live
This we owe to Almighty God
Who made all these things
To understand fully the mystery of His creation

I cannot even hear the words he say
The moon of his face lit by the candle
The shadows of his eyes gathering dark
His hands root like white same as his father

Then Mr Harland Cottrells words
Come back to me
You kill nothing that live in this world

So now none of it makes sense
These things are dead and should be returnd
To the earth from which they come
Tis gainst nature that they are trappd here
Still floating strippd far from Gods mercy

Master Blyth turn to look at me
Ah ah S S S sorry he say

I see this not to yr taste
I interrupt you in yr work Mary Ann

So he return the candle to me and carry on
Yet my mind is full of what I have seed
Spin spin Turn this way and that

I find it fearful
I know it to be wrong
I never seed anything so ungodly
Or anything so chargd with worship

But no wipe dust only
That evening do only the floors
The surface of that wooden bed and chairs
Make all as good as I can
It were many days work to do all

Yet though I do not look at Master Blyth
I feel him there and can hardly hold my brush
Such is my fear

My mind circling again and again
That Devil with the moving eyes
Also the certainty that should Master Blyth
Take off his boots then we should see
His legs scaly his feet clawd

He planting limbs in blood
They grow in the garden
Hands and feet pushing up

Tis just as my mind does scream
With all these thoughts
I come upon a bucket stand beside the wooden bed
Something dark is in it

I shine my candle down
My head turn as though I am falling

Inside it are many frogs all cut up
I see legs heads all thrown together

What am I to do with this
I take the pail and go out into the lane
I do not look again inside
I do not want my hand near
Hold the candle high
But stumbling still
Must not spill the bucket

Who did this and why
Does Master Blyth take his own way
Or obey his fathers instructions

Walk down Lower Slad Ground
Tip all the stinking mess in a hedge
Then go back and clean the bucket at the pump

What house am I living in
Yet I cannot but be grateful

Yet I must think on this
Here I could fall into sin
Here I not understand

Tis as Nettie says Work work
And do not see Do not ask

None of this for me to know

MOUNT VERNON

In the first bruisd light
I wake early

The winder of my tower room open
The air knife sharp and stinging

Slowly I unwrap the stiffness of my limbs

Look out at the fleecd pink of the morning
The garden all shroude the cloud settld on us
As it does oft these rearing Valleys

So it did the first dawn at The Heavens
When I think myself indeed in paradise
I am not far from there now

I pull on my dress
Wince the lump above my breast
I feel it more there a knot of wound
It takes all my power
I am growed thin as a child

Sit at the kitchen table and write
The pen move smooth cross the paper

I do not write as neat as once I did

For now I am tird bitterly bitterly tird
I think to eat some food but none I want

The time is short

Yet still I continue
Not because he says I must

A cause now I start the words run on
They have their own way to go

All around the zummer is pacing on
The verdous trees now heavy with the weight
So many breathing flourishing leaves

Below terraces cut in the earth
Steps which lead down
Through two lines of trees

Beyond the thick woods
You reach see through a white iron gate
Which is behind the small zummer house
Such a trim and eggshell little place

This acre a corner of heaven descend
What a mystery now to think that
Tis this exact house
This place I saw the building go ahead
When I was a stripling
Tower up through the cloud of winter trees
That day with Ambrose
Oh it were long ago

I wish I could but walk through the garden

Yet my pen tumbles on and on
Still I must listen for my Master
Though he rises from his bed less and less

Talks oft of how I must write for he
Three lines I do take down
Of this date and that Act of Parlement
Afore he drops again into firm sleep

Though now today he calls me
His theme it has changd

His concern is that letter
He did write to his relatives
Which he instruct me to post

Worrid he is now that no response
Has been receivd

I do not light upon him as to the fact
No response now will evr arrive
For I no a ways sent the letter to be postd

It lies still in the kitchen

I did not destroy it
That I would not do

For that letter is in the manner of a will
Which will be need when he is gone

Yet I consider it best
That the letter stay here
In that way no one will come
To disturb us here

Yet he is not to be stoppd
By such an easy trick
Does discuss now as to how
He must take contact with a solicitor
Who may assist him in the matter
Of this his acursd book

I stand afore him while he turns
The question this way and that

Though I know you will serve me well in this
As in all else he say

Yet I feel I must also seek other assistance
For I know this is a weighty task to ask
Even you and I working together take some time

Yet still I cannot help but to say
Perhaps Sir I had best send word
To the son of that Mr Hawkins Fisher
Who as you know was always a friend
To yr dear departd father

The son being also now a solicitor in Stroud
You know him so I think

This were wickd of me
For that man he will no a ways have
Not in this house or anywhere about
He cannot take the risk of that

This I already know
As he does now make clear

Instructs me then to write to another
Whose name he has heard

Being Mr Watton of Rowcroft

So I sit down and take up my pen

How a man must be found to help
With the preparation of a singular book
On an important subject of much local interest
Arrangements also made as to a book binder
Might under take to make public such a document

I write the words down without hearing them
Think He finds someone new now to lie for he

Keep the anger in my mind lockd tight

Does he believe any assistance be a coming
Mr Gains left a cause he was not paid
The lawyer in Stroud will be the same
Twill be knowd

His family never could keep a hold of money

The sun pass the summit and slide syrup down
Afore all is crossd dottd blottd finishd

Then he takes the letter sends me for a spill
Lit from the kitchen range melt the wax seals

When I return with the lightd spill
He drips the wax and stamps
Then takes a penny from his pocket
Course he say
I shall go again to Stroud myself
In but a few days

I say Yes Sir yes

But will he again

The hill being a straight drop his leg rotting
The horse fine tempering young and skittering

I take from him the letters and the coin
Promise that all shall be deliverd well

Then gather also up some bloody rags and bucket
Cross the hall and down to the kitchen
Lean gainst the table
Breath blockd in my throat

I stoke up the fire
Must then wash out the rags
Think what I might find for lunch

There is little enough
Only what the garden yield
Some salted beef gone green
Eggs the boy from below does bring

The Master call again
I must go to him

Yet first I take up that letter he did write
Step to the range pick up a spill
Place it where it light
Lay it close gainst the letter
A copper flash sparks paper burns a circle black
The wax of the seal spits
The flames take and flare

The letter is gone
Droppd into the range
All is ash

STOCTON HILL

So now I do come to a part of my story
Another strange terrifying wonderment twas
Of that Mr Harland Cottrell
Or so I thought at the time

For as I did tell
He hopd v much he might cure
The deformity of my mouth

Already he had tried herbs and plasters
None of it had changd much
I did know he discussd this much
With Master Blyth

Anyways Mr Harland Cottrell come one day
Just as I am out the back working the mangle

Palm Sunday had been and gone
Yet it were a scurvy inhospitable day
Ice still lie all cross the path
I wrappd tight in coat and gloves
My feet pulsing cold

Mr Harland Cottrell wear no coat

Only wool jacket

Was always casual not take care of hisself
He should a knowd better

So he comes to stand beside me
Near foot slipping on the path

Mary Ann what think you about this hole
That has always been yr upper lip

I feel blood rise up my body gather my face
For I am ashamd and shockd
That he should speak such way

For I know right well my face is deformd
Yet prefer not to think much of it myself
Or others to say it

Tis a burden the Lord placd upon me
That I must carry brave
As He carry the cross at Calgary

So I say nothing yet he keep on
I do not think it good for you
Tis true you are ill favourd generally
Not properly growd
Yet the face is what people see
Course he says and coughs a little
Are those ignorant
Think such a mark the work of the Devil

I speak up hotly then angry at those words
Say loud I never had no talk with the Devil
No a ways shall

Mr Harland Cottrell then bang hands together
Gainst the cold
Wipe a kerchief ovr his running nose

It were still early then
Behind him the sun stain in the skye
Flame red but muffld in frost

Say he I know that right well
You are a good girl of cheerful heart
Honest and hard working

He wave the kerchief afore put it away

What I say is others may not know this
Which may cause you some difficulty
You must think of the future
Not all as educatd as me

All this v well but I not understand
The direction of this talk

Yet then he say
I have study much recently
Seed several demonstrations and sure
·Could close up the hole for you

I feel like he slap my face
For I no a ways heard such a thing

Think also of the hollering from his study
Things live in bottles the high wooden bed
I do not want to end like that

Also say Mr Harland Cottrell
I have certain ways which mean

You will feel no pain

Afterwards would be some discomfort
Say Mr Harland Cottrell
But I give you a draught to take away most
It would not take long
Come courage Mary Ann
I think this best for you
We have time this afternoon
Can do it then
What say you

You have no need to worry
For Nettie will offer you much comfort

Does he not see that Nettie
Has as much comfort in her
As a thorn bush in a frost

She thinks I get what I deserve
For my arrogance

With that he is gone back inside
Driven there by a chill gust
Filld out by flecks of snow

Little for me to say in truth
He employ me this what he decide
But I am gut with dread

After he has gone
I go back the kitchen tell Nettie
My legs will hardly hold me
She get water and say No No
He go too far but she like me
What choice we have

We cannot say him nay

They will mesmerize you say Nettie
Tis known he has that dark art

Netties first moment of kindness pass
Soon she sitting by the range
Wheezing as she jests again
Rocking back and forwards snoffling
About how many he has killd today

Mary Ann she say
I think you do better with they
Butchers carpenters barbers poisoners
In Stroudwater

Do you not know have you not seed
His hands are terrible shaking
Like leaves in a storm
So she says rubbing at her wobbling nose
Laughing herself almost to tears

This I do know I have seed it myself
Heard others say it

I cannot work I cannot think
I am so afeard

Master Ned is meant to be in the school room
Yet as always he has finishd all his work
In but a few short minutes

Whereas Master Blyth is still there
Head bent down labouring slow and steady

Soon Mr Harland Cottrell will come shout

At Master Blyth How you is so tardy
How can it be that one so slow
Yet make so many simple mistakes
Threaten even to beat him sometime

So twas in that house
You do not kill a mouse
But Mr Harland Cottrell he could be iron hard
With his shadowd and baffing oldest son

So anyways Master Ned being finishd
Hear news of what is to be done

Come in the kitchen smiling and light
Twill be nothing he say
Come Mary Ann
My father and my brother have much experience
In this You will do v well

Yr brother Oh yes Yr brother I think
What do you really know about he

Then Master Ned takes a knife feels the blade
Whirls it around his head several time
Oh yes he say This one be sharp enough

Think I then of the showman in the black cloak
As I did see that distant night
He who controls all
Did bring the Devil out

When he see I do not accept what he say
He cease to jest lay his hand upon my arm
You know they would not harm you
They would not do this if they did not care

I am not calmd a jot by his sudden kindness
Ask Nettie if perhaps I should run
She say No no You not do it
Where can you go

But I do not know if she takes care
Of my interest or only her own

I wring my hands shake my head
Try to hold tight my tears

I not take off my clothes I say to Nettie

Oh no Nettie agree
He will not ask that
Tis not proper
Anyway all person of sense know
Never cast no clout
Til May is out

I think of all I have heard said
The Kettle Boil Cutter and that
Most of it in prank
But always that type of jape is serious

Some not live long after they see he
But maybe they were always fixd to die
Their time already come I do not know

The afternoon come The minutes pass
I stay with Nettie in the kitchen
Stand croochd gainst the wall

My mouth gone cherky
Shivering bones knocking together
Partly the cold but also fear

The light at the winders gone white
As it does when the air is laden heavy
With snow soon to fall

Think maybe if I keep mouse quiet
He will perhaps forget me

Yet soon he comes with Master Blyth
His sleeves rolld up rubbing those
Long white hands together
They boots rattle cross the stone floor
Nettie also backs out the way

So then you come with us now Mary Ann he say
I stayd fixd gainst the wall
Cannot move even if I want

Now now say Mr Harland Cottrell
This is all agreed
Then he steps forward ready to take me

Come come This the time
We do not help her by dallying here

Master Blyth then catches hold of me

But Master Ned come past his father
Step toward me quiet and firm stretch out hand

His eyes are deep and steady
So when he hold out his hand I take it

There he says and this time his voice not falter
Now we shall do v well

He keeps hold my hand

We walk together like bride and groom
Through the chill afternoon yard
Where I look up at the whitening hills
Rising all around under the ice laden skye
As though I see for the last time

Into that Cabinet room we do step
Mr Harland Cottrell following behind

Once again I am seizd with the desire to run
But Master Ned stay firm

Come sit you here say Master Blyth
Twill not taste good I do admit
Yet this draught spirit away the pain

So I do find my courage and drink it down
Though so bitter it glutchs in my throat

Now I will be damnd for all eternity
For though herbs are in the tankard
Also cider or maybe beer
I know the swimly smell
From those nights at The Heavens

Briefly then that scent
Makes me think of Ambrose
Where is he now

When will I see him again
I should like to see him afore
I am calld home

For a moment I look up and see
That moon touchd piglet floating
The adder all curld up in his jar

The glass thick and distorting like a lens
So that all is spread and twistd
Mouths with stretchd lips grimacing horrible

Then I am told I must unrag me
Take off bodice and blouse
I had thought would not be need
Yet I am numb and surrenderd now
Seed the scissors on the table
The needle cotton strips of bandage
Metal instruments all packd neat in a case
Should be usd only for carpentry

I think then of the frogs in the bucket
Cut into bits all throwd in together

They picks me up and lays me on the wooden bed
I pray and pray to the Almighty Save me

Then Master Blyth does stand ovr me
Saying You have only now to watch my hand
Watch it close

Then he does move his hand back and forwards
Moving cross my eyes and forehead

Watch he says Watch now close

His voice does wrap round me
My eyes follow his hand back and forwards

Watch watch Only watch close

My head dip and swoop turn in many circles
I feel a hand on my face

Then cold metal pulling and pulling
Pain ramping up through my face into my head

I cry out but then my head turn to liquid
I go back to The Heavens and my days there
Weep terrible for I see Baby Fern again
Her steps tottering in the garden
All among the willowing grass and buttercups
Her tiny hands trail

She closy by I step forward to be beside her
We are on the edge of the world far up high
Like the Devil take Jesus to the top of the ledge
Say all this will be yrs if you follow me
Then Fern and I fall ovr the edge both lost
Falling down and down

I screaming and my mouth on fire
Flames flizzie all inside my head
Catch hold my hair
All alight like a fire cracker

Then nothing at all

*

Much later I wake in my own bed
My mouth smouldering hot my throat parchd

I lie there weeping
For though tis bad to have a
Hole in yr face tis much worse
To have what I now have

I do not need look in the mirror see
Dare not place my hand there

So I lie crying for the memory come to me
How tis oft said Mr Harland Cottrell
Enjoy a rare ailment and so I think he only evr
Brought me here as a trial
To see what might be done

Yet when Master Ned come in later
He never usually come up the steep stairs
To our attic but he come now and say

Now now Mary Ann You not be a silly goose
You know you must wait It take time to fix
Then you will see

Place beside my bed a little milk jug
Filld up with red berry holly
Oh what joy it were to see it there

Also bring me a warm blanket I need
For the snow has come now muffld all about
Drifts near three feet deep
Tween the hedges of the lane
All snewd up so none may pass

Truly I must say
I were a fool
Can only say I were young and ignorant
Had no knowledge of the world no one to tell

For soon it heal well
Then only to pull out the stitches
Not much pain at all Just a few sharp tug

Then Mr Harland Cottrell find a chair
Stand me on it so I may look in the mirror

This were after the snow had gone
A day when a struggling sun
Touch yeller some parts
Of the quaggy fields

Master Blyth beside his father too
We was in the hall

Tis true still be a red mark pointing upwards
On my top lip but mouth all close up proper
My tongue tuckd away as should be

I like a different person to myself
Nettie say You are still v ugly
Yet I not listen to her for now
I am only ugly in the normal way
She no better never was

Now I am like everyone else in life
The same chance make myself a better situation

Mr Harland Cottrell change me
Make my face more pleasing
To others and to me

Pleasd he was about it talkd long
Of the racing success as had been made

*

During that time I wait for my mouth to heal
It were oft hard to sleep

The spring was slow to greet us that year
Easter came went still we waitd

Rain on Good Friday and Easter Day
Brings plenty of grass little good hay

The night skye Bible black
The frost bring all to stillness
Every sound echo sharp like metal on metal
Carry many miles back forth cross the Valleys
I lie awake long

Oft I hear them down below in the house
The voices talk argue then quiet
I not hear the scratch of pen
Yet imagine I do

Then talk again
Oft Mr Harland Cottrells voice
Grand ponderous reading from the Bible

Stare up at the tiles above
Though there be plenty loose not a star shew

Thought the snow had passd
Then it come again
When it melt water come in
Many parts of the house damp with it
Yet this attic always adry
May God be blessd for that

Twist turn toss Nettie beside me snoring deep
I try to keep away from her
For she is always itching terrible
Not just her face now but all her body

She no a ways had a fragrant smell
But it grow worse and worse
Though the smell so familiar now

A certain comfort in it

Finally I get up wrap myself in a blanket
My face is nagging at me
The skin pull tight
The scab ready to fall
Though Mr Harland Cottrell
Say You must not touch
Not at all

Yet they are scratching bad

I go the top of the attic steps
Creak my way down step on step
Feeling the wall

Hearing still the distant thump
Of the fulling stocks
That does go on now all night
Despite the complaints Mr Harland Cottrell
Has made most vigorous

Only on Sundays he say now we hear
The birds singing

Surely every man has right to that

Anyways I should have light a candle

I come down to the kitchen
See the shadow of the girt oak press
Lurch near the winder Glass dark

Light spill at the door
A coming through from the school room
Where many lamps are lit

I move close the door
Now I can hear the scatching of pens
The tight breathing The shuffle of boots
Cough cough Tick tick

I stand where I can see through
But not be seed

Bowd heads all round the table
The books laid out
The light shine on forehead
Edge of hand cheek mouth pursd tight
The hands move slow and regular
Like the movement of many clocks

Mr Harland Cottrell stand up
Pace round the room
Look down at the work
Tush tush he say
Here here

Do you not see You must take care
He point down at the work shake his head

I step forward Crash Splash Bang
Oh no Oh no I had forgot
Many pots are standing on the floor
A cause of the water that come in
After the snow thaw

Everyone turn around I leap back
I hate myself for a dumpty fool

Mary Ann say Mr Harland Cottrell
What do you here

I would like to run
Yet that may make this worse
I have no answer to give

Master Blyth I then do see
Pushd so far in the corner is he

Still at home he is though sixteen now
Should have been apprenticd
Or sent in profession long since
As others in that room are

Still I stand unable to run
I am afeard but also I must say
I do not want to leave that place
The light the warmth the pens scratching
The sense of all together in this high purpose

Perhaps you wish to learn to write
Say Mr Harland Cottrell

Others about look at me and laugh
My head feel large my hands heavy
The scab on my mouth itch
Like tiny scratching scraping hands
All the air presses in close

I would like to write I say

I do not know how or why I say it
Twas not me that spoke

Again laughter rustle through the room
All except I think Master Blyth
His face is shade so I cannot see

Well well say Mr Harland Cottrell
If you want to learn then so you must

The men are laughing more at this
They nudge each other push

Come say Mr Harland Cottrell We must find room
But none move

Mr Harland Cottrell walk slowly round the table
Eyes bright and hard as flecks of ice

At first the men think he jest
Now they wonder

Here he say
Point at a corner is a small gap

But the man
Perhaps more a boy sit there say

She is but a child and a girl

Oh oh say Mr Harland Cottrell
So then she is less in the eyes of God

For a moment there is quiet
The fire crackle someone sneeze

Then Mr Harland Cottrell say
In this present time of the world
Things are not well developd
Yet you all must prepare yrselfs
For another time that is yet to come
Then shall be increasd fairness
A weighing of the talents of all

A woman has as much need
Better herself through education as any man
Or how will she teach her childers

What say you to that he say
He wait but no one say anything
I know they think he a fool
I wonder also if they be right

She not sit down at the table with us
This a voice say but I see not the speaker

So so say Mr Harland We shall see
He turn to where a small table stand
Near the winder

He pull the table forward a chair
Then lift a candle from the side board
Place it there Take a board and chalk
A book narrow and thin
He lays out flat

This practice does demean us a voice say
We are not to be mixd with the likes of her
Many murmur in assent

Mr Harland Cottrell seem to hear nothing

Come come he say but I do not move
Want only to run from the room

Now now Mary Ann say he
Be not dispiritd

I sit down for there is no other way
Now I am sore afeard

I do not know why I ask
It were wrong of me
I never was good at letters
I can remember nothing now of school
It all swimly in front of me
I am not a man
I cannot do this

You have only to copy Mr Harland Cottrell say
Yet still the slate all swirl in front of me
Like water circle a drain
Tis too late at night
I cannot think

I take a hold of myself
Only copy Only look at each letter and form it
Slowly I begin

All goes on well a letter or two
Til the chalk a coming alive in my hands
Squawks gainst the board
Breaks in half

Yet even then Mr Harland Cottrell say
Be not cast down

Come along now come along
You have not all the eve to be frittering

That were how it start
How I learn to read and write
So I may now set down this story

Tis mortal hard I learn slow
I am too tird

Work all day and sit there then
Into the top of the night
My hand cramp the ink blot
I cannot recognize the letters make them right

Yet I keep on and though it be so hard
I remember those nights so well
The music of breath in the room
The clack of Mr Harland Cottrells boots
As he walk the room check each work
The darkness pressing in at the mullions

Tis as though we are one person
We work to the Glory of God
Mr Harland Cottrell tell it so

Be not conformd by this world he say
But be you transformd always
By the renewing of yr mind
That you may prove what is
That good and acceptable and perfect
Will of God

No one speak to me
The men do not like me there
I hear them mutter it so

They also do not like always
The way Mr Harland Cottrell teach
Though they may not say so direct

For Mr Harland Cottrell teach not
The classical World of Romans
Yet the words we speak in mill field lane
The voice of the flowring meadow

But say the men what use is such
Who write the voice of the cabbage patch
Shall not advance far beyond the pig pen

If you wish to rise in the world
Then sure you must learn Latin and Greek

Tis well knowd Mr Harland Cottrell
Does know these languages French Italian also
Yet he will not teach

So some does complaint yet also I do hear
As I fight with the chalk and stubborn letters
News that the men bring back from Stroud
A world opening up to me

How the Gloucester Berkeley Canal now finishd
A new weathercock to the spire in Stroud
Plans for an omnibus from Stroud to Gloucester
Yet I do not know what an omnibus is
Horse racing on Minchinhampton Common
A horse cut up bad outside a beer house

Also talk of a new shearing frame
Does replace the old Harmer
Can cut the surface of cloth
As close and neat as even the best Shearman

The big new mills built at Ebley Lodgemore
Even Vatch Mill soon to be rebuilt

All with many looms inside
So folk no longer working in their own homes

This much discussd and criticizd
The mills is much lust and drinking of cider

Tis not the will of God
That man should work like this

All this I hear but give no mind
I have board and lodging and so much more

The best is the end when I put things straight
Look then at other books

That the first time I see poetry writ down
It does all go from left to right
I see now that it must

But not all the space is filld up
The words have their own pattern
Make a picture on the page
The space that is writ
Speak as loud as the space that is not

I cannot read them right but I like to see
The spaces and all that lie in them

Soon soon I will read them correct
I see the path ahead long and steep
Rising through many tight knit trees
Lit all the way with bright lanterns
So one may step on boldly
I must work and work

Course I tell Nettie nothing
Yet she soon lights on this

Mary Ann you noaf
Waste yr time with that
Tis no one makes money
Scritching with a pen

Once I would have said nothing to her
Yet the times they are a changing now

So I says to her
You speak like that to me as you may
Yet tis a cause of me you spend yr days
Sat by the range warming yr feet
Perhaps you might think on that

She waits til I turnd away
Cornobble me with a rolling pin

Master Ned also does mock me sore
So so Mary Ann he say
You are become so clever
Off to the university soon
I am sure

Yet soon they has less to say
For Mr Birch Nazareth hearing of my skill

Well well he say
I am not surprisd Mary Ann
You may be an elf looking girl
Yet you were always subtle in the mind

So he brings back from Stroud
Halfpenny pamphlets or chap books
Penny bloods or catchpennies
Nixons Prophecies and Mother Shiptons Legacy
With stories in which I am to read to Nettie

This I love to do
Sometime Mr Birch Nazareth come the kitchen also
For to hear me read

Master Blyth also for Nettie does oft make
A bowl of slickut or bread pudding for he

Always has done for she is fond of he
A cause of his care for those infernal cankers
Which do test her most severe

She the only one however as does take that view
Others use Master Blyth as a whipping boy

Even I myself it pains me now to report
Did once lay blame on he
When Mr Birch Nazareth did speak me most severe
For I had left open the yard gate

I did say then twas Master Blyth
Who did leave the gate

Oh I wish I had not
Yet he was that character of person
It would happen to he

Anyways as Master Blyth does eat his pudding
I help Mr Birch Nazareth to ease off his boots
He take some snuff that Mr Harland Cottrell
Had best not see as he does not approve
Snuff being the cause of degeneracy
Swollen tumours also in the nose

So I do read stories of brigand chiefs
Stolen childers gypsies witherd hags
Ladies of title with knowledge of poison

So I do make voice for the many parts

Voices fiercesome funny and tragic

All clapping when I does the voice
Of Blackjack Pirate or Dick Turpin
Who does growl in a manner frightening

Yet Mr Harland Cottrell is not to know
For he says such as they is but
Sentimental rubbish full of superstition
Only for those dummel as a donkey

But I do love those stories
With highwaymen and robbers and fair maids
Who is kidnappd

They remind me then of the ballads
As Mr Abel Woebegone did sing

Nettie loves them also
Though she tells me oft
I read them wrong

I care not what she say

For these are the blessd days of my life
For everything give thanks
For this is the will of God in Jesus Christ

Not just those nights of writing
But all the days as well

For now in my mind are many stories
Which I tell to myself again and again
As I work

Taking the characters and making
New adventures for them
So I am carrid through

The easy days the zummer come again

Mr Harland Cottrell and Master Blyth
Sometimes out all day with the doctoring
Or instructing the men on the farm

Perhaps some other scheme to help the weavers
Make some representation of their behalves

Introduction of the threshing machine also
Which has brought many to poverty

Injustice also in those far distant lands
Such as the slavery in the West Indies
Always of deep concern to Mr Harland Cottrell

How Parlement must be reformd
The town of Stroud representd in that place
In recognition the Stroudwater cloth
As made here famous throughout
The Christian world and even the pagans
As live in darkness beyond

Mr Harland Cottrell also inventing now
A man made leech

Oh God save us all from his schemes

Orderd also from Mr Johnson of London
A pedestrian curricle with two wheels
He do sit astride it up the lane
Yet it wears out the boots fast
We did never see much future in it

Meanwhile Master Ned lie out in the garden
Oft reading then of Lord Byron and Mr Burke

Also Mr Hobbes and that
Godless Frenchman Mr Rousseau

Complaining bitter all the time
How he is not sent to school
So it do seem a shame
When he is so clever

The afternoons full of a blessd stillness
The light moving from our Valley
Cross the town out the other side
Not far from where The Heavens is

Oft the sound of chipping and hammering
Occasionally a burst of singing comes
From those that work to fix up the cottages

Sometimes they come also round the pump
How go you they say You a funny looking girl
They say But a good lass aint you
A good worker A kind lass
Oh yes We know We heard say
Sometimes they give me a bun
One day a cane hoop to jump through

I never knew such happiness could be mine

Even now I thank God for it
For it meant that even in the twistd times
As does descend later
I always had those days to return to in my mind

Like jewels I keep hoard away in a precious box

*

Then comes the day when I understand more

It were autumn a coming then
The last of the mell brought in
We had walkd up to White Hill
To see that last cart all hung about
With flowrs and ribbons
Some playing the pipe or the fiddle
The men walking behind
Carrying sickles or scythes

Anyways tis at that time
It starts with the money
A sum which is left on the hall table

Mr Harland Cottrell place it there
For a man who deliverd
Hinges for the doors of the cottage
As is near finishd now

Oft tis like this
Money left where it ought not to be
For though they say he has no money
Mr Harland Cottrell also think nothing of money
Treat it no better than stones

So the money is there
Mr Harland Cottrell leave it
When he go out early

Master Blyth left behind in the school room
Mr Harland Cottrell tongue mauling him
As is always the way

Mr Harland Cottrell away to Randwick
For to organize outdoor relief

For those low types as lives there
Oft brawling and gambling
Cock fighting and whoring they

He might think a little more of the poor
Who are close to home

So say Mr Birch Nazareth and Nettie

Tis true what they say
Always in that house
Much talk of the trials of the common man
Yet the opinion of Nettie or me is never askd

Course the difficulty being the common man
Looks desirable when you behold he at a distance
Yet is less favourable to consider
When he is closy upon you
So say Mr Birch Nazareth and Nettie

So Master Blyth when he not out with his father
Always in the school room head bend down

Anyways I see that money there
When I go up the stairs
Must go out on the roof and clear a gutter
Tis apparently the cause of water
Come down the wall

This Mr Harland Cottrell say
Though Nettie scorn laugh and say
You may clear all you like the roof is shot

Anyways I have no choice in the matter
Know only that I must go up that scaffold
As it still all about the house

Waiting for repairs that are never done
Clear out leaves and muck

So I do Tis not done quick
While there look down from that lofty height
See Master Blyth go to the Cabinet
Walking uncertainly head down crooching
Always something womanly in his stride

I climb down then the stairs

The money is gone

This circumstance is strange
For the man would have come to the door
Rung the bell I would have heard
The bell in that house is clamorous

My mind is dutherd by this
Go through to the kitchen see Nettie there
So I say to her

Who came to the house

No one she say

I look at her about to speak
Yet something tells me hold my tongue

Instead I go back to the hall
Perhaps I am mistakd

I walk to the shelf
Outside Mr Harland Cottrells study
But sure as sure the money was there
Is not now

My fingers tremble I swallow many times
A pudding which jumps a thimble as walks
No one needs know about such as these

Yet this were a goodly sum of money

Just as I stand there staring
I hear footsteps behind me
Master Ned is there

He always can do that
Appearing sudden from nowhere
Like the magic sprites in bottles
In Netties halfpenny pamphlets

His eyes now also light on the empty shelf

Come come Mary Ann say he
You have not even skill in crime
Come back to the place where the evil is done
Just to see it again

Certain you have not even botherd to hide
The money be in yr pockets still
You are a fool a thieving fool

I feel the tears flush to my eyes
My throat closes as though a hand grips it tight

I cannot speak
Straightway turn out my pockets

Master Ned watches me
His eyes shrewd and mean
Head shake back and forwards sadly

So so Mary Ann Reading and writing are you now
Stealing as well so it seems
So clever have you become

Even when my pockets are empty
He shakes his head still

So so You hide the money

No No You know Sir
Please Sir I no a ways did

Who then

I do not want to be accuse
Yet neither want to think
On the question he asks
Stare at the floor tears falling fast

The voice of Master Ned change
Mary Ann Mary Ann
Weep not he say

He looks around him secretly
You come with me
Come now he say

He push me into the squob
Under the stair where is darkly
Many buckets spades saws
Up gainst the wall press my legs
Hang close my head

He is beside me tight

I am sorry Mary Ann he say V sorry

I should not accuse you as I did
But I am placd in a difficult position

I stop crying then and listen
His eyes forage mine in the dark

You been in this house long enough he say
You not a child
Tis better I explain
You see already
You know

Yet my father does not know
Neither does Nettie

So he goes on
I do not want they know
I am sure you can keep a secret

I nod my head
For all my fear I like to be closy by like this
I like to be told a secret
I yearn to know something
As Nettie does not know

In this house say Master Ned
We have a difficulty You already know it
There are people not to be relid upon

You probably know my brother Blyth
Tis hard to say

Course he may have some healing talents
More so than my father
I know some do say that
Steadier hands certainly

This I do not deny

Yet the truth is he have his own sickness
It comes upon him silent and sudden
Father would beat him soundly if he knew
Perhaps he would be sent away

He may be a difficult type
Sad to say he will always be unnatural
Yet he is my brother
I must protect him
Try to lead him always in better ways
He means no harm

That is why tis best for him to stay
In the school room studying
Or in my fathers Cabinet

You notice even my father keeps him close
That is how it must be
My father feels something
Though he does not know

You see Do you see Mary Ann
I need not say more

No Sir No I understand

Sure I feel I do
For I have heard that screaming in the night
Which I never understood afore

Good thank you Mary Ann he say
I think I can rely upon yr help
Now come quick we must go

So he push me out
I stand blinking in the hall

Go Go say Master Ned
So I go and busy myself
Say nothing to Nettie
Never know how the money is returnd or not
Though hear the door bell ring later

Watch Master Blyth careful after that

Oh yes thought I Now tis clear
That is how it must be

The idea comes also twas
Only but two days afore
We had seed the harvest moon
A vast ball of orange hanging
But a foot or two above the horizon
The surface of it pockmarkd and scarrd

Tis well knowd course
That those who contain an infection of madness
Do always their deeds worse than evr afore
By the light of the full moon

Master Ned is wise and has good reason
He loves his brother dearly
We must all make sure to keep this secret tight

*

So the year turns about again
That winter as cruel as the one afore
Gnawing sore in the belly of many

Til mellow days warming butter blessd long
St Marks Eve and the dumb cakes
As some do believe

Then the sheep sheard and harvest home
Back again to autumn

Then all change
For Master Ned is now to go down
To Mr Gronah the school master in Stroud
To prepare his examens
For when he is a lawyer
So that he may set about the many reforms
As are so badly need
In this our tarnishd world

Oh how pleasd he were for that
What preparations were made

All the time Master Blyth did watch
For he were long since come of age
Yet he did go nowhere and nothing
So it seemd no a ways would

Though he did still bring back books
Hid them well under his bed
They come from Mr William Burrows
At the dispensary in Stroud
This I did know well
Though he askd me not to tell

All these decisions Mr Harland Cottrell decide
Many years afore and never would be movd
Was this because he knew something regarding
The temperament of Master Blyth as we did also

Given the words of Master Ned on that money day
I took it to be so

Though it did seem to me unjust
Master Ned off in the mornings down the Valley
Soon oft does not come back
For he has much studying
He can do better if he stays
With a friend in the town

Master Blyth busy as cat in a tripe shop
Always working for his father
Tis only allowd to the town Sunday afternoons

Perhaps I should have felt sympathy more
For he always eclipsd by Master Ned
Had not the power to speak much for hisself
Did not invite much sympathy

All this I think on only slightly
For I myself am much occupid
Study also all the days endways

Come then All Hallows Eve
When the dead do leave the grave yards
Walk among us

The winter rolls in day on day
The frost sharper rise each morning
Ice gather on paths and puddles

I am frustratd with my work
For though I can read
Tis still the childers primers
I do work on
Must figure the letters slow

Mr Harland Cottrell see my anger
Say to me Nay nay Mary Ann
You may be a challenge to the eye
Yet you are subtle in mind
Be not discouragd

All must keep on til they fully letterd
For who can live to the Glory of God
If they cannot read the Bible theysselfs
So he say and tis right
Yet my eyes close tird head nod

Still I keep on
Move from the childers school book
To copy from the Bible
Gradual the knots of the letter unfold

Then come the time just afore Christmas
I remember it well

As was oft the case I was clearing away
Certain books after all else is left
So I come to pick up
The story of How Paradise Was Lost
By Mr John Milton

I have seed it afore
Yet the words all cling together
Lock me out in misunderstanding

Now I pick it up and read

Of mans first disobedience and the fruit
Of that forbidden tree who mortal taste
Brought death into the world

Sudden it all clear as drops of dancing water
The words flow away from me
I know them all
My eyes fly down the lines
Inside I am leaping

For I can read
I can read proper without stopping
Can hear the rhythm inside me
Know what the next word is
Even afore I come to it

Ask and it shall be given
Seek and ye shall find
Knock and it shall be opend unto you

Strange the joy of it must shine
On my skin for when Mr Harland Cottrell
Come in say Come Mary Ann
Tis v late
Clear up

Then stops for he sees and comes ovr

What do you read he says

I look up at him then
Oh how I would like to
Fling my arms round he

I can read I say
Read anything any book all in this room
I can read them all now

Tis the world of the Angels I say
For I am stupid with excitement

Mr Harland Cottrell say
Oh yes my girl so tis

When he say this he sudden laughs
This I seldom seed afore
For though he has a merry enough temper
Usual something grim in his visage

Now he lays a hand on my shoulder
Which pleases me girtly
For I have noticd many a time of late
How tird and worn he is
His teeth bothering he much
His hearing failing also

Worn down in spirit more so
For though he work so hard
Tis his path in life to be evr misunderstood

So many new worlds I say
Tears is falling down my cheeks

Seeing as I am ovrcome he sit me down
In a chair by the fire
Where are yet some embers burning

Yes he say So many worlds
Then he nods his head

After that we have nothing else to say
So sit together in silence
Hear the ticking of the clock
The settling of the coals

So then it comes to me to ask
What I have long wantd to know

Sir please may I ask about a certain book
That I have seed

Yes yes he say I go to get that book

Tis a book I have lookd at oft
For it reminds me of The Heavens
That pile of yellerd paper under the boards
Some letter printed big and some small
A black line cross the bottom

I take it in my hands cautiously
Do not look at the words
For I am afeard

Hold it out Mr Harland Cottrell

Oh yes oh yes say he
The Rights Of Man by Mr Thomas Paine
Perhaps not the right book for you Mary Ann

No Sir I say
Tis just I have seed it afore Sir

Oh yes he say his head on one side

Perhaps you heard of it in connection
With our lost friend Mr Abel Woebegone

Yes Sir I say
He had a copy Sir
But twas hid

Oh aye say Mr Harland Cottrell
Well might he hide it poor man
For it were on account of that book

He was imprisond
Do you not know that

I was told Sir I say
Yet I did not like to believe it

So so say Mr Harland Cottrell
He was the son of a printer in Nailsworth
A family of dissenters and radicals
But all honest and good men

Many were sent for hard labour
In Northleach gaol for the printing
Some as long as two year
He being young it were but six month
Though that were far too long

So so it were a bad business
For there was a young woman he had
Was with child

Many such as I did speak up for he
For what crime had he committed

I do not believe that any book
Should be kept from any man
Only we educate all well
Then they shall have the wisdom
To judge for theysselfs

But others do not see it that way
So he were lockd up

When he came out
That shrew did want he
For a husband

With all her Wesleyan cant
So he were pushd upon her
In the belief she would keep him right

Many say of course he drank
Which is certainly true
Yet he never did til he was imprisond

So say Mr Harland Cottrell
Something inside me settles
For now I light upon something
I no a ways did afore

I always knew Mr Woebegone a good man
Now I am sure tis true

That a question long troubld me

Not so Mr Harland Cottrell
Whose eyes now are full of tears
As mine were just afore

Yet still I ask
What of the book Sir

Here Mr Harland Cottrell shake his head
Many of the ideas in it are interesting
We must be prepard to discuss consider all
Yet finally tis a dangerous book
Not the ideas so much the language

Now you can read yrself Mary Ann
I think you see how
One word can be laid out after next
All appears to do no harm
Yet you take it all together

The effect is more powerful than strong liquor
Which will lead to no good

Again he shakes his head and says
Come come Mary Ann
Enough questions

So he is away up to bed
I stay to put away the last books

On the side are some of the young Masters
For they been studying there as well
Master Ned home that evening
Though oft not

Usually I do not touch their books
Being frightend to disturb something
Yet now I must move them to put
Some other back

So tis I take up a book
Which is writ upon the name Master Ned

Another writ Master Blyth
Yet strange tis
You cannot tell the two apart
For the writing is so similar

Which I had not knowd afore

MOUNT VERNON

Memory is not this date that date
Tis what touch the heart
A story you tell again and again
Til finally it comes true

Yet I must not go on too fast
Must write down only what I saw and knew
At that time

Otherwise it may not be said clear
How things fell out

So do I think writing now late
Into the owl calling night
Which presses cloudy black
At these fine tracery winders

Til then my Master is call again
Harsh and angry frightend maybe

I stand so stiff I can hardly unbend
Slow I make my way the steep stairs

Holding the rail pull myself up

The stairs my bones unlocking as I go

Ah ah he says Mary Ann I have need of you

I must change the bandages again
So I back to the kitchen to mix and stir
Calomel two scruples tar ointment one ounce

A mixture of oil of almonds and caraways
Droppd in the ear may also comfort he

I set straight the bolster to prop him up
His face long and fine bond
In the flashing of the candle lit
That same face his father
Mr Harland Cottrell had
His brother also

I bathe and wash
He lies quiet some time
Now starts up again

So how is yr writing Mary Ann
You work long into the night

Yes Sir I say and pull a bandage tight

He say Perhaps since sleep is not upon us
I shall dictate some parts of the book again

Such as my family and the contribution
As was made to the struggle for the Reform Bill
Also gainst the most injust system at that time
For the distribution of Poor Relief
You remember all this well no doubt

Oh Sir say I
But tis gone past midnight now

His eyes move ovr me then
Measure every surface
Weigh my power gainst his
Shut his eyes sudden

He is subtle careful proud
He does not need to shout or scream insist
His power is gentle cunning
Slip silken snake around you

Or perhaps you would prefer he say
To read me some part of what you write

His eyes hunt mine I do not look away
I tell him No no Sir
What I write is not ready
I still have many things to consider
How exactly is best to lay things out

Ready he say ready
No need for you to consider such

I say naught watch him close

He thinks now to jest with me
Shaking his head his white hand wave

So I see Mary Ann
You are become quite a writer then

His mockery does raise my ire
My hands still work steady
Pull hard on the bandages

Tis necessary they be stretchd tight

That not possible Sir
I am sorry

So so he say
Perhaps you then at least tell me
What tis you write

Tis only now Sir say I
That I come to the part of the story
Does take place at Stocton Hill

He sinks back then upon his pillows
I feel anger and fear rise from he

Turning his head he looks again at me
Mary Ann was it not some chance
That you and I should meet again
That you should come and work for me
Was that not a fine thing
To happen to someone such as yrself
Placd in a troublesome circumstance

Oh yes Sir I say Course Sir
I am truly grateful for the work
You do give me

This I say quite easy
He may have now my gratitude
If so he want it

For tis not gratitude we trade here but power

Why is he not afeard of me
Any day I could go down into Stroud

Tell all and anyone I fancy
Or write it in a letter
If so I want

Gratitude gratitude
No it were luck
His as much as mine
That we did meet that day
I come back to he

My mind travels now ovr the memory of it
It were but three months ago

Come on the cart Gloucester to Painswick
Walk then the long wearying way down

Been in Gloucester more than forty years
Yet want at the end

To behold at last the massing hills
Of my once and always home

Amidst those same streets
Where I had walkd so many years afore
Though all so changd I hardly know

Stood there outside the arch of the Shambles
Where tis knowd you do stand
If you want to find work

No one wants me why should they
A broken down old crone
No work left in her

So I am there til evening threaten
When all else is gone

Someone throws a rotten turnip
Boys poke with sticks

Then there he was
Walking toward me
Just as though only a day has passd
Come back that same evening
Back along the shoulder of the Valley
With his brothers hat and cane

Oh yes the years and illness
May have left he slower fatter
Sliding at the edges
Walking now with a rolling limp
Yet he was still the same

Raise his hat
Just as he did that last day

Say Ah there you are again
Mary Ann Sate
Do you know me

I say straight
Course Sir how could I forget
I know you well

Yes yes he say Mr Blyth Cottrell

I nod my head
Look him long in the eye
He also try to hold my gaze
But cannot do it

All I can say is
I were hungry tird thirsty beat

In truth it were comfort to see his face
Bringing with it the hope
That he might at least give me a few pennies
Enough for some food
Perhaps a roof for the night

Tis true he did not fail me then
Startd to talk straight how he have need of me
Bought a house up the other Valley side
Pointing to where this house lie
Up on the ridge in the knot of trees

Offer me then ten shillings a week
More money than half the folk at that fair
Been offerd

So I then think he not only pay me for my work
Yet also for my silence
For though he gone forty years more
Few can recall the details of a face
Yet still he wantd no bad word spread

Course I was willing enough
For what choice have I
At least I think to myself
Now when he uses me he pays for it
Never did afore

Though I would write down here
So tis knowd
I seed none of the money yet

Then it were just as we stand there
That a gentleman did approach
A browsy young man in brushd cape
Raising then his hat

So he does introduce hisself
As the son of Mr Paul Hawkins Fisher
Says how his own father did oft tell
Of Mr Harland Cottrell

Welcome back to these Valleys Sir
All of that he say

Yet all I notice is how sprightly my Master
Does hurry hisself away

Tis fortune for him his arm
It has been sawd off
Perhaps if it were not for that
He never would come back

I have finishd now the bandaging
Try to shift his leg
His head rises up again
His mouth is clamp shut tries not to cry out
Yet the pain is ovr brimming

He does not look at me yet speaks again
Ah well so we will work again tomorrow
Since you write of Stocton Hill
That I can dictate to you

Thank you Sir I say
You are tird and there is no need
Can be sure I write well
Tell all the richness of that time
Such as to represent with truth
All who did inhabit that place
Those long departd days

Aye aye he say and looks me deep

Soon I shall go down to Stroud myself
In but a day when I am stronger

That he does say and bid me then good night

So I stagger my way up to bed
Foot after foot no light except
What the obscurd stars bring at the lacd winders

My mind still running fast
Ovr and ovr on this one question

Why did I not speak
On that day at the Shambles

Good and evil they are always at war
Their battleground the human heart

STOCTON HILL

When does the moment come
The time when you find yrself growd
In years if not in stature

Sudden you see the grander world
You question all about

I do not know For me it come late I think
For a long time still Stocton Hill were my all

The town far distant low down
Lost in the curve of the Valley
Carts pass on the new turnpike road below
Going to Painswick even to Gloucester

Also Sundays to the new chapel at Ruscombe
Or even now to Pakenhill so namd after
The pagan savages as come up the River Severn
In times long past
So Mr Harland Cottrell do tell

We do hear talk of the death of the King
May God Bless and keep him now in perfect peace

Also how the Rotten Boroughs must be finishd
The new towns such as Birmingham and Manchester
To be givd the vote
Even Stroudwater also
None of it meant naught to me

The winter come and gone
The days dut and shet
Another whole year fled past
High zummer return begin again to wane
All blossomd fine under the maturing sun

So it happen about that time
I am gone in Stroud in the cart
With Mr Birch Nazareth for he must visit
Mr Henry Howell the brazier on the High Street
To enquire the mending of some harness buckle

It being a Friday the town is busy
The pig pens up and the corn being sold
Women offering eggs milk butter
Meat in the Shambles

I am to watch the cart
For much pilching there has been
In those recent time

While we are there many is gatherd about
To see the workings of a new machine
Has been made by the Shearmen

This machine is like you use to shear cloth
Yet this one can be usd for grass

Such foolery say Mr Birch Nazareth
Who have need of such a thing

So many these Valleys inventing this and that
All for to solve difficulties
As do not exist

So we go on but soon does meet
One of the ploughmen from Hammonds Farm
Lies just cross the Valley from us

His face is set serious for soon he tell
The Master there has receivd a letter
Do come that now famous Captain Swing

Soon as hears that name Mr Birch Nazareth say
Come come Mary Ann we tarry not one moment more
We must for home with haste

This I know for all about much talk
Of this Captain Swing
The letters do come from he
Threatening Destruction and Devilry

Now Mr Birch Nazareth does say
Shaking his head sore in sorrow
So now it does come to Stroudwater
It were always sure to be

Tis said that at West End Culkerton
Also Cranmore Farm and Bagpath
Rodmarton and Crudwell
Barley ricks and barns
Have been put to the fire

Tis particular the threshing machines
Which do get batterd into sticks
For they have takd the winter work
From many a labourer

Now at Stocton Hill we have not any such machine
Yet still Mr Birch Nazareth say we must stand ready
Secure all the buildings and the barns
Send reliable men also cross to Hammonds
To see what may be need there
Pray my dear Lord He hold us closy by

So we hurries home the cart rocking and swaying
Cross many ruttd ways Mr Birch Nazareth
Switch the whip to drive the horse on
Saying Aw whoop aw whoop

Get back to Stocton Hill
Mr Birch Nazareth does give many orders
All about as to how matters must be organizd
Then goes to get his horse
Ready to set out to Hammonds

Tis only then we realize the horse is gone
I go in to ask Nettie

She says Oh yes course tis Master Ned
Did take the horse
For he has gone to visit some friends
Who is out at Tetbury

Mr Birch Nazareth and me
We know not what to say
Master Ned should not a takd the horse
Without at least speaking first

Has he also no care of the danger
In which he may place hisself
For tis out toward Tetbury
Where the mobs is knowd to gather

Yet for all that there is little we can do
Only we can wait and pray
That he may come home safe

Wait also for news of further violence
Which does certainly come

For many groups of brawling ignorant types
Were now striding drunken and singing
Armd with sticks pick axes stone hammers
Bludgeons scythes and shovels
From one village tother
Finding out where were the threshing machines

Magistrates oft do go out to meet them
Talk reason and bring calm
Also special constables now sworn in

The landowners gathering together
Tenants and servants who was known to be loyal
Ready to drive back the mobs

For sure they will be hung or transportd
To Van Diemens Land
Tis the home of the Demons
They may wish then they had swung

The weather also at that time hot and close
For though it were September come
No sun but heat as stick yr cloth to yr back
Face stream sweat

The air all about dusty and dense
Green of the Valleys all wilt and grey

Which to add a young man is brought

To the Cabinet of Mr Harland Cottrell
An Irish papist he up from the Cut

Possessd by the Devil so they say
His eyes staring his tongue lolling
We did see him in the yard arms striving

Saying how he has seed the Beast
A white horse ridden by Death hisself
Earthquake and the moon become blood
The sun turn black as sack cloth of hair
The stars of the heavens falling to earth

So he does go on twisting and writhing
Though they hold him down
Telling how many a good Minister
Has faild to drive this chattering Devil out

What happens in the Cabinet I know not
Mr Harland Cottrell Master Blyth
Both go in to minster to he

I suspect there is mesmerism practisd
Certainly the young man is soon much quieted

After Mr Harland Cottrell shakes his head
Say Maybe tis the voice of God hisself
Who speaks through this young man
Though he be a boy and a papist too
To warn that the time appointd
Will soon be upon us

I am much afeard to hear this
For how will such as me be judgd

Though only a day later news does come

Which no one dare tell to Mr Harland Cottrell
That now the young man has seed
Mary Magdalene herself all glittering white
Washing her stocking ovr the side
Of one of the canal boats

I did always think our dear Lord surely choose
His messenger more prudently

*

All the time also we are waiting for news
Of Master Ned but three days pass now
None does come

This you might suppose would be
Of much concern to Mr Harland Cottrell

But no no Tis not so
For Mr Harland Cottrell has a mind
For one thing only
Which is these acursd West Indian slaves

Does work now day and night
Always down in meetings in Birts Rooms
At the White Hart the top of High Street

With those other ardent enthusiasts
Such as the banker Mr Henry Wyatt
The lawyer Mr Paul Hawkins Fisher
Mr Benjamin Parsons Minister of Ebley

Mr Harland Cottrell making a girt petition
From the establishd churches
And other of Randwick

Though oft times sorely disappointd
For so many others as he do say
Seem not to understand the importance
Of this weighty question of Justice and Liberty

I should think they do not
When their ricks is at risk of burning
His own son but sixteen year of age
We know not where he is

Yet this were the nature of Mr Harland Cottrell
He was evr possessd by a fatal goodness
Can never hear a warning
Though it be shoutd from a mountain top

Master Blyth also seems not to understand
The events are a coming to pass
He work long in the Cabinet

His main fear seem to be that
Since the Cabinet is but a barn
The mob might burn it in error

Nettie and I shake our heads privily

Forgive us we do not see
The importance of protecting
Piglets adders and all those already dead
Floating comfortable in glass bottles
So all goes on waiting waiting

Then we were in the kitchen one eve
The scatterd sun dropping low
Yet the heat not abatd

When Mr Harland Cottrell does come in

To shew us a picture he has been sent
That does give a clear view so he say
Of the many evils of slavery
The brutal suffering it causes

Calls in also Mr Birch Nazareth to see

So we all looks at the picture
Nods our heads and agree tis a scandal
No person of Christian sentiment
Can accept such a thing

Though in truth we do not understand the picture
If those dark figures are the slaves
Then why are they all lying down
Is this a cause they are sick

We do not know and do not like to ask
But when Mr Harland Cottrell has gone
Nettie say she cannot understand the question

For why they not give them a good scrubbing
Surely much would be curd with soap and water

No no no say Mr Birch Nazareth
Nettie for the Lords sake be not so ignorant
He is about to explain
Which I should much like to hear

Then sudden we is all interrupt
By the sound of horses hooves in the yard
Nettie jump for the carving knife
Mr Birch Nazareths eyes are alight with fear
Tis Captain Swing we think

But surely it cannot be for boots sound now

Round at the front door
We hear Mr Harland Cottrell go to answer

Quick Mary Ann say Nettie
You go and listen what is said

That is how she is
She has no regard for me never has
Yet she is quick enough to use me
In any oil slick purpose

Though on this occasion it must be said
I am spice enough to go
For all want to know

So stand I near the school room door
With ears prickd sharp

Tis constables at the door and they is asking
Where is Master Ned

Mr Harland Cottrell asks Why you seek him

The constable says He has been seed
Near Charlton House out at Beverstone
Where much violent and threatening behaviour
Has takd place just that same afternoon

Mr Harland Cottrell say straightway
This clearly a case of mistakd identity
Such stain never to be put upon his sons name

The constable then ask his question again
As to where is Master Ned
Mr Harland Cottrell then reply
Master Ned is with a friend in Stroud

That then were the end of it
So I go back to the kitchen to report

All of us perhaps is wondering
Did Mr Harland Cottrell lie when he said Stroud

I know it cannot be so for he would not lie
Tis only his attention is so far removd
From here and now he has made an error

Had no idea the mistake might be important

For Beverstone is a village just near Tetbury
So I tell you

Yet even though we all know that
I do not think any of us thought anything
But an innocent confusion had been makd

❋

So another day turn come Saturday
When one of the farm men
Does say as Master Ned seed in Stroud

Tis a worry then to all
For widely knowd hand bills
Pastd all about and come Sunday
Many have plottd to gather in Stroud
Forces also are massing
To drive them back if need arise

No one of good character
Best go near the town that day

Mr Birch Nazareth shakes his head and say

Someone should go and fetch he back
But I notice that Mr Birch Nazareth
He does not offer hisself
Being I think angry about his horse
Course still is not returnd

Then comes Mr Harland Cottrell now wakd
Rather late to the danger
Says that Master Blyth should go
Be sure to bring his brother back

Master Blyth I must say does make no question
He has always lovd his brother dear

So that day he went off
All of us itching with worry
Yet still we continue in prayer
Watch in the same with thanksgiving

Five of the clock come Master Blyth return
Master Ned not with he

Master Blyths eyes are all rimmd red
Black smears cross his face
Tells us stuttering and stammering
How he did find his brother
Plead with him many a time
But no no he would not come back
Though the dragoons is sweeping
Through the town with long swords
Does make yr blood stop to hear it

This he cannot tell his father
For Mr Harland Cottrell has gone out

So the eve pass

All the time I am listening
For a footstep or a voice
None do come

Come eight of the clock I worry worse
Do get out sheets heat the smoothing iron

Nettie say she do not care any
The Devil can take them all
Tis none to her

Yet still she comes to help me
As she does not generally do

Holding the sheets
As I work the iron
She say to me
I always say no good come of Master Ned

I push the iron gainst her fingers so it burn
Say you do not speak any ill
Gainst Master Ned
Who is oft kind to you

After that she say nothing
Yet still she smirk
Goes not up to her bed
As usually would

Come ten of the clock and still no Master Ned
I work at a book on the kitchen table
Then come the sound of hooves in the lane
That the horse of Mr Harland Cottrell

Oh oh now the trouble will start

When Mr Harland Cottrell ask
I know not what to say

So then is shouting for Master Blyth
I shake my head get up from my book

Soon the house rattling with angry voices
Mr Harland Cottrell speak straight to Master Blyth

You have allowd he to consort with ruffians
Those who would engage in insurrection
Left him there in the town
What brotherly love have you
How can I trust you more

Master Blyth croochd gainst the wall
I I I sorry Sir he say
Twas w w wrong of me
I should not have done

So goes on
I hear it all but then step out
Into the night time cricket chirp garden

So tis I see him first
Master Ned a coming up the hill
Through the field calld
The Shoulder of Mutton
Then the home orchard

I sought the Lord and He heard me
Deliverd me from all my fears

So I say to myself yet then remark
How tird is Master Ned so exhaustd
He can barely walk a straight line

Totterdy and dawdles through the trees

What has become of he

Come in the back door through the school room
Heading toward the stairs
I hear him puffing and stumbling
He must be took sick

Then hear Mr Harland Cottrell Master Blyth
For they have seed he both

Then Master Blyths voice
Never fear Father
Tis but fever
There is much in the town
Comes fierce but blows out quick

Do not t t trouble yrself at all
C C call Mary Ann for me
I shall t t tend him she will help

I am already hurrying into the hall

What come at me there
I know it immediately
My mind tumbles backwards
I am in the kitchen at The Heavens

Tis the smell of beer or cider
Grows and spreads all about us

I wait then for the storm
Mr Harland Cottrell now will beat the skin
From Master Ned

He must do so
For there is no other proper way
To treat a stumbling drunkard
But to beat it out of he

I may not have card much for Mrs Woebegone
Yet she at least did knowd that

Mr Harland Cottrell must well know it too
For he had writ many pamphlets
On the evils from fortify drink

But no storm come
Master Blyth takes hold his brothers arm
I take hold the other
We pull him up the stairs

A difficult job this is indeed
For he is swaying and tosticatd
Starts to sing then a vulgar song
Til Master Blyth does clap a hand
Gainst his giggling mouth

Still waiting and waiting
Yet Mr Harland Cottrell only say
A draught of chamomile may be best
Mixd with sal volatile tincture of lavendar
Til the morning
We see what happens then

Yet Master Blyth he say
You see him settld
Then you come back down to me

His voice is grating
His eyes gone small and stone sharp

Some wrinkle in the cloth of time
Does then come for I know what will happen
I hear all

I am there in the bedroom
Pull off Master Neds boots
Get his britches down pull tug
Wipe his face with water

He waving his arms and laughing
Starting again to sing
Til I do shut he up

Down below I hear
The swish of the cane
The shouting

Tis the first time
I evr hear that in this house
For I always believe
So it oft said
That Mr Harland Cottrell
Does not believe in beating

Now it seems he has changd his view

I find a night shirt in the press
Put Master Neds boots straight gainst the wall
Pull the covers down
Then up again ovr he

No no no I say to he Keep quiet
Yet he does start to sing again
Take my hand staring into my eyes
Say Mary Ann Mary Ann will you marry me

I ought not to have laughd
Yet I could not help myself
Wheezing and giggling
Tears run down my cheeks

So twas I did not properly think
Not til all was quiet
Myself also abed

Only then my mind turns round about
But all is tangld there
No answers come

Ask myself why why

Why is the truth not spokd

My mortal soul struggle and fight
Wanting to be able to say

I was evr a fool for the truth

*

When milk begin to sour it go all at once
In the space of minutes it turn bad

Yet in our lives troubles not come so obvious
Only one thing builds on another
Gradually the shadows gather

Yet still there are moments days
When all begins to slip and tumble
You understand how unstable the ground
On which you stand

I wish it were not so
I long to live always
In the God touchd days at Stocton Hill
Yet we must all grow
Meet the world as it really be

One such day come back to me now
I know it well

Many times I have gone ovr it
Was there something I did not see
Or something I chose to lay aside

Even now so much is unclear
I try to write now only what I see then

When you look back yr gaze is warpd
You know more You see the story end
All seems to lead to that

Yet really it were only an accident
As happen in many places

It were that same year but later
Perhaps the middle of November
For the Guy had certainly be burnd up

A procession passing along the Valley
With lanterns burning tar barrels firecrackers
Much offence being causd for some do say
Tis not the papist Guido Fawkes we light
But that Duke of Wellington
Who is set firm gainst reform
That was the talk

Soon after that the rain had start

Then did not stop
Many a ditch and highway flood
Water rising in diverse house

So twas that day the skye pewter
The rain fall in waves
Would soak to the bone after but five steps
Falling and falling and falling
Sure it would never stop

The distant hills all shroude deep
Everything shine silver

Master Ned fritchety and bord
His father said he not go to his studies
Must stay home help Mr Birch Nazareth
Prepare some boards less the water
Does come in the house

Then that day a messenger
Come to the house with a letter
Poor soul his head coverd in a cloak
Dripping water at the door

I am askd to take it to Mr Harland Cottrell
In his study bent ovr a book as he oft is

At that time not so much engagd
In they slaves in the West Indies
Instead returning to his pamphlets
About the importance of the education
Of the working man and woman too

Quacks like a pelican in the wilderness
Yet is no a ways discouragd
For this you must admire he

Now he take the letter from me and read it
Run a hand across his head Oh oh he say
Then he tell me Mary Ann
Go and find Master Blyth
I have need of he

So I go and find he
In the school room as he always is

Then back to the kitchen
Where I am blacking boots

The next thing is Master Blyth
He come to the kitchen door
Has a look on his face
Such as I have seldom seed afore
Like a flowr long closd come into bloom

M M Mary Ann he say
C C can you help me prepare
I am to travel to Oxford early tomorrow

Now this had me boffld for I knew that
Mr Harland Cottrell due to Oxford tomorrow
As he sometimes did
To listen to learnd societies there
So why now Master Blyth

Father cannot go he tell me
Has been an outbreak of smallpox
Near to Minchinhampton
Has said he will go
To do the vaccinations
So I am to go to Oxford instead

I feel then some of the excitement he feel

For such as this has never happend afore
Usually he is trustd with nothing

Straightway I am heading for the stairs
To see what must be made ready

Just as I go I meet Master Ned
I smile at him expecting that he might
Share in this small excitement

But no no
Instead on his face an angry frown
His brow knittd
Lips pulld together
He looks as though he would like to spit

As he passes me he says something about the rain
Water pooling on the top landing
I remind myself I must go up there soon
Empty out the buckets

I think nothing more of it
Hurry on past him
Already I am worrying
Has Master Blyth sufficient clean clothes
Too late to wash
No dryth now

So I set to organize the things he may need
Put all in a cloth bag be easy to carry
Lay out linen find boots
Will need clean

I think perhaps I hear a noise above
Yet probably I do not
I cannot have done so really

Not with the rain a coming down

Then I hear a voice calling
Tis Master Blyth shouting up through the house

I go down again see the back door open
The rain pounding the quaggy earth
Go out through the back door

The weather is worse than we know
The rain sting and the wind buffet
Water running like a river down all the lane

Master Blyth is standing there already
Dark with rain his face pale eyes hollowd
My brother he says He went up on the roof
Trying to put a tile back

N N now he is stuck up there

I thought that strange
Both the young Masters spent many hours
Vanning about the roof when they were but boys
It had oft worrid me

Yet now course for some years
They had not been up there
Being long past the age for such pranks

I shall go up help him say Master Blyth
W W would you hold the ladder Mary Ann

It were simple enough to do
Moving in closer to the wall I come out of the
Wind and rain just a jot

So he start up the ladder and I held on
Soon he disappear ovr the ledge of the roof
Up into the grey skye above
Climbing in betwixt the chimbleys
I left there rain gathering in my hair
Shivering as shoulders of my chemise soak
My clogs filling with muddy water

I look down at the Valley as I stood
Could only see one slice of it
But the rain gather thick
The light gleam grey
The hills are lost
Only the dark line of their shape

Then I hear movement above
Master Blyth call down
Are you ready Mary Ann

I fix my hands on the ladder
They been up and down that ladder many times
But still I hold on
Master Ned come down first
His boots step rung after rung
His jacket caught wild in the wind

When he come down I step back
Thank you he say
Now you go on inside Mary Ann
Tis not fit for anyone out here

So I look up briefly
See the jaggd edge of the roof
Master Blyth foot come ovr
His leg stretchd out
To catch the rung of the ladder

I turn away take one step toward the house
Shivering still wipe the rain from my hair
All in a second it were done

I look back
The ladder then sways out from the wall
Moving slow and wavering
The pattern of it clear gainst the raining skye
As it start to fall

Then he is falling as well a coming down hard
His jacket spread arms stretchd out
A black crow flapping
Held for a moment gainst the leaden skye

He turn sudden toss
His head come down on the scaffold
The rest follow hit hard
Fall down duff

Immediately he is screaming
A terrible high pitchd yell
Ah ah ah He lie on the scaffold twistd

Already blood dripping
Dribbling ovr the edge of the boarding

Master Ned stood quite still staring
As though he were frozen
The look on his face smitten
Full of a strange wonder

My legs movd without me thinking
Ran straight through the kitchen into the hall
Mud and rain dripping

Mr Cottrell Mr Cottrell Come quick Come quick
Master Blyth is hurt Come come

Mr Harland Cottrell appear in the hall
Moving slow still holding his eye glasses
Swinging in his hand

Then he see me and he understand
Hurries with me through the kitchen
Splashes out to where the ladder stand

Master Ned is still standing there
The look on his face as though he has seed
Something strange and beautiful

Then he seed his father and start to howl

Though Mr Harland Cottrell
Is far from a young man
He is lither still and quick
Up he hurries kneels down beside his son

Mary Ann he call down
Go quick and find me Nazareth
I have need of a hurdle

I hurry up the lane boots gritting and splashing
Bang on the door Mr Birch Nazareth soon appear

A flakett I tell him Please be quick
He knows straightway what I say
I follow him to the byre help him pull one out
From where they stack gainst the wall

My hands are numb now
Sobs heave in my chest

When we come with the flakett
Master Blyth is liftd to the ground
Not shouting but his breath harsh
Whimper like an injurd animal
The blood is a coming from his chest
From one of his hands
The tord flesh hanging limp

Master Ned and Mr Birch Nazareth
Do hold the wavering flakett high
Mr Harland Cottrell edge Master Blyth on

The scaffold planks swash with blood
Master Blyth limp and duff
A hole cut in high above his heart
Where the spike of the scaffold pierce

There I stand rain pouring down my neck
Blood running tears flowing
Then I must turn away for
Nettie does shout at me from the back door
To help her pull back the bolt to open
The second door as is never usually usd
So then can carry him in
Take him straight to the Masters study

Light a fire Mary Ann I am told
I set about it concentrate only on that
I not listen to the screaming See the blood
Mr Harland Cottrell soakd to his elbows
All bloom down the front his shirt

Mr Birch Nazareth do say
Mr Harland He is sore hurt
I think you must send for a doctor from Stroud

This Mr Birch Nazareth say not as he has formerly done
Not out of any desire to provoke
But in genuine care for Master Blyth

Still Mr Harland Cottrell stare at him sour
You think I cannot tend my own son

I think of all I heard said about
The shaking of his hands
Surely Mr Birch Nazareth is right
Yet even now he will not be listend to

Mary Ann Mary Ann Netties voice angry
That no way to lay a fire
What you thinking of

She snatch the kindling from me

But Mr Birch Nazareth lay a hand on my arm
You go and find dry clothes he say
Come come You can do no more here
So I went to dry myself

All that long eve Mr Harland Cottrell work
The house full of screams and groaning
I eat no supper sit at the table crying

Nettie and Mr Birch Nazareth come and go also
With precious few words to say

No one will make any joke now
About how many killd today

Stop yr snittering Mary Ann say Nettie
Yet her voice is less harsh than usual
Not all the redness of her face

Is the rash always afflict her

She has always care for Master Blyth
As others do not

So it roll on and we are told to go up
But I stay on

Finally it come out that
Master Blyth will not die
Tis a wound can perhaps heal
Tis hopd also God willing
He be left with all his senses

Yet there is a deep hole in his chest
Which may yet take infection
His hand also is much brokd
The thumb near pulld off
All the soft flesh beside it splayd apart

This I seed how twas
When I was calld upstairs to take away
Some sheets all soakd dark in blood

Saw his face then turnd gainst the sheet
The colour clay His teeth clenchd tight
The shutterd room candle flicker low
Full of the metal smell of blood

What I seed then in that face
I had never seed it afore
Twas a poisond rage
Gainst his brother

I goes back down then still weeping
Nettie soon slap my head and say

He is lucky May God be praisd
Stop yr wailing girl
Tis a blessing
The stake might have gone right through
Killd he dead as a nit

I do know we have much to be grateful for
Thank the Lord that Master Blyth will live

But still I cry
Not so much for his hand
But for a deeper confusion and pain

For some days after I am vexd and sad

It all unroll as I know twill
I been in this house long enough

Master Blyth say straight twas all his fault
As he put his foot ovr his balance went
That was how he kickd the ladder away

Aye aye Mr Harland Cottrell say
This is the problem is it not
You were evr careless in such matters

Yet I see what no one else see

So many times I try not to think
I try so hard not to know
The rain so solid surely I was mistakd

But no no

*

All this I should have fishd in my mind
More deep to know it further

Yet at that time come into my life
Such shining Happiness and Grace
It did push out all else

So I tell it were but a week or so later
The feast of Advent just gone

The work on the cottages behind did finish
This having takd much longer than it should
Due to the want of money

Yet now they look splendid and fresh
The stone almost white even in the winter sun
Winder frames gleam
Front door rubbd smooth

Mr Harland Cottrell it were said
Had these cottages built to improve his income
Were Mr Birch Nazareth who said he must
Otherwise the bailiffs be at the gate

Aye aye Mr Birch Nazareth say to Mr Harland Cottrell
You can live on fresh air
Or maybe vegetables in water
But if Master Ned is to be a lawyer
This must surely cost many a penny

Anyway soon the cottages were put to let
So we heard one day new people were to come
Sure enough a family arrive
He an engineer from the mill

Then we heard another was to come

One day carts in the lane and shouting
I no a ways saw any of it

Nettie was took sick with a lax
Mr Birch Nazareth busy with the cow leech

It were washing day so I had all to do
Just myself It were scalding work
The steam gathering all around
My face sweat My arms ache

Were not til gone six of the clock eve
I finally stop to rest
One of the farm hands out the back
The one as gave me a hoop
Call me a good lass
So him I ask The new people are come then

Yes he say They all set up now

So what people are they I say

He say Mill people A young chap
His wife a small childer
Then two more as lodge with them
So is said

That morning I had bakd bread
Decide to take a loaf
Mr Harland Cottrell would like me to

So I walk the few paces up the darkend lane
The front door of the cottage open
I step up The bread wrap in a cloth

I stand on the door step feel duberous

Have always been afeard of them I do not know
Even though my mouth were better
I still feel the shame of it
Know my appearance not such to encourage folk

I can hear the sounds of a child playing
Yet still no one come
I peer into neat hall
Bags baskets boxes piled
Further back a doorway must be the kitchen

In this doorway a child appear
Maybe but three years old
Sturdy and strong with shiny brown hair
Eyes peering wide in the darkness
Wave a wooden rattle at me
Good evening fine lady a lady to you
My name is Conker
Then stands on one leg
Near falls laughs is gone

I stand watching the space where he stood
Still hear the clatter of the rattle
Smile to myself
For Conker does indeed seem
A goodly name for a brown shining lad
Such as he

I wait a while again bang firmly on the door
Immediately a figure appear that hidden door
It were hard to see
The light were dark outside
Yet bright within
So that my eyes glare

The figure moves then I think Oh oh

For even in the movement I saw

Then quick and merry lightness spreading
Ambrose step out on the door step

Why why he say Tis Mary Ann Sate

I so ovrcome I start cry near drop the bread
Yet he moves swift and neat to catch it

Nay nay he say Do not cry

Oh Ambrose I say
I never thought to see you again

But Mary Ann he say I told you Did I not
Twill not be long til we meet again
In better circumstances
So was I not right

Oh yes I say Oh yes

You work here he say

Yes Yes I work for Mr Harland Cottrell
You know he He lives right here in the farm

So you and I are neighbours
I am lodge here with the man who is my Master
At the mill I and another here

I see then from the way he stare at me
That he remark how my lip is remade
He is not a man to make comment
On such a private matter
Yet I know he approves what is done

Which does give me pleasure

Then he say Come in Come in
I do not feel comfortable to
So still we talk a little longer on that step
The lanterns burning within
The smell of good ox cheek stewing
Ambrose tell me after we left The Heavens
He not stay at Bowbridge Dye Works
No not he Never did he want to be there

Went cross the hills to Nailsworth
Did receive help from some Quakers there
Found then a job at Playnes at Dunkirk

Becoming then involvd in a new power loom
Such as needs no human hand to work it

This does sound most fantastical
But I take it as no surprise
That Ambrose should be involvd in such
He evr lovd to ride ahead of the times
Catch the future in his grasp

Then after did take a job at Dudbridge
Which is where he work now
For an engineer who does also work
With these miraculous looms

So he tell me all

Sad I feel when I say I must return
I would like to stay

Yet with Nettie sick tis my job
To take care of Master Blyth

STOCTON HILL

Who rise not yet from his bed
Screaming oft times in the night

Well well Ambrose say
I hope I shall see you oft now
I say Yes yes

Yet the truth is I walk back to the farm kitchen
Feel a little downfallen

It cannot be what it was afore
Then Ambrose was a brother
Now he is raisd in the world

Still I am weeping tears of joy
What thanksgiving to God our Father

To know this most precious friend of my heart
Is found some footing in the world
Lives now so closy by me

MOUNT VERNON

This morning my Master is awake early
The weather now is cooler
A rain does fall so fine
Tis more like mist

So so he say drinking now the tea I pourd
Today I shall go down into Stroud
Shall call upon the solicitor
To speak so of my book
To ask him also to communicate
With my family in Gloucester
Tis clear the letter has gone astray

So he nods toward me as he say this
I keep my eyes to the floor

So I set about to help him
Find waistcoat and thin black cravat
To be tied in a bow
All combd neat and straight

Tis a shame my Master say
Mr Gains has left us
How much easier it would be

Should he bring the horse down
From the coach house
Yet no doubt I shall get there

Yes yes Sir I say
No doubt you shall
I can help you

I know well the horse of which he speaks
Have been taking hay to he most days
Pumping water also tis heavy work
Since Mr Gains gone

Steep and brokd are the steps
Do lead up to that coach house

Yet still my Master be not deterrd
Standing for a moment to stare up
Toward the gate post and the yeller road
Though you do see neither from here

Perhaps he says I had best use a cane

So I go in up the stairs
To that long light room
Pieces of staind glass twinkling
In the high winders
Turning the air blue green red

Lean down then beside the open trunk
Yet tis not til I clasp the cane
I see tis one I know

Though have not seed it forty years since

I cannot lay my hand upon it

Yet what choice do I have
Since I did promise the Master

So out I do stretch my hand
Clasp it round the ebony wood
My eyes following the carvd silver knob
Fine as a spiders web

My heart constricts as my hand grasps
Yet so I do take the cane
Carry it down the stair

With the rain sprinkling fine
The light round us fracturing
I hold the cane out to he

Soon as he see it he waves me away
No no no I do not think so
Get me the musket will do better

So I stand the cane gainst the wall
Bring the musket to he

He snatches it from me and turns
Taking bold strides toward those rocky steps
As did lead up to the coach house

His teeth are grittd his hands clenchd
He will go on though the pain is bad

Stopping at the foot of the steps
He grunts in effort as try to move
That poisond leg up

Sir Sir I say Please take care

Yet he will not
He is fighting now with the musket
With his leg pushing and shoving hisself
His face turnd purple teeth bard
Grunting shoving again and again

Til sudden he do raise hisself up
Shaking then on that step
Face snarling like a tiger

Yet only for a moment
Afore he does fall back tottering
His girt height swaying then falling
Down onto the rain soakd path

So there he lie staring up at the skye
For a moment I wonder if he is takd
Then shakes his head
Lies on his side
His jacket all slabberd
Good leg kicking
Back and forwards

Eyes now shut face the colour of clay

I put my hand down to help he
He holds me then a minute
His breath much constrictd

Afore with desperd effort
He does raise hisself up right again

So back to the house he goes
Yet will not accept my help
Throws hisself down on the bed
Still soaking wet

I move then to shut the front door
Yet remembering that cane
Do step then out to fetch it

Moving through that light touching rain
Lay my hand upon the shaft
When sudden do hear a footstep behind

Turning hastily a shadow moves
Grasping the cane I do hurry then
In through the door

Oh God have mercy on me
I know who tis walks the garden here
Yet when I look back
No one is there

Stand I then quaking
Hear a querulous whinnying
Come where the coach house is
Tis that horse does speak
Wanting now some hay

Perhaps he also has heard all the cafuddle
Down here below
Feel also restless spirits walk

I listen at the door of the sitting room
Yet the Master never stir

So I go up through the garden
Round the lichen grey castle walls
Where narrow tree thick stone steps
Lead up the coach house

Once there I look in upon the horse

Lay my hand upon his bristling damp muzzle

What can I do

Is v little hay still left
I have not the strength for the pump

The Master will never ride this horse again

So I pull the door open the horse step out
He a dainty skittering thin skin type
For a moment only stands
Eyes rolling

Then tosses his head trots to the stone gates
Cross the yeller road hooves clatter the stones
Galloping now to his freedom
Out onto the heath land above

There now tis done
The Master leave not here again
I do make sure of that

This surely should bring me some peace
Yet now I cannot settle
All my thoughts do whirligig about

I should not have writ
Of that raining ladder day

These words are dangerous
They take their own path

See how you drop a stitch in knitting
All does unravel fall apart
So tis now

335

The Masters brother
He is evr with us now
Haunting all this place

For so we do know a good name is to be chosd
Rather than riches of gold and silver

I made my decision long ago
I have learnd my lesson
With telling the truth

Yet some at least I can write
Those sapling years of his life

That at least in that early time
He be knowd through to his core
As Ambrose did know me

As one other only did know me

Yet now as I sit down again to write
My hand shake and draw back
From this its givd task

What power have I to render
All the precious feeling
Of her my dear friend

But still still all of that time
I must now go on to tell

STOCTON HILL

My friend Lucetta

I never write that name afore
Even the shape it make on the page
Has a perfection to it

I remember the day I first saw her
It comes back to me oft in dreams
The colours of it washd pale
Yet still imprintd deep

It were on the high lane as leads
From the farm at Stocton Hill to White Hill

That lane follow high the sloping ridge
All drop away below

It were a glorious spot a splendid day
Early spring in the year after last I write

The earth unfold slow the winter
A few sharp flits of green
The skye endless high so one surely see
Straight up to paradise

So it happen I were walking that way
As I were sent with a message
To them at the chapel help Mr Harland Cottrell
With the poor of the parish

The message I take is for Mrs Comfort Zummers
I remember the name for never such an
Uncomfortable or wintry person may you meet

Anyway so I am walk the lane
There comes a neat person
Walking along the way toward me

Though she wear a simple gown and apron
She look like a fine lady

Her hair hang down golden brown long soft
Flow like a river twisting
Her figure full and plump
With the shine of ripe fruit
The sun light crown her queen

I stand to one side and slowly she pass by
Each foot place firm and steady
Walk the earth like God made it
For her alone

Oft people see me but they do not see
They go on pass Say nothing
For though I am fifteen now I am growd no taller
My hair sticks out brown and tightly curld
No matter how I comb it down and tie it back

But Lucetta turn her head toward me
Looks at me kindly nods just a little
Smiles a small smile

338

Behind which were laughter pure laughter
Not a drop of cruelty in it
Just a laughter that come
As part of the pleasure of the day
Me a part of that

After that she gone on and I step on also
Look back several times see her firm figure
Swaying along the lane

A hand stretchd out to catch a blade of grass
Her hair dance also as a breeze takes it
Walking on through the brindld light

Ovr her shoulders she wears a flittery shawl
So pale like cloud or feather
Now it does blow back from her shoulders
The wind sweeping it wide

I think then of the Angels
White and wings folding
Chargd with gentleness and grace
White gainst the sparking grass

How I see them sometimes
Long for them always
Keep them hidden in my mind

*

I knew who she was course
Had heard talk of her a coming

She the niece of Mr Birch Nazareth
Comes from a place near Oxford
Where a corn mill there gone bankrupt

Her father was a Minister
Gone to the Lord a long time back
Her mother a Mistress in a school
Now takd also to her eternal rest
She two older sisters
Gone in service Oxford way

Is said she wish to be a Monitor
But now she come instead help Mr Birch Nazareth
See what work she may find here

Yet that afore Mr Birch Nazareth got a pleurisy
As last several months
So I must go ovr to look after he

Say he then Mary Ann
You promise me no matter how sick I am took
Do not let that Mr Harland Cottrell near me

How can I promise such as that
Yet when Mr Harland Cottrell does send ovr
Draughts of herbs for Mr Birch Nazareth to drink

He does say Now quick Mary Ann
Put that in the hedge
Without anyone see

Mr Birch Nazareth slow get his strength back
Which may or may not be a cause
Of what is tippd in the hedge

But when this niece does come
She is set to look after he
Til he is back strong again

That is all I know in this matter

Yet it give me blessd pleasure
As I step on to White Hill that day
Just to know such as she
Is living but a few paces
From the kitchen where I toil
So I may see her pass up and down the lane

Yet then tis only a few days later
I see her again near the same spot
On the lane but a different day then

The sun still high yet a brisk wind blowing
Pull at hedge and tree
Chase the clouds fast cross the skye
Draw a tear running from the eye

She hurrying toward me hands waving
Can you help me Can you help me

The cows she said
Tis a fencing flakett has blowd in
They soon get where the new seed is plantd

I hurry on with her soon see what she say
The cows are in the lane and crossing ovr
Into the sown field on tother side

We must go back to the farm I say
Send the men who drive them back

She stand firm and shake her head
What have we need of men

Tis true that usual such as I can chase a cow
Yet it does not seem right
She should be involvd in such a task

No I say You should not
Yr cloth will spoil
The mud is quaggy the thorns sharp
I shall go to the farm

Yet this she will not allow

Come come she say You and I can manage
So we must for we cannot wait
Look even now the cows stray toward
The open gate where is the corn field

So we set about to get them turnd back
She take off her apron and flap it hard
Shout loud Back back you back
Get you out of there Back back

It were not painless to move them
Their heads hang low their swaying bellies
Their flesh loose on haunch and shoulder
Girt eyes liquid and yet steel hard
Tongues roll cross their bristly lips
Jostle and bellow refuse to turn

Yet she will make them do it
Stride on through the mud block the gate
Wave her apron at them hiss
All the while the wind dashing
Harder and harder
The hooves of the cows slide in the lane
They do not want to go back
Where the flakett has falld

You stop the gap to the corn
She shout at me I will move the flakett more

She push past the cows tug at the flakett

Get on with you Go back Go on now

I also am flapping my arms and shouting
She heads them off as they go down the lane
Both of us are laughing spitting stumbling
Our hair blown in our mouths
Cheeks slappd and stinging
Clouds trees hedge still tossing

We need a stick she says
That will move them on
Saying that she pulls
Two long switches from the hedge
Pass one to me
Slaps hard a cow cross its haunches
So it bellows loud
Plunge down past the flakett
Back where it come

So with stick shouting sliding in the mud
Much laughter we get them all back in

That I think enough
Yet she is concernd for the hurdle
It might blow down again so must be fixd

Come come she says Look such luck
The twine is here
So I am to lean gainst it push it close
She will secure with the twine

Her shoulder is closy gainst mine
Pull it in tighter she tell me and I pull
Her hands knot and tug tight

Graceful hands but strong and supple
Tear firm the twine

So then tis done
We rest then in the lee of the hedge
She laughs again blows on her cold hands
Pushes her hair back from her shoulders

So then she says
You are Mary Ann Sate
As Mr Nazareth tell me

Yes Miss I am

Ah she say Ah And so Mary Ann Sate
Shall you and I be friends

I never heard such a question
I did not know there could be such words
Feels as though she say something undecent

I blush and stare down at the grass

Oh no Mary Ann she say
I do hope you not such a person who would think
That I should consider anything at all
Of a persons appearance
I hope you would know that I see only
The goodness of God in the human heart

Yes Miss I say I am sure
Though I do not know of what I am sure

I hope also she say
That such as you
Would not give any thought whatsoever

STOCTON HILL

As to my appearance whether tis pleasing or not

Oh no say I quickly
No not at all
I no a ways think of such a thing
I also think only the goodness the heart of God

So my words all tumble out
Yet she laughs kindly
Says V good then so we are friends

For a moment we stand in silence
I twist my hands wish to be gone wish to stay

Then she say
Oh no now we are stuck
The wrong side of the flakett
Must climb ovr and up she jumps
Foot up and up and despite her heavy skirt
Her leg swing high

Sit for a moment astride the flakett
Cheeks burning browsy legs hanging long
Puts down her hand to me and pulls me up

I am ashamd but fird with joy
Sitting aside her a top the flakett
With all the Valley swirling by the wind
Tossd and tussld below

*

So such changes come then in my life
I have hardly time to think
Of what might happen to others

Yet now I see sure enough
Other alters there were also all round

Many of this a cause of Ambrose
With both he and Lucetta closy by me
My cup of happiness should ovr flow

So it does except that
He is not changd Ambrose
Tis not long afore I remember that
Though I love him v much
I also find he frightening

He thinks on things too hard
He does not follow what others say

This I do remember particular
One eve when we all did go to Stroud

This because it had been givd out
The gas lamps would be lit in the streets

This had been talkd of some time
How Mr Marling and Ferrabee
Has got Mr William Stears from Leeds
Come lend assistance to this scheme

Ambrose course was hot to go
For this was all his belief
How all the girt injustice of our time
Be put to rights by better machines

This he did tell me as we walkd
Also saying that Mr Harland Cottrell
Is not a real doctor only a cunning man

This course I know well
Yet do not like to hear it said

Shewd also contempt for Mr Harland Cottrell
The education of working men
Is no way to change the world

You also Mary Ann he says
Might consider the fairness yr own situation

Not the first time he has said such as this
Yet I do think it none of his business
So did give him a chilly stare
Which end that talk

Yet it were always the way betwixt us
I could say I love him less for that
But it were never true

It were the worrying
Thinking troubling part of him were the best
That I still say

So that eve we did walk
Past Stratford House toward Stroud

Mr Birch Nazareth saying then
What have we need of gas lamps
A rag dippd in tar and set alight
That had always sufficd
Such was his opinion

Mr Harland Cottrell had also warnd
That in London several of this lamps
Had blowd up showering many with burning glass

The town then crowd thick with many folk
You could see then the lamps not lit
Some set on walls high posts

We waitd long then til it were truly dark
Crushd in there with many other
The evening chill settling
Our feet aching and froze stiff

Ale fetch out from the Lamb
A smell of grease from a sheep
As turn on a spit

Then finally come a man with a long pole
He does then reach it up
Then flash flash flash

Such was the light
You did never see such a thing
It burns a pale gold like parchment
Edge furry as dandelion head

Stretching out through the winding streets
As though the stars theysselfs descend
One by one lighting all round
Heaven sudden so close you touch
The walls theysselfs made glitter gold

The light it shind then in the dark
And the dark comprehend it not

You stretch out yr hands all did
As though you might touch this light
Take some part in that warm glow
As did spread cross stone and winder
Roof and chimbley

Were not only the town transformd
All the people there faces turnd up
Staring staring all caressd the yeller glow

No one speaking only looking such the wonder
The lamplighter still walking on
Like Jesus hisself walking in the garden
As lies to the eastward of Eden
In the cool of the day

Bathing us all in a new light
Each thing now namd afresh
Becoming therefore quite changd

So I was forcd then to consider Ambrose
All his talk of machines

How this and not religion
Will save our world

Perhaps he was right who can say
Yet also that time strange terror fall upon me
Awe perhaps and pity for as a new world comes
So an old one must die

So in some strange perversity
I mournd also the old
In all its dark simplicity
Its dirty grace and disappointment
The blessings of its privacies and hiding holes
Which would not now come again

*

Though at that time I not want to listen much
Talk of the turning wheels of change

There was another as did

For this is how it does go
One group of people is together
Is a balance fall betwixt them

Others come and all is alterd
The mixture is quite different

What happend then were not Ambrose fault
Yet maybe it would not have happend
Had he not come

That much I can say

We had always been close to the mills
Many who work there stride up past the farm
To go to their homes Much is the gossip
Those blob mouthd men

Has always been so
Yet now we have mill people
Living up close

Or maybe tis just I am older
We do not live so tight in on ourselves

The young Masters also grow
So the changes come

Master Ned been working now more a year
For the lawyer in Stroud
Work which at first he likd

Yet soon he is full of complaint
How the work is inferior to his purposes

What a waste he should copy out documents

This come as no surprise to me
That were his nature
Slow and steady like the tortoise
Were never his path

Also we did know but could not say
That Master Ned is going now to the Fancy
Know more than anyone should
As to who brings down who in the fight
Of Obadiah Curtis and Break Neck Jones
A Battle talkd of all cross the Valley

Such also were the spirit of the times
Which were much of question and argue
The proposals for the Reform of the Corn Laws

This Ned and Ambrose did discuss
With much serious thought
Argument back and forth
Ambrose telling much is said at the mill
By those of spicd temper

Ambrose but three years older than Master Ned
Was not right the two evr came friends

For all he works hard and has some money
Ambrose is still like me A rough lad

Master Ned is different He a gentlemans son
A queer sort of gentleman perhaps but still
He has all of Stocton Hill Farm

If Mr Harland Cottrell were a different father
He would not have allowd it

Yet course Mr Harland Cottrell say nothing
He not of that opinion and anyways
Too busy with his many schemes
And of course the continual worry about money

Mr Birch Nazareth in the study more oft
Angry words pass back and forwards
He like a wife nag a profligate husband

Then Mr Harland Cottrells voice
Soft sweet as singing
How the Good Lord will provide
So we have no need of worry
Only we have faith in God

Even King Solomon in all his glory
Lilies and fields adornd
So he go on

That was how that zummer was
Master Ned and Ambrose sit out the wall Sundays
Mr Birch Nazareth stirrd up

I was glad to get on with my work
Spent many an hour in thanksgiving
For my friend Lucetta
Had not time for many other thoughts

So also perhaps did not see as I should
What a change had come in Master Blyth

It did start that day he did fall
I am sure

Growd during the many weeks
He was confind remaind grievously ill

The wound on his hand never did heal proper

At first when he did start again
To work for his father and to study
You did not see the change so much

Yet strange tis to report
He never did stammer again

Which were a hard thing to fathom
Except you do see as life go on
The chain of cause and effect
Does not go straight one link the next

Can happen that bad leads to good
So tother way about
I have good cause to know it

Perhaps the terror of that fall
Did knock the stuttering out of he
I do not know

Yet that were not the only change
Though his brow low and eyes shadowd
He had a certainty about he
That was not there afore

Bringing back still from Stroud
Those books as he do hide under the bed

Still it were hard for he
For he wish also to be friends with Ambrose
Oft greet him warmly

Yet how can I say
There was always something in Master Blyth

Even though the stuttering was done
Made others fall back
Particularly men

Maybe he did want friendship too much
Which were bitter for he
For of course Master Ned
Was always welcome everywhere

*

Soon a come the harvest moon and the hunter

Autumn did linger long that year
Always was my favourite season

The apples we have got in and stord
Taking in also many fine blackberries and sloes

All brushd with that thin golden mist
Come so oft as the year wanes

Leaves russet scarlet flame
A sweet smell of rot all round
The sun low slung in the skye
The light polishd bronze

Mr Birch Nazareth come strong again
So it must be Lucetta take new work

Though Mr Birch Nazareth regrets this much
For how Lucetta takd in hand his cottage
Which I shamd to say
Were in a most degectd state

I myself had offerd afore to assist he

Yet he no a ways wantd that

Lucetta did not even ask he
Just set about with me to help her
To put all straight

Several days work it were
All cleand polishd scrubbd fresh

Mr Birch Nazareth complaining all the while
Though admit hisself finally
Mightily pleasd with the result

Yet where now may she find a position
No place to be had at the grist mill Stratford
Nor with Mr Biddles and Bishop at Salmons
Rumours of bankruptcy again at Grove and Rock
They do lie closest to us but she go not there

Then she say perhaps she must enquire in Stroud
Yet Mr Birch Nazareth say No no no
No respectable young woman should go there
So many having fallen there in grievous sin

The Stroud Society for the Prosecution of Felons
Has been establishd at the Lamb Inn
Such is the Satan staind times now

So finally she go to Mr Fluck at Pitchcombe
Tis the mill further up the Wick Stream
Where the young Masters did swim that first day

This also the mill where Ambrose work now
Promotd he is to an engineer
So he does recommend her

Tis a shame all say for her father
He were a Minister of good name
Yet what else can be done

Mr Fluck a man of uncertain reputation
Of he I shall say more
Though has at least many orders to fill
Three stocks and two gig mills many looms

Such twistd stories fill the Valleys
The life of the mills is sore hard
Dangerous crowd full of infection
The men there rough the money bad

Yet Lucetta pulls at the leash
Keen enough to go

The more she talks of it
So I long to go as well

What have I to fear says she
Helps me unblock the guzzle hole near the pigs
I am a hard worker will have money enough

She does not say least she will see some life
Which is what I start to feel now
Tetherd at Stocton Hill

I never think afore but think it now
Would long to go with her

At Stocton Hill Mr Harland Cottrell turns grey
Is becoming deaf so shouts at people
Though he does not know he do it

Still teach sometime in the eve

But less come now
The times is hard

Perhaps also Mr Harland Cottrell has less pull
Than he once had
People do not believe
That books can change the world

For now all is talk
Of the Reform of Parlement
How the Rotten Boroughs must be finishd

Ambrose tell me of this
For many at the mill do speak so
Pamphlets are passd around and letters writ

Mr Harland Cottrell say
They think they learn the lessons from France
Those who would stand gainst the tide of change
Yet they would do well to listen
To Mr Attwood and his Birmingham Union
For what does not bend will surely break

If they do not listen to such as he
They shall soon have much worse to come

Best give something to these new men
Or soon we shall have a situation
Where every man who has a hearth
Big enough to situate a pot
Will be wanting to cast their vote
Even those as cannot write their name

So he says but I do not understand all
Only many of the men from the mills
Think the time for the likes

Of Mr Harland Cottrell now long passd

One day I am in the kitchen and Ambrose is there
We talk of these questions and so Ambrose say
What think you on this question of reform Nettie

Progress Nettie snort I do not believe in it
Some forward some back Tis always the same
Once you let them out of the bag
Who is best kept there
What then will come

Oh aye say Ambrose Quite right Nettie
For he does evr love to tease
You must take care of these radicals
For they are no better than pagan savages
They eat their own childers
Having flavourd first with pepper and herbs

Nettie not even realize how he jokes
Shakes her head wipes her running nose

Books ideas buildings machines she say
They come and go Come and go like night and day
I tell you twill make no difference to us
There are always winders to be cleand

*

But where is Master Ned in all this
We cannot know

Sometimes he is here but sometimes not

Tis said he must still pass examens
Afore he can be full a lawyer

Yet seldom he is to be seed studying

Master Blyth course still work for his father
When he is sent to the dispensary in Stroud
He comes back still with those books
As he does keep well hid
As is givd to him I know
By that Mr William Burrows there

I am not surprisd he keep hid
For one day I do open
Inside is unholy images as I cannot describe
So I fear what company he has fallen in

Many are the rumours of resurrection men
Who do ply their evil trade now in Stroud

Master Blyth still at his books
Long into the eve
Oft just he and me
Each with our candles
He in the school room
I in the kitchen
Tis a placid life

I should have valud it
Yet I was come of an age when I could not

Each morn I watch Lucetta
Come pass winder wave at me down the lane

Each eve I look for her come home

Tis not many days but she does not come alone
Walks up the hill with Master Ned

When I see it my heart does leap and fall
I do not know what to think
Course it would be they should walk together
Fine they do look
He is a match for she
Though not the same station

For he was seventeen by this time
And growd v fine
Soon to be a full lawyer
A dandy gentleman he shall be
Tall and straight like his father
That long serious face thick thatch of hair
On him a shine of glorious innocence
So you would think if you did not know

This is a chance for her I know it
Yet still tears come in my eyes

I want my friend
I can say that now
Say it oft in my head
Lucetta who is my friend

What should I say to her

I keep my lips sewd tight

Tis only right
That such as she should be raisd
In this life

Yet Nettie as always has plenty of poison to lay

Ah ah she says sitting at the table
Rocking long and laughing

Til a gusty fit of coughing take her
She hossockd up terrible in her bellers
Spits up filthy

See her See her Nettie say
What a curse lies in all that golden hair
She had better off look like you Mary Ann
Least no one will evr want you for a wife
Believe me girl you be glad of it

I kick at Netties shin as I pass
Would gladly give her a clout to the capper

More and more oft I see them
Walking to chapel together
His head bent in toward hers

Yet I also have many hours with her

Come come Mary Ann she say oft
Give me a hand to fetch this wood
Still keeps house Mr Birch Nazareth
Despite her work at the Pitchcombe Mill
No matter she is oft mortal tird
Her back aching and her feet sore

Tis terrible hard so she say
All must put sheeps wool in their ears
Otherwise they soon be deaf

A man killd out at Kings Stanley
Cleaning the carding machine
When twas working
So was caught in the rollers
Took the skin off his hands
Then his hands theysselfs

Afore he is pulld right in

A fool he was they say
Yet Lucetta says no
It could happen any day
For such is the pressure
To keep the machines running

The childers is most upsetting also
Falling into the Slubbing Billy
As it not properly fencd off

All this she says yet without much complaint
She is always gay and laughing
Make every job light
So it seem to me

Though even I can see how
Each day the mill does wipe
A little more of the shine from she

So oft I help her
We work together

One day she gives me a dress
That she has finishd with
Stitches up the hem so it fit

Also she helps me with my hair
In her hands it lies down flat
Turns her fingers through it
Makes it into neat plaits

Then she and I do sit at the table
In Mr Birch Nazareths cottage
At the end of a long day

Stretch my neck back
To feel her fingers in my hair
I am happy then as I have evr be

Even when she ask me a question
Which is about where I come from
I tell her I do not know

Then she is put about and say
How sad this must be for me
Like the book of my life
Has the first two pages tore out

Yet to me it does not matter
I tell her
Nay nay do not think on it

I do not say
What need I of family
When I have a friend

Soon even Nettie less to say gainst Lucetta
For Lucetta who is evr tender heart
Does buy her new wool stockings
This a girt kindness to Nettie
Who has such terrible sore rubbing skin
So her boots are always chaffd

Yet such a character is Nettie
She takes the stockings looks at them in scorn
Says I know not why you waste yr money
Never wears the stockings the day

Only I does see how she puts them on
Afore she settles down at night
Stroking the wool of them flat

But oh oh I worry
For what might happen to Lucetta
She walk together with him more and more
Mr Birch Nazareth has spoke to her firm
She ought to take care

For you see Lucetta a particular character
Who has many advancd ideas about friendship
How tis more important than love
The instrument of spiritual improvement

All this she does tell me
Much else besides for afore she came here
Her mother did give her to read
Of Mrs Radcliffe and Wollstonecraft

I do not understand all she say
For I am not as clever as she

Yet though she is so intelligent
In all this something important
She does not comprehend

What she does take as friendship
Others may understand another way

This a blindness in her
Yet it does make me love her more not less
So it be for other too
Of that I am sure

Only once at that time she evr speak

Master Ned she says to me
He means to continue at the law

Oh yes I say So his father wish
For lawyer are need to bring about
These girt changes are a coming

Ah Lucetta say Ah
I ask only because I was not sure
For I have seed him several times now
He comes to Pitchcombe Mill to talk to Mr Fluck
Tis about the wages I am told

Many are grateful I am sure
That such a fine young man as he
Should involve hisself in these our troubles

For certain tis shocking what we abear
Animals should not work as we do
Let alone men and women of Gods creation

Yet it makes me ask myself she say
Things are said you see
What plans he does intend

She has her hands in my hair
Twists it lightly on her finger
Would you know Mary Ann
Do you hear talk

What then can I say
I am much troubld in my mind

What of the day when the constables did come
Also Master Blyth and the fall he took

Should I tell her of these things

Perhaps I should have done

Yet I myself was so unsure
I did not want to bear false witness
Also I did not like to disappoint her
With such talk

So I do tell her naught

*

But that v eve all were alterd
I cannot say whether it a cause our talk

Perhaps not
For I had long been curious
With questions forming in my mind

So that night as evr was
I go in the school room
Where Master Blyth does work

It strike me then how tird he does appear
Perhaps he always look like that
But I have seldom takd trouble to see

So I go as though to mend the fire
For the night was turning aching cold
No star to shine or moon to comfort
Ice gathering creep up from the Valley bottoms
Clotting at the winders
Forming thick ovr trough and puddle

So there I was lifting a log
Just as he stands up to finish

Then I note carefully
The book he was writing in

Say quite easy
Oh Master Blyth how tird you are
Leave those books to me
I will tidy them up

This I do a purpose
So it hurt me to see
How his eyes do light up
At this the smallest offer of kindness

For that see was how he was
Like a dog always eager to please
No matter what unkindness is done to it

So he leaves the room
I gets the bellows to the fire
Though that was no a ways my purpose

Then I step up to the books at the table
Afore I look at them take a deep breath

For in truth I know what I will find
I knowd it for sometime
But did not want to know

So I look at the page on which he work
Though I have knowledge
Neither of a doctor or a lawyer

Still I know right well
That the book he write
Is a book of law

Then what do I do
But look at all the books
Which are there

And some as put on the shelf

And oh tis so
It no a ways was the two hands
Do look strangely the same
But that all is writ in one hand

God help me how has this come to be
Why has it not been uncoverd afore
I at least should have seed it

Never there was such love for a brother
Or love so misplacd

That I do think yet also ask
Was it also fear

So I stand there at the table
My head in my hands breathing sharp

In my mind everything shifts and turns
I go back to that day and the ladder

But even then despite I know
My mind does fight long

For this the truth of Master Ned
No matter what you know of he
You never think he did much wrong

That is how it always was

*

Mightily increasd then is my burden
For what now should I say to Lucetta

Surely I must tell her
That Master Ned is deep dishonest

But afore I have time to consider on this
Many events do crowd in one upon the other
For this is how life turn about
Nothing and nothing then all at once

The first we hear was gasping news of Bristol
Where ruffians have takd ovr the city
Lootd the bishops palace
Burnt many of the buildings

A good many the Qualities hidden in the cellars
Taken the plate and cutlery down with them
Dragoon guard sent through swinging swords
Cut many down

Tis sure they be sent to the hulks
Then transportd to Van Diemens Land
As were those break up the threshing machines

Is the same in Derby and Leicester
Lucetta hears all at Pitchcombe

Soon Mr Harland Cottrell shouting
As tis not uncommon to hear
But now tis Master Ned he shout at

So so they go at it again say Nettie

What has happend say I
For I have been helping Lucetta in the cottage
Only just come back

Master Ned has faild all his examens say Nettie

So I think that not surprising
For all the work he seemd to have done
Was none of it his

I say to myself
So so his father no a ways discipline him
Now he meet with the nature of this life
That will not be so kind

Nettie does not agree spitting and coughing
You think to see him bring down she say
But you wait wait
Such as he do not go easy

I do not listen much to she
Grows more sour as day follow day
Smells no better than a night soil pot

*

But soon tis clear that Lucetta
Not walk with Master Ned any more

She explain to me straight
As she does sew a button

I was uncertain she say and troubld
So I decide that I might
Discuss this with Master Blyth

Who as we know may say little
But is doubtless possessd of much quiet wisdom
And Godliness

Now this were something new

Twas Master Blyth she says
As did set me straight on certain questions

It pains him much to give a bad report
Of his brother who he loves dear
But he was worrit for the sanctity of my soul

I feel it right he should warn me

I care not what work a man does
Yet Master Ned has lied to his father
Making out he takes his studies seriously

No one should deceive in such a manner
Tis gainst our Heavenly Father

Also is involvd in business at the mills
I fear he is not honest

To me honesty is all
So I tell him firm

Course I am pleasd
That she has seed this
For I myself has wonderd much

Still I am amazd that Master Blyth
Should finally speak gainst his brother
Though it must surely come some time

Also I do not know how she dare
She the orphan of a family
With nowt to call their own
He the son of a gentleman

But that is how she is

She has no fear of men
Or of those who are her betters

Mr Harland Cottrell and Master Ned
Speak sharp theysselfs
They may not like
When other take up the same tune

So after all of that
Is a cankerous feeling in the house
Mr Harland Cottrell speak little to Master Ned
Speak only Master Blyth of his disappointment

Yet none of it the fault of Master Ned
That course the view of Mr Harland Cottrell

Who also say many harsh things gainst Ambrose
For tis he who has led Master Ned
Allowing his mind to be venomd
By ideas of struggle and breaking up
Are gainst the ways of the Lord

Mr Harland Cottrell I know does even say
How Ambrose must be throwd out the cottage

This however does Mr Birch Nazareth prevent
For sees also the goodness in Ambrose

Say No No No You do not move gainst he
He does pay the rent regular
We have need of such as he

So say Mr Birch Nazareth
Telling us also
Tis even said by some that Master Ned
Was part of all that riot in Bristol

For he was away those few days
Tis true

Know also Ambrose care nothing
For what Mr Harland Cottrell does say

Though course it must be the case
That if Master Ned is never to be at fault
Then many other must be in his place

*

Soon then Master Ned is took to bed with quinsy
Tis a cause of his many disappointments

No one say directly
That Lucetta has jiltd he
Yet tis gathers thick the air storm

I am set to mix kali and pure nitre
Cochineal five grains and spirits of ammonia

Tis Master Blyth sits by his brothers bed
Feeds him broth bleds him
Washes away the sweat

Still he will do that for he
The turning come but slow

Master Ned still talking wild
He did never want to be a lawyer anyway
It were a loss of his time

I hope it were the fever as did talk

Lucetta she were evr kind and caring

She worrit she had wound he
So oft she spoke to Master Blyth
To ask how does he fare
Is he stronger

Master Blyth take trouble to explain to her
All the details of the quinsy and its fever
Is most kind considerate to her worries

So oh oh it all come round

Later you think were there other paths
When all might have been different

I think not
Whether it be God or fate or what not I know
But all is laid out

We are but stands of corn
Who chose not whether we be bathd in sun
Or beatd flat by storm

MOUNT VERNON

I must stop writing now for dawn is come
The candle low and guttering

How strange at first I could not
Find those first words to put down
Yet now I cannot stop

So much I thought I had forgot
Rise up to greet me
So perfectly clear and shouting out loud
To be set down by the pen

I must go on I am the servant of the words
Must make the past tidy shew it proper

The world that felt like dark disorder
Now under my pen is all put right
The divine work of the Almighty
Celebratd now and uncover
All done in praise of He

I say this but I know
The part I tell now simple
Know what the good what the bad

Not all goes on like that

At the winder the dark now tingd pink
The air damp and clinging mist
I feel the dew has settld on my skin
Though it cannot be

My breath comes short
The pain in my chest digging sharp
As I descend the kitchen stairs

Find there that one has been afore me
That boy is Ambroses grandson
A loaf of warm bread
Has placd upon the table

I tear a piece with my hands and eat
The bread smelling of sun and warmth
Break soft in my mouth

Sitting then I do remember
How I did meet that son of Ambrose

As I walk up to this Mount Vernon

That first time That same day I was hird
Strange twas for he has only seed me once
That being near thirty years gone

Yet even in that moment he did know me

He stop me in the road call to me
I hurry on scard to be seed
Many do taunt and shout in the road
Cripple they call out and idiot Or imbecile

But though I hurry on the voice is still calling
It does not mock so I stop

I also do know he straightway

He met me with his father in Gloucester when
He hisself were just a boy

Ambrose long dead now
Killd in an accident cart out near Maisemore
Never brought the body back roads being flood
Block with mud and water

I hear tell of it
Never thought to hear more til that man stop me

You are Mary Ann Sate he say
So I had thought you long dead

Oh what joy it were to see a familiar face
It were the second that day
This the more welcome

Then I explain where I go to work and he say

Aye I hear he come back
Bought the big house a fine place

You not had yr fill then of the Cottrells yet
Yet then he laugh for he look at me
See how I am placd
What choice I have

Then lay he a hand upon my arm and say
If you need me I am here I keep the toll house
A small lad stood beside him

This I know to be Ambroses grandson
They all have the same face the same easy limbs
It could have been Ambrose hisself stood there

He is not one quarter mile away
The land church spire steep thickly wooded

Yet the boy does come
Ah how manifold are the Lords blessings

Do know also the Lord shall repay
Yea many time ovr
All that is given in kindness

STOCTON HILL

Ah yes the nursing of Master Ned
That were perhaps the start of much

Yet not many weeks later there comes another
Which also were the cause

I could see it not at the time
I live just from day to day
Happy in my love for Lucetta
Grateful that she is deliverd
That she has seed the truth of all

Advent was gone two three weeks or more
Soon to celebrate the birth of our Lord
With holly and mistletoe cut down the trees
Laid out on the mantelpiece
Wrappd in a wreath at the front door

I look forward to the singing
Of all those Christmas songs and carols
Which evr movd my heart

To hear also of the birth of the Christ child
Read out at the chapel all crowd tight

In good cheer though breath rising white

Yet just when all should be joyous
To celebrate that blessd season

Did happen the child got sick
That little one as livd in the cottages
The son of the man who Ambrose once workd

That little one calld Conker
Though his real name was Colin

Had been fever in the mills oft at that time
So no one thought much

But soon Lucetta come ovr to the farm
Ask if she might see Master Blyth

She had perhaps waitd til she knew
Mr Harland Cottrell was out
For otherwise she must speak to he

But instead she speak to Master Blyth
I hear them in the sitting room
Can you not help this child Sir say she

Aye aye he say
But I must speak with my father first

Why must you speak with he
That was always the way she spoke
Too direct some would say

Then I hear no more for the door shut

When Mr Harland Cottrell back went cross

He would have done anyway
That was his way
Was never slow to help

Know not what the family thought on this
Probably glad enough for money would not run
Even to go down to the dispensary
To that well known Mr Burrows
The danger were not mortal

While Mr Harland Cottrell was busy there
I met Ambrose in the lane
I only desird to talk to him of light things
I did not want to mention
Mr Harland Cottrell and the Conker child
I knew he would have his views

Yet he was not to be movd away
Straightway begin to say
No good would come of it

Least he hardly make the situation worse I say

Aye aye Ambrose agree
I not say he make the situation worse
Yet he certainly will not make it no better
For all he thinks he knows so much

That was all so we wait
Mr Harland Cottrell say in a day or two
The child will revive

Two days pass snail slow
Soon as Lucetta get home
She helps to nurse

Master Blyth go ovr also
To give instructions in the matter
I know not what pass there
Yet it seem surprising to me
That two growd people be need
For the nursing of a small child
I say no more

Yet for all that the child did not revive
Come then but two days afore Christmas Eve

The mother she stand weeping in the lane
Dressed in nowt but a white night gown
Stands out clear gainst the darkening eve
Pulling at her hanging hair
Scratching her face sore to see
Her hands reaching up and up
Though she might pull down help from heaven
Her feet bare the ice hard mud
Her breath white as though you see
The pain comes in each scream

It were a wrenching sight to behold

She already laid two in the church yard
Afore she evr came to Stocton Hill
Poor soul

Now she cry out saying this child too
Will soon be gone
He cannot last the night

It did shatter my heart to hear it
For he was a merry little soul
Knottd curls and warm hands
Taking a crust from me at the table

With his other hand
Pat my knee v gentle

Tis hard this world
The Lord test us most severe

Mr Harland Cottrell
Hearing that mournful sound
Which seemd to travel all cross the Valley
Soon come forth and after him Master Blyth

They have lit lanterns which sway bright
As they step ovr to the cottage together
Are there some moments endways
The night now rolling in

When they come back tis clear
All has not falld out well

I stand at the winder listening
Can see the two clear
The light of the lantern
Touch the sides of their faces

At first I hear what I expect to hear

Mr Harland Cottrell say to Master Blyth
No no The child will come to quite well
You shall see Only have patience
We have no need of any further assistance
The draught I have administerd will do all

Master Blyth follow him
Then stop and how strange to relate
He speaks with a baff
Has not done now in many months

Say I I I do not think so

At this I move closer the winder
This I have not heard afore

What say you Mr Harland Cottrell says
Fix Master Blyth with a shaking stare

I I I

Do not tell me says Mr Harland Cottrell
You know my view on this
We have no need of any other
You deceive these good people
Who have no money to spare

He gets no further for Master Blyth
Shaking and mouth fish open shut
His hands trembling shout

The child will die
Do you not understand
The child will die

After is a sudden long silence
A stone go down a well is long falling

Then Mr Harland Cottrell stand staff straight
Purse up his mouth point his finger
Aim his eyes like they two musket

I will not have you say this
Tis not true
You are deceivd and you deceive
That whole lot doctors chirurgeons apothecaries
No better than poisoners carpenters barbers

Butchers all

Yet he does not get to the end of that

Master Blyth has his head down is spitting
I feel his temper boiling ovr
What bottld rage does lie there

I say
The child will die
If we do not get a proper doctor

Proper doctor Proper doctor
Mr Harland Cottrell is raging now
Finger stabbing
Near toppling ovr such is his wrath

Yet what neither have noticd
From where I am I see
Ambrose is a coming through the darkness
Bringing a lantern in his hand
Come up the lane

He see all for he always see
Yet he is subtle knows always that
Sometimes kindness is more deadly than rage

So he steps forward
Touching his cap say to Mr Harland Cottrell

Ah Sir I see you have decide on a doctor
I am free now Sir
Will gladly walk to Stroud

At this Mr Harland Cottrell boil ovr

You keep out of this
It has naught to do with you
Already you meddle in my affairs

Yet even as Mr Harland Cottrell say all this
The rage is leaking out of he
His body begin to sag a little

He knows he can control Master Blyth
He not so sure of Ambrose
Though he is the lower station

Also I must say Mr Harland Cottrell
Eldering now and tird
Perhaps he know when he is beat
Though I think him wrong
I do not like to see him so

But he hisself is proud
Will not admit defeat

So he say grandly
I have said my last word on this
I more experience than any doctor
In these five Valleys
If you wish these good people
To waste their money
Then that is yr affair

So he strides away into the house

Master Blyth and Ambrose are left there
Standing together ockerdly
Their lanterns hanging close
The yeller light furred in the dark

STOCTON HILL

Ambrose did no a ways like Master Blyth
But now he say evenly
What you said is right
I know tis
So I shall go now into Stroud

I think you must say Master Blyth
But what of the money

Among us we shall find it Ambrose says

Thank you thank you say Master Blyth
I only hope he will not throw you
Out yr bed

What care I say Ambrose
Speaks as he always does easy and calm
There are plenty of other places I can go

I only hope Master Blyth say
His voice tremble bad
I wonder if he might cry
I only hope tis not too late for the child

I hope so too say Ambrose
Fitting his cap to his head
But at least now we have done all we can
Nobody may do more
If the child is takd
It shall not be for want of a proper doctor

He stand still for a moment nod his head say
Thank you Master Blyth for yr help

So that was that and Ambrose went

I did wait up then
Much later heard Ambrose come back
With that Mr William Burrows
From the dispensary

Mr Harland Cottrell shut in this study
Say nothing of it

Master Blyth go in with that Mr Burrows
They do seem to know each other
Rather cordially

Which do not come as a surprise
For tis Mr Burrows
Who has lent Master Blyth
The books as is hid under the bed

Containing those images of bodies
Cut into pieces the skin off
You never saw such iniquity

Yet what then came to pass
The child last through the night
Wake the next day
The day after sit upright
Wanting bread

So you say that Ambrose and Master Blyth
Were provd by this right
Yet that is not the case perhaps
Who can know

That question not much interest me
What I want to know is something else
For I watch all close

Why Master Blyth now speak his mind
To his father when in many a long year
He never has

Now he starts where might it end

What well of anger lies there unplumbd

What might he become

*

So Christmas pass
We dip down into deep winter once again
Oh how many hours of joy
Did I pass with Lucetta

Sometimes together we read
The Romance of Robinson Crusoe
The Pilgrims Progress of Mr Bunyan

Some also of that Mrs Radcliffe
Theories about the liberation of women
Which interest me less than the stories

But Lucetta talks of all that long

Or sitting peaceful near the fire
Deep in the evenings

It were a lengthy winter
Easter well passd afore
We come up into spring
Hold face to the weak sun
Some mornings

So many without food that winter
The mills oft stoppd and then
They has no choice but to throw theysselfs
On the mercy of the parish

Yet Mr Birch Nazareth keep us well enough
And what care I
For I am with my friend

All the while I watch her with Master Blyth

They conduct theysselfs course v proper
Pass in the lane or stand near the pump
Sometimes find they have cause
To walk to White Hill at the same time
Backwards and forwards to chapel also

What I see most is how he change

That day he spoke up to his father
Were only the beginning

She was the cause of all
For that was her gift
I think she loosd his tongue

Deep|wisdom has Lucetta
For she see what other never do

She does divine that goodness
Is not necessarily dressd up
In smiles and laughter

Badness not necessarily the dark and silent
Can be all the other way about

STOCTON HILL

As she say when we first met
She is not distractd by the surfaces
Sees through to the goodness of the human heart

This a powerful thing to behold
A lesson in life all should see
How love can change a person
So soon you hardly recognize he

Soon Master Blyth held up his head
Look direct in the eye
Question what is said
It never was so afore

No longer hide books under the bed
Yet leave them out on the table
I take care not to look
For fear of what I may see

Yet even on that question
I am provd to be misguide so it seems

For I do ask Lucetta about those images
Is she not frightd for Master Blyths soul
Does she not fear he has been hoodwinkd
By those resurrection men as does steal bodies
Use the dead for unholy purposes

Yet Lucetta only laugh at me
Course she says Master Blyth is engagd
In many enquiry into questions
With that good Mr Burrows in Stroud
Examining many questions of anatomy
A science may not always be discovrd
Only through the theory

This is the future Mary Ann
You have no need to fear

So she say and so I try to believe

One day I see her with Master Blyth
She does take his hand I see her fingers
How they close on the place the flesh was torn
When he did fall that day

How can she touch him there
It troubles me to see it
As though someone had touchd
The scar on my lip

I feel I have seed something indecent

Yet still I watch them
For there was little else to watch
Mr Harland Cottrell takd up now
With the study of phrenology
Measuring all our heads
With many diverse instruments

Master Ned oft not home til late
Or not home at all
Stay with his friends in Stroud

That even more so since Lucetta did spurn he
Perhaps he feels some ockerdness
I do not know

He has takd a job with a bookseller
One Mr John Brisley in the town of Stroud
A man who is well knowd to be a radical
Much gainst his fathers wishes

Tis not a job fit for he

But what does Master Ned really do
I do not know
There is much gossip

Even in these Stroud Valleys now
There is political unions formd
With petitions and protests and speeches

The times are stirring
Everything is put out of joint
Many a calf is born with six legs I am told
Yet I never see one

Druids tis say do come in the church at Stroud

Preachers are abroad
Talk the end of the world is nigh
One comes and bangs a pan out in the yard
Sings a wailing song
Of how God will take us all soon

Nettie throws a ladle out the winder at he
I rather go onto the next world now
So she say
If the other choice
Is to listen to he gibberwoling

I find the days long
Oft no one at all but Nettie and me
My work gives me less pleasure

For the situation of this house worse than evr
What pleasure is there
To polish a board to shining

When the board is deeply crackd
Falling away into the earth below

How can I clean a winder that is brokd
Or get mould off the walls
When they do run water

Perhaps tis a cause of this malcontent
That I begin to dream many stories
Make worlds inside my head

This I have always done
With highwaymen and pirates and goblins
Such tales as come
From ballads and pamphlets

But now the worlds in my head
Are inhabitd by some who live real
Soon they do become more fact
Than the world I inhabit

In these worlds are always my dear Lucetta
With her Master Blyth they is marrid
How I think of them is live in a house
Like the ones new built just outside Stroud

In that house are no crackd boards
Or mould or buckets catching water
There you polish a board and it shines fine
In that house is blossoming happiness

She become a Monitor in a school
No longer the nastry toil of the mills

Yet where am I in this dream
That is what is troublesome

Always I think myself there with them

I am hird as a maid there
Or perhaps we both become Monitors
Maybe it could be so since I read now
As well as any

Have read many many books
For that at least I may evr do

In that little house of my mind
Lucetta and I sit together in the evenings
As we do now

Reading the word of the Lord
Or perhaps the sermons of Jeremy Taylor
We do both much enjoy

These dreams are my girt pleasure
But behind them lies a worry
What if the dream should come to pass
I am not part of it

Soon I am sure twill happen
Lucetta will marry
Even though she says she no a ways will
Has no interest to

Then she will go away
That I cannot even think
Yet sometimes lying abed next to Nettie
Unable to sleep
I find myself weeping with fear of it

Then one evening come when I am tird
My cakers swolld for several days

I have womens aches sawing inside

Lucetta sitting with her sewing
Talking merrily of her old life in Oxford
How she should like to see that place again
Or perhaps go to visit her sisters

All of a sudden I am engulfd in fears
Start to weep like a child

Oh I am ashamd

Yet Lucetta takes me in her arms much concernd
Mary Ann Mary Ann what ails you

So ovrcome am I
I cannot stop myself from speaking
Oh Lucetta I am afeard you will leave me

Lucetta shake her head Hold my hand
Oh I remember how soft was her touch
How her warmth did fill my whole body

She say to me
Mary Ann You must know I love you dear
You are a sister to me
We shall never be partd
Do you not know that is true

I sat for a long time with her
My head rest gainst her shoulder
The rustle and creak of the wind in the chimbley
Nettie snoring somewhere atop the stairs

I felt then such peace
The next day even more

For Lucetta gave me a lock of her hair
She had twistd it neat in a plait
Made a tiny basket for it
From pieces of straw

After that I was happy
Oh so happy

For though soon she might marry Master Blyth
Yet I had no need to fear
For the love of sisters
Is not changd by marriage
Or even by the distance of mile

The love of sisters abear all she say
And this the truth

For so do I love her deep even now

*

The spring then bustle in
And the situation in the country
Become perilous

Tis said two hundred thousand
Are massd at Birmingham
Though Mr Thomas Attwood
Does call for peace and calm
He does also say
These men cannot be held back much longer

In Stroud members of the gentry
Have been cruelly set upon and robbd
All must lock up every barn byre shed

Diverse chains stold one night
From Mr Fluck at Pitchcombe Mill

Even at Hammonds cross the Valley
They have a bee hive wickdly takd
Fish from many ponds have gone

Mr Harland Cottrell come into the kitchen
Was a soft evening the light hazy
Bellow at us all as is now his way

Many have tried to tell he is deaf
Must get hisself an ear trumpet
Yet he seems not to hear
Which is perhaps not surprising

Ambrose is there as well
Also Lucetta and Mr Birch Nazareth

For tis being said now the way forward
Is for all as have any money in a bank
To take it out now without delay
For only a crash in the financials
Will bring the Government to sense

The cry everywhere is Stop The Duke Go For Gold
And Mr Harland Cottrell
Having considerd long his conscience
In quiet communion with his God
Does feel action such as this
Is indeed need for the safety of this
Our noble country of England

We all nod seriously and thank he
For this his support of a just and worthy cause
May do much for the welfare of the common man

But after he has gone is some levity

For as Ambrose say
Oh yes certainly
If Mr Harland Cottrell takes his vast fortune
Out of the bank in Stroud
Surely this will bring that Government
Quaking and quivering down on bend knee

This be a far girter cause of national concern
Than two hundred thousand in Birmingham

Nettie and Mr Birch Nazareth snort laughter
Yet not too loud for they may be heard
Soon Ambrose making us laugh all the more
By pretending to be Mr Harland Cottrell
Wagging hard his finger and his nose
Shaking his head v solemn

We should not have laughd so

Particular as the conditions continue grave
With many new constables being sworn in

Yet still we never thought that danger
Should come in our own lives

I remember it well an eve twas
The skye then colourless and low
So all the depth shade the Valleys
Seem flat and draind

The air strangely warm and still
As I step out to breathe the air

What should I see but Ambrose

A coming up the lane from Cally Well
Pulling with he a horse labouring
To carry a body slung cross he
So I run down yet Ambrose shout me back
Go and fetch Mr Harland Cottrell

Nettie now at the back door also see
She call Mr Harland Cottrell
Who what mercy is at home
So also Master Blyth

Immediately they set to get Master Ned down
For so we see tis he

Mr Harland Cottrell praying again and again
The mercy of God

Master Ned say I try to stop they
He was attackd I tried to stop they

They set upon him say he
For he has much money in his bag
I tried to stop them so

So the story does emerge
How one of the men of Biddle and Bishop
Who is taking money back to Stroud
Has been beaten about

None of this comes as all new to me
There is always wild talk
How such money as is paid for cloth or flour
Is rightfully theirs how it must be took

Yet I never thought any fool enough to do it
Those who run will not get far

STOCTON HILL

Soon be wearing the county livery
At Horsley gaol or Gloucester

Hear also then a name I heard afore
Twas that of William Morris Moore
A young stockinger and commercial traveller
Of Tewkesbury once so they say
But a man gone to the bad
In dissolute idleness
Spreading of Jacobin talk

As they go into the house I am following
Ready to find bandages and water all
When a hand lays firm on my arm

Where go you Mary Ann say Ambrose

I do go to help Master Ned I say

Why are you helping he Ambrose say

For he is my employers son I say cold
I do not care for Ambroses voice

Nay nay Mary Ann he say
You never were a fool
Do you really think this story true

Even as he speaks some cog in my mind
Does slip into place
Turn the wheel about
Another way

Master Ned did no a ways help that man
So say Ambrose

He was one of those who did attack

How can you know I say
You should not say it

Ambrose say nothing more
Only stare at me

Oh so so I say
You are such a teller of the truth
Go you and say all to the constable

Ambrose shrugs turns away
I would not spend my time to say such
I would not be believd

I do care naught for Master Ned
The law is not need to deal
With a fool such as he
A rich mans son who meddles in affairs
He not understand

Others will swing His hands always clean

Yet we have only to wait Mary Ann
Time and the natural justice of the world
Will soon bring Master Ned to right

You had best look to yr own affairs
As I have told you oft afore

Tis true he has said much to me
About my position at Stocton Hill
Why I not seek myself some better employ

I have no a ways listend to he

And do not now
For Stocton Hill
Is all my home

His words have not settld
Afore Master Blyth steps out of the house

Mary Ann will you help me

Sorry Sir Yes Sir I should not have tarry

So I am about to go in
Yet Ambrose has Master Blyth fixd with a stare
Which stops all

Let me tell you now Ambrose says
Yr brother Ned will claim he helpd that man
But he did not

Tis as likely he was part of the gang
As did organize the attack

The silence follows is long

Master Blyth look Ambrose straight in the eye
He never would have afore

Then he say calm and clear
Yes I had supposd it may be so

Then is silence again
I watch Master Blyth
Oh my heart could break
For he does love his brother

Yet what then can any of us do

When love is not enough

Later that evening all is dark
I take water up to Master Ned
Whose ribs is broke and wrist too
Bleeding inside so they say

Master Blyth sit with he in the candle lit

I hear but scraps of their words

Master Ned say You will speak for me

Master Blyth reply
I was not there I did not see

But you could have been
I need yr help
I know right well you will help

But Master Blyth say
I will dress yr wounds
I will not say naught
Of things I never saw

I will not speak for you

So tis that Ambrose Master Blyth and me
We keep our silence

All through that dragging winter
The damp slow spring follow

Though the constable come to ask
The Master from the mill

All around name of William Morris Moore
He and some others who were certainly
At the heart of all that pass

Much is the braggards talk
Men can never keep their mouths shut

They do not heed the words of the Good Book
Wherefore let every man be swift to hear
Slow to speak slow to wrath

I am afeard guilty confusd hurt
I never have wantd to lie
Yet he is my employers son
If I say aught I will be put out

Also I never saw any myself
Have only Ambroses word in the matter
Though I know what he say must be true

Never did then speak again to him
Of what does pass

Think with sadness how I love he deep
Always have He is such a dear friend to me
Yet we are so oft set gainst each other
About matters are not our own

Not since that eve did Ambrose evr speak
One word more to Master Ned
The breach tween them never mend

Part of the reason why Master Ned is believd
Is because of who his father is
And that father speak for him

Many the town of Stroud
Critical of Mr Harland Cottrell
His reputation betwixt and betwixt
Quality do not like him for he say too much
About wages education doctors and all

Yet there is no one who disputes
He is an honest man
Holds the hearts of all other men dear

So tis believd his son must be the same

Others are sent for hard labour
To Horsley gaol
Yet Master Ned is a hero
Among the respectable of the Valleys
For he did defend that mans life

The doubts squat on us
A black cloud of flies
All around rot

I long to be gone
Spend my time dreaming
Of that fine neat yeller cottage
Where I will be with my sister and Master Blyth

I feel it a coming close
I see it in Master Blyths eyes
He does not bother to hide
From his father his anger now

The future is within our reach

*

That zummer
Twas then the Reform Act finally passd
Stroudwater now representd in the Parlement

Sheep roastd ale drunk
Many chasing a pig with a greasd tail
All through the town
The prize a pair of buckskin gloves

Some of the low type women
Organizing a smoking competition
As to who could puff through
The most quantity of tobacco in an hour
A barrel of gin the prize
So the scandal were told

Though soon enough it come clear
That no new world has been brought to birth

The next spring I remember the day
I had been that morning into Stroud
For to take a letter from Mr Harland Cottrell
To that lawyer Mr Paul Hawkins Fisher

Much wickd laughter in Stroud
For what was said cannot surely be true

That Mr William Ratcliffe of Woodchester
Had mountd his fine horse at the Swan Inn
Has rode right up the scaffold
Which around the new subscription rooms
Higher up than twenty men

There he dismountd and the horse
Which was worth fifty pounds
Did fall from the scaffold

Mr William Ratcliffe it were said
Were rather fresh when he rode from the Swan
Yet quite sober when he saw his horse all dead

This I did hurry home to tell Mr Birch Nazareth
For he and I did always enjoy a good story

But did arrive at Stocton Hill
To hear a thunderous rumble of shouting
Did soon forget horse and scaffold all

Shouting was not unusual as I told afore
But now comes with it a battering heart

For that future I do dream is perhaps come

The voice of Master Blyth
It does smash cut thrust cut
Gainst the voice of Mr Harland Cottrell

Something about the sound is welcome
It gladdens my ears

Never doubt in my mind
That Master Blyth has now said to his father
He wishes to wed to Lucetta

What now will be said
I should like v much to know
Yet cannot hear the study door being tight

If this were any respectable household
Mr Harland Cottrell be raising an objection
Basd on questions of station
She but an orphan and a mill worker
You sell yrself too cheap

Yet I known Mr Harland Cottrell long now
This an argument he will never use

No no the objection will not be that
Twill simply be that he wants no change
Master Blyth has always been his instrument
He will not let him go
Will cling to the story
Something amiss with Master Blyth
Must stay home be kept close
Only take instructions never lead

That is how twill all go
Except no one now believe that story more
Like a pile of leaves it has all blowd on

This is what I think
As I boil a pan in the kitchen
Preserving fruit tomatoes plums
Wait wait

When Master Blyth finally come out the study
He walks in the kitchen his face raw
Say with his lips knotting tight

Mary Ann I need yr help
I am leaving for London
I must pack many things
So he gives me instructions I set to
Though I have the tomatoes also
All the time I am waiting
He will say he is
Betrovd to be marrid to Lucetta
She will go with him
Leave far behind the staining mill
But he never say

This worries me yet I take strength
Perhaps he has to ask her still
I do not doubt she will say yes
All will be well

And I I
Tis so exciting I can hardly think of it
I will go on a coach to London
The idea fills me with shivering

Part of me longing part of me afeard
Yet I shall be safe if I am with Lucetta

All the time I am packing
Nothing more is said
I go on with the tomatoes
Later I will remember the smell of ripe fruit
Warm and boild down with spice
Tis a smell even now would sicken me

Oh so long I wait afore I see
Lucetta come up the lane
Even then I dare not go to her
I know she will be busy
Whatevr news she has
Surely she will come to tell me

She does not come she does not
All the lids are on the tomatoes
Their smell still swell the kitchen
Full of promises that will not be

My thoughts begin to strike me cold
Something is not right
Two young people who are promisd
Bring a lightness all around

So why now the day so burdend

I make the supper only for Mr Harland Cottrell
He says not a word
How glad I am Master Ned is not home

Then I set out cross the yard
But I do not find Lucetta
Finally I must ask Mr Birch Nazareth
I wait a while afore she comes down

As soon as I see her
I know all is undone
Her face is drawn back at the eyes and mouth
Her skin patchd red
Lines swolld under her eyes

Is it possible Mr Harland Cottrell
Has refusd their match
So my mind does question

Ah Mary Ann she say Shall we walk

So we set out into the lane
Though the evening is darkling
The weather discourage

There I can hold the words in no longer
You know I say Master Blyth go to London

Ah yes says she
I know that and I heartily glad for he
You know he goes to train to be a doctor

But how I say His father do not pay

No no so Lucetta explain to me
Of course Mr Harland Cottrell is not pleasd
Yet what right has he to decide

Master Blyth was recommend
By that Mr William Burrows
Who does work at the dispensary in Stroud
A man whose reputation is beyond question

Was askd to go most particular
For he has many skills now
As others do not

What skills I do not ask
Yet wonder again about the resurrection men

She say Master Blyth can work and train
That is the way he can progress
He has found a chirurgeon in Lambeth
A village ovr the south of London
Can take him on

Yet what of his hand I say
This I ask for that hand
As was damagd in the fall
Had heald up but still does work stiff

No no Lucetta say
He has told all and that is no problem
So they say

Oh I say Oh
But you You
I thought you would go with he

Me How Mary Ann could I go with he

I thought you and he would marry

She laughs then a bitter small laugh
Turn away from me

Oh Mary Ann she say
I do love you v much
But really you must stop
To see everything in terms
Of marriage and romance
This is childish thinking
Tis true that Master Blyth and me become close
Yet that were not a closeness of that kind
Not in the least

I think what she says is not true
I seed I know

The truth is that he has disappointd her
Yet she is too proud to say it

Already I do hate him for it

I cannot explain it to you she says
Tis a private shameful matter
Not to be spoke of
Master Blyth does labour
Under a girt pall of sin
Must forevr make amends for his nature

This he and I have now discussd
So tis right he should go to London
Become a doctor as he has always want

This he has decide I am v glad
This Mary Ann is what love really is

Tis not about marriage which only confines
But about seeing another use the gift
Which the Good Lord blessd him

I nod my head
Try to look as though I understand
Yet tears are running down my cheeks
I am so glad of the dark
She cannot see

Soon our conversation is end
She go back to the cottage

I stand outside the back door and weep
Perhaps for him perhaps for her
More for myself
For all my dreams are gone

Yet still the next day
Just at the first flush of dawn
The skye rose pink and damply mist
When Master Blyth is all packd up and ready
Will take his bags down the bottom road
Find a cart to Stroud
To meet the staging coach

Still I am dry eyd do not look at him
Only say good bye in a small voice
The least was as necessary

Not so Nettie as she does love him well
Has made cakes cut a dab of cheese
For he to take

Mr Harland Cotrell is up and working
Yet does not come out his study

So tis Master Ned who stagger out
Came home late the night afore
Still he says affectd by his injury
Though is months past now

Is it injury or liquor
Perhaps I am too harsh

Now he weeps long and loud
Pleads again and again with his brother
Do not go Do not leave me

Master Blyth then turns to Lucetta
Say My friend who has done much for me
Can I also ask you now
To look after my dear brother

She course does agree to this

Still Master Ned does say
You know I will die without you
Please I beg you do not go

Without you I shall be undone

MOUNT VERNON

Now how my Master does rage gainst me

For I have so forgot myself and left
Some page of what I writ
On the table in the hall

Do I never learn my lesson

Shouting now Shew me what you write
Fetch me all the book
You have imprisond me here
Writing lies about me

For what has he found
Not the story of my beginnnings

Not ramblings of the humble maid servant writ
So rich folk gasp at the lives of the poor

Instead some part of his own story
Which he did want to writ hisself

Still he rants on
How soon he shall be going to Stroud

I best give him now all I write
He will handle all hisself
Never should he have had me back
In this his house

I take no regard much of he
Soon he will be calm enough again

Give me the book he shouts again
Bring it to me

Sir I say I am truly sorry
That I cannot do what you ask
You see I do not writ in the kitchen now
I have takd my writing upstairs
The light is better there
Yet the stairs are many and steep

So I leave him there in the hall
Those two lost pages cradle in my arms
Cross the slanting staind glass light the hall

See him down below me
Balancd on that barrel of the musket
His stump arm waving at me in rage

You you he shout again accusing me
Who are you to pass judgement

Whatevr guilt there is
You have yr share in it

All would have been well
If only you had been loyal

Is that not true Mary Ann

Is it not true

I try as best I may
To shut my ear gainst he

Yet his voice does follow me
All up the high and echoing well
Of the twisting slanting stair

His words settling deep in my mind
No matter how little I want them there
Whatevr guilt there is
You have yr share in it

This I will not hear

STOCTON HILL

Many a time I remember
That day Master Blyth left

Without you I shall be undone

At the time I took it only for the artifice
Of which Master Ned is such a craftsman

Yet who can say
For as time rolls out his words start to seem
To have more truth in they

As evr the darkness gathers slow

At first things went on much as afore
Only Nettie does go pecking vile on me
Even more oft

This I understand she miss Master Blyth

So she may I think but I do not
For though Lucetta will hear
No word gainst he

I do consider he did lead her on
Then let her down most cruelly

For this I never will forgive he

So there I was alone in my anger
Alone also in my work as evr was
Nettie oft abed sleeping
Though Mr Harland Cottrell does not know
Itching pitiful all ovr

Master Ned working at the booksellers
Stay oft in Stroud
That was the story

At the mill all as afore
Though the Reform Act passd
Stroud has now his own man Colonel Fox
Who is sent to Parlement to speak for us

No matter does it make as any can see
Soon loud clambering complaining again
With hand bills and meetings

I do not know
I never walkd oft the way to Stroud
Though Lucetta must have heard at the mill
So she say it to me

How the Valleys always boiling
For there was never any trade more intricate
More uncertain and contradictory
Than this our cloth trade

Mr Harland Cottrell hisself changd now
Growd deaf so that you must shout at he

Through an ear trumpet

Got hisself also some Waterloo teeth
For his own was all falld out

Stayd home more particularly
When the weather is gloaming

His joints become stiff as rustd hinge
Sat many hours silent by the fire

You might have thought he at least glad
For the law now been passd Parlement
End the evil of the West Indian slavery

Yet Mr Harland Cottrell say Nay nay
You mark my words the way the law is cast
Many shall find a way past he

I think also he must miss Master Blyth
Yet he never mentiond his name
Never opend the letters as came
Leaving them only to Master Ned
Who no a ways tell us any

Strange he never say anything about Lucetta
Never accuse her in the matter of Master Blyth
His departure

Though to me it were clear
Her hand were in it
She had encouragd him to go
Hoping also to go herself
Afore he did disappoint her so bitterly

Yet that were Mr Harland Cottrell for you

He were misguid in many matters
Yet he were always fair
Would never use his station gainst any
That were the puzzle of he

So things go on
I were happy for every eve
Lucetta is home
She and I sit together for an hour
Just afore bed

Or sometimes a Sunday afternoon
Walk out in the fields many mile

Do enjoy to go to Painswick
Taking not the toll road
Walking the stream and Stepping Stone Lane

To see the many fine yews round the church
Which we do also try to count
For I do tell Lucetta how tis knowd
There be ninety nine yews
And should the hundredth evr be plant
Then both the tree and he who plants
Shall by a Devil soon be struck dead

This Lucetta does allow me
For though she does not believe my stories
Yet she does enjoy them and understand
My love of such
As others do not

So we walk oft through those tunnels of yew
Close and dark cloying branches clinging
She oft ahead dash this way and that
Seed and not seed cut by sun light

422

Wearing always that same pale shawl
As does blow about her shoulders

So one day we are there the wind blows sharp
A coming down through the yews
I hear a curious noise
Like the playing of a flute
Not music yet a few long notes
That do mix with the sound of the wind

I turn to look around for her
See her not then hear her voice

And lo she is far up on the roof of the church
Above the gargoyles waving at me
Her arms and shawl spread like Angel wings
Gainst the sapphire cloud torn skye

Still that ghostly music spreading like smoke

She gave me then also a bracelet
Made of jewel colourd glass beads
Never a thing so fine did I possess

It were a blessd time

*

Yet too oft at Stocton Hill
Our solitude were interruptd
By Master Ned
He always want this and this and this

I went to him course as I must
Yet I found no joy in it
For oft he were red in the face

Could smell the liquor on he

Always he askd is Lucetta not here
I shook my head as though I did not understand

Lucetta were different
Always pleasd enough to help
For since Master Blyth had gone
She had fall back
Into a pleasant way with Master Ned

I found it vexing to see
I never knew what she knew of him
What she did not

Yet still I question her

She turnd then and lookd at me with her
Pooling deep eyes and said

Afore he left Master Blyth
Askd me particularly
He said would I take care of his brother
So I must Twas a promise

For we are Christians Mary Ann are we not
We cannot let others stray from the true path
Tis our duty to help those who are temptd
Particularly with one such as he
Who has such a good clean soul
He means such kindness always
Though he so oft fail

So you know in a case such as this
Friendship may be his route to redemption
We can never under estimate

What true friends may do

This she did always say
For this was her theory
Which she had read much

I said little then
For yes I am a Christian
I believe there was goodness in him
I saw him as a small boy
Shot through with the blessings of the Lord

Oh we must all be kind and loving
Only sometimes it does not serve
Tis a question the Christian faith
Not oft address

*

That next zummer all were stirrd up
Breaking open the land itself seemd to dip sway
Even at Stocton Hill the air restive

Many false prophets abroad in the world
Who privily bring in damnable heresies
Also sorcerers performing signs of the Beast

St Swithins Day it raind
So for forty days did remain
Torrents thrashing down day on day

Would punish the growth from the land
The harvest would not be got in
The price of bread evr rising
The work less and less

425

In Stroud many gathering together
Waving loaves of stale bread
All tied about with black ribbons

Master Ned tell me and Lucetta
Mr Vincent come to Stroud
Along with that Mr Morris Moore
To address the people

All will go to hear him speak
Also me I want to go as well

Nettie tell me Nay nay
You will be takd by the constables
Transportd You not go there

Yet still I ask Mr Harland Cottrell
Which were bold of me

I have to shout it rather
First he shakes his head wipes his hand
Cross his wide forehead
Takes his eye glasses on and off

Yet finally he say
So so you may go Mary Ann
Yet you take care you do not believe
All is said there

Take care also of yr own person
There will no doubt be thieves and drunkenness
And lewd behaviour
So you girl take care

So the day come there I am
With the others from the cottages

Ambrose and Lucetta we walk down
Join many others there walk the path
Along the stream
The land wet and sticking our feet
A cause of all the rain

Many dressd in their fine clothes
Such as they usual wear for church
The women with their best hats
The men their shirts pressd and fresh
Someone plays a trumpet others sing
Women have a meadow of flowrs
Stuck into their hats laughing all the way

My heart beat fast my hands squeeze tight
To be part of such a merry throng

Though Ambrose do say such is the times
How can we know whether any is the man
Holds back the mob or whether he is hisself
That same brute force

Such he does oft say now
For he has been promotd to a new position
Is in charge of much of the engineering
Wheelwright also at Pitchcombe Mill

So he does say less gainst Mr Fluck
As once he did

This I do not criticize him for
I am glad to see him so raisd

Yet hope he does not lose his feeling
For those who can no a ways advance
Of who there be many

So that day soon come up the town of Stroud
Gather in the main street jostling and pushing
The hyms of Mr John Wesley being sung
Talk of all the unjust laws
Of that Whig aristocracy

There Mr Vincent stand high up on a box
All fall into silence when he begins to speak

How the hardy class of the weaver
Who was a proud and independent man
With a good living much food spread on his table
Has now been reducd little better than a pauper
Work a fourteen hour day for a few shillings

Then others such as Mr Morris Moore do come
Gone on then about Parlement and all
I am at the back and cannot hear
Many tankards being carrid out from the inn
Some already high in drink

Then Master Ned jumps up high
The platform starts to speak

I back away
Hiding myself in the crowd

I think then what his dear father would think
If he could see all

Standing up high sun catch the yeller of hair
One hand grippd cross his chest
The other outstretchd

Three and a half million of working men he say
Hold out the olive branch of peace

To the enfranchisd and privilegd classes
Only asking a firm and compact union
Asking only they may be free

Though I do hear but few of the words
I feel the shape of them
The galloping rhythm matches
The beat of every heart

The dip and sway the twist and turn
How they come in the ear
Pass straight to the heart

The crowd hears it too and roars claps
Laughs throngs twists

So that when he come down from the platform
Many are crowd about him
To slap him on the shoulder

Others also stand up after to speak
Wild men talking the revenge of the Lord
Foaming at the mouth and raging
Calling on all to act
To bring about a new world of Justice and Truth

The constables now standing watching all
Tis well knowd the King and Country men
All wait in readiness

The crowd in a high excitement sway and toss

Hand bills blowd down from trees
Or passd out through the crowd
Blowing everywhere about

I remember Mr Harland Cottrell did warn me
Of the safety of my person
Which never I did listen much
Yet now I begin to think

So I wander away a quieter spot
Sit on a wall eat the bread I brought with me
Prefer just to watch all that goes on past
Yet keeping an eye always on Lucetta
Who is up the front of the crowd
Listen to every word

No sun seed in the skye that day
Yet still were hot like a pan boiling
The speaking finishd
It comes to me in a sharp way
How I am separate from others
That I may not laugh and talk
With them of my age
This I know but being among so many
The truth of it bears down on me

I should like to go home
Feel strange heart ache for Mr Harland Cottrell
Who has always knowd me as others do not

Yet I must wait for Lucetta
The crowds is too much for me
Brawling start a man cornobble another

Just then Lucetta come up
Her face flushd her lips lickd red
Her chest heave with all the fire of the place

Mary Ann she say
I think we must get Master Ned

Must tell him he is to come home
The situation here is perilous

I shake my head
Who am I to tell him how to behave
Tis well beyond me to take any hand to he
Well beyond her as well

Yet she do not think so

I should have stayd then I should have done
Yet I were weary and wiltd
I did not like the idea she had

But twas my business to protect her
There I fail her
For all I wantd to do was to get away

Such was the heat smell shouting
Bitter spit does rise in my mouth

So I depart and began to walk
Out to the hem of the town

Yet then who should I see
Down below me at the turn in the road
But Master Ned

Where can he be going

He turns away then into a chur
Leading down toward the Slad Brook
And the new Slad Road

How come he there
It seems to be he moves by magick

For he has not walkd pass me

Yet seeing him disappear there
A memory does come back to me
Of that showman as did produce
The rolling eye Devil

So he did have that look to me

This region no one do generally go
It being many gardens rent from Church House

Yet all being degectd soild and mould ridden
With sheds slipping and flaking
As they tip toward the Brook

I step out after he

Such pokey yards are here
All crowd and pooling with mud

I turn on again heading down hill
The mud slipping under my boots
The light from above cut out
By the low hang of branches

Stepping past a pile of brokd ends
As must be kept by some scavenger man

Sudden I come through a gate round a corner
I am close to he

I duck into a doorway
Many chicken feathers spread cross the floor
The winders coverd with boards
Broken spades and tools proppd gainst the wall

From here I can see but not be seed
For the door is shroude by a hood of ivy

See Master Ned standing still
Looking all about
His head raisd
As a hound does taste the scent

Takes a key from his pocket and approaches
A low door half burid underground

This building I do know is calld Little Mill
Round about is some others not usd in many years
Now sinking low and rotten

He turns the key in the lock disappears inside

I do not know I do not understand
So turn then and walk back toward
The main way as does lead me back home

The path not so flockd going back

Walking home a hollow feeling came on me
Yet I could not say why
Perhaps twas but the end of a giddie day

Much later Lucetta did come back
Master Ned with her
He straight to his room

So so I think
He must have gone back in the town
She did tell him made him come
This I thought did shew
The strength of her character

That she could bring him so to the right path

Usually she and I would have sat long
In the farm kitchen to talk of all

Yet she was weary and strangely quiet
Her eyes downcast shaking her head
Said nothing of Master Ned

*

The next day risen was Sunday
So come all to Ruscombe Chapel
Master Ned looking clay cheekd and stretchd
Eyes heavy and dull
I see him watching Lucetta all the time

The sermon echo back and forth
When lust hath conceivd it bring forth sin
And sin when tis finishd
Bring forth death

Then later Master Ned is takd abed
An ague is what he say
Tis always the same tale

I go up with water and he says
Mary Ann Mary Ann Will you not fetch Lucetta

This is how he always is
Why can Lucetta not bring this or that

Usually I say naught about it
Yet now I try my tongue say
You know right well
Lucetta does not work in this house

434

He then is sharp with me
You do what you is told say no more

So so I go and find Lucetta
Who is out in the garden
With that Conker from the cottage
Playing at hoblionkers
With some as left ovr from last year

I hope she will say no
Then I shall be provd gainst he

But she says Oh yes of course

She should not have gone

Yet she goes up to him
Is there a long time

The day hot and shivering still
Breath gather choking at the throat
A slight disturbance ripple all the air
Like a pan of water just afore he boil

I went out into the garden
Lookd long cross the Valley
Prayd she would come down

What had she to discuss with he

Found myself imagine what she might talk about
Clothes cling hot about me sweat bead my lip
I wantd to think of her and I did not

When she does come down she is brimming up
Hold her cheek with her hand shake her head

Mary Ann Mary Ann she say to me
First looking around to check that no one hear
You will never think I know not what to say
Master Ned did ask me to marry he

My eyes fall open wide my jaw slack
Course I knew he did find her fair
As nearly all men did

I knew two or three at the mill
Had been in to see Mr Birch Nazareth
To talk to him of marriage

Yet she wanted none of them
I do not blame her
I saw two of them
One with jug ears and rabbit teeth
The other shorter than her by six inch

She say I said no course
I cannot Course I cannot
Yet he was most pressing
It were v ockerd

Said he spokd afore to Mr Birch Nazareth
Yet he cannot have
For I would have been told

Master Ned tells me I am all
Can save him
He loves me true
Will become a new made man
If only I will give my heart to he

But no no I cannot do that
He is takd up in matters are not right

Our friendship course is of value
Yet it can no a ways be more than that

I had never thought of such a thing
It does vex me much

This I know Lucetta does say in deepest honesty
Yet I cannot help but think
That only she who has such an innocent heart
Could have faild to comprehend

She say I have said to he
I am glad to offer assistance
But no no How could he have so misunderstood

Perhaps I should consider myself lucky
To be made such an offer as this
Yet Mary Ann you must see
You do see I am sure

Yes I see Of course
You cannot marry he

No she says No I cannot
I v sorry for he takes it hard
I am not interestd in marriage
Even if I were

Oh dear oh dear she say
She is all put about
Though she has much courage
I see that she is fearful
She will be in trouble
For saying no to he
A girl like her should be grateful
For such an offer

Should take it without question

I am sure she says if I talk to my uncle
He will understand He knows how things stand
It may be he employ for Mr Harland Cottrell
Yet he has always talkd fair with he

So she takes several deep breaths
And is gone

I am so top full of excitement fear shame
I know not what to do with myself

Imagine such a thing he should ask her
That she should say no to he

Soon after Nettie come downstairs so I tell her
For I must tell someone

As I speak I realize is some evil in me
Is glad to see him so rejectd

For the first time he will not have what he want
He can bend so many others to his will
But not her
So he shall see

Nettie shake her head pull down her mouth
Tip back and forwards hands flapping
Scratching always at the raw patches on her neck

Oh Mary Ann say she
You evr see only the good
Think all be put straight so with no trouble

Come come girl

So you are a fool
Do you not see what trouble now will come

The supper is late
Get on now stoke the range up
Get the potaters in the pot
Look to it

*

So that I think were that
Tis a vexing moment for all
No more will be said

I were secretly happy
For now I thought she will stay away from he
Make sure nothing further is misunderstood

But oh it were not so
The talk start slow
Perhaps it were always there
But I being the side of the Valley never hear

The first is Lucetta come home one evening
All slabber the front of her dress is muck
I thought she must have fallen but no

She was not one to cry
Yet she was close to tears when she said
They threw this at me

At first I could not believe it
She did not say more
I took the dress and wipd it with a cloth
Then bang at it with a brush
Hung it out by the glowing coals

Ah so that the mill I think
It were evr a place of ruffians and scallywags
Yet soon after the rumours rattld more

The tongue can no man tame
Tis an unruly evil full of deadly poison

She has temptd him He not the first
That I think the jug ear man say

Her behaviour is not proper
He only ask to take what is already his

So seems Master Ned not the only one
Misunderstood and read a wrong many things
How easily kindness can be takd for more

This I did also know but she never see

Another evening Lucetta come home looking beat
Chalk white and teeth clenchd

Find me water Mary Ann she say
I find it for her

She stands hands grippd to the back of a chair
As though she might fall
Yet says naught of what has come to pass
I am hurt to see her so

No sooner has she gone
Into the kitchen comes Mr Harland Cottrell
As soon as Master Ned is back he say
You must send he to me

Oh yes Sir I say

Then I think Surely rumour has not travelld
As far as Mr Harland Cottrell
Gone up through his ear trumpet

He was anyway as I make clear
Able to hear some noise like a mouse shuffle
Though not a drum banging

Maybe tis best it should be so
If Master Ned has spread false report
He could do that with no doubt
Then soon his father will tell him enough

Master Ned not come back that eve
But the next when he steps through the door
I tell him he must go straightway

What will be said now
I must know
I must protect Lucetta

The winders of Mr Harland Cottrells study are open
I stand close outside the garden
My back flat gainst the wall

I cannot hear all but I listen close

So so say Mr Harland Cottrell
You are enterd upon relations
With this girl is Mr Birchs niece
Such as can only lead to marriage

Master Ned say v quick
Twas her Sir
That I can tell you
She did lead me into temptation

There is a long silence
I am breathing rough with shock

How he suggest such a dishonour

Can imagine how Mr Harland Cottrell considers
The question his head upon one side
As I seed so many times afore

Then he say
I have no interest in any account
How this came to be
The fact is since you are come to this pass
You must marry this girl

That is the case whether you want her or not
If you do not then her reputation is staind
That you must not have upon yr honour

Perhaps Master Ned then movd to say something
I do not know I could not hear

All I hear is Mr Harland Cottrells voice
Calm and slow and firm
There is no question of what you want
Or what affections there are
You may not leave her in a situation of dishonour
She may be but a mill worker

Again there is some disturbance in the room
A rustle a silence
Words I do not hear

Then again Mr Harland Cottrell say
You should have thought more careful
Afore you broke the laws of the Lord

You take now what comes to you
I have no doubt you and she
Can make something of yr situation

I hear some movement at the back of the house
Pray God tis not Nettie come to look for me
I turn from the winder back through the garden
My ears and heart burning

How can all be so mixd up and mismatchd
How can Mr Harland Cottrell think that
He offer Lucetta salvation
Through marriage to his son

My head is turning and turning
With the thought of it
Yet I have not reachd the door
Afore Lucetta comes
Pulls me in gainst the wall
We both stand there gasping for breath

Her eyes are wet her mouth set firm

When she can speak she say
Mr Birch Nazareth said I am to marry he

No I say No

Lucetta shakes her head wipes at her eyes
He says that I am compromisd
Tis said everywhere that he and I
We are already a marrid couple
In all but name

He said my reputation is brought low
No other man will have me

I must take him while I may

But who says these things I cry

I do not know she says
Master Ned it must be he
Yet others there are plenty
Who take up the hue and cry
Like hounds they are on a scent
Keening and baying repeating also
What they know is not true

I am weeping myself now
How can such things be said
How can she who is so pure and good
Be use so

I cannot say more for Nettie shouts
Mary Ann Mary Ann You lazy varmint
Where are you now

I must go I say

Afore I can move Lucetta
Catches hold my arm
Her fingers dug in deep my flesh
Her eyes are sparking sudden

Know this Mary Ann Know this
I will not marry he
I will not
I would rather die

Nettie shout Mary Ann Mary Ann
You lazy little worm get you here now

I step again toward the back door
There is Nettie waving a pan at me

Sudden I know I cannot enter that room
Cannot stand there and make the supper
Tis beyond what I can abear

So I walk in and say
Nettie you must get the supper yrself
I have important affairs to attend to
I walk out again cross the yard
Going to find the only person
Who I know will help

Ambrose has only just finishd his supper
Still he steps out with me
We go to stand by the pump
Where we have oft stood afore
At least standing here
I can appear to be drawing water
If anyone asks

I do not need to tell the story much to he
He already knows all and more

What can she do I say
Who will bring these lies to an end
Ambrose you must know
Who I must speak to

I want him to be part of my anger
Yet he only shakes his head

I think Mary Ann there is little you can do

Yet she cannot marry he

Ambrose shrugs and raises his eyebrows

No no she cannot do it I say
What is said is not true

It matters not now what is true and what not
Ambrose say
You know Mary Ann
How this does go

This is now the story told gainst her
He will be believd she will not

Tis true many know Master Neds true metal
Yet there are also plenty drawn by he
He has a way with he
You know it well

Many at the mill simple desperd
He has a talent for sending words
True as an arrow straight to the heart
He spin a net catch them in

Such is my anger I am near to shout at he
So you think this is right

No I do not think it right
But Mary Ann she is but a chit
A pretty chit and clever
Aye too clever for her own good
She thinks to make her own rules
Yet that she cannot do
Now she has but two choice
Either she marry him to save her honour
Or she journey far away from the Valleys
Far enough people do not hear whisper

Of the stain upon her

No I say No She cannot go away

Ambrose looks straight shakes his head

You I say You you
How you usd to talk about a new world
Promotd now to such a high position
Perhaps you do forget

You think what happens here
Is right

I do not think it right Mary Ann he say
When new worlds come
Matters will not be organizd this way
Will not be such as powerless as she

Yet I am not talking of new worlds
Am talking of the strife ridden tarnishd world
In which we poor souls are condemnd to live now
He is a gentlemans son

He says those words with contempt

She is but a cheap girl as works in the mill
With no connections no name

I am shouting now
Do you think Tell me this
Do you think what is said of her is true

Ambrose rolls his eyes a little thinks on this
I would like to smash his head

I think says he she has been unwise
She is a fair and well made girl
Knows how to use all that to her advantage

He lays then his hands on my shoulders
Which he must well do
For my feet near lift off the ground
Such is my wrath

Yet since you ask me No No
I do not think that of her
Deep inside she is Christian and moral

Yet of what importance is this now
She ought to marry when she first come here
Instead of stirring up the men as she has done
No tis not her fault
She does not deserve this
Yet why do we speak of this
She is undone that is all

My anger now gives way to tears
I may not abear what he says
I cannot stand tis true

Do you not care I say
Do you find no sadness in yr heart

For a long time he says nothing
I turn away ready to go back to the house

Then I feel his hand on my shoulder

Mary Ann he says
I know she is yr friend
I know you love her

STOCTON HILL

I am sorry deeply sorry
It has come to this

If I could make the world other than what tis
Could I help you I would
You know that

I cannot turn to look at he but put my hand up
Lay it for a moment ovr his hand
The weight of which still rests on my shoulder

Then his hand slides away
I walk back to the house
Without looking back

I do not want to go in the kitchen
Yet where else can I go

I know what will happen there
Nettie will laugh and rock and cough
She will say something about
How no good will come of all that blond hair
How Lucetta is a scurry lass
Who gets what she deserve

This is what I expect
Yet when I walk in the door Nettie is silent
She does not ask me do this do that
So I sit down at the table
Sink my head down on the boards

Around me I hear her
The pans clatter the ladles bang
The door of the range slams
Boots kick gainst the back of a chair

I no a ways thought she to share my anger
But she does and more

Together we could blow kitchen to sticks
Such is the storm of our rage

Finally she say Go you to Mr Birch Nazareth
See what he may say

So I goes back cross the yard again
Knock on the door Mr Birch Nazareths cottage
Up above me I know is Lucetta

Take a long minute afore he open
Stares at me as though he barely know me

Please Mr Birch Nazareth I say
I must speak again to Lucetta

No Mary Ann he say shake his head firm
I know you mean well
But she must stay where she is confind
May not see you or anyone else

He sees then the anger and sorrow in my face

I am v sorry say he
You must believe me I try to do what is best
Now go you back and say no more of it
Lucetta now must travel the route
She map out for herself

I stare him straight in the eye
Brimming again with anger
How can he say what is best
What route she map when she does naught

I turn away without saying good night
Go then back to the kitchen

Nettie does not ask for she knows

Together we get the supper done
As we must

*

That night I hear Lucetta
As I lie abed eyes gazing wide
Rage still ramping in my blood

First tis a gentle tap
At the bottom of the ladder
Then the whispering hook of the voice
Mary Ann Mary Ann

In haste I pull myself up and climb out
Little thought to Nettie
Sleeps like a heap of stone
Come quick to the top of the ladder

Below I see the moon of her face
Hanging there in the darkness

Quick she says Get clothes come down
I have need of you

Afore the hand of the clock move one jolt
I have my clothes on carry my boots in my hand
Come silent down the steps

Already she has gone on
Is half way toward the kitchen

I follow place foot gentle
Mr Harland Cottrell will not wake
Yet Master Ned is in the house and might
Lucetta is holding my coat and a warm shawl

Tis only then I notice the cloth bag
As makes a small pile by the door
Tis hers

No No I say No I will not No

Mary Ann she say Please We cannot talk here
Come come pulling out the lane
Carrying that bag with her
Til we are clear of the house

But I will go no further
No No No I say

I must she says What choice do I have
Come Come Mary Ann she say
For I am weeping like a flowing stream

I will do v well
I shall go back to Oxfordshire
To the school where I usd to be
The lady there knows me well
She will find a place for me
I shall be a Monitor

No No No I say
That word seems all can come from me

Mary Ann twill not be for long
I will write to you
Sometime we will meet

It can be done

No I say No No
You must take me with you now I say
Twill take but a moment
Let me gather my clothes

No Mary Ann No
It cannot be You know that
Of course I would want that
Yet I shall struggle to find a place for myself
I cannot find one for you as well
I shall send word as I see a way

Mary Ann come now find courage
Tis not so bad
We shall meet again
I shall make sure of it
But please please help me now
I cannot carry this bag so far

We must leave now for the cart does depart
At cock crow and we must get up the hill
Tis well the other side of Stroud
Help me now please I beg of you

So I calm my tears string the bag tween
She one handle I tother
We set out stumbling hard
For the moon is lost
The stars shade
Not a sign of the dawn

I remember it always
That dark and drear night
Our footsteps splashing and stumbling

453

A fine rain sprinkle ovr us
Til it gather and run
On face and hands

The bag swinging tween us
She not stopping for any reason
The rhythm of her steps firm and true

So I go with her
All along the way past the silent mills
Even the babble of the stream blunt
Hardly the shuffle of a hoof
As we pass stables and barns

Even at this hour distant bang of fulling stock

Comes at first to the hill leads to the town
Yet Lucetta takes hold the bag more firmly says
We not go that way We might be seed

Tis true for in this all unbalancd time
The watch is always ready
Constables pace the streets

So turn along the Slad Brook round the back
Taking then the new road
Passing that Little Mill
Where I was but days afore
A coming around the back of Church House
All the gardens there

Seeing beside us the church spire
The mass of the buildings round
Yet going on the hill painful sharp
Our boots sliding our hands numb
For it were cold though zummer

Finally we come to the ridge and see below
The Valley of Stroudwater where runs the Frome
The many trees mass down in the green depths

This the Valley I did see in childhood
As Ambrose and I playd high up
Near the Drybrook cottages
But a few fields from The Heavens

Yet this is not all for first we must down
Then steep up again

No time to spare for the first grey light
Bloom now on the distant high horizon

So steep you must huff and puff and pull
The bag dragging us back sweat rising
I have walkd it afore but only in the light

Then into the trees and up the final pitch
Long long I would stop and catch my breath
Yet she goes on though the handles of bag dig
Our legs heavy complaining sore

Come finally to the white iron gates of this
Mount Vernon I know it now
Yet at the time twas nothing to me
Just a coach house ahead but the house itself
Hid down the curve of the track

Cross the new yeller road
On on til finally we come out on the roof
Where the land flatten are many quarries
They dig stones for the roads

This be a place well knowd for bandits

Thieves ghosts and evil spirits
Yet Lucetta care naught for that
She has told me many a time
That such spirits do not exist
Are but for ignorant people

So she say yet I am not so sure

Seeing my fear and weariness
She does quote me then from those sermons
We did so oft read together

That we stay here only one days abode
Our age no longer than a flie
So we look somewhere else for an abiding city
Another country in which we fix our house

Then she does lay a hand gentle on my arm
Not more than another mile Mary Ann she say

I do not want to arrive
I want to walk forevr with her here
As the dawn breaks light rolling in
Come far from the distant horizon
Touch some more distant peak

The air giving up the darkness
The shapes of bush and tree
Drawn black and clear now
The road ahead unravel
Like a spool of canary thread
Taking me always away

So we walk high road on and on
My heart is crying out within me
As finally we come to the Bear of Rodborough

This is that same inn
Where I did come first in this country
I have heard spokd of but never seed again
In this long time

Others now are gatherd near the inn
Lucetta is afeard to go too close
For someone might recognize
Refuse to let her go

Most of these others wait the coach
Yet Lucetta has not money for that
Instead she will take the fish cart
As comes this way just afore the coach
This she know for tis the way
She first came here three years afore

Those three years the blessd of my heart

I am praying the cart might not come
Or that twill be long delayd
I might yet climb aboard with her

Yet we hardly arrivd afore the distant
Rhythm of hooves heard along the yeller road
Some stand back at this time
As the smell of fish is sharp
But Lucetta waves out her hand
Cart does come rolling to stop
Horse blowing harness champing

Perhaps I think the man might want
To stop for a glass of ale a slice of bread
That will take a while
But no such mercy is

I am weeping again shaking now
Yet Lucetta catches hold of me grips me tight

Courage Mary Ann Courage
We are sisters so we shall never be partd
This is but a brief separation
When I have a new position
I shall have some money
When a holiday comes

Trust you in the Lord with all yr heart
Lean not on yr own understanding

Now now do not cry so
I will write you

Please now do not make me leave you so

When she says I take a pull upon myself
She suffers too I must not make worst

So I cease my crying say farewell
Godspeed Good luck I wish you well
You shall make a fine teacher
We shall meet again soon

So I say as we kiss again
Then the carter says
Come come now lasses adry yr tears

He a merry facd man in a staind apron
With bristles come out his ears
Throws up her bag
She soon to follow
Put up on the back
Out the way of the dripping fish

STOCTON HILL

Lies shiny under loose tied sheet
Blank eyd silver glittering
Still hold the silent depths of the river
Even in their death

Where she sits I hope the smell may be less

Then the cart is gone
Though her dove flickering hand wave long
As it disappear into the damp unrolling dawn
The mist still thick on either side
Fading and fading
Even the sound of the hooves gone

I left standing at the side of the road
All life draind from me
Cold cold cold

Til I come to myself and realize
I must back to Stocton Hill
Already I will be missd

So I walk all that long way back
Through the yawning Valleys
Where horses is put in harness
Cows is brought in pails is emptid
Dogs bark children run to get milk
All unknowing

I make good progress stride well
Keep my head up my lips pressd tight
Yet the inside of me is teard out

MOUNT VERNON

This now tis enough
My ink does run dry
Have writ all I can

Am too tird to go on

That were the end of my life

Oh that it were true

I spend now the afternoon outside
The ovr growd garden of this Mount Vernon
In the extremity of heat
Warm well my old bones

There amidst all the crowding green
Find some treasure moments of peace

Later as the sun spreads wide and colours
All the horizon like fields of golden flowrs
I get up go in the house
Needing some water to drink

Soon as I come in the door

I know someone other also
Has enterd this place

I feel a disturbance in the air

'Twill be the boy I think
Sure enough as I go down the kitchen
I see him there putting out on the table
Bread eggs and milk

Though now the boy does look at me in fear
I think then for the first time
How all this world must look to he

This fine house running now all to ruin
This old crone the only one to care
Small and stoopd not much bigger than he
Thin as twine
For so I am

Come come I say to calm his fritcheting
Will you not take some milk yrself

He shakes then his dark head
Holds one sapling arm with the other
His head shaggy with black curls
Mouth wide and ripe lips
Always near to laughter
That same look I know so well

Also bold now it seem
For sudden he does say

Mrs may I ask you a question

Course you may boy say I

Taking out a cup for milk
I shall have some even if he not

So as I pour the milk he say as he must
Is it true you can remember
The revolutionary Mr Ned Cottrell

The name drops into the room gently
Yet it seems to echo long

For I am told the boy says
Still twisting his arms but speaking bold
His brother does now live in this house

Who tell you this I say
My hand not steady with the jug

My father say it but also boys at school
Tis talkd of sometimes all he did

Aye aye I say I do remember he

I realize then I should say more
The boy does expect it
He wants a tale to tell in the school yard
Yet what else is there to say

The silence does unnerve the boy
So he says thankee v much
Turns toward the kitchen steps

Thankee he says again
I shall come back afore too long
Then he is gone and I am sad

I should have said more

For what does it matter what he knows
What he believes

The story he has heard has become true
Twas all so long ago

I drink the milk put down the cup

He meant no harm yet his question
Has set my mind tumbling again

Hear again my Masters voice

Whatevr guilt there is
You have yr share in it

All would have been well
If only you had been loyal

Is that not true Mary Ann
Is it not true

Look in upon him now
Firm in sleep still lost

I am glad of it

Oh Mr Ned Cottrell the famous revolutionary
Saviour of many and engine of progress

Perhaps they do say
That he was a hero
Maybe they are not wrong

Yet what of the others
What of the costs

Those are the stories history never writes
Only the pressing onwards stride of progress
So tis understood

What of those who blockd the forward way
Whose struggles came to naught
Who fought on the side of defeat

Who will evr speak for them
When will their voices be heard

STOCTON HILL

After she has gone
I care not what happen to me
I am finishd with
My life done

Or so I think
Such are the passions of the young

I come close a beating that first morning
Mr Birch Nazareth does want me beat
So he says to Mr Harland Cottrell

You fool Mr Birch Nazareth say to me
Maybe you think to help but you shall see
Now you watch the way the world unfurl
You are but the ruin of she

Yet Mr Harland Cottrell not beat me

Nay nay he say
Mary Ann God Bless her soul
She has barely the sense of a dog
If someone tell her to do something
So she does it

Nettie also say to Mr Birch Nazareth
She is but a simple girl
You cannot blame such as she
Tis well known not just her face is wrong

So she makes various obscene hand signs
All to imply I am but an imbecile

I do not care
Even if they beat me it means nothing
Part of me should like a beating
One pain might kill another
So I think

All round make false report of Lucetta
Call her a slany Jezebel strumpet
Flowsing hussy trollop

The flight she make taked as evidence of guilt
Soon it be widely agreed
We are best done with her

I keep my mouth tight shut
Feel the poison of their spite
Deep within me

So the days toil on
Light dark pull heavy one after tother
Like a plough sticks in mud

That zummer never does come good
The rain keep a coming
As the wind does piffle and whistle
Tear down all is plantd
What will winter bring

I do not care It suits my mood

Yet in all this the worst is Master Ned
He is a sight you cannot believe
Meeking he goes and palely weeping
Oft takd sick with fever
Maybe even a true fever this
Who can know

His father say his heart is brokd
Others say also Aye aye she did play with he
Tis the sickness of love

Oft I am in his room taking water tending fire
He says to me he cannot live without her
That he must go and find her

What can I say

At first I take no notice of he
So tight am I with anger

Yet the more I see him
How weak he is how hurt and pale
I do begin to wonder

Does he really feel what I feel
Did he really love her so
When I see him I think it could be true

But it cannot be
No no it cannot

For he was the one did blacken her name
He did destroy her and yet now
Calls out for her in the night

Tis beyond what I can understand
But twas evr so with he

*

The winter come in and strike the land hard
Though tis but October snow come down
So it stay for many long days

Even the stream at the bottom
Is only a thin trickle
Running through blocks of ice

The land still white silent aching
All move slow the blood throbbing sore
In hands and feet

Nettie is took sick her bellers filld up
Coughing and coughing
No chance to sleep

Mr Harland Cottrell cannot get out
For he is feard to go down on the ice
So only I must carry on
Breaking the ice from the paths
Carrying wood to keep the fire alight

No money now for beeswax candles
Only tallow made of hog
Which fills the house
Devil smelling thick black smog
Settles heavy in the lung

We are all famishd
There is only bread made from barley
Sour hard eat with pairy cheese

Maybe a dunch dumpling if you lucky

Mr Birch Nazareth bring not now the meat he did
For he also is takd hard

Tis generally thought he is a man
Who has never had wife or family of his own

Yet Lucetta had tell privily
This is not so

He was marrid when he was young
His wife takd in child birth but one year on
The child also

So Lucetta she did give him much joy

Always a jug with field daisies on the table
The linen kept white crisp the winders shining

No doubt he did look to see her wed
Grandchilders to play round his hearth
Now twill not be so

Tis clear who Mr Birch Nazareth blame for this
For now he never speak a word to Master Ned

If Nettie or I mention his name
He does growl and shake his head

Yet at this time tis only Master Ned
Who does help keep our spirits living
For he is now a little recoverd

Setting up a girt complaint
For the changes in the Poor Law

Tis most unjust
For none is meant to take food out
Any who wants assistance
Must go in the Workhouse
Families all split up

But Master Ned and some other defy this law
Even Mr Harland Cottrell agree this is right
For why can they not be givd bread
In their own homes

So so the talk goes on but I not listen much

Instead I stand oft in the garden
Stare cross to the place last I last saw her
Though tis too far to see

All is clothd in white mist thick as smoke
Only the darker lines where the trees are
Above the skye stretch up to eternity
No mercy to be found in it

*

Spring eternally come slow and damp
The fields still brim full of water
The sun too weak to soak up

More and more is the talk of a strike
It must come

All say what a mystery tis the clothiers
Why are they not afeard

Do they not know what happend in France
Soon all their slicd and bloody heads

Be pild up in baskets

I do not like such talk

In the end the strike never does come
Instead machines one night are brokd up
It happens at several mills up the Valleys
Pitchcombe Rock being two

The v next day the constables
Do come to the house and ask for Master Ned

Mr Harland Cottrell is away from home
But mercy Mr Birch Nazareth is with us
He go out to them for Nettie and me
We are much afeard

I do not know what is said
I am sure Mr Birch Nazareth
Never tell Mr Harland Cottrell their visit

So so say Nettie Look now what comes to he
Who was always intend for some higher purpose
So sneers she

That evening we hear more
For Ambrose does come to sit in the kitchen
Tells us straight how he did mention Master Ned
To the constables

This does shock me deep
Though I cannot say he has done wrong

Ambrose say he was left with no choice
Master Ned his tongue will stir up ignorant
Yet he will vanish soon as dust

They like sheep follow one after the other
Ovr the edge of the cliff

Also though he does not say this
Ambrose now is in a yet higher position
Having excellent skills in all manner of carpentry
Such is needed for the maintenance
Of the many carding and spinning machines
So must shew his loyalty to Mr Fluck

I do not criticize he for it
For he always has time for Nettie and me

The next day Master Ned announces
He is leaving for Bristol
Has got a new job there

I do not know whether all this
Is but the weaving together of circumstance
Or whether there is more to know

Soon after several is arrestd one transportd
Others is on the burster at Horsley

Yet tis important to record
At several mills at this time wages are raisd
So tis not true to say it were all for naught

Mr Harland Cottrell in his oft perversity
Take Master Neds departure as good news
I also am glad to see him go
Pack his things in a bag
Say naught as he leaves

Yet after he has gone I find myself sorry
Only because the house is even quieter

472

Just me and Nettie sometimes Mr Birch Nazareth

Other people have some grip on life
Yet it flows past me
And I watch
That is all

*

Then a message come for me
A letter arrive to the George
I go to fetch it

I hold it in my hands a long time
Afore I am able to open it
I have never had a letter afore

In the letter Lucetta says how she has a job now
Is an assistant teacher share a room
With another such

I hate her for it
So her life goes on and mine does not
Soon she will call that other teacher
Sister dear sister as once she call me
That other teacher will brush her hair
As once I did

Soon as I think it I hate myself
I am glad she is happily settld

The cold still biting even as April enters
Then come three days of storms
Battering raging and tearing
Pull up several ancient oaks
Tear roots deep from the soil

Which were not so bad
As one of the chimbleys at Stocton Hill
Blew half off

The stones spread cross the garden
What fortune no one was killd

Tis just after I finish to clear the stones
That I happens to meet Ambrose

Ah ah Mary Ann he say to me
I am sorry to see you look so poor

I suppose so I do look
What with the want of vittels

But that is all his sympathy afore he say
What can I say to you though
You will stay here
Though there is no life for you
You know it well

Why you not look to yr own affairs

Ambrose has said many such ovr several years
Usually I do not listen

Now his words do join my own questions
I begin to think on it

You can go to Pitchcombe he say
I will find work for you there Mary Ann
There are places you can live
Not so grand as this farm
But a deal more comfort

So he say and his words grow in my mind
What is there to stay here now Lucetta gone

Master Ned and Master Blyth also
The house gradually falling down
With little to eat and nothing to mark
One day from the next one year from tother

Netttie I owe her nothing
She has no a ways likd me

The thoughts grow and grow

Tis the small things some time
Which bring the change
For me twas Nettie a coming well again
So getting up and checking my work

So Mary Ann I see you not black the grate
The yard is not swept
Cobwebs up on the landing ceiling

So she goes on and on
This has always been so but now my anger
It gathers and gathers
So one day my mind is set

I speak to Ambrose he say
So at last you come to yr senses
Course I shall make arrangements

Then two days later he says tis done
A position is found for me at Pitchcombe
Tis picking wool which I done afore
So many years ago with Mrs Freda Woebegone

A respectable woman in Painswick
Does offer me also a bed

So my mind is made up

The day I choose
Is the first of strong sun
I feel the life in me rising
Thinks to myself
Why did I not do this years ago

Mr Harland Cottrell I say knocking at his door
Please may I speak with you
For all my courage still I am shaking

Then I must shout again
To make he hear

Come come he say
When I open the door see him there
As I have seed him so many times afore
Sitting bent at his desk
I am sudden full of regret
For his grey hair swept back
His gold rim eye glasses
His long fingers and fixing stare
All are so familiar to me
I remember all his kindness

Yet still I am decide I must go on
I must not hesitate say it all in one breath
Shouting v loud as he has not his trumpet

Sir I am decide I shall leave here
They have work for me at Pitchcombe
This will be a better situation for me

Sudden he stand up
I was not prepard for the shock upon his face

Mary Ann Mary Ann What talk is this

I am sorry Sir but so I must

No no no he say
Who put such nonsense in yr head
You must not go to any mill
Beezlebub hisself walks these paths

My knees is shaking now my voice thin
So it may be Sir yet my mind is made up

His hand come crashing down on the desk
No No So you will not
I do forbid it
This is yr home has always been
You are need here

I understand Sir but I must

No No No I cannot believe such base ingratitude
You have lodging here this long year
I take you as part of my family despite all
Now this is how I am repaid

I am truly grateful Sir for all you do
That I am but you must understand Sir
I should like to be paid for my work

I find it hard to believe my own voice
Do I speak these words

At this he seems to swell up and grow

I think he might burst out his own skin
Then the air goes out of him shoulder sag
Shakes his head back and forwards rubs his chin

Mary Ann Mary Ann I had not thought you to be
A person so interestd in money

These words make my ire rise again
I will go on I will say what I want despite he

Then he seems to think a little
Tis true he say then
Not right I do not offer you any wage
Yet Mary Ann you can see how I am placd
From where would I find such money

I thought you would understand that I here
Am engagd on many works to the Glory of God
For the advancement of His people
For the understanding
Of the natural philosophy of this His creation
As such the case I have no thought of money

I say nothing to this
What I could say is perhaps he should
Spend less time on God advancement philosophy
Manage better his affairs

For though there is no money
He have still sometimes new shirt and shoes
Books arriving in parcels from London
We feed the soul if not the body
So he say

What is no money to some people
Is v much to others

STOCTON HILL

But I say none of that

Sudden he turns from me bitterly says
Go then go and do not come again
I am bitterly disappointd in you
If you want to go to the Devil
That is yr business

So I leave the room shaking
Twas all much worse than I thought
I am sorry we have argud
But I am through it and free
I am going now

So only Nettie to deal with now
That is done quickly

Walk in the kitchen and say
I am leaving here Nettie
I go to work at Pitchcombe

She stands there with her vast jaw open
Her chins wobbling as her head goes side to side
Then she is gone to Mr Harland Cottrell
What will they say I wonder

Soon as I think it I do not care
The sun is dancing as I walk up to the attic
Takes not ten minutes
To put my possessions together
I have no bag so wrap them in a shawl

Place careful the little basket
Lucetta did make for me of her hair
Also the glass bead jewel bracelet
Placd within that now

The button from the chemise of Baby Fern
Which I have always kept

Also a shawl Ambrose give me
Once at Christmas tide too precious to wear
The kerchief of Mr Woebegone
All wrappd together now

Then I come downstairs
The house is silent I love it then
As I lovd it the first few years I come here

Tis hard but I must not delay
So I step out the back door
Head down the lane not look back
Though terror grips my soul

Yet I have not gone many steps
When I hear the voice of Mr Harland Cottrell

Mary Ann Mary Ann
Tarry a moment if you please
I stop and turn to him
There is a deep kindness in his face
He stretch out both white hands toward me

Tis only then I notice how his waistcoat
Is buttoned up all crookd
How this does appear to make him stand
All pushd to one side
Comic and sad both

Why does he never notice such as this

Mary Ann I am truly sorry
I should not have spoke to you as I did

I was hasty and unkind
I faild to acknowledge all yr kindness
Given as twas ovr many good and bad years

Thankee Sir I say

Yet I am thinking tis better when he shout
For what now can I say

Please Mary Ann he say Please reconsider
Where will I be without you
Who else would evr serve me as you have done
Please will you not think on this

Tis hard then v hard yet still I say
I am sorry Sir I do not wish to leave you
That I do not and I remember all yr kindness
Yet I must be paid for my work
Even such as me must be paid

Mr Harland Cottrell throw hands in the air
His lock of white hair blowing wild
Of course he say Of course
You are quite right
But here then let me make a suggestion

I wait then for his suggestion
I will not take it whatevr tis
I am going I will go Tis all decide

Mary Ann how say you to this
You work in the mill and then you have money
Yet you still live at the farm here
You help us out just some time
Perhaps when the work is too much for Nettie

This I had not foreseed
I do not know what to say
Yet what he proposes answers my every question

I feel myself weakening
I must not I must not
But what argument is there gainst this

Thank you Sir I say
I must certainly consider this offer

My mind is moving fast
I know not now where the words come from

However Sir I say
I do not like share a room with Nettie
Perhaps another could be found

Yes Yes Mr Harland Cottrell say
His eyes brightening much
That was v much my thinking Mary Ann
Yes yes I had oft thought this
Was on the verge of mentioning it to you
In fact why do you not come with me now
We consider what arrangements be made

So I follow him back to the house
Immediately he takes me up to the landing

Here he say here
Flings open a door has not been open
In many a long time

As the door open mice scurry out the mattress
Soon we see the ceiling hanging down

Ah ah say Mr Harland Cottrell
Um um Yes Well there we are

I biting my lip to stop myself laughing
Tis a long time since such mirth rose in me
A sudden love also for he
Stand there so v grand to offer me this room
With its mice cobwebs dust

Ah yes he say Yes
Obviously we have to look to some improvements
But there we are Mary Ann

You are excellent at cleaning
Putting things straight
You would be able to get it better
In no time at all
What say you

Course I had to say yes
It were not the room I card not for that
It were him finally
I could not say him Nay

For though he was selfish and foolish
Yet I lovd him still
I did not want to go

That eve in the kitchen
Nettie would not speak one word to me
I was glad to have frightd her

Though truth is I would have been
Sad to take my leave of her
Though I did not like her nor she me

So that night I went to sleep in the mouse room
Having first some cleaning found a mattress

Afore I went abed I stood by the winder
Lookd out into the blackness and smild
My mouth hardly knew to smile twas so long

I thought then of Lucetta
I knew she would be proud of me
For I had a new job but also stay where I belong

In truth it were down to her
She had given me the strength for this
As she had given others their strength
Made the light of God shine in them

Even though she were gone
We were all touchd by her still

So this then the beginning of my new life
I step out into the flow of the river
Watch no more

*

Course had been to Pitchcombe afore
Yet so tis different once you are inside

Tis a place of iniquity so all chorus say
Yet certainly at the beginning
I am spinning with the joy of it

The noise cracks yr ears
Ground a jumping under yr feet
Yr mind dubbld by it

Due to the fall of the fulling stocks
The whole building shake ceiling to floor

All must shout til their voices is adry
All is dust dirt hurry

Oft I am think Mr Harland Cottrells question
Does the man work the machine
Or the machine work the man
It seems a question worth to ask

Meet there such I have never met afore
Israelite Spanish with rings in his ears
Even one who has no hair being burnt in a fire

If we do not meet the orders
Soon there will be none more
So does Mr Fluck say
Oh many a time

That where the looms are
Yet I am in the picking room
Less furious just a little
We are many women

Work at opening first the girt sacks
Spring open with a bang
Spreading dust and grease everywhere

Wool is sent even from Australia

Then banging this wool to get the dirt out
Afore tis washd in troughs
The floor always slipping wet

The room gaping and winders high up

Cakd with dust

The only advantage being the wool is grease
So keeps yr hands oild soft

The first day I arrive a problem straightway
She cannot work here one say
Does not have the height to reach

I am afeard then for tis true
The trestle is high
Yet one steps forward bold
I know her later is Emma

Nay nay she says
Go fetch one of those crates
In which they keep the bobbins Go
So a child goes comes back with a crate
When I am stood on that
Emma send up a cheer all laugh
So I am startd

Course there is drinking and swearing
Many engage in seditious talk

Such as one Mad Dog Harvey
Who is but half savd
Cannot see what is the difference
So he say betwixt our new Queen
And a washerwoman
Why they not be treatd with equal respect

Let her put a sign ovr her door
Viva Regina Washerwoman Mangler to the Community
Then I have respect for her

STOCTON HILL

We all do laugh though we should not

A narrow passage round the back
Up where the cloth is stretchd to dry
Where you do not go

Tis said there you see
Men tug up womens skirts
Pulling at their britches
Pushing and groaning no better than animals
It would sicken yr heart to see it

Also much courting of the proper kind
But even that I do not like to see
How girls do make such fools of theysselfs
Tis none of it for me

Our foreman is a hard man
Shouts at any who stop work
Even to wipe their brow

Yet for me life is not so bad as some
For Ambrose now is raisd
Keeps an eye for me
All know it take care

The rough girls on the line Betty Kate Annie
They says to me Oh you have a fancy man upstairs
I do not mind their jests

As Ambrose is a fine man now of good position
I do not speak much to he or tother way about
Yet there is a memory betwixt us of other times

One day on the line all is tird and broke
We must keep on to beat the hazel twigs down

Yet all is degectd run adry

So speaks Emma and say
Is there no one can tell us a tale

So I say I will and starts
Soon a silence falls
Even the foreman listening
At the end many do say
What a fine way of words you have
What a story you do tell

Which makes me shine happy

After that many a time I do tell stories
Oft shouting above the noise

I am never without one to tell
For I remember each penny blood or novel

Mother Bucks Fairy Tales The Pig Faced Lady
The Poisoning of Fair Rosamund by Queen Eleanor
Johnny Armstrong How he Fought and Fell

Tell again all those stories
Add many more of my own
Speaking in all the voices of the character
Describing so we are all transportd there

Even the foreman say naught
For he can see all works better
If we do pass the time this way

Aye for a while it seem a fine life

For I have money I never afore

New dress new boots button smart
Take home to Stocton Hill pork and potaters
For Nettie and me

Buy myself a hair ribbon
Give a few pennies to Emma for her childers
Make her some time stewd ox cheek
Or a pot of stirabout

For she no a ways does have any meat
Not even tripe or slink or broxy
Can her money run that far

Yet she is always my friend and defender
Turns her snake tongue on any hissing woman
Who does mock or spite me

Buy wool stockings for Nettie
For her feet is v swelld

I do this for Lucetta did once do the same
I like to do as she has done

Nettie say You fool to waste yr money
Yet I know her now and see
How she does cradle those stockings
When she thinks I do not see

Still in the eve when I get home
It be late but I help in the kitchen and clean
Not so much for there is no time
Truth to say Mr Harland Cottrell not care
As long as he has a fire and supper

Rain running in and mould growing
All where the chimbley is brokd

Yet still I like to be there

Sometimes also sit in the evenings
When all is done
Hold the lamp close
Read a few lines to Mr Harland Cottrell

His eyes going milky and cakd up
Mind running oft ovr the same track
Again and again

For in this way his kindness come back to he
That he did teach me to read and write
Which no other person would have
So now I can do this service for he
Which is blessd comfort

You plant kindness so kindness grow
Though it may take many a long year
Afore you have yr kindness back

This I should like to believe

I see all his weaknesses and frailties
Still it gives me pleasure see him by the fire
His is a life livd close to our Lord

This no one may gainsay

                              *

During those first years at Pitchcombe Mill
I have quite oft a letter from Lucetta
They bring word to me from the George
To tell me so

Lucetta is fine settld now and training
For to be a teacher

I also do write back to she
Mr Harland Cottrell giving me the paper

Some of the pain and anger goes
Yet not the missing of her
Which will always be sharp
Still the letters bring some comfort

In my mind I am always planning
When it comes Whitsun perhaps
I could take the fish cart as she did take
Go and see her
Yet the journey so long
I do not know when twill be

Still the letters come from Master Blyth
Mr Harland Cottrell start to open them now
His anger has died now some
He does not say much yet hands them to me
Words from London town of the hospitals there
The work which is never at an end
In streets where are many poor and uneducatd
Terrible sickness they are crowd close
So the letters say

Though it also clear to see
What a success does Master Blyth make
Of this course which he has chosd
Attending many lectures and demonstration
Soon offerd a much prestigious position

Also Master Ned does write sometimes
But those letters I do not see

I do not need to for I hear oft
Even see him sometimes
He comes to a meeting at the mill
Raise his hat to me
When he sees me walking by

I say Good morning to you Sir
Hope you are keeping well
He gives me that smile
As he smild when he was a boy
Full of laughter and light
Say Oh yes Mary Ann thank you
V well and busy about this
Important and God givd work

So he nods again and smiles
Raises his hat with a flourish
Making me think of the cloakd man
Who did raise the Devil
In that strange place
Maybe the past maybe a dream

For I know and he knows
Tis knowd everywhere
That though he works for the factor
Does buy sell cloth up and down these Valleys
Then goes to Bristol and takes more orders there
He is also taking chap books with he
Some as come from the London Working Men
These he distributes all round

These are read much in the yard
Round about some even go in the fields
Proclaiming so with hand on chest
For them as cannot read theysselfs

Also talk of whether force be just
What may be done in the girt struggle to come

Reading also from that book Mr Thomas Paine
As many have been imprisond for the spreading
Like poor Mr Abel Woebegone
The words theysselfs a breathless magic
You start to read you want for more

Many at the mill fall upon this talk
For they have no education and all for them
Is bloody struggle break all down
Afore you build again

Always they are threatening
The evil they shall visit on that Mr Fluck
Which I cannot say surprise
For sure he is an unyielding man

Such as Ambrose do not care for this
You must shew yrself respectable
Make clear that you can be trustd
These wild schemes only bring working men
Into disrepute

These folk in London Birmingham Manchester
He say and so do some others
Tis only dreams and cloud building puff
What chance is there they give the vote
To those who have naught
Why should them who own no land
Be given a say in what is done

Such as Ambrose also place girt faith
In Mr Miles who is sent from London
To enquire into the condition

Of those many weavers as without work

I listen to these debates close
So when Ambrose come to ask if I will help him
Course I say I will do all I can

Tis not much he wants

Only to copy out some letters
For many letters are sent
The writing of them long work

This is nothing to me
For I have oft writ a letter
For some person who is not letterd theysselfs
In this way earning myself a few pennies

Also Ambrose ask I should report back to he
All that goes in that picking room

If the foreman push someone head down slap
When he has no good reason
These things I am to say

This does involve difficulty for me
For the foreman is a rough and ignorant man
Knows what I do
So slams my head gainst the wall
When no one can see
Or trip me as I walk and push me down

I do not care

*

So that was how it start

In ways that seemd small enough
That surely count for naught

Yet as time goes on many things change
At the mill itself but inside of me
You see things there
Anger like a putrid boil grows

I were four years there by then

This I must say as being
A difficulty of the human character
The more you have the more you want
What satisfies you once
Does soon begin to seem but little

What you see also is that letters are writ
Reports are made meetings is organizd
Mr Fluck is ask again and again
Could not he change this or that

Pamphlets passd around and read
Strikes is threatend and people are beat
Yet that Mr Fluck is a man of iron and stone
No a ways will yield

Oft cruel to the childers
Pushing one in a freezing water trough
For the sin of falling asleep

This I say though I respect Ambrose dear
More and more I think no progress can come
Unless there is force

Yet still when some of the rougher men
Come to me ask my help in certain matters

I do say No

Put on the whole armour of God
That you may be able to stand firm
Gainst the wiles of the Devil

Mr Harland Cottrell has taught me well

But oh oh it were not so long after
Two events did come to happen
Both did change my mind and venom it perhaps

The first was that my letters to Lucetta
No longer receive any reply
Though I write again and again
Comes back only silence

I go to ask Mr Birch Nazareth
His letters also receive no response
He hisself never been quite so merry
Since she left
You see the age in he

What can we do I say
How can we find out if she is safe

Mr Birch Nazareth shake his shaggy head
You must hand her ovr the care of God
Cease yr canting

We cannot know what might have come to pass
But be sure she is belovd of God
All will be well

So I try to do
Yet still my mind is hauntd

Surely some wrong has come to her
Otherwise why does she not write

I think again of Master Blyth
Does she write to him in London
Could I find some way to ask him this

Yet I feel sure he has quite forgot her
Though he were the start of all her troubles
That I do never forget

So my mind is stirrd and turns tumultous

Then just at this time come other trouble
Which has been gathering a while
For the men who work been making moan
For some time now how the beams is unsafe

These beams being anyway too low
So you may easily catch yrself in they

Already trouble with a wheel running too fast
As does break the shaft

Ambrose I know many times spokd to the owner
Those beams must be takd down
New ones put up
We cannot patch nail forver

Yet this will not happen for to do it
Does cost much money and time

So the argument goes back and forth
Til one October day low skye and air closd in
Feverish damp with all dripping

There comes a grating heaving breaking
Goes all through the building
So that all stop and gasp

A girt shouting and banging
A sudden silence as a raging cry goes up
All the looms and wheels must be stoppd
Straps levers rollers all pulld loose
Then we hear screaming
The running of many feet

The foreman say You get on with yr work
Is no cause for you to go

Yet some women work in the picking have men
Who are in that loom workshop
So they take no notice of the foreman
Push their way through
For tis clear that
All is smashd

It were the beam as has been warnd of
It come down and two were killd
Crushd under its weight
Their heads and back brokd
One other with his arm broke
Another knockd out senseless
By the fall of the timber

All is shouting and weeping
Emma from the picking shop is wailing sore
For her husband was one of the dead

Sure there are promises all will be right
Money paid those lost their family
Twill all be takd care

But oh times goes on and tis not so
We seed it once we seed it a multitude of times
The only recompense offerd to Emma
Is that her three young ones
Must come now to work in the mill

Those poor childers not ten feet away
From where their father died
The beam really no better than twas
Though we are told tis quite safe
Only patchd again

Tis the honour of the scarlet of Stroudwater
Knowd throughout the world

So all this we are told
But what good is that for Emma

What good also for all the mills that close
Many of the small ones gone years back
Now the larger also turnd to grist or pins
Even Griffin Mill made ovr to sawing

Many sneer then at Ambrose and his like
Talk talk talk all the owner does is fill time
He has no intention of redress any question

Also at that time comes news sheets
Make their way from London or Bristol
I am sure is Master Ned who brought them
The Poor Mans Guardian the Northern Star

Other like them saying
How all men must have the vote
Which seem no more possible to me
Than Queen Victoria do take in laundry

But many at the mill say
That tis the way
The only way

All cross the country news of the struggle
Growing apace

What an age is this we live in
When all is shouting clambering

Everyone talk but no one listen

How come there so much knowledge
Yet still we chokd by ignorance
Impossible to sort the wheat from the chaff

So is my mind stirrd up
Nothing in the world seems simple
I am torn this way and that
So despite all my loyalty to Ambrose
I come to think they are right
Who says no point in talking more

When I see Master Ned again
I look at him and think
Maybe he is the man for this
As others think it too

We do not need the sane and wise now
In their place we need those who will act
I do not want to think this
But I do

So then when I am askd again to help
I say that God help me I will

Yet tis only they want me to keep the watch
While some meeting or discussion does take place
This I feel no fear to do

All I must is stand near the gate of the mill
Watch to see if anyone comes near

This no danger to me as should anyone come
I pretend I am but taking a rest
As I walk toward Stroudwater

Anyways no one much notice me
Think me too small and stupid
To be involvd in any matter of import

Only once or twice do I hear some talk
Which I try hard to forget
So I may say if askd
I know naught

Yet still one thing does stick in my mind
The words Little Mill

*

All the time more and more are without work
Come again and again to the gates
Pleading not even for work
Just for a crust of bread

Never were this country of England
Brought so low

So another year drawing toward its end
The air all around weightd with the loss of hope

Then all changes quite sudden
Such is the gift life can all turn round
For we receive news that Master Blyth
Will be a coming home at Christmas tide

Nettie and I set to though tis late the eve
Cakes puddings fires laid dust raisd
Holly and ivy carrid in

All past strife forgot for this time
What a fine gentleman he has become
So says Nettie beaming wide
Her sticking out teeth dancing
Merry in her mouth

Tis true Master Blyth was much changd
A silk top hat a double breastd vest of velvet
A girt coat with a narrow waist and high collar
Side burns and moustache all neatly trimmd
Boots shind to a mirror

Netties pleasure does only increase
As he does once again boil up many receipts
To ease her scald and flaking skin

Hardly he had arrivd than Master Ned come too
Who had not been expectd

So for those days everything near olden time
Much bitterness laid aside
I was glad of it

If only Lucetta had come
My happiness would have been full
Yet even Christmas tide brought no letter

Still I did enjoy the noise in the house
Had forgot how much they all do quarrel

All about the Peoples Charter twas
I had never heard of this afore

Master Ned say this what the future must be
Yet as you suppose Mr Harland Cottrell say
Improvement and education
Not sedition and violence

The women make theysselfs into demons
Akin to their French sisters
Have they no shame

So say Mr Harland Cottrell
Master Ned speaks not gainst he
Though when his father does not see
He rolls his eyes does make
Certain obscene hand gestures
Such to indicate his father a fool

During that time a stain on the shine
I must write it down

All was sat to dinner that last night
A man come to the back door
I did not see him for twas Nettie who went
Thinking it to be a beggar man

Yet then she come in and say
Master Ned is wantd at the door

Knowing all I knew about he
I was immediately afeard
Surely they not move gainst he

At this season of goodwill

But quick quick Master Blyth got to his feet
I went back in the kitchen taking a dish
Though my real purpose to hear what was said

I never saw the man
Only the back of Master Blyth
Black gainst black in the frame of the door
His voice v firm and clear

I am afeard you are mistakd
My brother is not here
He is in London

So he turns away and shuts the door firm
Yet I have not movd fast enough
So am stood there with the pan

Staightway Master Blyth looks put about

I am sorry Mary Ann he say
I do not like untruth and neither do you
Yet this man can come any other time
This is our moment for all to be together
Do you not think so

I nod my head and for a moment
His hand touch my arm

Such is the Yuletide warmth
That spreads joy all about
That I think Oh yes he is quite right
To send that man away

Yet later the next day

When both is set to leave
There is some bitter dispute betwixt them
This I know

It did happen just after Master Blyth
Had steppd cross to the cottage

I had supposd he went merely to bid farewell
To Mr Birch Nazareth

Yet I do suspect there was some more substance
To their talk

For soon after I did hear voices raisd
Not just Master Ned who always could rant
Yet his brother also
Much bitterness there was

Know also they do speak of Lucetta
But more I cannot tell of this
For that morning a blessd crow
Has got hisself fixd in the brokd chimbley
Is flapping there bringing down much soot

So busy am I hear not what is said
Only later Nettie does report that Master Blyth
He never knew the real reasons why Lucetta
Did up so sudden and leave this place

Only that morning Mr Birch Nazareth
Did tell him all

This did surprise us both
That Mr Birch Nazareth did stir matters up so
Yet that does honestly shew
That his feelings gainst Master Ned

Had growd no less calm the passage of time

So this then was the cause
Of all Master Blyths anger
Did leave then his pale face burning scarlet
His eyes sparkling though he tried not to shew

I should have askd him then
If he had any news of Lucetta

Yet that cursd crow got hisself in the dining room
Up the dresser did smash a glass decanter
Til I hunt he down in the back of the book case
Hold his beating flapping black eyed squawk
Throw him out the front door
Oh such trouble he was to me

Which by then Master Blyth had gone

So only know though much remain the same
Yet also all now does turn about

He that was kept under
Surely now does rise

MOUNT VERNON

I have decide
Enough now of this

I did think to take possession of the page
Yet now it does possess me

I should never have come back
I wantd the Valleys I wantd not my Master

No need for me to stay
This house full of fine things
They could be easily pawnd
The money would be good enough to keep me
For the short mortal time I yet to spin

I am an honest woman never pilchd nothing
Not though I nearly starvd
Yet now perhaps I must

Or could go into Stroud
I have yet strength for down the hill
Find perhaps that son of Mr Hawkins Fisher

We did both see him there at the Shambles

He is a man of standing in the town
His father knew Mr Harland Cottrell well
Has record much the history of that time

I am sure if I spoke
He would listen

Tis not too late for justice

That now is what I must do

Go I then upstairs to that tower room
Which I have lovd so much
Have knowd some blessd peace there

Hurriedly to pack up my one cloth bag
Carry that down the stairs

Oh I am gone gone
What a relief tis to decide

Step I then toward that stain glass
Ornament tracery front door
My hand reach out for the knob

Step out into the sparkling morn
All hushd by the thickness of green
Only the sound of birds chirping
As they twist and chase above

But then his voice

Mary Ann Mary Ann So he does call

I know not what he say
But all I hear is those words again

Which have echoed all about
For so many days now

Whatevr guilt there is
You have yr share in it

Standing there by the door
Tis as though I hear what he says
For the first time

Always I have knowd and not knowd

The words do take all my strength
I step back through the door
Sink down on the steps

A marvellous light breaking in my mind
For the time is at hand

My heart discovers its own self
Above all else we are told to get wisdom
With it comes understanding

Sudden I see with a clarity
How all that lost time of my life
As I did spend in the City of Gloucester

I was always hiding from what he now say

I see it all quite clearly now

Write write I will again

My energy has come back
Though a red lump now does break
Through the skin of my chest

Sucking fast my life away
Yet still I am not finishd yet

My Master wants a book
He shall have a book
All the world shall know it
Not the story he wants
But at last the truth

God God have mercy on my failing soul
Give me now the fire of courage

The courage I had when I was a child
When Mrs Woebegones knife to throat

Fear not them that kill the body
For they cannot kill the soul

Oh for that time again
A power could tread on serpent or scorpion
The pen on the paper can return me there

I must believe that now
For I have nothing else to believe

Yes twill all go down
Every last word

Not for him no no a ways him
Not even for God or some ideal of truth

Tis said we wait on the judgement of the Lord

A false witness shall not be unpunishd
He that speaketh lies shall not escape

Yet I wait and wait and it prove not so
Time exact no revenge

So who then will listen

Maybe just the Valleys
Who have keen ears though they say naught
The lifting wind I hear now touch the zummer air
He says Yes yes I hear

Aye these Valleys they shall know
Scratch it out with my pen
Make them the final judge

Aye soil soul sin
We have plenty enough sin my Master and me
He and I both in it bury deep
Draw no breath

Yet I now stare in the face
The part which is mine
That responsibility I do bear

In that I am different to he
For that he never will do

Write now my confession

Both of our damnation

STOCTON HILL

How then shall I write of that time

Yuletide the last of the Lords light
The months followd cruel

Never afore had any livd through such times
Where new machines were inventd every day
Time speeding forward so fast
No one can keep abreast of he

Yet the state of man
Lower and lower he fall
Further and further from the Lord

At the mill Ambrose now is all passd by
No one listens more to he

I was angry and afeard all day and night
Frightd for Lucetta because she did not write
Angry for Emma at the mill
Who had scant enough to eat
So I gave some of mine to share

So the plans were made for that girt gathering

As was plannd for Whitsuntide
When all would go up to Selsey Common
To gather there and make protest

But it fell out I did not go
Not due to any lack of feeling
I was hot to go

Mr Harland Cottrell Nettie both took sick
Their stomachs much disturbd keep down no food
So I must stay at Stocton Hill
Though it were hard
Particular when I heard other below
Gathering mass the road
With staves and banners
All such things

Singing the gentry must come down
The poor shall wear the crown
Stand up now Chartists all

So I heard them go then come back
Late that night with more shouting and singing
Down the Valley
All hearts sailing high

At the mill those next days
The air pulld tight as the skin of a drum
Though little is said for the foreman
Watch all the constables is close

Then toward the end of some day I gets a message
Will I keep the watch that night

This I have done afore glad enough
No doubt some meeting does take place

Or I must say the truth maybe some sabotage
Which has been done oft afore
Tis wrong I know
Yet they is driven to it

So that night I go home to help Nettie
Then come back

No one at Stocton Hill ask where I go

So tis that eve
I standing on the mill path pretending idle
Dropping stems of grass in the mill stream
Wandering up and down
As though I pass the time

I do not know who is at the mill
When I walk past I see the backs of men
Who enter in the buildings
Several horses tetherd there
Which I do not usually see
Yet I take care not to look too much
For tis not my business to see

But then that zummer eve
Things happen as has never happend afore
First there comes the sound of much commotion
Shouting and banging maybe the noise of a fight

Just as I wonder on this a lad does come
He walks just as though he idle as do I
Yet I know he is a lad of the mill
Know also he is quaking fear

When he comes to me he goes on past
But not afore he says

Mary Ann Get you back up the hill
Quick now go quick

So I turns heads straight up
Cutting up the field away from the road
Yet I am but half way up when I sees

The mill is alight
A column of smoke rising

I run then down the hill to raise the alarum
Others course were there afore me
Had always been there
Hollering and shouting

Now many times I think back what I see
I am sure were some as did ride away
I heard the horses hooves others running

The buildings catching quick
The heat come off them like a wave
The air trembling breaking
So I ran with others we find buckets
Form a chain to bring up water
Out the mill stream

The darkness now were gathering
Many many did come down
People from all cross the Valley
You see them scurry down the hill
Legs flying like so many ants
Stumbling then in the half dark

Though so many work dash the water
That we throwd was spit in the ocean
Twas but a matter of an hour

When the loom shop all burnt up
So thirty looms all gone

The carding and fulling savd
Only for they were some distance apart
Soakd well now in water

The skye now black above no stars
The whole Valley thick with the smoke
All were there coughing and crying
Faces blackend throats sore

Though I had no love for that place
I walkd back up the lightless hill weeping
Wiping my eyes from the smoke
For twas no good to burn it down
Where would me and others like me
Find now work

When I get back home
Mr Harland Cottrell and Nettie
Are not abed for news has come even to they

Mr Harland Cottrell stand in his night shirt
White head shaking rubbing chin mumbld huffd
Tis the vengeance of the Lord he said

Soon they both to bed and I also
Though I were too fird and fearful
For any much sleep

Several times up in the night
For Nettie still vomiting sore
I must empty the pot for her

At dawn then I start to drift sleep

Yet just a few moments later
A banging on the front door
No one usual evr comes there
Not at this unearthly hour

I must go answer it
For Mr Harland Cottrell sick

So hurrid I pull on my clothes
The banging comes again shakes the house
I opens up not feeling the fear I should
Sees then one I knows to be a constable
Two others standing there

Behind them the morning dew and mist
Still cling all cross the fields
The sun not quite break through the clouds

I am sorry say I but the Master is sick abed

Yet just as I speak
Up behind me comes Mr Harland Cottrell
He has only an old coat ovr his night shirt
His face is green and shadowd

What kind Sirs is the problem here

The constable has a blunt face small eyes
Speaks he then We seek for Mr Ned Cottrell
I believe he is yr son

Course he is my son say Mr Harland Cottrell
What want you with he

I think you know right well the constable say
An impertinent way to speak

Indeed I do not say Mr Harland Cottrell
You will not find him here
He lives all the way to Bristol now
Did you not know that

No the constable say
He is here in the area
We are seeking him
For serious charges may be brought
In relation the purposeful burning of the mill

What what Mr Harland Cottrell say
What lies do you tell
You must retract those words Sir
Is a slander on my sons name
I tell you he is not here

Then the constables eyes fall on me
You are Mary Ann Sate

Yes Sir that is I

Have you not seed Mr Ned Cottrell

No Sir I have not

Then one of the other men speaks up
She works in the mill Sir
If anyone will know she will

Aye aye say another

Then my girl you must come with me
Say the constable
That we might discuss this further

At this Mr Harland Cottrell
Starts to shout and rant

God mercy deceit and lying
Laying at the door of an innocent girl
Can they not see
I can hardly be held account

Oh aye I think to myself
Simple imbecile all
Yet I could set light to a mill
If I so chose
Though I did not

Thinking this I am calm
Say loud and clear
I know nothing of the whereabouts
Of Mr Ned Cottrell
Or naught else either
Yet if you wish me to come with you
Then I will
I have nothing to fear
The Lord knows my innocence

Bold twas of me to speak so
Yet I did feel certain of my position
Thought to calm rage of Mr Harland Cottrell
For I did not like to see him so vexd
Particularly not in front of these men
Who had no understanding of he

Thank you my girl say the constable
Then we shall go

I wait to see if they will lay hand on me
But they do not

So I step out and they follow
Behind me Nettie is weeping

Then she call out Wait Wait
She comes with a shawl for me
Though tis mellow morning

God Bless you girl
Laying the shawl about my shoulders

So she says weeping
Afore turning to tend to Mr Harland Cottrell
Who has gone dark red shaking sore

I go on down the hill head high
The sun now a coming quieter dries the dew

As I come down others walk the opposite way
Come no doubt to see what remain of the mill

Their eyes still blank from the fright
Of the flames

They are silent as I pass
They know I am guilty of nothing
Wonder what now will come to pass

One shouts out at the constables impertinent
So you think to break Mary Ann Sate do you
Oh you got the wrong one
You shall see

Eventually we come to the hill
Go up into the town of Stroud
I know where we go
Which is to Spillmans Court

At the foot of Rodborough Hill
That being the house of Henry Burgh Esq
He being the Justice of the Peace

As I walk down cross the canal
Thoughts twist in my head faster and faster
They want information about Master Ned
Yet I have not seed him since Christmas
That I can say in all honesty

Course they will ask also
Whether I were at the mill last night
I will say I were not
Only did go down to help gainst the flames
This does not seem a serious deceit
For in truth I only standing on the path

So that the decision I take

Who keepeth his mouth and his tongue
Keepeth his soul from troubles

Soon come then to Spillmans Court
Such an elegant gracious house
I have never approach

Though course am taken round the back
Placd then in a low room
A table and one chair
The winder croochd with little light
The door thick and stud

One come and one go
Walk up and down say this and that
The question is askd again and again
Do you have no idea where he would be hid

No No No

I will keep my mouth with a bridle
While the wickd is afore me

Were you at the mill last night
Are you aware cloth has been stold
Tis said meetings have takd place
Are you aware of this that other

No No No

The day is maggle hot and room close
For seven or eight hours no one comes
It must be gone now six of the clock
I have eaten and drunk nothing
My throat is closing up
My head does spin with hunger
When will they let me go

Their questions press in my head
I myself should like to know
How a meeting should end in a fire

Then they come back and shouting starts
A hand come cross my face my neck jerks
Slap me hard so my nose bleeds

A man stands close and swears in my face
Pushing up gainst the wall by the winder
Calls me a whore and spit on me

I just say no no and no
I will keep saying it
I have no fear of them

I did not bend to Mrs Woebegone
So will give no ground to they

Even if I could
I would not turn him ovr to these men
For though he may have some bad in him
They have more

My shoulders is grabbd and shaken
My teeth rattle in my head I bite my tongue
My hair is pulld so my scalp burn
But still no no no
I have seed nothing

The day is closing
The light at that low winder grey

Fear is on me now
For I know they could kill me
I am as nothing to them
It would be easily done

Mary Ann Sate has died of shock
Or she has trippd fallen on a dark stair
It could be so

Maybe it were better I speak
Just say some small thing to hold them back
Then just as I think this
The room changes

The sound I am hearing I know well
It brings such peace and comfort
The Angels are here
Their white wings at the winder
Curling close

So it seems that the men know it too
For soon they stop their threats
Leave me alone
My head down on the table
Listening listening always to that sound
Knowing I am safe

Perhaps I sleep I do not know

Later comes another a mild man
He is not drunk or shouting
Brings me a glass of water
A platter with a dab of bread
Asks me to sit down
Which I do

Then he say most polite
Are you sure you cannot think of any place
Where Mr Ned Cottrell might be hid

I set out then to say once again
He cannot still be in this area

Yet as I speak a memory appears in my head

Little Mill and the low door in the wall
In the chur wherein Master Ned did enter
Comes back to me

The name of that place
I have heard it once or twice since

What is certain is no one knows
I saw that door
Twas an accident
I might well have never seed it

Or forgot it

So I can answer clear I know nothing

Then he speaks again most polite
You are a good girl
Course you would want to help
In this grave matter
Where as you understand
Valuable property damagd seriously
Many is put out of work

When he say this I am set to thinking
For he is right
I myself have no work now
Least I have a bed at Stocton Hill
What of the others
I do start then to weep

I could tell him about the meeting
The commotion those that ran away

But I think then of the Angels
I know I will not do it
Not for all his kind words

Then finally all is stoppd
The first constable come back and say
We waste our time here
She knows nothing
Or perhaps she cannot remember
We cannot anyway rely on testimony
From a girl not half savd

So I am takd to the door and pushd out
Stumbld down into a back yard

See ahead of me a gate
Hurry to get through it

Falling straight then into
The arms of Mr Birch Nazareth
His vast width height his shaggy beard
All appear now even more than is

Surround also by some other like
Emma and Annie from the mill
Ambrose and some other from the cottages

Tis only when I see Ambrose
My courage fail
Yet two takes hold my arm
Another find a kerchief wipe the blood

Quick quick they say we must away
So I am pulld from that place

When we come up to Stratford House
Mr Birch Nazareth turn me to me and say
How go you Mary Ann

I am quite well I say
For I am proud want none see me beat

What did you say another ask

I said nothing
They wantd to know about Mr Ned Cottrell
Yet I did not say naught
They said he burnt down the mill

Others nod then and Mr Birch Nazareth as well

Do you think it can be true I ask

Mr Birch Nazareth looks clear in my eye
Lays a hand on my shoulder

What think you Mary Ann

I can only speak the truth and so say
He may not have done it hisself
Yet his hand could certainly be in it

He will swing if they take him say another

I bow my head then unable to think of this

Come come Mary Ann Mr Birch Nazareth say
I will take you back to Stocton Hill
Though I am v sorry to say
That Mr Harland Cottrell
He is took sick

Aye aye I say
He has been sick several days

No Ambrose say No Mary Ann
A much worse kind of sickness now
Shaking and unable to move one arm or leg
I think it may be mortal

This news now comes on top of such other trouble
I cannot understand it all
Can only step up the dusty hill
With Ambrose and Mr Birch Nazareth home

*

That eve all I want is peace
For I am badly shakd and feard
Yet none is to be had

Never heard the messenger must come up the lane
To the cottage of Mr Birch Nazareth

Mr Harland Cottrell lay on the sofa
His body stiff and ockerd
When speaks one side his mouth only open
Tis a horrible thing to see

Nettie is much put about
She will not look at me or speak
Probably she does believe I am responsible
For some wrong doing

Now also she is frightd as I have never seed
For Mr Harland Cottrell been all of her life
Despite she mock and tease behind he back
She does love him dear

I also at least can find other work
Another place to board
Yet Nettie she is old and has no strength
There is no hope for her

Finally I make Mr Harland Cottrell comfortable
Hear perhaps some voice in the kitchen
Yet consider it not

Mr Harland Cottrell then does sleep
So I go back to Nettie in the kitchen

The back door still open
For the evening is caressing still

Though the light dying fast

Nettie cast her vast bulk down
In the chair near the hearth
Hide her head away from me

This I do find vexing for she never has afore
What evr happen Nettie has much to say

So I clean up the kitchen
Scour the pots put the smoothing iron in the fire
Ready to start on the linen

Tis comforting to do such small tasks
They keep my mind from larger thoughts

Yet just as I draw the iron out
Ambrose is at the door

I look ovr to Nettie for surely now
She will begin to go at him
Instead she gets up and hurries out

I have no time for her now

What what I ask him
For he surely comes with news

Six are arrestd he says

Master Ned I ask

Oh no say Ambrose Not he
They have not found
Tis true now that wages is going up
In the mills in Stroudwater

For there is certainly fear

But to me tis no way forward
Those who celebrate now
They will soon weep

Yet Mary Ann he say
I come with a message from Mr Birch Nazareth
He ask that you step up to see he

Oh yes of course I say
This is of some comfort
Mr Birch Nazareth take some charge ovr matters
Til Mr Harland Cottrell come to hisself

So I walk up with Ambrose
He tells me then Mr Harland Cottrell
Has writ a letter to Master Blyth in London

Or not hisself he could not do it
So Ambrose write it for he
Which is how he knows what was said

Oh I say Oh And what did the letter say

In the letter say Ambrose
He asks for Master Blyth to come home

I am glad to hear of this letter
Without Mr Harland Cottrell we are all adrift
Blown as leaves in the wind
Circling and drifting with no purpose

Oh aye Ambrose say
Yes he dictatd the letter to me
Even his tongue roll could not speak proper

Yet you know what he said in that letter
He says to Master Blyth
You must come back home at good speed
For yr brother Ned is falsely accusd

So so you see Mary Ann
Some things do not change

I do not like entirely the way Ambrose speaks
Yet tis true you must wonder
Even now it seems that Mr Harland Cottrell
Does not believe that his belovd son
Could evr be guilty of any base action

This the cause of his illness now Ambrose say
That he lie to his own self so long

I do not want to hear this
Yet there may well be truth in it

This our conversation as we walk up the lane
Then we come to Mr Birch Nazareths cottage
Stop outside the door

Then Ambrose takes hold of my shoulders square
Look me in the eye and say
I am sorry Mary Ann
You are a girl of girt courage
You have need of all that now

I nod my head but think not much on it

So I go into the cottage
Ready for a list of what must be done
How things are to be organizd

Yet as soon as I go in the door
I feel the chill of the air
See Mr Birch Nazareth as I have never seed him

How he is changd from only hours afore
When we did walk together up from Stroud

He stand by the table on it lie a letter
I look at his blanchd face shallow eyes
The heavy hang of his shoulders
He wipes a hand cross his face

Mary Ann Tis better not
I am sorry I am v sorry
I can only tell you
I know not what to say

Yet I must tell you Lucetta is dead

The words do hit me with a dull thump
Saying them Mr Birch Nazareth
Does sink down in a chair at the table
Commence then to weep

So so he say See how rumour will always spread
Fast as a rambling weed chokes always
Any seed of truth

I should weep as well but I cannot
Nor move nor speak nor breath
Just stand there watching him

I want now to read the letter
But he has it lockd tight in his fist

On he weeps

I stand watching him

Breath snaps sudden in my throat
I put my hands to my head
As though to hold it together

I tell myself I must comfort Mr Birch Nazareth
Yet instead take hold of the back of a chair

Finally I turn stumbling walk out the cottage
Into the last of the light
My feet touch that same lane
I did walk so oft with her

For a moment I hear her laughter
See a flash of shining hair
The curve of her narrow waist
The way she walkd
Always so strong and sure
Stepping away from me now
That pale shawl lifting at her shoulder

So I turn then turn and turn again
Where can I go

I stand for a while in the lane
My hands claspd together
Yet finally there is no choice
I must go back to the farm

When I get back I try to tell Nettie
My lips will not move

Then I understand Nettie knows

Aye aye Mr Birch Nazareth came earlier

Tis a sad business what can anyone say
Many a girl does go wrong

Nettie say this spitting without look at me

Go wrong I say

Oh aye she say Oh aye
Did he not tell you
Course not he probably did not like to say

She died in a Workhouse course
Nettie rocks and wheezes now as she speaks

She was with child not marry
She and the child both takd
It were probably best
Since she were ruind

A poker stand by the fire I pick it up
Raise it at Nettie who shields her head

Tis not true I shout Not true
The poker strike but Netties hands stop it

Not true Not true
I raise the poker again

We are both stoppd by a cry
It come from the sitting room
From Mr Harland Cottrell

Come come now girl stop yr wailing
Nettie say and take the poker from me
The Master has need of us
Come now quick

STOCTON HILL

You may go say I
But I will not

So I sit myself down and refuse

Nettie is soon back
I have need of you she says
You not help the Master
You soon be put out this house

I say naught only stare at the floor

You cooten Mary Ann
Do you not know if Mr Harland Cottrell die
We are all finishd

Yet I care not what she says
Sit there stubborn and still

When she comes back again she slaps me
Still I will not move

I always told you Nettie say
No good would come of that girl
But oh you would not be told

I stand up and shout
Shut yr filthy mouth
How dare you How can you

Nettie looks at me but she does not hear
There is no help in speaking to her

This is how she has always been
She will no a ways shew any proper feeling
Or allow it in anyone else

I stride out the house spitting silent rage
Spend that eternal night in the barn
Lying awake amidst sheaths of hay

I cannot know what has come
Every time I think of it my mind shys away
Like a frightd horse

Tis more than I can abear
I will never believe what Nettie say

*

All around us now is strife weeping

Neither sun nor stars in many days appeard
No small tempest lay upon us
All hope we be savd takd away

Still we must all go to our employ
Though all there is to do now
Is clear away the blackend beams
Pile up the stones about

Also wash in the stream some cloth
Which is burnt and staind
Will never come good

Resources is sought to rebuild the mill
Yet this will take many months

All who were there must soon seek other work
So they go up and down the Valleys
Some gone already to Gloucester

Now there is no talk of how to shew the owners

How they must listen how all will be changd

Still the talk is of Mr Ned Cottrell
How he has led all to a world more just
I do not know how they can still speak so

What purpose is there to stride and strut
Teaching lessons shew the mill owners
But still there are plenty
Who thinks a blessd work has been done

The more they search for he
So the legend grows

To me it matters not what is done
Naught will change

This is what I think when I do think
Which is not much at all

Instead I lie in the barn
While Nettie does tend Mr Harland Cottrell

He comes no better
It were not much expectd
He has done his three score year and ten

All have seed seizures like this afore
When a person gone stiff they not come right

He can still speak a little and move some
But he does not get up
I fear he will not

News come more men is arrestd
Soon to be tried in Gloucester

Yet Master Ned is not takd
Though tis said more and more
He was the one responsible
He did stir others to do it

Still the constables search for he
Bashing in hedge and wood
Going through every barn and byre

To me it all float by
I think only of Lucetta

At night pictures turn and twist my mind
How at the Workhouse
Many is toss in a pit together
Put lime on them
I have seed it so

Always I push these pictures from my mind
I do still not believe that letter said

She were always lied gainst
Now it comes again

I choke when I think of it

I lie in the hay barn long
Say nothing to anyone

Think oft of Master Ned
All this is down to he
This knowledge come again and again

My mind go back to that day
I did hear in his fathers study
How he did pour dishonour

On her name

I hate him for it
A hate as grows like a canker

Then one day Mr Birch Nazareth come
Mary Ann he say You must get up

I lie looking up at him but do not move
So then bends down to me
Takes hold of me gently
Raises me up

Come come he says
This will not do
He takes me back to the farm
Where Nettie boil aniseed caraway turmeric
For to dose Mr Harland Cottrell
The smell does bring some comfort
I know it so well

Mr Birch Nazareth sits me at the table
Now now he says I have better than herbs
From his pocket produces a bottle of cider

Nettie and I both draw back
For Mr Harland Cottrell does not have such
In his house

Yet Mr Birch Nazareth pours me the bottle
You must drink he says
For you have need of yr strength
Tis better than any medicine

He drinks hisself I see then
How he has need also for his beard is knottd

Much flesh has gone from he
His back stoopd as it never was afore

I drink The taste bangs the back my throat
Warmth fills me head spins so I drink again

Then Mr Birch Nazareth sits down next to me say
Mary Ann I am sorry to tell you this
But Ambrose is arrestd

I shake my head at him
I know it cannot be

No no I say for all knows
He was not involvd in the fireing of the mill

Yet even as I say this I am crumbling inside
For I know and Mr Birch Nazareth knows
Even bone brain Nettie also
No justice in this

Mr Birch Nazareth now shake his head and say
They cannot get the man they want
All they have is ignorant lads
Who only did what they is told

Also that Mad Dog Harvey
With his talk of The Washerwoman Queen

You know how it goes
They must have someone

I shake my head pull at my hair
Tis this this now
This what breaks me

For what if Ambrose is transportd or hangd

Yet Mr Birch Nazareth take hold my hands
Holds them tight in his
Come come now Mary Ann
You must not lose yr head
Think now clear and calm

I know you said to the constables
That you know nothing of where Master Ned is
All know you do yr best for he
Yet think now hard what yr position is

I have knowd Mr Birch Nazareth so long
I trust him certainly and so I say
I do not know where he is

Yet I do know a place where they might look

Aye Mr Birch Nazareth say
Would it not be best to say this
If only it might shew you willing to help
Give you perhaps an opportunity
To tell them straight Ambrose
He has naught to do with such as this

But Mr Birch Nazareth I say
I cannot say anything I must not
There are many in this neighbour
Who do look to him for hope
Many who do support all he does
I cannot be seed to act gainst he
Even in giving information which cannot help

Then a long silence comes
Mr Birch Nazareth does look at me long

Then he say Mary Ann I cannot tell you
Right from wrong
Yet he is a dangerous man
You know it well
You must now think on this

So you must think also of Ambrose
You come back with a bloody nose
Who can say what might befall he

I do think but my mind is boffld
Perhaps Mr Birch Nazareth is right
I should have said what I knew
When I was there

Maybe twas because I lied
That Lucetta met her end
Maybe it was punishment
She herself would never have lied
No matter what

So it all go round in my head

Mr Birch Nazareth sit with me still
He is too fair to force my hand

Nettie comes in then with a basin of water
I ask her what I should do
My mind is dancing with the cider
It all seems now like a game of dice
What matters it now how it falls out

I wait for Nettie to say
Oh no Oh no You do not touch Master Ned

Yet instead she looks me long

Her lip curl up

I think then for a moment
As how her flaking hands do stroke flat
The rib of a wool stocking

She say straight
If you can Mary Ann
You bring him down
Tis right
The time has come

*

So I goes down to Stroud
Mr Birch Nazareth wish to go with me
Yet I desire to go myself alone

Think myself drivd by a yearning for truth

But were it really so

No I do not think so
I think what hurrid my feet
Not truth but revenge

For I thought of her
Separatd always now from the Lord
Though she had life strength love enough
To triumph ovr the whole world

Twas the lies he told about her
That destroyd her

So I went gladly
To do what damage to him I may

That was what I thought

Yet revenge is like a rolling stone
Which when a man has forcd up a hill
Will return upon him with increasd violence
Break those bones whose sinews gave it motion

*

When I arrive Spillmans Court
My good fortune the gentler man
With who I spoke afore
Does come to answer

After he sit me down
Not now in that low pinchd room
But in another with dark wood panels
A suit of armour shields on the wall

First I say to him most polite
I understand Ambrose is arrestd

This he does not deny
So then I say what a worry tis
Since all does know his innocence

It seems amazing I may speak
With such calm and clarity
Yet I am in the grip of a death like calm
A steel cold courage
No care for my own safety

The man is quite reasonable
Say that enquiries must be made of all

Though he is civil I see he thinks me

But an imbecile

Then I say I have rememberd
Some information may be of help

Also I say perhaps this information
Might make it no longer necessary
Ambrose should be held

Even in that moment I am again amaze
I should dare to bargain so
With such a man as this

Still I am fird with the bravery
As comes to those who have lost all

So then I tells him about Little Mill
Since he thinks me a simple fool
He accept most readily I only just rememberd

This place I say I do not think tis important
Am sure you can find nothing there

But he is pleasd enough by what I say

Mr Ambrose Woebegone I say again
He was not involvd in this
Will he now be releasd

Oh aye aye the constable say you need not worry
He was only evr helping us to consider
How we might proceed

So he say which is a lie

He lay then a shilling on the table

I look down at it lying there
It pains me to take it
But how may I leave
When my future is all to the wind

So I take the shilling walk home

The evening is a coming
Shadows like the closing of shutters
The air is chill now and damp

On the way I see nothing hear nothing
All is like something describd in a book
With no substance to it

Til I come to a bend in the path
Emma standing there
Says to me
What say you Mary Ann

I can say nothing

So so Mary Ann say Emma
You did always like a good story
Had you no story to tell the constables

She spit on the ground beside me
I say nothing walk on

Yet in my head the words of the Bible
Sound again and again

But of the knowledge of good and evil
Thou shalt not eat of that tree
For the day thou eatest thereof
So thou shall surely die

*

When I get home Nettie say Master Blyth is back
Yet I cannot stand to see his face
For what have I done
In betraying that brother he so loves

Still I wait in the kitchen doorway
Hear the voices of Mr Birch Nazareth
And Master Blyth

Nettie say It turns out well he come home
For so he would have come soon anyways
He has been offerd a new position
Now he is qualify
A proper job tis in Oxford
He due to start in just a few days
Here is the letter

I look at the fold paper on the table

So so say Nettie spitting and coughing
Think then how well has Master Blyth done
A rich and fine gentleman he shall be

He who we were told could do nothing at all
A proper doctor poisoner butcher carpenter
Of which we all be proud
No cunning man he

Oh aye I say Yes we may be proud

So I say though the words have no meaning to me

It were always in him say Nettie
From the day he sewd yr lip

I know now what she say is true
Were him as sewd my lip not his father
But I cannot think on this
Only what now have I done to he

They wait for you Nettie say
I must go tell them you are back

I should like to flee away
Yet that would be cowardice
So I stand and wait

Then Master Blyth come in the kitchen
I stand pressd gainst the wall
He looks at me long
I do feel ashamd

He is so changd
Stronger clearer sure of hisself now
Like someone take a strong black pencil
Draw a dark line round about he

Now he says
There are two things I must say

First Mary Ann I know of Lucettas death
So I want you to know how truly sorry I am
She were a good friend to many of us here
I know you feel her death v deep
You may be sure I do so too

As he speaks his voice shudders

Thankee Sir I say Then I ask
Had you heard any news of her Sir
Afore this tragedy did befall

No he tells me I did hear at first
Yet then the letters did stop
You can be sure many enquiries
I have made ovr the last years
To know more of her situation
Yet my every question drew a blank

Then he say again
I am truly sorry

He the only one who has said this direct
Others may feel it I know
He is the one that speaks

Then he say also Mary Ann please be not afeard
I have spoke with Mr Birch Nazareth
He has explaind to me how we are placd
You have only done what a Christian must

But please please now
I need something from you
You must tell me where is this place
Where will they go to look for he

But then Mr Birch Nazareth comes in and say
Nay nay Master Blyth
Do not think of it
Now matters to the law must be left
There is naught you can add

Yet Master Blyth does say to me
Please Mary Ann He is my brother
I know he may be but a common criminal
Yet he is still my brother
I care what comes to he

Mr Birch Nazareth then gives me a sharp look
As though he want to say
Do not tell him anything

Yet I cannot hold my peace
He has a right to know
If I told the constable
Then so I must tell he

Anyways I think
The constables already come and gone
Nothing there to find

So despite the look on Mr Birch Nazareths face
I tell Master Blyth all

Still Mr Birch Nazareth does say
No no no Master Blyth please
Do not become involvd in this
All has gone too far
A gentleman such as yrself
Must not act in a matter of this nature
Let the constables do what they must

So say Mr Birch Nazareth then add
It could be thought you have betrayd him
Yr motives might be so misunderstood

Then Master Blyth does say
In a voice with not a shred of bitterness
I have always been misunderstood
So what matter does it make
If I am misunderstood again

No one knows what to say to that

See then his healthful hand lay out the table
White and clean strippd bare
His fathers hand
Gentle and light

Like some small animal new born
Lying there on the table boards

All is sudden peaceful and blessd
I feel sure now things will be put right

His eyes look up at me search me long
I seed him then as I never have afore
How his life like mine
Has no a ways been his own
How we live both all
Within the limits others do make

The question come to me clear then
What have I evr knowd of he

Soon though the moment is brokd
He stands up to go
Though Mr Birch Nazareth say again
No no You best let well alone

Yet he is already at that door
See those starry untouchd fingers grasp handle
His damagd hand move up straighten his collar
Turn to us with a nod of his head

Yet he is shaking now
Is it with anger or fear
His eyes also flooding
As he steps out the door

Oh some things do not change

I stand in silence staring where he was
Feel as though I have murderd someone

Perhaps some fragment of the future
Come to me then
For I feel grippd by fear

*

Tis late that night when we hear
Footsteps screading in the lane

Nettie and me are stayd in the kitchen
The candles lit and the range
Mr Birch Nazareth with us
Mr Harland Cottrell on the sitting room sofa
Not sleeping but not moving neither

I hurry out in the lane and Ambrose is there
He stretches out a hand to me
I hold it tight
He walk in with me and we see
His lip is split ear bleeding
Yet still he smiles easy and say
Oh tis good to come back

Then he laughs raises a hand
As though tis all but nothing

I cannot stop my tears

Nay nay Mary Ann he say
You did what you must do

Please now do not worry
I will find a way to protect you
So you know it well

We sit him down then fetches out
Potater pie for he

How good tis to see he sit at the table
Eating well while Nettie boils a kettle
I do find some rags
So we may clean his ear

Mr Birch Nazareth also takes from
Hiding in the back of the press
That earlier cider

So Mr Birch Nazareth pour a tipple for each
We send it down fast and laugh

So for a moment the kitchen is alight
With merriment
All our good heart feeling
For Ambrose is safe

Yet our laughter has hardly died afore
We hear more scuffling at the back

Tis Mr Birch Nazareth now who goes
Is out there some time
The low rise and fall of voices
Solemn cadences bring no good news

Yet still those of us inside
With cider on our lips
The candles lit now warm
Do feel still some strange urge to laugh

Or if not to cry or to scream
Such were the rankling of the time

Soon soon those feelings all snuffd out
For Mr Birch Nazareth come in
Shaking sore his head

They went to arrest Master Ned he say
He did run so they shot he
The bullet broke his head
He now at Spillmans Court

Happen down in the foot of Stroud
By the mill stream on the Slad Road
A desertd enough spot you know

All know that spot but does not say
Tis near Little Mill

I do not know what we felt
Was it pain sorrow grief relief

Nettie say But sure he will recover
Master Blyth has gone to he
We know what skill he has

No no say Mr Birch Nazareth
He was shot clean in the head
The life gone from him in that instant

Nettie does let out then a stifld sob

I go to stand near the door
For I am frightend I might faint

Someone shall have to tell Master Blyth

When he returns

Mr Harland Cottrell as well

Mr Birch Nazareth says he will do that
Goes from us into the drawing room

Ambrose sits down holding his hat
I am sorry he says
You both knew he from childhood
He was a man of many parts
This much is true

Tis no way for a man of but twenty six years
To lose his life

Nettie and I nod and nod again
We have naught to say
It feels as though we are at the end
Of everything

From the drawing room a terrible wailing
Nettie then begins to weep

I stare at the floor
I know of course he might live still
If I had not told

Will this help the men takd at Gloucester
I ask this to Ambrose

I think it might he say
After all he ran and that is takd as guilt
It were better they had capturd he alive

Then Mr Birch Nazareth returns

Mary Ann he say
The Master is asking for you

I am trembling then for I wonder
Does he know what I have done

I must go to him and so I do

He lies on the sofa his eye glass beside he
His shoulder crumpld face soakd in tears
He pulls one leg up as though in pain
His body wrackd by sobs
I never thought to see him so

Mary Ann he says when he can speak
Will you help me I have need of you

Course Sir I say
I do whatevr I can for you

Please he say Please
They tell me his body is at Spillmans Court
Will you go there

Yes Sir I can go

His voice is brokd the words come spitting

You go to my study and open the drawer
In there is a red box v small
You find it for me please

I go to the study and open the drawer
Though the room is at the shut of dark
I can see the box in the drawer clearly

I take it back to he

Open it he say and I do
Inside is a gold ring
Plain but thickly shapd

I always meant to give him this
So Mr Harland Cottrell say
He was to have it when he marry
But now now he must have it in the grave
Twas his mothers

So he says his voice a whisper
His words all brokd up
Hissing for his mouth not move
Yet he goes on

I am sure they will let you in
Even the dead must have certain rights
Do you not think so

Yes Sir I say I am sure
I will insist
Thank you Mary Ann
You are a trustworthy girl
I know you do yr best for me

Now he gasps for breath his lip wagging
I have to lean my head in close to hear

I would ask Mr Blyth but he is not back
Perhaps he is already there
Keeping a vigil for his brother
We shall see

His hand does grip mine then

I am surprisd at the force still in it
Fear not Be strong and of good courage
For the Lord thy God He doth go with thee
He will not fail thee or forsake thee

I promise him again that the ring
Shall go with Master Ned to his grave

In all honesty I am relieve
He should ask me this
Because this at least I can do

Though one thought does trouble me

So I go back to the kitchen
Where all want to know what I have been askd

I explain about the ring
Speak then my worries

Course I say I must do as he does ask
Yet should the ring not go to Master Blyth
For his wife He is the older son
Mr Birch Nazareth and Ambrose shake their head
Ambrose squeezing up his hat
Looking at the floor

When Mr Birch Nazareth say
Come come you know Mary Ann
Tis never likely Master Blyth should marry
This I think you know

I did not know and in that instant
I have no time to think on his words

Though later I will many times consider them

Already now Ambrose is saying
Aye aye tis justice he should wish this
Yet Mary Ann you must not go there now
Tis dark and the times perilous

Yet I say I will go
I want to be sure to arrive there in time
It may be easier to enter at night

No no Mr Nazareth say Tis not safe
You wait til Master Blyth come back

Yet I am determind to go

So then I go with you Ambrose say

Again Mr Birch Nazareth say he will go
But I say no tis better not
For he is already exhaustd

So I set off and an unnatural peace settles ovr me
As I walk that road I know so well

All is strangely quiet
Though there are many on horses
Guarding the mills

I move soft and shadowd
Afeard that any should see me

All round must have heard
Of the death of Mr Ned Cottrell
For many this comes the end of hope

All all along the route
I wait to meet Master Blyth

Walking back
But I do not

Feel sure I shall find him at my journeys end
Keeping watch for his brother

When I come to Spillmans Court
One of the ignorant types who was there afore
Is there now

So so he say
You like it so much here
You decide to come again

Or perhaps you interestd in that girt quarry
We have takd tonight
Oh yes we done well with yr help
An honest lady you are so I heard say
All for King and Country keeping the peace

So the man mocks me
I see how he must be playd

Say I Right you are I am a good Christian
So now I ask you do something to help me

Maybe maybe What you want

Oh please Sir you know I did know him well
I have workd for his father long
May I not see him now one last time

Others are gatherd now laughing
So proud are they of the murder they done

Oh yes they say You see him one last time

Yet I hope yr stomach is strong
For half his face blastd off with a musket
You not mind that girl
You got a taste for blood
Not mind that half his brain is hangd out

I am afeard of what I shall see
But still I say Take me to he

So I follow that man down a corridor
Twas somewhere in cellars of that house
Dark as a rabbit hole and nearly as damp
Following only the dancing light of his candle
Leaps up and down the walls

Then he open the door
Pass me the candle

You not scard to meet the Devil he say

I shut the door on he and am alone
By the light of the candle
I see the body laid out
Mostly coverd by a coarse blanket

I hold the candle up
See what is left of the face
Black blood sticking the white of a bone
Shatter tooth and jaw all tore out
You see straight through the black rip
To the rigid throat

The eyes closd the brown hair flat to the head
What remains of the mouth grinning

But even for all that I know

I know

Still I reach for the hand under the blanket
Tis cold and stiff yet I pull it out
I must see

There is the scar livid
That day on the roof when his hand rip

I know
The man I see here is not Master Ned
God save my soul

Keep my hand on his dear hand
Though cold and brittle
Slide that ring on his finger

Oh belovd Father
How oft and always do we fall
So far short of yr Glory

Father forgive I pray Forgive

MOUNT VERNON

So there now tis writ down

Words like the twisting grain of wood
Or the course of a slow running river
Have ways they must evr go

Who might I to wield the axe cross the grain
Or try to untwist the flow of water

But so I have done

Now you know
I also know

Tis as though I see it for the first time
Though twas always so

The man downstairs
The maggot leg man dying hard
For forty years has usd
His dead brothers name

We are deep in the caves of night
The silence plunges down distant all round

Yet strange tis that my Master also
Does know what I have writ now

For sudden he is keening wailing

I go downstairs
Stiff and breathing sharp
Without a candle hand feeling rail
Foot edge forward not a star shine a winder

I find him raging
Like some girt chaind beast
Convulsd by pain

The end cannot be far away
I perhaps have hastend it

Soon the torrent of pain do pass
He lies hissself down draind

Oh Lord God why not he be takd
Such cruelty is there in this
He was never a man would make
A Godly death

I do not wait
For him to come to repentance or confession

I have never thought to call any Minister
He no a ways did want any of that

He is as he is And always was
Some beauty in his steadfast stubborn nature
He is glorious in his error
It were evr so

Mr Ned Cottrell

Now my thoughts push at something
They cannot fathom

Why did he want me to write his story down
The story of Mr Ned Cottrell that famous hero

Shot dead so long ago
Yet alive all these years

He wants to hide the past
Yet also he pushes at it plays with it
Wants it hid wants it out

Perhaps his soul is not easy
Fear the judgement of God
That he may burn forver in hell
As sure he will
There can be no doubt

Still I say to myself
Oh Mary Ann Mary Ann take care

Will you never end with trying to save he

Then tis as though he know my thoughts
For he wakes and turns his head says

Ah Mary Ann Mary Ann do you not know
You think you take some power ovr me

Yet I care not what is said about me
Only that something is said
That I shall be immortal
Whether in fame or infamy

I know it for truth
Why did I not see this sooner
He wants glory and cares not good or bad

What power can I evr have gainst he

Nothing folds out here as I expectd
I thought once the truth was told
Then all would be straightd out

There is perhaps some loosening in the air
Some shifting inside me a weight gone
Yet that is all no more
For this can no a ways be put right

Pain burns through the lump in my chest
Which pounds in my heart
Brings fever to my cheeks
Pulls tight every muscle

For a moment I look up then
Seeing now the first fire of autumn
Touch the leaves
Why stand I here for arguing with he
What will any of it change
I should better go out in the garden
While I still may

Yet still I think on this question of glory
Which he wants so much
He did always

It seems to me he is confusd

For glory does last for but a season

Whereas for those of us who are
But naught

We shall endure for eternity

STOCTON HILL

That night I come back from Spillmans Court
I am like a person lost in purgatory
See hear feel touch nothing

I should have said something then
Could have told Mr Birch Nazareth
Ambrose or Nettie

Not Mr Harland Cottrell no
He was too sick he could not have understood

I could not abear his relief

For so it would have been
If someone had told him that Master Ned
Did live yet

Yet my lips were seald by outrage
Confusion anger pain

Oh to see him lying there
His body brokd to bits
Laid out where others make merry

He who had always been so poorly usd

All I could do was go to my room
Lie me down
Shut my eyes gainst the world

I know not if I slept
Yet twas as the night was rising
Up toward the dawn
I heard sounds within the house

Thought perhaps Mr Harland Cottrell stir
So got up went to the kitchen
Thinking to take some water

So imagine then my shock
I turn back from the dresser
Who is there but Master Ned

Tis like I see some fantom hover there

In his hands does he hold
That same letter as his brother held earlier
Tells I think of this new position
Starting soon in the City of Oxford

Now he turn his head in greeting
Fold letter in his pocket
Raise finger to his lips

Ah Mary Ann he say
His voice no louder than a spring breeze
I have need of yr help
We must work quick and quiet
Go upstairs now bring me all is in the room
Does belong to Master Blyth

He is standing close to me now
I look up in his eye
There I find nothing at all

So I spit on him
Turn away

I will fetch carry nothing for he

Yet still he goes on
His feet creaking slight on the stair

I stood there
Could have run then for Mr Birch Nazareth
For Ambrose for a constable

Yet I did nothing at all

Not long afore he come down
Wearing boots cravat
Double breastd vest of velvet
That great coat narrow waistd
All as belongd to Master Blyth

The bag as well the cane
In his hand the silk top hat

So he goes past me with a nod
I follow behind him up to the gate

Places then that hat on his head
Stretches out his hand to me
Say Come come now Mary Ann
You and me are old friends
Do not let us part like this

I keep my hand by my side
Stare at him straight

So then he shakes his head says
One man is already dead

That he says
So he knew

Then he smiles a little say
What help tis for another to swing
I have no talent for sacrifice

Remember this now Mary Ann
No one would have been shot
If you had been loyal

If you want to make a new world he say
You must break up the old

In this business many will suffer
Progress is a girt mill
All men are but grist to it

He looks at me then long
Stretch out his hand
Once more

I do not take it
Yet still he gives me a kindly smile
Waves with a flourish that silver head cane
As belongs to Master Blyth

So he is off
Not down the hill but stepping out
Along the shoulder of the Valley

Heading up through Cinque Foil Piece
And Elchers Orchard

Going perhaps to Painswick or to Gloucester
Where his face be not so well knowd

From there no doubt to Oxford

That was the last I see of he
Moving easy flowing away
In that spruce hat and coat
Catch now in the dawn breeze
Cane waving the silver knob
Carvd with lines fine as spiders web

His hand moving up to hold the hat
Less the wind pull it away

Even now I have to say
Something in his movements
That wave of the cane steady of the hat
The long strides as though he cross the world
That would make you yearn for he

For though his brother twas
Had the gift or curse of the mesmerist
So he also had that power
That grips on the minds of others

Away away along the hill
Turning only once to wave a hand
Afore stepping on again

MOUNT VERNON

So that was all
Never did see him again
Not for forty stretchd years

Heard of him maybe once twice
Mr Blyth Cottrell gone off
To the West of Indies so they say
After the tragic death of scoundrel hero brother

A doctor and a fine gentleman he

Some say also he went so hurry
For twas he
Did shoot his brother
In some dispute ovr a sweetheart

Could it have been true

No No It never was so
He went to his brother that day in love

It were evr so
His godsend and his blight

See how the truth is twistd

Yet so it go on til that day I already tell
Five months ago now
In the spring

When I am stood there outside the Shambles
Someone throws a rotten turnip

Then there he is
Walking toward me
Just as though only a day has passd
He has come back that eve
Along the shoulder of the Valley
With his brothers hat and cane

Raise his hat to me
Just as he did that last day

Say Ah there you are again
Mary Ann Sate
I thought you were dead

And yet do you know me

I say straight
Course Sir how could I forget

Aye aye he say Yes
Mr Blyth Cottrell
You remember

When I hear that name
I do look at him long

Then I also do say that name

Which is not his name
For why do I do it

Because if you tell a story oft enough
So it become true

I had a few shillings in my pocket
Yet how many nights would that last
Afore I must sleep in the street

That is how it came to pass
I work for he again
Day on day I not think
Of the lie he told

Who can wonder Master Blyth
He find no rest

Tis not only my Master he haunts
But me also
Has done all these years
Wandering endlessly
The many chambers of my mind

My questions being many

How twas that he was namd
An unnatural man
When surely all that is creatd by God
Must be natural
He Me All

Also what crime did he evr commit

None That is the truth

Nettie saw it and I did not

Did seem always to be such a mystery
So long it has takd me to see
There was nothing to understand
Only goodness
Which does sometimes blind us
With its bright simplicity

He and I we might have been
Unitd in a brotherhood of oppression
But what I see is this

In this world we are all positiond
On a ladder with a thousand rungs
Each tries to edge off the ladder
Those who lie just below
Tis the tragedy of the human state

So when a gate is left open
I blame it on he

This the error into which
Our too feeble flesh
Do evr fall
We are told what we should see
So we see only what we are told

Our only prayer should evr be
Let me see with mine own eyes

They say that time will always shew
The truth of a situation
Yet tis not my idea

For me it seems

That passing time
Only shew that what seemd important
Is nothing at all

Time not bring the past into clearer sight
Instead just wipe all clean
Render all the struggles of the past
As naught

STOCTON HILL

So twas I left my home at Stocton Hill
Walkd away that same morning

Took with me that shilling piece
Scorch like guilt in my hand
Yet what choice do I have
For now I have need of all I can gather

My foot follow the same way as he did go
Heading maybe for Gloucester
I always heard tell of but never see

As I come up toward Elchers Orchard
I stand look back
Tis too bad for tears
How will I live without this place

Soon all will be rising
Nettie shouting vicious for me
Why I not get the range lit the water fetchd
Mr Harland Cottrell not in for breakfast early
Only lie there bent now

Yet still he gave me

The best of my life

The farm solid and growd into the hill
Its gables ruggd gainst the lightening skye
The barns huddle about and the gardens
Where grow I so many herbs tomatoes beans

But no no I cannot stay longer
So I on into the starting day
The hill hard and steep

Oh that wretchd day
On on I did walk

I dare not go down to the toll road
Or through the town of Painswick
Must keep to the fields at the back
I afeard of ruffians who may know my name

Mary Ann Sate the witch as did betray
Mr Ned Cottrell

On I go up and up
Still the way twist and turn
Few do come this path

Come I then to a place I know
Tis Freams Farm leading on down
Where is Sutton Mill
I have been sent some time in the past
For to deliver a message

Lie down then under a bush
Steep gainst a sheltering wall
Think to sleep but no sleep come
Just lie looking up at the lace of leaves

The sun above the cornflowr skye
Hold my mind steady think of naught

Foxes have holes
The birds of the air nests
But what place now can I find

The night then does come
Still I lie gainst the wall
Feel that soon I shall die
Am glad of this

I must then have slept

So twas there gainst Sutton Mill
In the new born gleam of dawn
The mist still muster thick
The dew swathd heavy

That the Lord God did appear to me
Walking through the field
Just up afore me

As He walk through this His paradise
His garden He made eastward of Eden

Carrying in His hand a staff
His long robes trail the dew thick ground

Turning then to look back but once at me
Signalling then on up the hill
Back up the steep way

So I do rise up then and follow He
Knew that He had come
That I might not die

But have new life

In death dark vale
I fear no ill
With Thee dear Lord beside me

Though soon soon He is takd into the mist
Yet still I go climbing up
Fire now by the power of His Grace and Glory

I get to the summit

Come to a corner in the road
Look down many mile cross Valley and wood
Through the fold of hill and hummock

Far below see a lofty tower rise up
Tall and straight stretch up in the skye
Dazzle in the light

This then is the cathedral at Gloucester
Like I see the City of God

Such a soul flooding sight
Gladden even the sorest heart
Such should be raise to the Glory of our Lord

Such splendid perfection
Enough to wipe away all sin
All the petty inadequacy of our thwartd lives

Seeing this I feel new life might be possible
Even for such as me
It could be so

God shall wipe away all the tears

From their eyes and there shall be no more death
Neither sorrow nor crying
Nor shall there be
Any more pain for the former things
Are passd away

So thinking I find the strength
Step on again into the blustering day

GLOUCESTER

You write a book of yr life
Think perhaps it should be one page every year

Then you find that sometime
Forty years can be writ
In the turn of a page

So tis for me

What can I say of those many years
I did spend in the City of Gloucester
They were as naught

I was unknowd to the Lord unknowd to myself
Lost in sadness and in rage

Dwelling in the wilderness cast in a deep pit

Many jobs I did do
Emptying the night soil
Pot scouring stitching in a cobblers shop
Following after the coaches to sweep up
The soil in the streets
Working in hostelries workshops

Sweeping out the school house
Unloading wood for the fire

Little comfort to be found
Except the cathedral itself
Such as me not right to go in
Yet could stand near the entrance
Look up at the girt tower above

Which I do oft but always always
My mind stick on this one fact
I told the truth
I did what is right

In doing so I killd a good man

Curse be he that taketh reward
To slay an innocent person

God God I ask again and again
Yr law tells always the truth is all
So how then can Master Blyths life be takd
All my belief is turnd upside down

Then come the blessd day
I get myself a job in the gaol

Not many people want such work
Dressing the bodies
Even of those hangd
Yet I did like the work
Did it well

Buy a new wool dress
Go to the barber get some teeth
At the back of my mouth take out

They are rotten and ache bad

I think on it now and
Perhaps I take such care
In the dressing of those departd

For in my mind they became
The bodies of those who I had lovd
Yet had faild them at the end

Baby Fern and Mr Woebegone
Master Blyth Lucetta all
Mr Harland Cottrell and Nettie even

Perhaps twas because I think of them so much
A tiny bit of the past come back to me

*

It happen like this I was in the street
A winter day echo clear scatterd with frost

When I did hear a voice call out
At first was afeard but then I turnd
There was Ambrose walking toward me
Just as he always had

He come by then a railway engineer
Advise on a new line they bring in
Did not surprise me

If twas not one machine twas tother

Was marrid with a wife and three childers
One a boy who was with him that day
A fine growd lad of fourteen maybe more

The one who lives now down below this house
Has hisself a child
The one as brought the eggs

That day Ambrose slap me firm on the shoulder
Laugh long and shake his head again and again
Oh he says How good tis to see you Mary Ann

He says to his son who stands by
This lady were my sister
When we were but childers

Then he tell me both Mr Harland Cottrell
And Nettie dead

Though they did both live some several years
After I did leave

He takd to his eternal rest and then she expire
But a week later

The land at Stocton Hill now farmd
By a man come down from London

Many had supposd so Ambrose say
That with his fathers death
Master Blyth would return
If only for to see the place shut up
Yet he never did

At the mention of that name
I do turn about saying
Sorry sorry I must be going now
I must not delay

Yet Ambrose pull me back say

So so We think to make things different
Yet it all comes round again

You lay yr back to the wheel
For what time you may
Others will come after to push on
The girt load of human progress
I do not live in bitterness
And you Mary Ann
Do you

I look him then hard in the eye
No I say Not in bitterness
Yet I count the cost
I try to sort right from wrong

You were evr a good woman he say

Then shakes his head stares on down the street

Speaks again to remind me of that day
So far lost back in time now

When we did stand under the dripping trees
Far up above The Heavens
Talking of how we likd well the rain
As well the sun
The dark as well the light

Then he say
I hope Mary Ann even now
You see also the light

I nod my head and consider that question

Then he do say

I do never forget all you did for me

Thankee I say

Then thinking again the words come
We were so v young then

At that I bid him farewell and turn to go
He raising his hat to me

Only look back when I reach
The end of the street
See him still staring after me

Which did surprise me much
For he was never a man to look back
Always a man of the future was he

*

My dear Ambrose I never see again
Just that one time

Except did hear
He was killd out at Maisemore

So he become another body
As I imagine myself to have dressd
Care for at the end

Twas but a year after I meet Ambrose
My situation was happily improvd
It come about by accident

Twas a time of plague in Gloucester
Many many gone dead and a cause of that

Many deaths must be writ down
Many records to be kept straight
Yet even those who are to writ them down
Are dead theysselfs

So I say then
I can read and write
Can put all down if so the need is

Course at first I am not believd
But by that time I am knowd to the Old Porter
Of him I shall shortly tell more

Twas this Old Porter who did say
If Mary Ann says it then twill be true

So I am tried out
Worry then I may disappoint
For many years passd since I held a pen
The steel nib then being usd everywhere
Tis much easier

Yet Mr Harland Cottrell did teach me well
For when I get startd I write a good hand
Like to do the work
See all is record there

The name the date and the profession
Clock maker razor grinder stillborn
Weaver imbecile shearman
Died in infancy Died in childbirth
Milliner ladies maid baker

The work is less hard
I am givd a new dress and apron
The room where I work has a fire

Even I am paid ten shillings a week

Only one day I remember in particular
As I did fall in conversation the Old Porter
Had happend a few times afore

This Old Porter did put me in mind sometime
Of that Mr Harland Cottrell

The two were not alike in physical appearance
This Old Porter being as small and dubby
As Mr Harland Cottrell straw thin

Yet in mind the two were similar
As thinking deep long and questionly
On all matters of religion and morality

So it come that time a man was to be hung
In Gloucester One Edward Hewitt
Had grievously murdered his wife Sarah Ann

So that Old Porter say to me
What think you Mary Ann
Surely we should not be hanging men
In this now more civilizd and Christian time

I do take some while to think on his question
Then finally I do say

I think they should be hung Sir
Yes no doubt they must swing
For if you do not take a firm line now
Then what will come

You give any advantage to such as they
Can only lead to trouble

GLOUCESTER

Take the lid off
You will not get he back on

As I speak the words I think of Nettie
Remember how Ambrose did tease

They do eat their own childers
Having flavourd they first with salt and sauce

So we did laugh but maybe
She knew more than we evr saw

*

That day I do remember
For it were the beginning of many discourse
Did arise betwixt me and the Old Porter

He did lend me books
Of spiritual improvement and enquiry

Also the novels of Mr Dickens
Became my girtest pleasure to read
The verse of Mr John Clare
I had read afore

Some poems also he had on a paper
Writ by a papist in Oxford Mr Hopkins
These I did value more than any other
Repeating them oft in my head

So it came I did confide in that Old Porter
How I had growd apart from the Lord
Hid myself from Him and He from me

So I say this to he

As I fill his pipe
We both sitting down by the fire
For the evening long advancd

This he did tell me then
Mary Ann if we choose to live always
In the freedom of the mind
Whatevr may be the constraints of the flesh
Then the price we pay may be high
Yet that does not make our decision wrong

Also he say The question now is this
Mary Ann Where did you evr find our Lord
Where might you find Him now

The answer comes on me straightway
I speak without the least impediment

I always found the Lord in the Valleys Sir
The Valleys of my childhood

Ah then Mary Ann
Then that is where He is
Tis there you must seek He

So he does say

*

Only a week after this talk
This Old Porter is gone
His short season passd
Takd by a violent seizure

For we are but tenants here
A wind that passeth does not return

Days swifter than a weavers shuttle

I knew then all must change about

So all fell out and I must say
They give me two weeks wages
Also may stay in my room same time
I appreciate much

Yet what work then could I do
I had not long to pass I knew
Being gone my three score years and ten

Just as I am thinking on this
A lady does come to visit me

She is dressd all in black
With a stiff white collar
Her spine straight as a rake
Her hair pulld back
So her eyes waterd

Yet she spoke to me most respectfully
Saying she was a Quaker friend of the Old Porter
Had come to ask what assistance she may

I had never been askd such a question
But still I answerd straightway

I need to get home Madam
If some means could be found travel to Stroud

So she come back the next day
Says to me I am go to the Cross
To find there a man calld Sykes

He is a carter is already paid
He cannot take me to Stroud
Only to Painswick
Tis the best could be found

Then into my hand she pushes a cloth
Inside bread apple a slice of ham

When I look up she has gone

Sorry that I could not thank her
Yet still packing up my few possessions
Those kerchiefs buttons pieces of hair
I did evr keep

Setting out in haste
For the Cross
Where are many carts
Setting out and returning

I finds Mr Sykes with no trouble
Soon am sat up in the cart
Cloth on my knee

So we set out through the sides of Gloucester
Where are built now smart villas of red brick

Then all up the long rocking hill
The cart flick the whip the horse go on
Into the sparkling fresh of the hills
The green dancing in my eyes
All the way to Painswick

There I must descend
Take the road now on my own two feet

Yet I am in good cheer
For tis down hill all the way from here
To Stroudwater

Go back that same road I did tread
Well more than forty years afore

Tird and stiff I was but sure
Wanting to get on

Godspeed I say to myself
For you are on the way now

Home

MOUNT VERNON

Outside the rain fall now
Breaking gentle on the winder
Cutting down through all dust grime

Why does the Good Lord not call me now
My time is long past
I am done here
My suffering is enough

Instead I hear the Master calling
As he has done so many times afore
Like me the Lord should takd him long back

So I do think and yet this morning
The Master does rally strong stands up
Asks me to find clean linen
Boots waistcoat braces all

He is going down to Stroud
He will walk there
This will be the easiest way

So I do set about to help he
Easy and heart whole he is in spirit now

Which does suit me well
For there is yet one truth
Which does remain unspokd
A last coffin lid to be fixd down

So I stand by the bed
Pour water for he
Say now What of Lucetta Sir

Now that name come in the room
The air comes alive
He turns to me and I see
He will not push my words aside
Nor treat them as naught

Ah he say Lucetta
I know Mary Ann I know you lovd her well
I too She the only woman I evr lovd

It were a terrible mistake
She should have marry me

Mary Ann he say and raise up his head
His eyes now fixd firm upon me
This you must understand he say
I never said anything were not true

No I shout at him No No No
Tis not right
She were a Christian woman virtuous true

He shakes his head stretch out his hand
Mary Ann Mary Ann I am sorry
Yet what I say is right
Lucetta a good woman I lovd her true
You and I we livd in that house

Suffer the same pain at her loss
Love her still I know

Still he speak on Yet I must say
It pains me I want no stain on her name
She and I were together

No No I shout at he

Though in my mind I do consider
He did never marry why was that
He must have had plenty chance

Mary Ann he say Think a moment
You know how she died
You know

That as well a lie

No no twas not
Nobody say it to you for you so brokd down
Yet I made enquiries it were true
That were her nature

Can this be true
Did he try to seek her out
Who can know

His tongue is near split
He has told so many lies

No No No

So I say and back away from him

Mary Ann he say Come come

MOUNT VERNON

Stop now all yr anger
Let us be at peace

As he says he stretches out a hand to me
Outside the wind sudden rushes
Throws the rain now gainst the panes
Tosses the girt trees
Heavy still in all their green

So he say So
You live with yr lies
I live with mine
We all just do as we may
To find a way

Saying that he stand up strong
Steps out cross the room

I follow he to the door
Step out behind him

Ah ah he say What a fine morning
How I shall enjoy to walk

Sir Sir I say Might you not be better
To wait til the weather pass

Turns to me then laughs merry
Saying What now Mary Ann
Are you worrid I might catch a chill

At this even I must laugh

So then he steps out quite firm
Looks every part the gentleman
For I have got he finely dressd

I watch he go
Many many strides he takes
What Lazarus miracle is this

Yet then he stops turns back to me
Smiles waves his long fingerd hand

I should do better I think he say
To walk with a cane

So I go in fetch that cane
Walk out through the dewy morn

Hold out the cane to he
Takes it then firmly in his hand

Thank you Mary Ann say he
Thank you for this

Then does raise a hand say
Perhaps I will sit just one moment
Afore I go on

So I go back in fetch that light chair
As we have usd afore

So I do place it and he sits down
His brothers cane still grippd

Looking at him then I see
Tis not only rain runs his face

From trees around sudden birds do rise
A girt flock of them all burst forth

Tilts he back his head breathes deep

In that moment his spirit is snuffd out
He reach his journeys end

*

There is no shock comes with such force
As that we have expectd long

I know not then what happen
Where I go or what I do
This I cannot explain

The next I find myself waking
All the Valley spread afore me

The mist rolling now off hill tops
As though the land itself turns in its sleep
The air blew fresh through all the lung

You never saw the world so blessd
In this veild and deep breathing land
Infusd all through with that sweet earth smell
That does come after rain

See then the fresh day is dawning
Behold all things are become new
The light so arise in my heart

Glimpse then cross the lawn
By the zummer house

Where the shroude of mist still cover
Yet I see clear

Force myself up then
Go to find water and bread

For I am near too weak to stand

Then as the new day spills forth fine
I straighten myself out

Hard work tis to pull he in the house
Yet soon set to work to strip he down
As I have done it many a time afore
As I here tell

Wash he all clean
Comb out his hair

At least he already have clean linen
Black velvet overcoat waistcoat breeches boots
Which circumstance do save some work

I know not who may come to take he
Yet they will not find he disgracd

As I work I think still of all the hours
I did waste in trying to fathom he

Now the truth comes
There was never anything to fathom

There never was any Mr Ned Cottrell
For never anything fixd in he
His life one masque disguise follow another

Now I help him into his last costume
No doubt he will successfully deceive
Even the Lord Hisself
When he arrives at the judgement seat
Wheedle his way into paradise some way

The work is long his limbs heavy
A coming now stiff
A sheet must be find to bind up
His stinking leg tight
Put coins on his eyes
Fold neat his arms cross he

Find another sheet to wrap all in
Then needle and thread
To stich all around
Even now I sew a good hem

On and on I work though
Pain and weariness shake me

I feel death close
Am like a ship come through a girt storm
Now becalmd sails hanging limp

Without my anger I am nothing
Was maybe only that as kept me alive
All those years in Gloucester
I carrid with me poison through all my body
His guilt and mine

Yet I do find the courage to go on
For now now the Angels
They are here again
Gathering all about me
As they have done afore

Their white wings flutter
Gentle as the beat of a heart
Abiding now with me always

When finally I am done the day is far gone

So I go to the kitchen again
To find bread and water

Sit me down at the table
Where my hands move through all these pages
I did writ

Whose story is this

The story of men and their battles
For such was the stuff of my life

Yet through all of that and beyond
Is still another story
Hidden in the warp and weft of the words
An occasional flick shot through the fabric
Which is mine

Tis a story of these Valleys
Of the small things of my work
They are as nothing to the world
But I value them
Can feel my hand still on the smoothing iron
Stir the pot wind the mangle

Hope I this
If any should read these words
They might be a person like myself
Able to take enjoyment
In some small task
Such rub dust sweep

They may find that thread
Within this larger story
Which is mine

Share with me the morning I do love
Mist hanging down low to meet frost sharp
Ice hammer hard on the frozen paths
All this I have lovd

What of Lucetta and my love for her
I know not the truth of what the Master say
It may be that I was always unfair to he

But in this he is right
I saw her through my own eyes
Which perhaps do not tell true

I return her now to her proper state
Merely and beautifully another mortal being
A tangle of virtue and corruption
Cannot be unknot

She in truth was like those men
With their struggle and strife and judgement
A diversion from the proper course

We are told that love will save us
Yet me it did destroy
Many a time

Master Blyth also

You may much sooner die of an excess of love
Than lack

This not the Masters story but mine

I thought to scour his soul by writing
Yet tis my soul which is cleansd

As Lucetta did instruct me
I shew now how the Grace of God
Has been evidencd in every breath I take

In these pages I bear witness to that divinity
That exists in me in all of us

Feel neither pride nor shame
I did as all must do
I livd

So I shall write my name at the front

Mary Ann Sate

*

Now I shall set out to walk

Oh aye on my way again

There have been so many leavings

To everything there is a season
A time to every purpose under the heaven

A time to dance
A time to die

Take my book up to the tower room
Hid it there behind
That brokd panel under the winder

Mr Ned Cottrell so you see
I do now as I want

Tis the best place for it
These are but words etchd on the wind

For who would want to read
Of the life of Mary Ann Sate

Who care now what happend
Some night long ago
Be takd for the ramblings of an imbecile

Once I have pressd the book behind that panel
All will be done I shall start to walk

This I have decide
I must use my own legs while I may
For should I die here
Then some poor souls will be sent
Up the side of the Valley
To carry down my bones

I do not like to think of any
Who should go to such trouble

The walk will please more
Than any other could

Pass that toll house I shall go
Where do live the family of Ambrose
How blood is passd on to blood
What seems gone does come again

Down down into the depths of the Valley
All through the green fields
So I shall soon go

Climbing up the grand way

As I did once with Ambrose

So I lift up my eyes unto the hills
From whence comes my help

Hear soon calling clear
From that other country
That most distant shore
Where do dwell all those
Who have gone afore

Lucetta among them I shall see again
Her firm step lead ahead of me
That pale shawl spread cross her shoulders
Ready to take my hand draw me on
Should my foot evr fail

God speed Mary Ann
You are on yr way home

It may take me more than a day
To get myself to the Workhouse
Perhaps my soul depart my body
Afore I get there
I do not know

Whatevr come I will be bury with the rest
I hope they dig down deep enough

So they will write me down in their book
As I write down so many
Mary Ann Sate
The date and whatevr else they say

I am already on my way to God
As I set out to walk

Also to that girter life that is to come

Surround always by the Angels
Who do hold me now gainst their tender breast
Never leave me so again

Gentle white spreading light always
Through the gracious flutter of their wings

Safe and sure in the knowledge
That the Lord shall open wide His arms
Take me to Him
Hold me tight

We all meet soon in a better place

Mr Abel Woebegone
Do you remember me

I shall stand not far from where you stood
That day on the side of the Valley
More than sixty year past

I shall say as you did then
I am savd I am savd

For so are you and so we all
For whatevr crime we do commit
We remain dug deep in His creation

Aye I am returnd now to the girl I was
Who had no fear of anything
My certainty is the world
So I praise the Lord

Now as I shall walk through the Valley

On my way to Heavens Gate

I know now you argue not with He
Ovr the details of His Justice
Place yr faith in some ovr arching Good

You forgive Him His failings
As He forgive ours

We can never fathom the strangeness
Of His redemption

Yet still I think on all those come after

Those who writes books and chronicles of history
Always do study those things that change
Yet always I do wonder
Are they ask the proper question

Should we not rather study
Those things are evr the same

There are always winders to be cleand

The Valleys also be here always
Though the feet that tramp them so
May come go come go many a time
Though they build or destroy
Cut tree or plant

Seedtime harvest cold heat
Zummer winter day night
Shall not cease

Accept my love this place as yr inheritance
I have no other legacy to give

So commend these many acres to you

Hold fast to all all of this
My dear friends of the future
For in the glory of these Valleys you will find

Yr strength

AFTERWORD

After typing up this document, as you might expect, I spent some days in attempting to discover some additional information about Mary Ann Sate. However, despite extensive research, I never found any further evidence of her existence. All I could find was the record of her death in the Stroud Workhouse as noted down in the registers held by the Urban District Council. There it is written, 'Mary Ann Sate, 9 October 1887, Imbecile.'

Sarah Jane Moffatt
September 1938

AUTHOR'S NOTE

The following books were useful to me in the writing of this novel:

Ackroyd, Peter, *Blake: A Biography*

Anonymous, *Every Man His Own Doctor, Or A Cure of the Human Body, 1835*

Baker, Jim, *The Cunning Man's Handbook*

Bate, Jonathan, *John Clare: A Biography*

Bate, Jonathan, ed., *John Clare: Selected Poems*

Beacham, M. J. A., *Mills and Milling in Gloucestershire*

Berry, Liz, *Black Country*

Briggs, Asa, *The Chartists*

Burnett, John, *Destiny Obscure: Autobiographies of Childhood, Education and Family from the 1820s to the 1920s*

Burnett, John, ed. *Autobiographies of Working People from the 1820s to the 1830s*

Chambers, Jill, *Gloucestershire Machine Breakers: The Story of the 1830 Riots*

Chedzoy, Alan, *The People's Poet: William Barnes of Dorset*

Cooper, J. B., *Early Days*

Evans, Jill, *Hanged at Gloucester*

It Began in a Cottage, compiled by Stanley Gardiner (Baptists in Chalford)

Stroud and The Five Valleys in Old Photographs: A Second Selection, collected by S. J. Gardiner and L. C. Padin

The Gloucestershire Diaries, transcribed by John Hearfield, thought to be the work of Paul Hawkins Fisher

Hawkins Fisher, Paul, *Notes and Recollections of Stroud*

Hearfield, Marion, *William Cowle of Stroud: Life in a Victorian Town*

Hoy, Molly, and Hoy, Alfred, *They Met in a Barn: The Story of Congregationalism in Stroud 1687–1887*

Latham, J. E. M., *Search for a New Eden: James Pierrepont Greaves (1777–1842), the Sacred Socialist and His Followers*

The Stroudwater Riots of 1825, compiled from historical records by John Loosely

Mahler, Oliver, and Marshfield, Steven, *Stroudwater Valley Mills*

Marcus, Sharon, *Between Women: Friendship, Desire and Marriage in Victorian England*

Martineau, Harriet, *Autobiography Vol I*

Miles, W. A., Royal Commission of Inquiry into the condition of Hand-Loom Weavers in England and Wales in 1837–41. Gloucestershire section

Mills, Stephen, and Riemer, Pierce, *The Mills of Gloucestershire*

Lord Moreton, ed., *A Glossary of Dialect and Archaic Words Used in the County of Gloucestershire* (Volume 25)

William Barnes: Poems, selected by Andrew Motion

Paine, Thomas, *The Age of Reason*

—, *The Rights of Man*

Robinson, Eric, and Powell, David, eds., *John Clare by Himself*

Cotswold Tales, selected by Alan Sutton

Stroud Local History Society, *Stroud Versus Slavery*

Tann, Jennifer, *Wool and Water: The Gloucestershire Woollen Industry and Its Mills*

Thompson, E. P., *The Making of the English Working Class*

Tucker, Joan, *Stroud*

Urdank, Albion M., *Religion and Society in a Cotswold Vale*

Vincent, David, *Bread, Knowledge and Freedom: A Study of Nineteenth-Century Working Class Autobiography*

My sincere thanks to the following individuals and organizations for the assistance they have offered me in the writing of this novel:

Dr Claire Lynch of the Writing Lives Project at the Burnett Archive of Working Class Autobiography, which is held at Brunel University and John Moores University, Shorter and Timlin Archivists, Stroud Museum, Marion and John Hearfield and John Loosely of Stroud Local History Society, Dr Jenner's House, the Local Studies Room at Stroud Library, The Royal College of Surgeons/Hunterian Museum, Ray Wilson at the Gloucestershire Society of Industrial Archaeology, Gloucester Archives, Neil Baker of the Heavens Archaeological Project, Kel Portman of Walking the Land, Stuart Butler of Radical Stroud, Derek Benson of Tewkesbury Historical Society/Bristol Radical History Group and the Tyrone Guthrie Centre. Ian Mackintosh of the Stroudwater Textiles Trust generously read the manuscript for me at a late stage and his corrections were invaluable.

In addition, I owe a huge debt of gratitude to all the people who pledged for this book through Unbound. Without their support this book would not have been published. Others have also helped out in many different ways. They include: Liz and Martin Whiteside, Peter Moseley, Clare Dunkel, Jude Emmet, Tom and Barbara Castelein, Angela Findlay, Paul Scott, Peter and Diane Gilbert Scott, Clare Andrews, Clare Morgan, Roopa Farooki, Jacqui Lofthouse, Susannah Rickards, Christa Mahana, Caroline Sanderson, Katie Jarvis and Gill Eastwood. Before the publication of this book, Paul Milton and his colleagues at the Everyman Theatre worked with Hammerpuzzle Theatre to create a stage adaptation of a scene from this book bringing Mary Ann to life for the first time with great sensitivity. My colleagues and students on the MSt in Creative Writing at Oxford University provide endless inspiration, and all at the Quaker Meeting House in Nailsworth bless my life with their quiet and steadfast wisdom. Lastly, my family are ever patient. Thank you Stephen, Thomas and Hope Kinsella, Victoria Jolly and William Cornford.

Finally, a huge thank you to my agent Victoria Hobbs at A. M. Heath and to John Mitchinson of Unbound, who has made it possible for me to continue writing. Many others at Unbound also worked hard on the publication of this book. They include Rachael Kerr, Tamsin Shelton, Amy Winchester, Caitlin Harvey, Georgia Odd, Anna Simpson and Imogen Denny.

SUPPORTERS

Unbound is a new kind of publishing house. Our books are funded directly by readers. This was a very popular idea during the late eighteenth and early nineteenth centuries. Now we have revived it for the internet age. It allows authors to write the books they really want to write and readers to support the writing they would most like to see published.

The names listed below are of readers who have pledged their support and made this book happen. If you'd like to join them, visit: www.unbound.com.

Clare Andrews
Ange & Kate
Arvon Foundation
James Aylett
Jane Bailey
David Baillie
Katy Bevan
Jane Hart Black
Georgina Blastland
Graham Blenkin
Sian Block
Mark Bowsher
Stephanie Bretherton

Eva Brüning
Callum Campbell
Xander Cansell
Kate Carpenter
Louise Cartledge
Mary Cavanagh
Julian Clyne
Audrey Cready
Judith and Geoff Dance
June Dennison
Imogen Denny
Alison Dipple
Jenny Doughty

Cressida Downing
Jane Draycott
Clare Dunkel
Gillian Eastwood
Jimmy Edmonds
Frank Egerton
Lisa Elsing-Holden
Jude Emmet
Amanda Falkson
Roopa Farooki
Catherine Feore
Nailsworth Festival
Katie Fforde
John Fieldhouse
Angela Findlay
Daisy Finer
Sarah Frankish
Natalie Gamble
Robin Ganderton
Miranda Gold
Anthony A. Gribben
Kiran Millwood Hargrave
Lindis Harris
Philip Harris
Sophie Harris
Kirsty Henderson
Penelope Henriques
Amanda Holmes Duffy
John James
Kathleen Jones
Nina Jorgensen
Dan Kieran
Andy Kinsella

Laura Kinsella Foundation
Roman Krznaric
Elizabeth Lindsay
Jacqui Lofthouse
Liza Lovdahl Gormsen
Sally Lovell
Maya Matthews
John Mitchinson
Bel Mooney
Carlo Navato
Joanna Nicolas
Jamie Nuttgens
Katie Pitman
Justin Pollard
Norman Price
Noel Qualter
Jane Richardson
Rebecca Rue
Helen and Richard Salsbury
Caroline Sanderson
Deborah Shedden
Catherine Stewart
Jemima Stratford
Katie Sutcliffe
Elizabeth Symonds
Simon Taylor
Jackie Thomas
Lynda Mia Thompson
Claire Trehearne
Ann Tudor
Miranda Ward
Liz and Martin Whiteside
Suzie Wilde